Dedication

To Linda Strock and Yvonne "Cookie" Dias.
Your willingness to "get involved" with a stranger changed my life.
Without you, I never would have found my sisters.
Thank you for reaching out!
I will forever be grateful.

"All men should strive to learn before they die what they are running from, and to, and why."

- *James Thurber*

Acknowledgements

A huge thanks author Kellie Coates Gilbert for answering questions and reading a chapter for trust information. Any mistakes are my own.

To David Lawler, thank you for your expert advice as a GA attorney on divorce, wills, and trusts. I couldn't resist using your name since it's such a fine one for a lawyer.

To Vickie Sell, Retired US Forest Service Law Enforcement Officer, thank you for patiently answering all my questions and catching my typos. Any errors in the manuscript are mine alone.

As always, special thanks to my critique partners Michelle Griep and Elizabeth Ludwig (better known to me as Genghis Griep and Ludwig Von Frankenpen). Your marauding critiques and slashing hold my feet to the fire. I couldn't have done this or any other work without you. Love you both and I owe you each a ton of coffee and chocolate!

I could never miss an opportunity to thank Ginger Aster and Beth Willis, my fabulous beta readers. You two catch my mistakes and make sure I correct them. Love you both!

Sandra Bishop, my friend and agent, thank you for believing in me, for being my champion. You make this gig so much better.

Thank you to my phenomenal editor, Susan Price, and all the team at Lighthouse Publishing of the Carolinas. I'm excited to see where God is taking us all.

This book came with a tight deadline, so thanks to my sweet Hubs for feeding the beasts, and to our son, Greg, for cooking. Good thing I raised a chef.

My deepest gratitude goes to my Heavenly Father for fulfilling my dreams of finding my own birth sisters, for giving me this story, and always for whispering to my heart. Most of all, thank you for your grace and love.

Home to

Chapel Springs

by Ane Mulligan

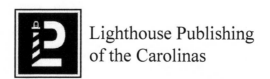
Lighthouse Publishing
of the Carolinas

HOME TO CHAPEL SPRINGS BY ANE MULLIGAN
Published by Lighthouse Publishing of the Carolinas
2333 Barton Oaks Dr., Raleigh, NC, 27614

ISBN: 978-1-941103-61-6
Copyright © 2016 by Ane Mulligan
Interior design by Karthick Srinivasan
Cover design by Elaina Lee, www.forthemusedesign.com
Original artwork by Terence Mulligan

Available in print from your local bookstore, online, or from the publisher at:
www.lighthousepublishingofthecarolinas.com

For more information on this book and the author visit: www.anemulligan.com

Brought to you by the creative team at Lighthouse Publishing of the Carolinas: Susan Price, Eddie Jones, Shonda Savage, Judah Raine and Lucie Winborne.

Library of Congress Cataloging-in-Publication Data
Mulligan, Ane
Home to Chapel Springs / Ane Mulligan 1st ed.

Printed in the United States of America

Praise for *The Chapel Springs Series*

Chapel Springs: where anything can happen, and usually does. Claire and her best friend Patsy are as loveable as ever; even with all the new problems they face, they keep their sense of humor. The storyline is believable, and readers will identify with issues that are mentioned in the book. Mulligan writes with humor and wit. This book does not disappoint.

~ *Romantic Times*, 4-Stars

Home to Chapel Springs is an engaging story, one that will have Chapel Springs fans begging for more.

~ **Michelle Griep**
Author of *Brentwood's Ward*

Pour yourself a tall glass of sweet tea and head out onto the porch with this richly woven tale of life in a small, but suddenly booming southern town. Mulligan's characters are warm and engaging, not to mention delightfully human, as they struggle to navigate problems both big and small, proving in the end that nothing is impossible when we hold tight to faith and keep our hearts open.

~ **Barbara Davis**
Author of *Summer at Hideaway Key*

With her trademark wit and Southern charm, Ane Mulligan takes us on another trip to the idyllic town of Chapel Springs. With Claire Bennett and her zany crew of friends and family, Mulligan spins an endearing tale of how far we'll go for those we love, and the ones we hope will love us in return.

~ **Jennifer AlLee**
Carol Award Finalist and Best-Selling Author

Fans of Ane Mulligan's Chapel Springs novels will be delighted once again to spend time in this quintessential little town in Georgia with its colorful coterie of friends, family, and lovable souls.

~ **Kellie Coates Gilbert**
Author of *A Woman of Fortune*
(Library Journal's Best Book List of 2014)

You'll laugh at the antics of the southern folk in this sleepy town. A fun and heartfelt story from a masterful storyteller.

~ **Carla Stewart**
Award-winning author of *Stardust* and *The Hatmaker's Heart*

A wonderful story of love, forgiveness, patience, and understanding. I highly recommend this book and series to anyone who loves to laugh, cry, and enjoy a great story.

~**Amazon review**

This is a small-town story with big-hearted characters.

~**Southern novelist Judy Christie**
Author of *Magnolia Market*

A touching story involving real women who face crisis, love, doubt, and desperation with love and humor. Together, they survive when courage calls.

~**DiAnn Mills**
Christy Award-winner and author of *Firewall*

Ane Mulligan … succeeds in creating a town full of quirky characters, each endearing in their own way, who discover—sooner or later—what their hearts and their town really need.

~**Cynthia Ruchti**
Award-winning author of *All My Belongings*
and *When the Morning Glory Blooms*

Reading the Chapel Springs series is like coming home to the place you wish you were from, to the friends you know and love.

~**Gina Holmes**
Best-selling, award-winning author of
Crossing Oceans & *Driftwood Tides*

Good, clean fun. Ane Mulligan paints delightfully imaginative word pictures, and makes you wish you could take Claire & Patsy out to lunch. I nearly fell off the sofa laughing at Claire's antics. Hopefully redemptive without sappiness.

~**Amazon review**

"Be strong and courageous. Do not be afraid .... for the Lord your
God goes with you;
He will never leave or forsake you." Deut. 31:6

Chapter 1

Chapel Springs

Of all the days to be late. Claire Bennett stormed up the boardwalk toward *Dee's 'n' Doughs*. Any other morning, the storefronts, with their brightly striped awnings, created a cheerful rainbow on Sandy Shores Drive. Not today. Skullduggery was afoot in Chapel Springs.

The bells clattered a loud jangle as she plowed through the bakery door. Patsy already occupied their favorite table by the window where, when the fog wasn't so thick, they could watch the lake and the boardwalk. Claire nodded hello and went to the counter for coffee. Normally, the aromatic bouquet made her mouth water and sent her taste buds into a frenzy of expectation. Today, all she tasted was bitterness.

"Morning, Claire." Dee poured a mug of coffee, adding a splash of cream and a packet of stevia, and then pushed it across the counter. "You're late. What's up?" Her cheeks, still red from the oven's heat, glowed in her round, jolly face.

Claire lifted one corner of her upper lip in a grimace. "Come sit with us. I don't want to have to tell this twice."

She settled herself in a chair so both the street and the front door were in her line of sight, where she could keep an eye out for that traitor, Howie Newlander. Next to her, Patsy had a pad and pencil out and ready. Claire had already alerted her to Howie's deviousness.

"Thanks. We're going to need that for a battle plan."

"I still can't believe he's back." Patsy took a sip of steaming coffee.

"Believe it. It's not out of character, you know."

The bells jingled merrily and Ellie Grant entered, followed by Lydia and her sister, Lacey, who didn't see them until Lydia pointed to them. They waved, Lacey blushed, and after getting coffee and bagels, joined her and Patsy. Dee followed them to the table, and Claire dragged over another chair for her. Once everyone settled down, she'd tell them what Howie was up to.

"When's your art show?" Dee asked. "My aunt in Philly wants one of your whimsy pots."

"The twenty-first." Claire glanced at Patsy. "I don't have one single piece ready."

Patsy's hand paused on its way to her mouth. "That's because you're so picky." She popped a bite of pastry between her lips. "Dee, you have to make these a regular item. The pear is to die for."

"I'm not picky." Claire removed the stir stick from her coffee. "I just want to try some new ideas."

"Uh-huh. You have plenty of things in the storeroom."

She wrinkled her nose. "Those are ordinary pieces for tourists. I wanted to have something new and innovative for the show."

Ellie's head followed the conversation like it was a Ping-Pong ball. "What more can you do that's truly innovative? You're the best there is."

Heat rose in Claire's cheeks. Compliments made her squirm, especially from friends. "That's a good question. Give me a few frantic hours and I'll come up with ... with something."

Known as one of the country's top pottery artists for her unusual coloration and form, Claire had to come up with a new idea, unless she wanted to relinquish her standing in the fickle art world, which she didn't. Just thinking about it gave her a headache.

"How's your mother, Ellie?" Dee asked.

The librarian squeezed lemon into her tea and stirred it with a sigh that sounded as heavy as a sandbag. "The air pressure change has her in bed. It's murder on rheumatoid arthritis." She mumbled something and sipped her tea.

Claire leaned closer. "What was that?"

Ellie wrinkled her nose. "Let's just say she isn't exactly a candidate for Miss Congeniality today."

Was she ever? Ellie had been under her mother's thumb all her life. Claire couldn't understand why she allowed her mama to be so domineering. If it were her, she'd—hmm, what would she do? There wasn't anyone else. Ellie's sisters left town years ago. The wimps.

Claire swallowed the last of her coffee and signaled Patsy. It was time to let her friends in on what Claire had heard. "I saw Howie Newlander buying groceries yesterday in Lund's. A whole cartload."

Patsy brushed her hands together. Fritter frosting crumbs scattered across the table. "What's he doing here?"

Lydia frowned. "I thought he went back to wherever it was he lived."

"Greenville, and apparently not." Claire didn't trust Howie. He was always a sneaky one, even as a kid. "He was seen skulking around the springs, and then Felix called me. Apparently, Howie has picked up the paperwork to run for mayor."

"What?" Dee slapped her hand against the table. "He's trying to pay us back for ending his land sale. That wasn't our fault."

"It has to do with money, you can count on it." Ellie wrapped her hands around her teacup. "Money and power."

Eyes narrowed, Lydia pursed her lips. "Whatever could he gain by it? It's not like being mayor pays much more than a stipend."

"Well, you can bet he's up to no good. He'll figure out a way to take advantage of the position if he wins." Claire gazed pointedly at each of her friends. "Let's all keep an eye on him. I want to know why he's lurking at the springs. And we can't let him become our mayor."

Dee looked skeptical. "You don't think that could happen, do you?"

"I wouldn't put it past him to try to buy votes. We have a lot of summer people who can vote in our elections."

"Why would anyone vote for that skunk?" Lydia wrinkled her nose.

"Because he could give them a pack of lies."

"You don't know that for a fact." Patsy wagged a finger at Claire.

"You're kidding, right? After what he tried to do to us?"

Lacey folded her napkin. "She's right, Patsy. I found quite a few discrepancies in that land deal. Howie isn't any George Washington."

Surprised their normally silent friend said that much, Claire smiled her thanks. "All I'm saying is one of us needs to be watching him all the time. While I'm not Felix's biggest fan, at least he loves this town as much as we do. Howie couldn't wait until he was out of school to hightail it out of here." A bitter taste filled her mouth. How dare he come here and run for mayor? "Don't we have some ordinance about living here for six months or a year or something?"

Ellie pursed her lips. "I can tell you this. He kept his legal residence listed at his grandparents' house."

Claire's heart hit her toes. "We're going to have to fight him. Patsy, take some notes. We need to know who he's talking to and what he told them. Then we go tell them the truth."

"You'll need facts, Claire," Lacey said. "Proof of your statements."

"If we can find out what he's doing, I'll get the proof."

Dee refilled their cups from the pot she'd brought to the table. "We'll all keep our eyes and ears open, Claire. None of us want that weasel as our mayor." She set the pot on an adjoining table. "Patsy, how's the romance between Chase and Nicole?"

Whoa, Dee changed direction on that conversation faster than a UGA Bulldogs running back. Claire stirred sweetener into her refreshed coffee. Chase and Nicole. At one time, she had hoped their gallery assistant would marry *her* son, Wes, instead of Patsy's, but she had to admit they were perfect for each other. Claire hadn't liked it when they bamboozled her plans, but in the end, it was all right.

Patsy beamed. "Chase proposed last night. Mama gave him Nana's engagement ring for Nicole."

Ellie sighed, Lacey grinned, and Claire swallowed her coffee so fast it burned her throat. "And you didn't think to tell me?" She thunked down the mug and wiped drops of coffee off the table where it splashed over the cup.

Patsy shrugged. "We both knew it was coming. Anyway, I thought Chase told you."

"He only hinted." Claire loved her BFF's kids like they were her own. And vice versa.

Lydia smirked. Technically still a newlywed, she was all about romance. "Those two were made for each other."

"Chase and Nicole are like our Wes and Costy," Claire said. "They complete each other."

Patsy elbowed her and laughed. "You didn't always feel like that."

She was right. Claire loved her new daughter-in-law *now* and couldn't imagine a better fit for her Wes, but it had taken a while—and a large dose of surrendered pride. "Yeah, well, I thought mail-order brides were something from the nineteenth century, not the twenty-first."

"God works in mysterious ways."

Patsy's gotcha smile irked Claire. "How come you're always right? It's downright unnatural."

The others laughed, and even she couldn't help but smile. "I say that a lot, don't I?"

"Claire, sugah, y'all might have a chance if you slowed down an itty bit," Lydia said. Her sweet smile and Alabama drawl always softened the sharp edges of any criticism. Why, she could lambaste the mayor and he'd stand there, waitin' for another helping.

Claire had to admit Lydia was right though. Her mouth started moving before her brain engaged, which usually got her into trouble. She tried to keep her thoughts to herself and not blurt them out, but her tongue had a mind of its own—one that seemed disconnected from her common sense.

She received a sympathetic grimace from Ellie, who then turned to Lacey and asked, "How's the new script coming?"

Bless her heart, Ellie succeeded in taking the focus off Claire's near *faux pas.*

"Good."

A few months ago, Lacey surprised them all by presenting an original script to the director at Curtain Call, the community theater in Pineridge. She had loved it, produced it, and when it was a hit, asked Lacey for another one.

"Well? What's it about?" Claire rotated her hand, motioning for Lacey to tell them more as she took the last bite of her raspberry Danish.

"Murder."

"Murder? You mean like a mystery?" Claire licked the corners of her mouth, checking for stray frosting crumbs. Hmm, maybe they could put Howie in this play.

Lacey nodded.

"Is it funny?"

Lacey had a hidden funny bone that came out in her writing.

"Jake thinks so."

"My brother-in-law would think your left elbow was funny." Lydia laughed when her sister wrinkled her nose.

"But she *is* funny ... on paper." Patsy kicked Claire's ankle. "Ouch. Why—oh. I guess that didn't come out right, huh? What I mean is Lacey's so quiet, nobody would know if she were funny. Van Gogh's ear, that doesn't sound right, either."

She drained the last of her coffee, crossed her arms, and swallowed while everyone laughed. At least Lacey chuckled with them, so Claire hadn't offended her. "We need to resurrect the Lola Mitchell Opera House for the Lakeside Players. That would be something else for tourists to do in the evening, and if we produced original plays, why, we'd sell out every night."

"I know y'all painted the outside, but what's the inside like?" Lacey asked. "I've never been in it."

Claire pulled a napkin from the dispenser. "It's been boarded up for the last thirty-five or forty years. Somebody started a rumor in the late eighties or somewhere thereabouts that it was haunted." She wiped her mouth. "Some say it's a friendly ghost, maybe Aunt Lola. I never saw any evidence of one, but it's not a bad rumor. People love things like that."

"But do you think," Lacey paused and leaned forward, her chin on her fists, "it's possible?"

"I don't know. I'd love to get back in there and restore it, though." Claire glanced around the table at her friends. "It's gorgeous inside. Decorated like the nineteen-thirties. Do y'all think there's enough interest to start a campaign?"

Lydia's eyes sparkled. "I do. A number of my clients have asked what they can do at night around here. So far, most tend to go into Pineridge. We need to keep those dollars in Chapel Springs."

The front door opened. Dee rose to see to the customers but stopped and pointed to the front window. "Claire, is that your Melissa with Bobby? Is she dating him again?"

As if she'd bitten into a persimmon, Claire's mouth puckered. "They're both working on his daddy's reelection campaign. 'Lissa wanted to get some experience for her senior thesis. I don't know why she couldn't have chosen Ellie's campaign instead."

Lydia's head swiveled toward Ellie. "You're running for mayor?"

Ellie shook her head. "Town clerk reelection."

Claire pushed the sugar packets toward Ellie, who'd just refilled her cup. "But y'all haven't heard the craziest thing. Felix has asked me," she jabbed her index finger to her chest, "Me—to help him."

"What?" Patsy's shocked expression mirrored how Claire felt when Felix asked her. "When did he ask you that?"

"Last night." She lowered her voice. "Howie is running on some trumped up green crusade. Doesn't that beat all?"

"My word," Lydia said. "You working with Felix … is like … well, I declare I can't even think of a simile for that. It's beyond oil and water. As for Mr. Newlander, how can he think he'd have the slightest chance of gettin' elected after what he tried to pull over on Chapel Springs?"

"I don't know, and it has me worried."

The whole subject turned Claire's gray funk to puce. She pushed her chair back. "I've got to go. I have a new employee arriving today. Ellie, tell your mother I hope she feels better soon. And Lacey, let's you and me get together about restoring the theater. Let Kelly know, too."

Patsy jumped up and followed Claire, grabbing her hand. "What new employee? You didn't tell me you hired someone. Who is it?"

"Mel. Remember? Goth girl from our night in the pokey."

Chapter 2

Atlanta

Surrounded by her best friends—her only friends if she were being candid—Carin Jardine dug and prodded until each gave up their story. No one was safe from her, and once she discovered their deepest, darkest secret, she'd find their names. Pulling a reference book from her shelf, she studied the photographs on her storyboard.

"Soon, you'll each have the right name, one perfectly befitting your personality." It really was a shame parents couldn't leave their kids unnamed until their personalities became apparent. Then again, sending "baby boy Jones" to preschool might put a wrinkle in his personality.

The door to her office flew open and banged into the wall. Edgar Allen Poe, her English mastiff, growled. When he saw Wick, he settled down but remained alert.

"Kay, I can't find my iPad."

She bristled at the nickname. "How many times have I asked you to knock first?" She laid the book in her lap.

"I did. You didn't answer." He crossed to her credenza, where he lifted papers, opened drawers, and riffled through their content.

"If I don't answer, it means I'm writing. Even JJ knows not to disturb me unless there's blood involved." Counting to ten silently, she gave him the once over. "I don't see any blood."

"You can work when I'm gone. My flight leaves at noon." He stuffed the papers and pens back into the drawer and pushed it shut. The corner of a notebook jutted out. Now she'd have to waste precious time straightening the contents.

"You don't get it, do you?" She really thought he would after ten years of marriage. "When you interrupt me, you pull me out of my story world. It takes time to get back in." Sometimes hours. "And what are you looking for? You're making a mess."

"Yeah, well, *I've* got a plane to catch and I *need* my iPad."

She rose and walked over to him. He exasperated her, but she laid the blame on his mama, who wasn't a Southerner. If she had been, she'd have raised him better. Slipping her arms around his neck, Carin kissed him. He smelled of Bleu de Chanel—and evoked an image of eating citrus fruit in the woods.

"Your iPad is on the end table in the living room, where JJ left it after you let him play Angry Birds. Good luck on your race. I'll pray a band of angels around your car."

His kiss was brief—barely there at all.

He pulled her arms off his neck. "I'm all packed. I'll grab my iPad and be out of your hair. Tell JJ *adios.*"

"You need to tell him, Wick. You're getting like my dad was, always going *out* the door. Okay, okay." She held up her hand to stall his tirade. "I'll tell him. But when you get back, let's go up to Chapel Springs. I want to see how much progress the contractor has made on Nana's—on our house."

Wick opened his mouth then closed it. He turned around and walked out of her office, pulling the door softly shut behind him. That was odd. Wick did nothing softly.

Carin returned her attention to her book of names. She had two hours to get her characters named and a synopsis written before JJ got home from school. Reading from a baby name book and bits of her protagonist's backstory she'd written so far, Carin slipped back into their world.

Her heroine had reunited with her college sweetheart in Paris. Smart, self-assured, and—Carin ran her finger down the page and stopped on Diann. Yes, that was it. It suited her personality with one twist—her Diann had a delightful sense of humor.

Names were so important. They defined a person. So, why did Wick still call her "Kay" when he knew she hated it as a nickname? She wasn't a "Kay." Her aunt was Kay, and she was plump and silly. Wick never seemed to understand that.

Blowing a stray hair out of her eyes, Carin forced herself to focus on her storyboard. Two hours later, she had each character named, the synopsis done and a start on the first chapter. She needed some caffeine.

In the kitchen, she popped a K-cup into the coffee maker and pressed start. Outside their eighteenth-floor Buckhead condominium, the sky darkened as storm clouds moved northward from down near the airport. She pulled up the weather on her phone to catch the forecast. If there were thunderstorms, she'd pick up JJ a little early.

The rich aroma of imported Columbian coffee filled the room. She lifted the cup and inhaled before she sipped. The taste was as good as its aroma, invigorating her as the caffeine zipped through her. The morning's mail was scattered across the kitchen counter where Wick had left it. There wasn't anything but four advertisements, two newspapers, and a flyer for a new Chinese takeout.

He must have taken the bills with him to pay online. He'd taken over paying them a few months ago when she was on a tight deadline. That book was out now, but he hadn't given them back to her. Not that she minded. She hated that chore.

She sipped her coffee and flipped through an advertisement from Macy's, then tossed the ads in the trash but kept the takeout flyer. Maybe she'd try it for dinner. JJ loved Chinese. She tucked it into her purse, which she had left sitting on the counter. The corner of an envelope sticking out from under the dog food bin caught her eye. She bent and picked it up. It was from the HOA people. She and Wick didn't own the condo but leased it. So why was the management company writing to them?

She ripped open the envelope and frowned at the word in bright red letters. *Eviction.* What did that mean? Oh, she knew what the word meant, but what did it have to do with her? She grabbed her phone and hit Wick's speed number. It went right to voice mail. He couldn't be in the plane already. He must have turned it off to go through security.

Picking up the letter again, she looked for a phone number. There it was, across the bottom. She tapped in the number, and when answered, she asked to speak with the person in charge. A few tense and humiliating moments later, she ended the call.

Wick hadn't paid their lease for the past three months. *Three months.* Why not? They had the money. Her last royalty check had been deposited in their joint account. He'd been gone a lot but still ... there had to have been some mistake. Rain beat against the windows and lightning flashed across the sky.

JJ!

Snap, she was late again. "Come on, Edgar." The beast stared at her, not moving. "Get up, we're late picking up JJ. Oh thanks, at the mention of JJ's name, you can move. You're a goofy dog."

She fastened Edgar's leash to his collar, grabbed her purse, and ran— or ran as fast as the dog would move. On the way down to the garage, she called Wick once more, leaving a second message for him to call her the minute he got off the plane. Her next call was to the Christian academy where JJ was enrolled, telling them she was on her way.

When she pulled up beneath the porte cochere, the headmistress stood with JJ, who glared at her with tear-filled eyes. She felt like pond scum. Her poor baby. Ever since lightening hit the condo building a few months ago, he'd been frightened of storms.

Mrs. Worley helped him get buckled into his booster and then walked around to Carin's window.

"Mrs. Jardine, can I talk to you a moment?" She nodded toward JJ. "Away from little ears."

Carin glanced in the mirror at her son. His nose was buried in Edgar's neck, and he wouldn't look at her. She put an arm on the back of the seat and turned to him. "I'm sorry, sugar. Forgive me? Please?"

When he finally returned her gaze, his eyes glistened with unshed tears. He gave a small nod and turned back to his best buddy. That would have to do for now. She got out and followed Mrs. Worley to the rear of the Volvo.

The headmistress held a large umbrella over the two of them. "Mrs. Jardine, you're late again. It's the third time this week alone. JJ gets very upset when you're not here, and I can't keep asking his teacher to stay late."

Would the ground please open up and swallow me? Right now? She couldn't tell the woman time stands still in the story world. Visions rose of being sent to the principal's office for lying when she was JJ's age. She hadn't been "lying" but telling stories.

"I'm so sorry, Mrs. Worley. I don't mean to be late. I'll set up an alert on my phone." She should have thought of that before this.

"I hope so." She crossed her arms. "Now, we need to talk about JJ's tuition. The accountant told me it hasn't been paid in four months."

"What?" First the condo and now JJ's school? What was going on? "I had no idea it hadn't been paid. I'm so sorry. I'll bring a check for you tomorrow."

The woman's whole face pinched until she looked like a California raisin. "It will have to be a bank draft, I'm afraid. The last check Mr. Jardine sent bounced."

Enough heat crawled up Carin's neck and into her face to raise the outside temperature ten degrees. She'd strangle Wick when he got home. She swallowed and nodded. "I'll get one this afternoon."

Back in the car, she tried to act natural. "How was your day, doodle bug?"

He now had his head buried in a book and mumbled an answer. It took some cajoling to finally coax anything from him, and included a promise to write a story just for him with a superhero named JJ.

"It was okay. But I hate the books she makes us read. They're for babies."

"That's because you're such a good reader."

As JJ forgot about her offense and chattered about his day, Carin murmured appropriate uh-huhs at the right places … she hoped. Her mind bounced from one crazy idea to another. Could Wick have hit his head during a race and suffered some kind of temporary bill-paying amnesia? Did he lose a bet on a race and now owed money to some mafia-type goon? What *did* he spend their rent money on? Her stomach churned.

It was times like this she wished she had a close-knit family like normal people. A loving dad, whom she could ask if he'd noticed anything different about Wick. Or a good friend. But with both of them being celebrities, they tended not to let anyone get close. Wick said it was for JJ's safety, and she'd agreed, because by then, she'd already been acquainted with women who didn't want to *be* a friend. They only wanted to *claim* friendship so they could namedrop.

That was right after her first book hit the New York Times Bestseller list. When the second one made the list, Sue Clements sidled up to her at her book signing acting so friendly, Carin believed her. The subsequent betrayal blindsided her. She never let it happen again. The downside was the loneliness.

"Mama, what's for supper?"

A glance at the dashboard clock told her she had just enough time to zip by the bank and get that check. "What do you think of Chinese?"

"Yes!" A small fist pumped the air in her rearview mirror.

"Okay, I've got to stop by the bank, then we'll go to a new takeout place I got a flyer for."

"Can I see it?"

"Sure." When she parked at the bank, she handed it to him. "Bring it in and read it while I do business. You can decide what we'll have this time." He'd choose egg rolls, pot stickers, and spare ribs—a calorie-laden supper and a fitting penance for a forgetful mama.

Inside the bank, she filled out a counter check for the amount to the school and the rent and waited her turn. When she reached the counter, she handed it to the teller, who smiled and tapped in the numbers on her keyboard. Then she frowned. "I'm sorry, Mrs. Jardine, but that account has been closed out."

Carin couldn't make her voice work. Her mouth opened but nothing came out.

"Maybe you transposed a number. Let me check by your name." The teller pushed up the sleeves of her sweater and tapped her keyboard. "No, ma'am, that was the right account. The final withdrawal was made this morning."

That couldn't be. Why would he?

"There's a note here that you're moving, and a forwarding address will be provided. Do you have that?"

Could he be thinking of moving them to the house in Chapel Springs? It wasn't finished yet—or was it?

The teller raised her eyes from her computer screen and smiled. "I'm sure we would have told your husband he could have transferred the funds just as easily." She shrugged. "Do you have the address for us?"

Carin shook her head and cleared her throat. "I'm not sure of it." She wasn't sure of anything. Her power of reasoning short-circuited at "account closed."

"Well, send it to us as soon as you have it. Y'all have a nice day now and enjoy your new home."

What new home? Had Wick bought them a house and planned to

surprise her? She'd kill him if he did. A woman wanted to choose her own house. And why would he jeopardize their credit by not paying the condo lease or JJ's school? None of this made a lick of sense.

She turned back to the teller. "I have another account here, in just my own name. I'd better close it, too." There should be a little over fifteen thousand dollars in it.

"You can transfer the funds if you'd like."

"No, I need it now. Please close it." It would take every penny to pay the lease and tuition.

The girl smiled and tapped away, then opened her drawer and counted out the money.

Carin breathed a sigh of relief. She could pay the school in the morning. She glanced around the bank lobby. Thank goodness it wasn't filled with customers.

"Here you are, Mrs. Jardine. Four hundred nineteen dollars and sixty-one cents."

Chapter 3

Chapel Springs

Claire unlocked the door to *The Painted Loon*. As she pushed it open, Patsy's hand gripped her shoulder and startled the daylights out of her.

"Here comes Mel in all her Goth glory."

Claire shaded her eyes from the sun and followed Patsy's waving. There she was, passing *Front Row Seat*, pushing her dark bangs out of her eyes as she worked her way toward them. Goth girl, aka Mel, or Melanie. Claire just hoped nobody tried to call her that. Everyone would think her cheese had slid clean off her cracker for hiring this kid.

"Hmph. They'll deal with me if they do."

"Who will deal with you if they what?"

"What?"

Patsy chuckled. "You're talking to yourself again, and I'm guessing you're feeling a bit mama-bearish over our new employee."

"There's something about her that brings it out in me." The object of their nattering arrived. "Morning, Mel. Remember Patsy?"

The kid sort of smiled, if you called a one-sided-lip-hike smiling. "Hey."

"We're both glad you've come to work for us." Patsy patted Mel's shoulder then ushered her into the gallery.

Mel stopped just inside the door. Claire quickly sidestepped the girl to avoid a collision.

"You really make all this?" Wonder etched Mel's voice as she gaped at the room.

Claire smiled. This kid was good for the ego. "Just the pottery. Patsy is the brush artist."

"Wow. You two could do some bodacious tats."

Potatoes? Claire's gaze slid to Patsy, but she looked as confused—oh. Tattoos. Of course. So much for flattery.

"Right. So, let's get you familiar with the gallery and our prices. Come on back to see the workroom first."

After she had a tour of the back, they started with the large vase display shelves, and moved to the whimsy pottery, where Mel just had to touch each one, boosting Claire's confidence. She explained the lighting panel and the importance of the lights on their artwork, then moved to showcases near the door where the smaller tourist-type items were displayed.

Patsy made a discreet phone call to Nicole to let her know about Mel so she wouldn't be surprised or think they were letting her go. Claire actually wanted to have Nicole at the pottery wheel more. She was turning into a fine potter. It was time for her to begin selling, and especially since she would be Patsy's daughter-in-law in a few months. Hiring Mel would eliminate the need for Nicole to be in the gallery so much.

Claire checked her orders and the phone for messages while Patsy explained their codes for pricing. It didn't take their little Goth girl long to master it—which went to prove you shouldn't judge a person by the way they looked. There was a bright mind beneath all that metal stuck on her body. She hoped their customers wouldn't be put off with Mel's Gothic aura.

Two hours later, Patsy went to paint, and Mel settled behind the front desk. Claire stepped up on a small ladder and set a platter on its stand, rotating it a couple of degrees to the left. The colors had been pulled from a memory, a sunset over the lake. A smile warmed her from the inside out. Next to it, she placed a large, colorful duck.

The front door opened, and Mel looked up from the funny papers she'd been reading. She closed the paper and stood.

"May I help you?"

"Who are you? Where's Claire?"

The mayor's voice had more gravel than Flintstone's Quarry. "I'm over here, Felix." She came around the display shelves. "This is my new employee, Melanie. Mel, this is our mayor, Felix Riley. Now that we've dispensed with introductions, what do you need?"

He waved a flyer in front of her nose. "Look what Newlander's putting in everyone's door."

"If you'd stop flapping the darn thing, I could read it."

"Don't bother." He stuffed the marketing piece in his pocket. "He's calling us earth-desecraters. Says the town isn't using recycled paper and …" he slapped his ball cap against his thigh. "Blast it all, Claire! He's accusing me of wasting money."

Mel snorted then hid her face in the funnies. Felix snapped his head around. "What's so funny about that, girl?"

She lowered the paper and returned his stare. Claire stifled a smile. Good for her.

Mel twitched her right eyebrow ring. "From what I've heard, you squeeze fifteen cents out of a dime."

Felix looked at Claire. "Did she insult me or pay me a compliment?"

"A compliment. You do get the most out of our tax dollars." She frowned. "I wouldn't worry too much over this, Felix. Howie doesn't have a chance. He's wasting his money."

"Maybe you're right." His gaze bounced to Mel, who had returned to the front desk. "Where'd you find her?"

No way was she going to tell him in jail. "She's from Pineridge."

"Huh." Felix stared hard at Mel, his lips moving. "Have you counted all them holes in her? Why, if she fell in the lake, she'd sink straight to the bottom."

Mel snorted again, and Claire put her hands on the mayor's shoulders, turning him toward the door. "Go to work, Felix. And quit worrying."

Two ladies opened the door. Felix doffed his ball cap and stood aside for them to enter. The taller of the two stared at Mel but then nodded and leaned toward her friend.

"I've always wished I had the nerve to get one of those nose rings."

Her short friend gasped. "You wouldn't … would you?"

"In a minute." She turned to Mel. "Did it hurt?"

Mel actually smiled. "Not a bit. You should try it. Now, how may I help you?"

Claire's instinct about that girl paid off. Her deft redirection of their attention was nothing short of brilliant. She left Mel to help them and went into the workroom, where Patsy was adding a branch of Cherokee roses to a still life. Claire slipped on her potter's apron and opened the clay barrel.

"I don't think we're going to have to worry about Mel being accepted here. I guess because we're an art gallery, people expect an oddball or two. Look at us." She chuckled. "If we'd been born a couple of decades later, you think we'd look like Mel?"

"You, probably, but not me. I'm not that adventurous."

Claire punched the clay into submission, slapped it down onto the batt, and set her wheel in motion. "I need to make the bank deposit later this afternoon. Do you need anything while I'm out?"

Patsy dabbed her brush on her palette, picking up thalo blue, then pointed the painted end at Claire. "Ooh, yes. Stop by Lunn's and get me a pizza cutter."

"Okay. You making pizza tonight?" Patsy-cooked anything was Claire's favorite. She was as good a chef as Joel.

"No. I want it for the rigging on a sailboat."

One day, she'd learn not to question Patsy's tools for painting.

Chapter 4

Atlanta

Carin opened the door and JJ scurried in, carrying their takeout dinner. "Put that on the counter, then hang up your jacket, and wash your hands." How could she be concerned about such ordinary things when her world's security had suffered a major breach?

"Okay, Mama."

She slid out of her coat and hung it in the entryway closet. Surely Wick's plane had landed by now. After slipping her phone in her pocket, she went to the kitchen. She fed the dog and dished up their supper. She'd wait until JJ was in bed to call his father.

Her son ran into the kitchen and jumped into his chair. He stabbed a pot sticker with his fork. Holding it aloft, he took a bite. "Yum!" He swallowed and picked up an egg roll with his left hand.

"Hold on, young man. You forgot to ask a blessing."

He set his fork down and grinned that heartbreaking smile of his. "Sorry." He bowed his head and asked God to bless their food, then picked up where he'd left off with the egg roll.

In her pocket, her phone chirped. An email had arrived. A quick look told her it wasn't from Wick but a Google alert on her name. It was probably a book review, and she'd read it after dinner. She laid her cell on the table and picked up an egg roll.

"Can I play a game, Mama?"

"Okay." She slid the phone to him. "Just one, though. Then bath time."

"'K." He picked it up and tapped the screen. "Hey, Mama, what does 'lost her edge' mean?"

"It depends on the usage. It could mean a knife isn't sharp any more. Or a saw. Where did you see that?"

"Here." He pointed to her phone's screen. "There's a Google alert that says you lost your edge."

That "lost her edge" didn't sound good. Not if it were a review on her latest book, and they were due about now. Her stomach lurched and threatened to return the egg roll she just swallowed. She tried to keep her voice free of anxiety. "Let me see, sugar." She reached out her hand.

JJ pulled back. "Aw, I wanted to play."

Stay calm. She took a deep breath. "And I said you could. I'll go see it on my computer." That was probably a better idea, anyway. He wouldn't witness her reaction.

In her office, she woke her computer and opened email. Her heart plunged all the way to her toes. There it was. The *New York Times* review. With a trembling hand, she clicked on the link.

"Jardine has lost her edge. She should stick to women's fiction and leave the romance to others more acquainted with the genre."

The reviewer went on to crucify her. Reading it all would be too painful, so she went to the next email from the *Romantic Times*, which gave her book only one and a half stars. The *Chicago Tribune* review was scathing.

"Jardine needs to have a romance before she tries to write one."

Carin blinked and forgot to breathe. *Wow. They love you one week and gleefully pulverize you the next.*

She didn't read the rest but opened the Internet and went to a review blog. "One would think being married to sexy race car driver Wick Jardine would give her something to draw on for romance. It makes one wonder if the stories about him are true."

What stories? And why was he gone when she needed him? She could use his support and his strong arms around her right now. Tears pooled in her eyes and spilled over.

"Mama? You okay?"

JJ and Edgar stood in the doorway. The dog lumbered over and put his big head in her lap. Carin swiped her sleeve across her eyes. "I'm fine, sugar."

JJ pushed Edgar aside and climbed onto her lap. He took her face between his small hands. "Why are you crying?"

Carin hugged him. "I'm not crying anymore. I've got you to love." She sucked back any threatening tears. She was stronger than any reviewer's barbs.

"I love you, too, Mama." He snuggled against her.

She drew in his little boy scent, part sweat, part dirt, and part Edgar. A bath was in order. "How about we read a book. Would that be nice?"

"Which one?"

"What about Chronicles of Narnia?"

"Yay!" He jumped off her lap and pulled her hand. "Come on."

"Bath first," she reminded him. He charged toward the bathroom.

She looked at Edgar. "You could use a bath, too."

He shook at the word "bath" and slunk away to hide. As if. "No use hiding. I'll find you, beast."

"'Night, sugar." Carin turned off JJ's light and closed his door. She made her way down the hall and across the condo to her office. There, she sat in the dark and stared out the window at Atlanta's night skyline. She'd be losing this in a few days. Why had Wick let the lease go unpaid? And why hadn't he returned her calls?

She pulled out her phone and hit his speed dial number. She was about to hang up after the fourth ring when a breathy female voice answered. In the background, Wick's voice asked, "Who is it?"

"I don't know. They haven't said anything."

"Give me the phone." Wick spit out an expletive. He must have seen the caller I.D. "Carin?"

Everything fell into place. "Who is she, Wick?"

"It doesn't matter."

"Excuse me? It doesn't *matter*? I think it does. You're having an affair. How could you do this to me? To your son?" She'd strangle him when she got her hands on him. Better, she'd—

"Leave JJ out of it, Carin. This is between us."

"How can I leave him out? You've gotten us *evicted* from our home and taken all our money." Indignation erupted like lava within her veins. "And you stole mine. Did you spend it on your bimbo? And how did you get access to *my* account?"

"You should be more careful with your passwords."

His cold, compassionless tone threw ice water on her anger. How could he be so unloving? "I don't understand any of this. What happened? When are you coming home?"

There was a long pause. Carin's heart dropped. "Wick?"

"I'm not."

Just like Dad. She couldn't believe this. First her birth parents abandoned her, then her adopted dad left, and now Wick? "Not what? Tell me what's happened."

"I'm tired of taking second place to your books."

Had she done that? "Wick, I'm sorry. Look, come home. I love you, and I'm willing to work on our marriage." *Please.*

"I'm not."

She sucked in a breath. "You have to come home." Even if just to get his clothes.

"No, I don't. And I'm not."

"You can't mean that. What about JJ?"

"You'll figure out something to tell him. You're a writer."

Yanking her hair out of her eyes, she questioned Wick's parentage. "How am I supposed to feed him? Where are we going to live? You took all our money."

"You'll get more."

"I've never known you to be so cold and heartless. My new book is … is …" Now was not the time for pride. "It's bombing. The reviewers are killing me."

"Gee, that's tough."

Now *that* ticked her off. "Sarcasm doesn't become you, Wick. The point is, sales will be down. I won't get any more money from this book. And what I had, you *stole.*"

"Write another. Look, I gotta go. I'll send for my things. Tell JJ I love him."

"If you love him, don't leave. Wick? Wick! Don't you hang up on me." Carin hit speed dial again. He let it go to voicemail. She tried repeatedly with no answer. Her heart pounded within her chest.

What was it about her that made everyone abandon her?

A sniffle made her jerk up her head. JJ stood in the doorway. She stared at him. How much had he heard? She tossed the phone aside and held out her arms. He ran to her, buried his head in her neck, and cried. Her tears mingled with his. After a few minutes, he pulled back, his eyes dry and his little face stained with sorrow.

"Daddy's not coming home, is he?"

She couldn't lie to him, but there was always a chance—maybe not a big one, but still … "Not for a while, love bug. It's going to be just you and me."

"But why, Mama? What did I do?" His eyes filled again.

Her heart shattered. That was what she'd thought every time her dad left. JJ wasn't going to carry that guilt if she could help it. She may have been culpable by neglecting Wick, but he was a scoundrel.

"Sugar, look at me." She waited until his eyes met hers. "You did nothing wrong. This is between Daddy and me. Not you."

"Is he mad because you were late picking me up? I don't care, Mama. Well, I do kind of, but I know it's 'cause you're writing stories."

"Do you have any idea how much I love you?"

His little face was solemn. "Two teapots full?"

She hugged him. "Eleven teapots full." He snuggled deeper into her arms.

"Mama, what's 'victed mean?"

That yanked the breath right out of her. "It means … we're moving." There was only one place she could go. "Do you remember my nana's house in Chapel Springs? On Chapel Lake? Your daddy—" Her voice caught. Gibraltar took up residence in her throat. She swallowed and forged ahead. "Remember how the contractor was remodeling it? It should be close to done. We can play camping out while he finishes. Doesn't that sound like fun?"

She was rambling, but it worked. JJ brightened at the idea of camping out. She took him back to bed and tucked him in. "Don't forget your prayers."

"You too, Mama. Don't you forget to pray."

She had forgotten. For too long. Hoping God would forgive her, she turned out his light. "I won't, sugar. Sleep tight. Tomorrow, we start packing."

Packing up her life. And she'd have to call JJ's school to tell them he wouldn't be returning, but that somehow, she'd pay her debt to them. Somehow.

She couldn't wrap her mind around Wick leaving them like this. How had she not seen the signs? And just how long had that woman—girl, if her voice was any indication—been sleeping with her husband? Better, how could he cheat on her? Humiliate her like this? She groaned. The reviewers knew about it. Had she been so deep into her fictional world that she missed it?

She searched her memories for hints. Wick knew she had deadlines to meet when he married her. He said he liked the idea of a novelist wife. Come to think of it, he'd always been big on image. The condo. The cars. Nana's old house became "The Lake House." She was happy with it the way it was, but he *had* to have it remodeled. She thought he'd given up his playboy image when they got married. Apparently, he hadn't.

And now he didn't want her anymore.

Waves of loss rolled over her. Nana warned her against marrying a Yankee—no staying power she said. And now her marriage was over. Dead. She dropped her head into her hands and let her tears fall.

How did one mourn the death of a marriage? And how could you mourn without a funeral? If ever she needed a friend, it was now.

Chapter 5

Chapel Springs

Melissa and Bobby sat in the far corner of Felix's campaign office—which was, in reality, a storage room—in front of the only window. At least someone had taken the time to wash it—probably 'Lissa, who had her head together with Bobby's, collaborating on something, and didn't even look up when Claire entered. Great. Now she was invisible. Then again, maybe that wasn't so bad.

She dropped her new Chartreaux Katz customized tote on an empty desk. The designer had duplicated the sign from *The Painted Loon* on the tote. She made them for all the shops in Chapel Springs, and the tourists snapped them up like warm Krispy Kreme donuts. Nancy Vaughn couldn't keep them in the boutique. They sold as fast as Chartreaux turned them out. Claire wasn't sure who bought more—the tourists or the shop owners.

Claire pulled out the chair, scraping it on the cement floor. It emitted a screech that rivaled fingernails on a chalkboard, startling Melissa from Bobby's magnetism.

"Hey, Momma. I didn't hear you come in. What are you working on?"

"I don't know yet. Felix called me in a panic." She dropped into the chair and drummed her fingers on the desktop. "Bobby, do you have any idea what's yanked a knot in his chain?"

He stopped folding the flyer with Felix's face plastered on its front. "Yeah. One of the farmers, Murdoch, I think, is stirring up trouble. He heads the local chapter of the Farmers Union. All I know is he's hot under his overalls about something. He called Dad last night. Threw Newlander's name around."

Why would the farmers side with Howie? That made about as much sense as an interstate highway in Hawaii. Howie was for big business, and all that environmental stuff usually caused farmers grief. What was the connection?

The door banged open, hitting the wall, and Felix blew in. "Good, you're here. Newlander's trying to blame me for Benson Creek drying up." He threw his cap on her desk. "Me! How does a creek drying up involve me?"

Claire's mind clickety-clacked through memory banks until it landed on the springs. *Uh-oh.* She tensed her jaw muscles, grimacing. "Do you think he's trying to tie it to the warm springs?"

Felix blanched and sank into the chair opposite her. "Could he do that?"

"I don't know. What happened to the report Sean gave us?"

"Who?"

Claire sighed. Nicknames died hard. "Wingnut."

Poor kid's ears stuck straight out and Leonard Sokolov, the geology professor they'd hired to investigate the springs, called him that. She shuddered at how close she'd come to making a life-altering mistake over him.

"Oh, yeah. I've got it in my office. But there wasn't anything in—" He slapped the desk with his palms. "Wait a cotton pickin' minute. There was something about an underground stream that might have been diverted. But that wasn't our doing. That was the state's DOT."

"Felix, you've got to know by now, Howie doesn't play fair." She went to the coffee machine. "Want some?"

Felix scratched his ample belly. "Yeah. Any Krispy Kremes left?"

Bobby raised his thumb over his shoulder, pointing to the small card table behind him. "Over here, Pop."

By the time Claire had brewed a cup for Felix then herself, he had frosting crumbs collecting in the corners of his mouth.

"Thanks," he mumbled around a mouthful of donut. "So what's the plan?"

She pulled out her cell phone. "I'm calling Sean." She'd kept his number, thinking maybe he and Melissa might—she glanced over at her daughter and Felix's son. That probably wasn't going to happen. But at least she still had his number. She tapped his name and waited.

"O'Keefe here."

"Sean, it's Claire Bennett from Chapel Springs. Do you remember me?"

"Hey, Ms. Bennett. I sure do. What's up?"

The warmth in his voice gladdened her heart and made her smile. She and Joel had grown fond of the young man while he was in Chapel Springs. "We've got a problem again."

"With the springs?"

"Kind of. Yes. With the springs. We need you to do some more investigating." Claire explained the farmer's accusations and Howie Newlander's role in their concern. "We'll pay you, of course." She turned her back on Felix's frantic waving and his purple-infused grimacing. "Thanks, Sean. See you next week." She tapped her phone off. "Don't start, Felix. You want answers?"

His shoulders slumped. "Yeah. Dawg-gone Newlander."

Bobby looked over his shoulder at them. "Pop, quit being so tight. The dude deserves to be paid for his work. Come on."

Felix stood. "Yeah, yeah, y'all don't have to explain it to the City Council."

"I promise to approve it." Claire shot him a cheeky grin.

"You'd better. It was your idea."

Shaking her head, she grabbed the last donut. "Felix, lighten up." She tore off a giant bite of the donut as Felix watched it disappear. "Things aren't that bad." At least she didn't think they were. "I'll see you later. Melissa, will you be home for dinner?"

Her daughter exchanged glances with Bobby before shaking her head. "We're going to get a pizza in here and finish getting this flyer ready for mailing."

As she descended the outside stairs, she stopped two steps from the bottom. On the sidewalk in front of the bank, Newlander strutted up and down, handing out flyers. Of all the nerve, right in front of Felix's campaign office. A man she didn't recognize took one, read it over, and asked Howie something. Whatever he told the man startled him. He gaped at the flyer.

Claire stole to the corner of the building. Would Howie give her one of his flyers if she asked for it? There was only one way to find out.

"What's this, Howie?"

He frowned, and rolling his flyers in one hand, he planted his fists on his hips. "What do you want, Claire?"

"I'd like to read one of those." She held out her hand. "Everyone else is reading them."

He unrolled his fist and glanced at the flyer. His eyes narrowed. "What for?"

"What do you think? I want to see what you're saying about the Town Council, make sure you're not slandering us."

He held the flyers tight. "Everything I say is the truth."

"Then you shouldn't have any problem with me seeing one."

His eyes darted between the gentleman to whom he'd been talking and her. His face grew red and his lips thinned. He turned and his long legs ate up the sidewalk at a remarkable rate.

"You want this one?" The stranger held out the flyer to her. "I'm a summer renter, and I almost believed this until he wouldn't give you one."

"Thank you." She took the paper. "He's been caught bending the truth before." She read the piece. Sure enough, it ranted about money wasted on the warm springs. His grandmother would be so disappointed in him. She was glad Granny Newlander had passed away last year and didn't have to see what Howie was trying to do to Chapel Springs.

Chapter 6

Atlanta

Carin taped the last box shut under the watchful eye of the HOA representative. Really? He thought she was trying to run off with the furniture? The condo had come furnished, and none of it was to her taste, anyway. The least he could have done was give her a hand, but no. That wasn't in his job description.

She slapped the last piece of tape on the last box and straightened. She stared at the HOA rep. "That's it. All done and not a single sofa hidden in any of the cartons."

"Just doing my job, Mrs. Jardine. What about your husband's things?"

She'd tried to reach Wick to see what he wanted her to do, but he wouldn't answer her calls, so she left all his clothes and personal belongings in the master bedroom closet. "I guess you'll have to contact him about those. I can't fit another thing in my car."

"I won't promise they'll be here, since y'all owe back rent."

She stared at him until he looked away.

The least he could have done was offer to help as she struggled with the big box. Apparently, his job didn't include any heavy lifting, either. Nor did he have the propriety to exhibit any remorse but stood with arms folded, watching as she struggled to push the box out the door.

Once it was in the hallway, she glanced over her shoulder. With her small son beside her, maybe she looked helpless enough that he'd relent and give her a hand. Instead, he closed the door and locked it. His mama would be ashamed.

JJ glared at the closed door. "That was mean of him."

"Let it be a lesson to you, JJ. Always be a gentleman."

"Yes, ma'am." He wiggled, trying to stretch taller. "I'll help you."

"Thank you, sugar."

With a little leverage, she and JJ managed to get the final large container into the front passenger seat of her Volvo. Thank goodness she'd paid off the SUV with an earlier advance. Edgar and JJ would occupy the back seat. The rear was packed to the brim with their belongings—a pitiful lot, to say the least. She closed the rear liftgate.

"Well, doodle bug, let's get this show on the road."

A tiny seed of excitement at seeing Nana's house again took root. Wick talked about renovating it after Nana died. He asked for her ideas but said he wanted to surprise her. She hadn't seen it since construction started. That was six months ago. Wick hadn't said anything about it for a while, so it might not be finished yet, but it had to be close to being done. That could be part of the adventure for JJ.

She smiled as memories of summers in Nana's lovely old house— and the friends she'd made there as a kid—played through her mind. Could it be they still lived in Chapel Springs? She could use a friend.

Back during those summers, Adrianna Bennett was a pretty good friend. Though younger than Carin, they'd still been close. She remembered Adrianna's parents, Miss Claire and Mr. Joel. He was the kind of daddy she'd always wanted.

Then there was Ryan—what *was* his last name? He lived next door to Nana. All she could think of was Seacrest, but he was the American Idol host. Graves. That was it. Did he still live there? Nana told her he'd lost half his arm in Afghanistan. Poor guy. How was he now? Did he have that PTSD? Would he even remember her?

There were other people she remembered, but they knew her as a teen, one of their peers. Now? Sue Clements' betrayal loomed in Carin's thoughts. Things were different now. She wasn't sure if renewing those friendships was worth the risk.

The three-hour drive took a little over four with pit stops—three for JJ and one for Edgar—and snacks. It was mid-afternoon when they pulled into Chapel Springs. JJ rolled down his window and stuck his face in the opening. Edgar put his head over JJ's shoulder, his tongue lolling out the side of his mouth.

"Mama, look! There's the lake and boats and people fishing and swimming."

"JJ, sit back. I know sugar, and you'll get to swim and fish, too. But we've got to get settled first."

Chapel Springs looked like Disneyland to JJ, but to her, it represented all her failures. A vacation lake house was one thing, but to live here full time? Last time she was there, she moved Nana into assisted living. When she died, they held her memorial service in the chapel out at the cemetery. Wick rushed them right back home without even going by the old house. Now, Nana was gone and that old house was all Carin had left of her.

"What's that, Mama?" JJ pointed ahead to a guard hut and a mechanical arm across the road.

"I don't know. It wasn't here the last time I came." When she was here to bury Nana, they didn't enter town. She eased to a stop and lowered her window.

The elderly guard welcomed her with a smile of recognition. "Well, bless my soul, if it isn't little Carin Rice all growed up."

Bud Pugh. The bank security guard. He must have retired from there. She raised her sunglasses and smiled. "Good afternoon, Mr. Pugh. It's good to see you. What is this for?"

"Well now, missy, with all the traffic we got since the beautifyin' of Chapel Springs, we bought ourselves a couple of trams. If you're visiting, you just park over yonder and ride the tram."

"I want to ride, Mama." JJ had unbuckled his seatbelt and stood behind her, looking over her shoulder.

"Hush now, JJ. Let me finish. Mr. Pugh, I'm moving here. Do I have to leave my car?"

"Now, that's good to hear. I was worried about your grand-maw's house a-sittin' there all sad and empty. Since you'll live here, you get a permit to drive in town. Let me git that for you." He stepped into the hut.

What had he meant by the house being sad and empty? Surely there was activity. Unless the remodeling had been completed. *Please let it be completed.* The alternative was unthinkable.

"Will I ever get to ride the tram?"

"You sure will, youngun. Any time you want." Mr. Pugh handed her a sticker for her window. "You put this on the inside of your windshield, Miss Carin." He leaned down and peered in the car at JJ. "Welcome to Chapel Springs. I'm guessin' you'll soon be our newest fishin' champ."

JJ grinned and talked with Mr. Pugh while she pulled the backing off the sticker and pressed it to the upper left corner of the windshield where he'd pointed.

Mr. Pugh returned his attention to Carin and held out his hand. Oh dear. She hoped it didn't cost too much.

She fumbled with the clasp on her purse. "How much?"

"Don't cost nothin' fer you, Miss Carin, but I'll take that trash and git rid of it."

She handed him the backing from the sticker. "Thank you."

His face wrinkled like a walnut with his smile as he waved them through.

JJ's feet tapped the back of her seat. "He was nice, Mama. Did you remember him?"

"Feet, JJ. And I do remember him. He was the bank security guard when I was a little girl." *I sometimes wished he was my daddy.*

The answer seemed to satisfy JJ, who pushed back in his seat so he could stare out the window. Pine Drive was the next street, and a moment later, she turned into the driveway of her grandmother's house. No. Her house.

The sun had begun its slow descent behind the trees, and the house stood in the shadows. Carin leaned forward, peering through the windshield. The outside of the old two-story hadn't been touched. One shutter hung askew, and what was left of any paint was peeling, giving the façade the appearance of a reptile losing its skin. Now she knew what Bud Pugh had meant.

"Mama?" JJ's voice trembled. "Is it haunted?"

This was a steel-magnolia moment if ever there was one. Carin lifted her chin and forced a smile. "Why no, sugar. It's just sorry lookin'. The work started on the inside, where all good remodeling begins. Come on. Let's go see what's been done. Grab your backpack. Come on, Edgar."

Carin took the leash and JJ's hand as they approached the wrap-around porch. "Watch that step." She pointed to a crumbling tread. "Let me go first and you follow. Put your feet only where I put mine."

She pulled Edgar to one side so he wouldn't fall through the rotten stair, then tested each tread before putting her full weight on it. They all needed replacing, but only the side of one was completely rotten. At the door, Carin pulled out her key and handed it to JJ.

"Before we go in, turn around and look. See?" She pointed to Moonrise Cove. "Our street is a hill, so nothing blocks our view of the lake. We're less than half a football field from the water."

"I can see the boats!" JJ wiggled in delight. "When can we go fishing?"

"We need to get settled in first." She held out the key. "You may do the honors."

He slid the old skeleton key into the ancient lock and turned it. There was a loud click and the door swung open.

Nothing blocked their view in any direction. Absolutely nothing, save for a single metal pole in the middle. The main floor had been gutted and reconfigured, but none of the new drywall was in place. A lone light bulb hung from a long wire in what was supposed to be the great room. Where the kitchen used to be, only one portion of the old base cabinets remained.

Why wasn't more done? Carin's stomach took a nosedive. Of course. Wick wouldn't have paid the contractor, either. What had he condemned them to?

"You're right, Mama. It's not haunted. There's nowhere for a ghost to hide."

With tear-filled eyes, she laid her hand on his warm little head to keep her fingers from shaking. JJ's glass was always full. Even so, dark shadows called for light. She flipped a switch. Nothing. "Sugar, can you go get the flashlight from the car? Be careful on the steps."

"I will." He zipped out the door. While she waited, Carin peered up the stairs. Would that be gutted too? They had planned on renovating it somewhat, adding a master bath and updating the main bathroom.

"Here, Mama." JJ handed her the light and she turned it on, aiming its beam up the stairway.

"Let me go first." The stairs creaked but didn't sag or give as she stepped on them. At the top, she tried the hall light switch. Light illuminated the dark corners and with it, a little of the tension left her shoulders. "Come on up, buddy."

They investigated the five bedrooms. Thankfully, they hadn't been touched yet. The bathroom was another story.

"Mama, there's no potty. Just a hole in the floor."

"I guess we'll do some real camping. We'll have to get a porta-potty until it's fixed."

JJ's eyes grew big with excitement. "Really? Cool."

Oh, to be six again.

"Hello? Carin?" A voice floated up from downstairs. "It's Claire Bennett."

Edgar flew down the stairs, barking.

"I'll be right down." She turned to JJ and pointed to a bedroom on the right of the hall. "That will be my bedroom. You pick out yours. I'll be back." She descended the stairs.

Claire laughed while Edgar slobbered all over her, then she rose and wiped her hands on her jeans. Thank goodness she knew mastiffs. Carin remembered when they got Shiloh as a puppy. It was why she chose a mastiff.

"Welcome home, Carin." Claire opened her arms.

Memories flooded of Adrianna and her giggling and eating lunch in Claire's or Nana's kitchen. It took every ounce of strength not to collapse into those arms in tears. How could Carin tell her this wasn't home? Home was Atlanta. Buckhead. Success.

"JJ is going to be thrilled to meet you." She stepped back and called over her shoulder. "Doodle bug, come on down and meet—"

"Come get me." His voice was muffled.

Uh-oh. "We have literally just arrived, and I don't know what's up there. Excuse me." She flew up the stairs. "JJ? Where are you?"

"Mama? Get me out." Fear bordering panic wobbled his words. She followed the sound into a bedroom on her left. "JJ?"

"I'm here."

In the wall? Then she saw the outline of a small door and a swing latch. She knelt, turned the lever, and yanked open the small door. A bug-eyed JJ leaped into her arms.

"It looked like a cool hidey hole, but the door closed when I went in and it was dark and I couldn't open the door again. That's when I got kinda scared." He pulled away from her. "But I'm not scared anymore. It's kind of neat, huh?"

She stuck her head into the little doorway. It was a finished storage room. She'd have to make sure the clasp worked on both sides before he could play in there. And leave a flashlight inside.

"Spoken like a very brave boy." Claire leaned against the doorjamb. Carin hadn't heard her come up.

"Uh, sugar"—she rose to her feet—"this is Miss Claire. She's the potter who made Timothy." She put her hand on JJ's shoulder and offered Claire a shy smile. "That's what he named the unicorn vase."

JJ's eyes exuded hero worship. He ran over to her. "You *made* Timothy? How'd you do that?"

Claire squatted to eye-level with him. "Sort of like God first made Adam." She glanced at Carin then back at JJ. "I took some clay and worked it, and then I put it on my potter's wheel and formed it—him."

"JJ knows all about how God made Adam *and* Eve."

"Yeah, he took one of Adam's ribs. There's a restaurant here named Adam's Rib. You ever eat there? Jake's got good ribs. He's the owner, and—"

The doorbell rang. At least that still worked. Edgar barked out the warning and charged down the stairs again. Who could it be—the welcome wagon? They'd just arrived. "Son, why don't you show Miss Claire around while I see who's at the door?"

JJ took Claire's hand. "Come on. I'll show you Mama's room. I'm gonna have this one. I like the secret fort. And you gotta see the funny bathroom."

Downstairs, Carin found a man examining the door's lock. She recognized Ryan immediately—of course, the folded sleeve would give him away even if she hadn't. He looked the same, just a little older. He glanced up as she came down the stairs. "You need a better lock. Anyone could bust this door wide open. I'll get a new one installed for you before nightfall."

He had always lived next door. She had a crush on him when she was fourteen. She couldn't remember who he married, but his wife left him a few years ago, Nana had said. He always took care of Nana though, and now it appeared he planned on taking care of her. It made her furious at Wick for putting them in this precarious position. If she ever saw him again, she'd draw and quarter the man and then give him a piece of her mind.

"Thanks, Ryan." She gestured toward the rest of the house. "Right now, I have no idea what to do with all this."

He nodded and twisted his mouth to one side. "Yeah, I'm sure it's a bit overwhelming."

"That's an understatement. There isn't even a working toilet in the house. Actually, there isn't even an un-working toilet in the house."

They walked toward the kitchen area, and a screech rang out. A leg crashed through the ceiling right above them and rained plaster on their heads. When Ryan reacted calmly, she realized he'd escaped the PTSD.

"It's ooookay. I'm aaalll right." Claire's muffled voice filtered through the hole in the ceiling.

Slack-jawed, Carin stared at Claire's leg. It wiggled and turned a bit to the left. Ryan snickered. "That's our Miss Claire."

"Don't you be impudent, Ryan Graves. I'll—uhm ... maybe ... I ... think I need some help here. I can't get my leg out."

"Are you hurt?" Ryan called to the ceiling.

"Nope. Just my pride. Promise y'all won't tell anyone about this? And Carin, I'm sorry. I'll pay to have the ceiling fixed."

That made Carin laugh. "With the state this house is in, you're worried about that?" She followed Ryan up the stairs. In a fit of giggles, JJ sat on the floor beside Claire, who half sat and leaned on one hand at the edge of the hole.

"JJ." Carin worked to hold in her own snickers. "It's not funny. Miss Claire could have been hurt."

"But she's not, Mama. She told me so. She's just stuck."

Ryan investigated the hole. "What happened?"

Claire gestured with her free arm. "I never saw this weak spot. It was behind me when I pulled JJ back to keep *him* from falling into the hole from the commode." She shook her head and swept her hand around, gesturing to the room. "You never know about old bathroom floors. They could be rotten, and well, I guess I proved it and ... here I am. Now, can you get me out?"

Ryan scratched his head. "The way the lath broke is like one of those Chinese finger puzzle games. You know, you stick your fingers in, but if you pull, you can't get them out. If we pull you up without breaking the lath away, I'm afraid it will cut into your leg." He stood. "I need a ladder."

Claire groaned.

"Does it hurt?" Carin asked.

Claire waved her hand. "No, but if this gets out …"

"We won't tell, Miss Claire." JJ patted her shoulder. "I promise."

He sat beside Claire, and Carin plopped down with them to wait for Ryan.

Claire winked at JJ. "I feel like such a klutz." Then she snorted. "I *am* a klutz."

JJ burst into another giggle fit that started Carin laughing. It really was pretty funny. Poor Claire.

Banging and thumping downstairs signaled Ryan was back. A few minutes of breaking pieces of lath away, and he told Claire she should be able to pull her leg out. She put her arms out for Carin and JJ to help pull her up.

Chapter 7

Chapel Springs

With Claire back on her feet and Ryan nailing a board over the hole, Carin took inventory of what she needed. The enormity of it made her ill. With a wince, she turned to Claire—there wasn't anyone else.

"What am I going to do? We need a toilet, beds, and some way to warm soup, at the very least."

Claire reached in her pocket and pulled out a small rubber-banded stack of checks. "I've got to make a deposit in the bank, and *The Tool Box* is just three doors down. I'll ride over with you. They'll even set you up with a port-a-potty."

A little of the weight on her shoulders seemed to shift, no longer threatening to buckle her knees. "I appreciate that. I wasn't sure where to get things. I hope they take credit cards."

Ryan came downstairs with JJ at his heels. "The hole's covered. I'll check back later to see if you need anything else."

"Thanks, Ryan. I'm glad you're still next door."

As Ryan started for the door, JJ dodged around him, trying to beat him out to the porch. With a woof, Edgar was hot on her son's trail and almost knocked Ryan over. His thigh took a beating from the beast's tail.

"Ow!" Ryan laughed and rubbed his leg. "See ya."

She reached out and caught JJ's collar as he tried to follow Ryan. "Stay here, son. We've got to go to the hardware store."

"Okay." He waved goodbye to Ryan and sat on the steps, tossing a tennis ball for Edgar who chased it and brought it back, collapsing on the porch next to JJ to chew the felt cover off the ball.

"What about the contractor?" Claire asked after Ryan left. "Have you called him to see why more isn't done?"

"No, but I will. Right now."

The call gave her no more than she already knew. Wick only paid for the demolition. After that, he instructed the work to stop. Why? Did he hate her so much he wanted to ruin her—make her homeless? What about his son? And why had she never seen this selfish side of him?

The same reason she hadn't seen his cheating. She believed in happily-ever-after and her mind was in her books.

Carin shoved back the hurt and regret. She'd had to work since he hadn't had a factory ride in two years. His income was sketchy, and it was her royalties that provided for his lifestyle.

Walking around the empty house, Carin braced herself, fearing the contractor's answer. "What will it take for you to complete the renovation?"

"The price I quoted your husband was $149,800." That seemed an awful lot for what needed to be done. Had Wick even checked the man out? Her heart skipped a beat. Had he signed a contract?

"That included the demo, so to finish is one-forty-five. But I'd need a cashier's check. Full amount. Up front."

"Yes, I'm sure you do." No way that would happen. She watched HGTV and saw those shows about unscrupulous contractors. "Thank you for your time." She hung up, shrugged at Claire, and relayed the conversation.

Claire crossed her arms. "If he were here right now, I'd jerk a knot in his tail. Don't you worry, sweetie. We'll all pitch in and help. That's the Chapel Springs way."

The room blurred as tears pooled in Carin's eyes. She wished it were her husband who cared that much.

Claire wrapped her in her second hug of the day. "Don't you cry, now. It'll all work out. You'll go to the hardware store and ask for Pat. Tell him I sent you and to give you our discount."

But where would she come up with the money? She gathered her keys and purse. They couldn't manage through the winter without heat.

Her thoughts spun like a roulette wheel, but no answer dropped into the solution slot. And right now, she had a little boy and a big dog needing their supper. Later, after JJ was asleep, she'd figure it all out. And cry.

As they drove the two blocks, Claire pointed to Cottage Row, telling JJ how his mama and her daughter, Adrianna, always wanted to stay there when they were kids. The cottages had been refurbished with bright paint and flowers. It was a welcoming sight to Carin.

She parked at the hardware store, which still had the same quaint front. Claire waved, saying she'd see them later. Unsure they'd find what they needed, Carin and JJ entered. The place was remarkably modern and smelled of sawdust.

"May I help you?"

Carin turned. A vaguely familiar, gray-haired salesman wearing overalls and a warm smile approached. She tried to pull his name from memory.

Carin unfolded the scrap of paper she'd jotted her notes on. "Please. I ... well, I need a few things. First, is there any way to get a portable toilet delivered this late?"

"Yes, ma'am. My son can do that right away." He pulled out a small spiral notepad. "What's the address?"

Some of the tension left her shoulders. "Number five, Pine Drive."

His head snapped up. "The old Rice homestead? You buy it?"

"I'm Cora Lee Rice's granddaughter." She held out her hand. "Carin." She avoided giving her last name.

He gripped hers and slapped his other hand against his thigh. His smile widened, making his eyes all but disappear. "Well, if that don't beat all. I remember you as a kid spending your summers with your grandma. People here got right chuffed when Miz Rice showed us your books. My wife loves 'em."

Pat Holcomb. The "Pat" Claire told her to ask for was the same man she knew as a kid. "Mr. Holcomb." If his wife still liked her books, she probably hadn't gotten her newest one yet—the one the reviewers flayed her over.

"That's right." His hand engulfed hers and held on. When she met his gaze, his was filled with compassion. "Now, Ms. Carin, Ryan Graves told me the state that house is in. That contractor your husband hired ain't from around here. He sure left y'all in a pickle, but we can sort that out." He tipped his head toward the note clutched in her fingers. "What else is on that list of yours?"

She had to swallow the lump in her throat before she could answer. She'd received more care today from people who hardly knew her than she ever did from her husband. "I need two air mattresses and something to cook on. The kitchen is gutted. Oh, and something to hold a five-gallon water bottle." She only hoped Nana's furniture had been stored in the garage. She forgot to look.

"I've got just what you need." He started down one aisle, pulling a buggy behind him. "You really going to stay there?" He stopped and dropped two AeroBeds into the cart.

"I ..." The whole town would know soon enough. Small towns were like that. She directed a look toward her son. "JJ, would you go find us a hammer? We'll need one." She waited until he was out of earshot then turned back to Mr. Holcomb. "I'll be honest with you. My husband left and took all my money. Right now"—she handed him her credit card—"this is all I've got. Miss Claire said you might ... maybe give me her discount?"

He frowned and scratched his head. "And to think I used to like Wick Jardine." He patted her hand. "Well, don't you worry your pretty little head none. We'll take care of you and your young'un. After all, you're one of our own."

She blinked, her eyes burning. He was what she always longed for in a dad. She wasn't sure if she'd ever become one of them.

Soon, she and JJ had everything they needed for the next few days and more. Mr. Holcomb's wife, who worked as his bookkeeper, came out to meet them. By the time Carin autographed Mrs. Holcomb's copy of *Social Circle,* they'd become Mr. Pat and Miss Cherry and adopted JJ, who slurped the lollipop Miss Cherry gave him.

"He's one of the grands now."

After the car was loaded, JJ waved the stick end of his lollipop back at the Holcombs, who stood in the doorway, waving. "They sure are nice, Mama. Mr. Pat said I could work for him anytime I wanted."

"They're good people, sugar. I think we're going to be okay living here. Now, let's get all this home." She started the engine and backed into the street.

Home. As bad as the house was, it was all they had. *Thank you, Nana.* Somehow, she must have known. But could Chapel Springs ever become home? Right now, success wasn't even on the horizon.

Mr. Pat's son, Tommy, was already at the house and had unloaded the port-a-potty. Tall and muscular, he was almost a clone of his daddy, right down to the overalls he wore. "I put it in the back, Miss Carin. It's a little hidden in the trees. That's the proper spot for an outhouse. I'll clean it each week 'til y'all get your plumbing back up and running." He let Edgar sniff him, then tugged on the bill of his baseball cap and jumped back in his pickup and left.

Carin put her arm around JJ. "It's been quite a day hasn't it? What do you say we get all this inside and set up? Then I'll fix us a soup 'n' sandwich supper."

"I wanna try out the outhouse. We read about those in a book at my old school and I want to see if it's the same."

"That's fine." She handed him a roll of toilet paper and let him try out the port-a-potty. He declared it a fine outhouse. In the kitchen, she found a three-foot piece of plywood and laid it on top of the lone cabinet base, then set up the largest of the three LED lanterns Mr. Pat gave her. He was right. It put out a lot of light. The butane camp stove assembled as easily as he said, and soon, the makeshift kitchen was workable.

JJ fed Edgar then dug through the boxes Ryan had brought in for them until he found their flatware and dishes because she'd forgotten to buy paper plates. She supposed they could schlep their dishes to the lake to rinse if she did it after dark. Were there any bears in these woods? It was a national forest, so there could be.

Sitting on the floor looking out the window to Moonrise Cove, tomato soup and pan-grilled cheese sandwiches never tasted so good. But soon, her strength ebbed, both physically and emotionally. Carin turned off the burner, disconnected the propane can, then led JJ upstairs.

He had chosen the bedroom right across the hall from hers. They got his mattress inflated and the bedding ready. Thankfully, the weather was decent and summer was coming, but she didn't know what they'd do when it turned cold. She pulled Edgar's giant pillow-bed up next to JJ's and after prayers, the two settled down.

Carin went back downstairs where she'd left the lantern on. She turned off the large one and turned on one of the smaller ones, leaving the room in a soft light. Out on the front porch, she sat on an overturned bucket. The moon had risen over the lake and the stars were brighter here than in Buckhead. There, she'd kept nagging questions from surfacing, never wanting to examine them closely. Now, the moonlight laid them bare.

Why had this happened? Was God mad at her for something? When had Wick stopped loving her? So many of her dreams included him. A soft breeze whispered through the pines, stirring a memory of a different dream. She was eight, or near about, and a new family moved in next door. They had three girls, and it set her heart to longing for a sister. She prayed it nightly for years before she realized God wasn't going to answer. Either that or He never heard her.

A stink bug scurried across the toe of her tennis shoe. She jerked her foot and sent it flying. At least one of her dreams had come true. She'd become a published author. A bestselling one, too, although it looked like that may have vanished. Her current manuscript, a romance, flickered through her thoughts and she grimaced. If the reviewers were to be believed, it was a waste of her brainpower. The irony was her successful novels were about women's friendships and sister relationships, of which she had none.

Writers either wrote about what they knew or what they wanted to know. She pulled the ever-present notebook and pen from her pocket, then cast her mind to and fro, fishing for a "what if" that would spark a story. Nothing came.

Some help would be appreciated, but the breeze had stopped and the air was still.

Like her thoughts.

She rose and went to the railing. Across the lake, sparkling lights dotted the shore. The first cluster was Pineridge, and the next was Scarlet's Ferry, but she couldn't remember any other names. Who lived in those homes? Were they year-round residents or vacationers? Maybe a lone woman, someone like her, rented the house. What if—

The thought got chased away by the image of her gutted house. Dread sent a shiver down her spine. "Come on, Jardine. Think!"

Writer's block wasn't something she had ever experienced, but this felt awfully close to how everyone described it. She rubbed her fingertips over weary eyelids. "Okay. I'm tired. My emotions are drained. That's what this is. Tomorrow, I'll be better and able to think."

With a final glance over her shoulder at the lights, she went inside. She left the small light on in case she or JJ needed to come down to use the outhouse. Irony lifted one side of her lips. Now that was funny. She'd never imagined herself living in a house with an outdoor privy. She started up the stairs. Edgar appeared at the top, and his low growl set her stomach to pitching.

"What is it, boy?"

He flew down the stairs, barking. Carin quickly got out of his way, and as she turned, she saw a dark shadow at the door.

"Carin, it's me, Ryan."

Edgar wagged his tail so hard, his whole back end wobbled. She opened the door and Ryan handed her a slip of paper.

"What's this?"

"I've got a buddy, a fireman, who's also a contractor." He ruffled Edgar's head. "He's honest and uses firemen or military veterans as his subs." He leaned against the porch railing and the beast flopped at his feet.

"I like that." She joined him, closing the door behind her. "Do you think he'd give me an estimate I can take to the bank? If I get lucky, the loan officer won't have read my last book."

"What do you mean?"

"Your daughter didn't tell you?" Nana had told her earlier that his daughter, Ilene, loved her books. "The reviewers crucified me."

Ryan sat on the top step, one leg bent at the knee, the other straight. "How come?"

Carin sighed and sat on the step next to him. "Let's leave it at I tried something new and it didn't work."

Ryan sat beside her. "So what are you writing now?"

Nothing. She shrugged. "I don't have an idea yet." If she didn't say the dreaded words, maybe her muse would come out and play. "It's probably because all I can think about is this mess." She waved her hand toward the door. "Did you see the port-a-potty? JJ thinks it's great fun."

"You know he favors you."

Warmth swelled her heart. "He's my pride and joy."

How could Wick have walked out on him? Exhaustion hit her like a ton of books. She yawned before she could subdue it.

Ryan rose. "I'd better let you get to bed. I'll call Norm tonight. Last name's Akins, so you'll know when he calls you. I'll need your cell number."

Carin recited the number, and he programmed it into his phone.

"I should have yours too." Her phone was upstairs. She pulled out her little notepad and handed it to him to jot down his number. When he finished, she took it and jammed it back in her pocket. "Thanks Ryan. It's good to have a friend. If I have to go to the bank, I hope I can put you down as a referral."

"You know you can." He stood and Edgar jumped up and leaned against him, nearly pushing him off the steps. "Careful there, big fella." He gently stroked and pulled the beast's ears one at a time, something Edgar loved. "I'll see you tomorrow. Hey"—he turned back to Carin— "you and JJ want to go to church with me on Sunday?"

She didn't really want to. She couldn't understand why God let Wick leave them, not to mention taking everything. Besides, God didn't seem to be speaking to her anymore. Plus, people tended to make a big deal over her when they recognized her. Set up false expectations. She'd rather stay in anonymity, but JJ loved Sunday school.

"Sure." Her mouth betrayed her.

Ryan bid her goodnight. Back inside, she headed upstairs. After she'd undressed and climbed into her makeshift bed, she thought she'd fall asleep immediately. Instead, guilt snuck between the sheets and covered her because she'd avoided their old church in Buckhead. After her first bestseller, people treated her differently, clamoring for her attention where before they hadn't known she existed. Worship became uncomfortable with people watching her every move. She quit going.

Maybe being in a new place would help get her back in tune with God. She could use His help for a story idea. Any story. Right now, her mind was like a desert.

Chapter 8

Claire removed her favorite vegetable peeler from the drawer and attacked a cucumber while next to her, her daughter sliced radishes. She wasn't going to enjoy this dinner. Not one bit. She scraped the peeler along the vegetable, wishing she could peel Bobby Riley away from 'Lissa as easily.

"Momma, I hope you don't mind too much that I invited Bobby to dinner."

Claire dug too deep and gouged the cucumber. "Oh blast." She sliced off the gouged part. "I suppose not, but you know my feeling on that subject."

Melissa put the last radish slice into a bowl and laid her knife in the sink. "I do, but ..." she stopped Claire's hand. "I've begged God to take away my love for him if this wasn't right. He hasn't."

"He hasn't or you aren't listening?"

"I'm listening and God hasn't. I've dated other boys, but none of them are like Bobby." She put up her hand to stop Claire's protest. "If he weren't Mayor Riley's son, you'd give him a chance." She walked out of the kitchen.

Claire's heart ached. Didn't she do exactly what her daughter was doing—fall in love with a non-believer? She shook her head. It was different. She hadn't known then what she did now about praying for a husband. About what they called unequally yoked. And 'Lissa knew that. Claire wasn't sure what God was up to or that she liked being on the outside of it.

Her daughter returned to her side and held out her journal. "Read it, Momma. You'll see I have been praying that way."

Good golly, Miss Molly. First Patsy read her mind, then Joel, and now 'Lissa. She needed to wear a bag over her head.

"That's between you and God, sugar. I trust you. If you say you've been praying, I believe you. And I'll support you in whatever decision you make." She laid her hand on 'Lissa's cheek. "I just don't want you hurt."

Her daughter leaned into her palm. "I know. I love you, Momma."

"Can anyone join this love fest?" Joel entered the kitchen with a platter of grilled, bone-in pork chops. Claire inhaled the aroma of apple and rosemary. The combination was heavenly. "Bobby's car pulled into the driveway a minute ago." He looked at Claire and winked.

Melissa went to the door, and Joel set the platter of meat on the counter to rest. "How do you feel about him joining us? Are you okay?"

Was she? "Not really." She searched his eyes. "What do you think of it?"

Joel wrapped her in his arms. "Having him to dinner's fine. But I'm as concerned as you about any commitment beyond that." He rested his chin on her head. "Now that I've finally seen the light, I don't want her going through what you did for so long."

Claire's heart swelled with love. "That wasn't your fault. Neither of us knew any better back then. But 'Lissa does."

"Then we'll pray for God's will in this, sweetheart."

Claire leaned back. "How'd you get so wise so fast?"

"You calling me a wise guy?" He made a move to grab a towel then stopped. His cheeky grin turned into a polite smile.

What in—Claire turned around. Bobby and 'Lissa stood in the doorway. Nearly the same height, they somehow looked good together. *No. That's not right.* Claire didn't want to see that. She untied her apron then retied it. "Hey, Bobby."

"Hey, Miss Claire. Mr. B. It sure smells good in here."

She never had trouble talking with any kid in town. Now suddenly, she was tongue-tied.

'Lissa filled the awkward silence. "We're going to play a game of chess, unless you need us to help."

Her tongue unstuck itself. "Go ahead. We're almost done."

The front door opened. Charlie's deep voice blended with Sandie's as they came in, followed by Wes and Costy's "*Olá*." Claire wiped her hands on her apron and went out to greet them.

Megan slid down the bannister, dropping to the floor beside Claire, turned, and put her hands on Sandie's already enormous belly. "How are my niece and nephew today?"

Sandie grimaced. "Active. I think they're going to be gymnasts." As she said it, the apex of her belly shifted from center to her right side, making her look comically misshapen. Charlie puffed up in pride, while Wes turned a bit green.

Costy slipped around Sandie and came to Claire's side. "*Olá, Mamá.*" She kissed Claire's cheek. Costy was her newest daughter-in-law whom she adored. It wasn't like that in the beginning, though. She shared a private smile with Costy, who giggled. Wasn't there a scripture about things hard won being extra sweet? She gave Costy a squeeze.

The kids all joined 'Lissa and Bobby in the den. Claire went to set the table. A moment later, Megan wandered into the dining room. "Momma, do you like Bobby?"

Claire frowned. "What brought that on?" Why was everyone suddenly so concerned with her feelings? She gave the tablecloth a toss to open it.

Megan caught one end in the air and helped lay it onto the table. "Don't avoid the question. Do you like him?"

"Of course." Claire smoothed the cloth and reached for the flatware.

"But not enough for 'Lissa to marry?"

"Because he's not right for her. Where is this going?" The eldest by four minutes of her twin daughters, Meg was not normally introspective.

She shrugged. "I don't want him to hurt her again." She lifted the stack of plates and set one at each chair. "When she broke up with him in our senior year, she cried every night for at least six months. I couldn't help her."

Claire studied Megan, who tended to hide her sensitivity. She was the daughter who always dated a lot but kept the boys away from her heart. What could—wait a minute ... did that mean—

"Megan Elizabeth, is there a young man you've actually dated more than once?"

Her daddy's cheeky grin spread across Megan's face, which turned a lovely shade of pink. Good gravy, love was popping up all over Chapel Springs.

"Tell me about him."

"Who?"

Claire rounded the table as she spoke. "You can feign innocence, but I know you, little girl. First you're concerned about 'Lissa and Bobby, when six months ago, you pretended you couldn't care less. And now you're blushing. Spill." She opened the sideboard drawer and grabbed a handful of flatware.

Megan followed her with the rest, setting them beside each plate. "We were both in marketing fundamentals my freshman year."

"How long have you known him?"

"Since forever."

Claire dropped the last knife beside a plate. "How come we didn't know about him?"

"No one did. We were good friends for years. Then something changed." She straightened the knife Claire dropped and laid the last spoon next to it. "I saw how much love can hurt with 'Lissa. For a long time, I was afraid to risk it."

Afraid? Claire had never seen this daughter anything but fully confident. "So what changed it? Can we meet him? What's his name?"

Megan laughed. "Believe it or not, his steadfastness changed how I felt. No matter how much I pushed him away or turned him down, he kept asking me out. I finally had to admit to myself that I love him. I almost invited him tonight, but I wanted to talk to you first." She took a deep breath and tucked her hands under her heart. "Momma, it's Dane."

"It's *who*?" She couldn't have heard right. Could she? Really? "Dane? Dane as in Kowalski?"

Megan nodded.

Claire's heart nearly flipped over in her chest. Patsy's son Dane and her Megan. They'd always hoped but never pushed any of their kids together. But God did. Wow. Somehow, she'd never pictured *these* two together, though. "Does Patsy know anything about this?"

"Not yet. Dane wants to talk to her first."

"Has he proposed? Is it that far? Oh, no!"

Megan frowned. "What's wrong?"

"Chase just proposed to Nicole. If Dane ... goodness ... we could have a bumper crop of weddings here."

Megan's gaze turned toward the den and sorrow touched her eyes. "I'd always dreamed 'Lissa and I would have a double wedding."

Claire passed the platter of pork chops to Megan, who sat to her right. At the opposite end of the table, Joel was deep in conversation with Charlie. Sandie, with a mixture of hand signs and a few words of Portuguese, chatted with Costy. This could have been any regular Saturday night family dinner. A sigh swelled Claire's diaphragm. If it weren't for that boy next to Melissa ...

He looked up, his brown hair flopping into his eyes. "Mr. B, these are great pork chops. What did you do to them?"

Oh, Bobby, that was sneaky. Trying to get on Joel's good side by complimenting his grilling. Claire narrowed her eyes at her husband who had the audacity to smile at the boy and share his spice rub with him. Did he forget what Bobby said about churchgoers? The twerp wasn't even original but quoted Karl Marx. He'd be better off quoting Harpo Marx. She snickered.

"What's so funny, Momma?" Megan asked.

"What? Oh, nothing. Just something I remembered." She cut her pork chop and tried to retain an air of innocence. What if she brought up the barbecue at church? 'Lissa invited him but never told them if he went, or if he did—

"Bobby, did you enjoy the barbecue with the young adult group?"

He exchanged glances with Melissa and laid his fork down. "I actually did."

"Just what was wrong wi— you *did*?" Was he playing with her? Claire wouldn't put it past him.

"The company was wonderful, the food good. The conversation was ... interesting."

"That sounds like you're comparing it to a dissertation of Tilly Payne's gallbladder surgery."

Bobby laughed. This wasn't going at all like she planned. Joel shook his head at her, but she chose to ignore him.

"Seth Hanson's nephew was there," Bobby said. "He's a good debater."

Ready. Aim. "What did you ask him?"

"If God was who he says he is"—Bobby leaned back in his chair—

"why does he allow kids to be hurt?"

Typical. Always borrowing clichés. Fire. "So you argued?"

Megan laughed, but Melissa did not look pleased. Her scowl had her left eye nearly closed.

Bobby shook his head. "We debated."

Claire had him now. "Who won?"

One corner of Bobby's mouth rose. "It was a draw."

"A draw?" What did the twerp mean by that? And why was he being so nice? Claire didn't want to like him. Wait … if he tolerated what Seth's nephew said, did that mean—

"Are you going to come to church?"

"Momma, did you see my new painting Aunt Patsy hung in the gallery? What did you think of it?"

Ooh, good deflection by Melissa. Score one for her. Claire pursed her lips. How could she get around that and back to what she wanted to find out?

"I did and it's beautiful. Does—"

'Lissa pushed her chair back. "Bobby and I have to print the flyers to hand out at church tomorrow. I'll be late. Don't wait up."

Wait! Something was off about that boy, and she wanted to expose it. Her heart screamed, *"He's wrong for you, Melissa!"*

Bobby laid his napkin beside his plate. "Terrific meal, Mr. B. Thanks Ms. Claire." He grinned at her. "I enjoyed the conversation." He followed 'Lissa from the room, chuckling.

Claire blinked. Joel and Charlie laughed. Sandie tried to hide a smirk. Costy looked as confused as Claire felt.

"What just happened?"

"Costy and I were at that barbecue, Ma," Wes said. "Bobby asked some hard questions and Vaughn answered them. However, I'm not sure our mayor's son is going to change, and that worries us." He laid his arm on the back of Costy's chair and tilted his own onto the back two legs. Claire wished he wouldn't do that.

She frowned and turned to Megan. "Do you believe him? Bobby, I mean."

Her daughter didn't answer right away. Finally, she shook her head. "I think it's an act to pacify 'Lissa."

Her gaze pinned her husband to his chair. "And you?"

Joel stabbed another pork chop on the serving platter. "We can only hope and trust God."

That wasn't what she wanted to hear. She wanted him to agree with her. To not like Bobby. Wait. No, that wasn't right, she liked Bobby. Claire sank against the back of her chair. But *not* as a son-in-law. Unless he changed. But if he changed, then Felix would be her daughter's father-in-law.

She jolted upright. Her archrival would be in her own family. She had to pray that wouldn't happen.

Chapter 9

Inside the church foyer, Carin hesitated, but Ryan pressed his hand in the small of her back, directing her toward a hallway on the right. She tightened her grip on JJ's hand and moved in that direction. Did everyone always congregate out here? When she slid off her sunglasses, a woman's eyes grew large as she stared. Carin lowered her head.

"It's all right, Mama." JJ squeezed her hand. "I'm here."

Ryan leaned close. "Is something wrong?"

If she told him, he'd think she was paranoid or terribly egotistical. She gave a quick shake of her head and smiled. "Just a tad nervous in new places. You forget, I'm used to being by myself for days on end, working."

Ryan pointed to another doorway, this one closed. "This leads to the children's section. Come on, JJ. Let's go find your class."

He slid an I.D. over a security light on the wall, opened the door, and ushered them through. They walked down the long hallway to a room near the end. Inside, three boys stood around an aquarium with a young woman directing the feeding.

JJ gave her hand a sharp tug. "Look, Mama, fish."

The slim brunette turned at JJ's voice. "Well, hey." Her soft drawl sounded more South Georgia than this part of the state. "I'm Tara Sue Winslow." She held out her hand.

Carin put the card she'd filled out for JJ into the teacher's hand. She wasn't as young as she first thought, maybe early forties. "Nice to meet you, Tara Sue. I'm Carin and this is JJ, my son."

"I'm sorry, I didn't catch the last name."

Because she didn't say it.

"Jardine." JJ said for her.

Here it comes. She took a step back as Tara Sue's eyes grew wide.

"See you after church, doodle bug." Carin turned and walked out, Ryan trailing her. As they left, the woman's voice followed them.

"JJ, is your mama the author Carin Jardine?"

Once again, Ryan put his hand on the small of her back, directing her toward the main worship center. "Is it always like that?"

Carin sighed. "Usually. It's not something I ever sought."

"I could tell when we first got here. You almost bolted. I suppose it could be annoying, but everyone here is really friendly."

"I'm sure they are."

To Ryan, they would be. But she'd learned the hard way that people wanted the celebrity, not really her. Only Nana had loved Carin for herself. And now JJ. No, when the people here got what they wanted from her, they'd turn away like everyone else.

They made their way into the worship center, and Carin steeled herself. She needed a story, and she'd do whatever it took to get one—even if it meant putting her heart in harm's way.

Blinking in the sunshine as they exited the church, Carin slid on her dark glasses. JJ hopped on one foot between her and Ryan. The service had been good, she enjoyed the music, and most everyone treated her hospitably.

"Interested in some lunch?" Ryan opened the passenger door for her, then helped JJ in.

She hesitated. A germ of an idea had landed and she wanted to get home to work on it. "I think we'll pass this time, Ryan. I really need to try to do some writing."

"No problem. Would it be all right if I took JJ out on the lake? He can swim, can't he?"

"Mama says I'm half porpoise." JJ buckled his seatbelt and tapped his toes against the back of her seat.

"Feet, JJ."

"Yes, ma'am." The tapping stopped. "But can I go with Mr. Ryan?"

"*May* I go."

Ryan started the car while longsuffering JJ sighed. "May I?"

Carin bit back a smile. "Yes, you may."

"Yippee! Do I need a fishing rod, Mr. Ryan? Do I have one, Mama?"

"No." Both Carin and Ryan answered him at the same time. Ryan glanced at her with an eyebrow raised in question. She nodded.

"Apparently you don't have one, but that's okay. I've still got the one I used when I was about your age." Ryan pulled into the line of cars waiting to exit the parking lot.

"Wow, that must really be old."

"JJ, Mr. Ryan isn't that old. He's not much older than I am."

"But Mama, you told me you were older than dirt."

"I was joking, sugar."

The light turned green, and Ryan turned left.

JJ didn't look all that convinced, but he let it go. "Mr. Ryan, Nana told me you were in the war. Will you tell me about it?"

"Sure." He smiled at Carin and mouthed, "I won't tell the bad parts."

With Ryan regaling JJ with war stories, Carin tried to examine the seed of a story germinating in her thoughts, but the conversation kept intruding. Finally, she gave up until she could be alone. When they got home, JJ let Edgar out then changed his clothes and raced out the door to Ryan's after pinky-swearing to be good.

The spring sunshine was warm, and the breeze carried the scent of pines and the lake as she settled on the back deck. She loved how the porch wrapped around the house, letting her decide if she wanted a view of the mountains or the lake. She'd be glad when the contractor Ryan recommended got out to see the house. The porch needed some rehab, too.

JJ and Ryan came out of his house, crossed the street, and headed down the path to the tunnel that went under Sandy Shores Drive to Moonrise Cove and the fishing dock. JJ turned and waved. She raised her hand to him.

After they disappeared into the tunnel, she leaned her forearms on the railing, a frosty glass of sweet tea clutched between her hands, and listened. The sunlight danced like diamonds on the waters of Chapel Lake. Birds, boat motors, and laughter blended together into a lake-cocktail of life.

But where was the story? The seed that had landed in her brain hadn't taken root. It was as if a rogue crow swooped into her mind and snatched it up.

Through the Georgia and Loblolly pines on a curved stretch of beach, three little girls played tag with some wavelets created by a passing motorboat. Behind them, two women stood side by side, laughing. One leaned down, picked up something, and both bent their heads over it. They were dressed alike in dark shorts, but where one had on a flower-print blouse, the other wore a cherry red t-shirt tied in a knot at her waist. Were they best friends? Sisters?

Draining her glass, she stood for a few minutes, waiting for the caffeine to work. Down on the beach, one of the women looked up, grabbed a pair of binoculars, then nudged her sister/friend. Waving her arms, she pointed to Carin. They both waved. She waved back but then slipped inside. When anyone got that excited about seeing her, she knew it was only the notoriety. Never just her.

With the story idea lost and now the privacy of her porch compromised, it was time to check out Chapel Springs. See what had changed since she was a teen. She grabbed her cell phone and sent a text to Ryan.

Going into town. Text when u r back.

Ok

Carin snapped on Edgar's lead. She planned to walk about the town without going into any of the stores, and the beast needed the exercise. They strolled down Pine to Main Street, then turned right toward Sandy Shores Drive. At the corner, she paused. There were stores to each side of Main. The town of Chapel Springs had two different shopping areas. The one that faced the lake held the art gallery, gift shops, and tourist type stores. The other was near her house and contained the hardware, library, bank, and grocery store. Nana's house—hers now—sat in the middle, making it an easy walk either way.

The ambiance on Sandy Shores with its unique shops was more to Carin's liking. She headed to her left and paused outside the used bookstore, *The Tome Tomb*, surveying the window display. One of her earlier books stood on the right side, its dust jacket torn and a little ratty.

"May I help—oh my word! Little Carin Rice!"

She found herself engulfed in a hug, at least as well as four-foot-ten

Tillie could engulf Carin's five-foot-six frame. It seemed everyone in Chapel Springs hugged. She pulled back and surveyed the elf-like owner of her favorite place in Chapel Springs. Many a summer's day had been split between here and the library. Tillie still wore her signature leggings and a long shirt. This one was zebra print.

"You look the same," Carin said with a grin.

"I wondered when you'd get back here, darlin'. Welcome home. And who is this and what does it weigh?" She patted Edgar on his big head.

"This"—Carin scratched the beast's ear—"is Edgar Allen Poe. He's a respectable two-hundred forty pounds."

"I could saddle and ride him."

"My little boy used to."

Tillie ran her hand along his back then bent to look into his face. The beast grinned at her and licked her nose. "His name is perfect."

"Thank you. I thought so." Edgar plopped down at Carin's feet.

"They were wrong, y'know."

Carin blinked. "Excuse me?"

"The reviewers. They're wrong. The book was good, sugar, just different. Mere readers don't like different. But a lover of literature doesn't mind."

"I hope my publisher isn't one of the former."

"Don't worry, dear." Tillie reached out and squeezed Carin's hand. "I've got faith in you. You'll bounce back."

Carin leaned forward and kissed the woman's cheek. "You know you're the one who sparked my desire to write fiction, don't you? You opened worlds for me and always believed in me." If only she could believe in herself.

Tillie patted Carin's hand. "And I still do." She stood a moment, nodding and smiling, as if she saw something no one else did. "Now, I've got work to do and so do you. Tootle-loo." She turned then stopped. "Bring that little boy of yours in to see me." She wrinkled her nose. "But stay away from that new bookstore, *Leave the World Behind*, on the edge of town. The owner, Esther Tully, is a bit pretentious, if you ask me. But then you didn't, did you?"

Carin wasn't about to get in the middle of that. "I'll bring him to see you, Miss Tillie. He loves to read." She'd make an appearance at the other bookstore too, though she'd do it quietly. Gentle tugging on Edgar's lead got him on his feet, and they moved down the block.

The village hadn't changed much at all in the past few years. New paint, some colorful awnings, an updated sign or two, but the stores were the same. The gift shop had a bright new awning, but there was a new boutique where the coffee shop used to be. Hmm, coffee would be good, and she had seen a place when she and JJ first got to town. Out by the boat launch, and it had a patio with tables and umbrellas. A good place to people watch. She'd check it out next time.

She turned and walked back the length of Sandy Shores, spending a few minutes peering in the window at *The Painted Loon* and the antique store next to it. There were a few people out and about but not many. A fatherly man, in his early fifties maybe, tipped his ball cap as he passed her. The courtly gesture tickled her. She smiled and inhaled deeply, taking in the scent of the mountains. It felt good here. She crossed her fingers. If everything went right and she convinced the bank to give her a loan, she and JJ could make a fresh start here in Chapel Springs. Then, she could find a story and success again.

Chapter 10

Claire set the last piece of pottery into the kiln and closed the lid. She played with the settings and turned it on. One platter was a decorative piece on which she'd experimented with color. She never knew how these would come out, but that was part of the intrigue of her art. It was what kept it fresh. And fun.

Patsy wasn't at her easel, nor was 'Lissa at hers. Claire never heard either leave, but that wasn't unusual. She wiped her hands on a towel and dropped it in the bin on her way to the front, where muted voices blended into an unintelligible hum. In the gallery, Wingnut—oops, Sean—stood talking with Mel, and Patsy was closing out the register.

Claire stretched out her hand and tilted her head up. Then up again. She'd forgotten how tall this boy was. The weather changed somewhere up around his brows. "Sean, I'm delighted you're here. I see you've met our assistant, Mel."

Sean looked down from his lofty six-foot-five and smiled. "Sure did. She's been showing me your newest work."

"We're about to close, so if you'll stand by, we can go over to Felix's campaign office to chat. I'll bring you up to speed on what's happening. I booked you a cottage. I hope that's okay."

"That's great, thanks." He sauntered over to Patsy's new painting of Moonrise Cove.

While Claire talked with Patsy, she kept an eye on Mel and Sean. "There's a bit of flirting going on over there on Mel's part, anyway." She'd have to watch that. Mel was too young for Sean.

Patsy peered over the cash register. "So I see. Chase and Nicole are contagious."

"They're not the only ones." Should she say something? Or had Dane talked to her already? She hadn't—"Have you talked to—"

Patsy's feet did a jig under the stool. "I was waiting to see if Megan had told you yet. I've been biting my tongue all day."

"I can't believe I forgot, but the business with—" she lowered her voice—"Bobby has had me all messed up."

"Girlfriend, that's not the real issue. Your pride is."

Claire pinched her lips together and shook her head. "Van Gogh's ear, do you always have to keep me accountable?"

Patsy's grin was as cheeky as Joel's when he was right. "Yep."

"You know I love you, and I couldn't be happier about Dane and Megan. I'm just not sure about Felix as an in-law."

"Ooh, I hadn't thought about that. Oh my. But what about Bobby's stand on Christianity?"

"That's the basis of my misgivings. He's putting on an act, Pat-a-cake. I'm sure of it. I'm so afraid 'Lissa will give up. She needs a husband who shares her faith. I'm not sure … oh, flubber. I'm not even sure about what I'm not sure of. What's wrong with me?"

"Nothing. You're a mother whose kiddos are stretching their wings and flying."

"Yeah. And it makes me feel old. I'm not ready to be old."

"Miss Claire? Are we ready to lock up?" Mel stood beside Wingnut— Sean near the gallery's front door. She lifted the "Open" sign, ready to flip it over.

"We are. I'm sorry, we got caught up." Claire stood. "Let's go. Patsy, I'll call you later. Mel, do you need a way home?"

"No, ma'am. I'm fine. My stepmother picks me up out in the parking lot by the guard shack."

"Well, if you're sure …" One of these days, she'd like to meet Mel's stepmother.

"I am. See you tomorrow." She cast a glance back at Sean.

Claire bit back a smile as Goth Girl attempted to flirt. It was kind of like when Aunt Lola tried to teach her and Patsy. They were so inept, they kept Aunt Lola in stitches.

In the campaign office, Claire reintroduced Felix to Sean then pulled out the maps and unrolled them on the conference table. Her daughter was nowhere to be seen.

"Where are Melissa and Bobby?"

"Out hanging flyers on doors." Felix pointed to a line on the map. "Now, Benson Creek goes underground about here for a couple of miles, then reappears somewhere around here." He pointed to a penciled "x" on the map.

Sean studied it and then looked at the DOT's map of the roads. "So, when they dynamited for the new highway, it most likely altered Benson Creek's underground flow, sending some of its cold water into the warm springs' feeder."

Claire tapped her finger on the lined plots on the first map. "Farmlands downstream have always used Benson Creek for watering their crops. Now they're saying it's less than half its original flow."

Sean frowned. "I'm missing something here. Why do you need me if you know this?"

"Howie Newlander is running against Felix. He's got the farmers up in arms, saying we diverted the water."

"No way he can back that up." Sean rolled up the maps.

Felix pulled out a chair and dropped into it. "He's twisting all the facts. He tells them Chapel Springs benefits from the new highway."

"Of course we do." Claire chose a chair opposite Felix and motioned for Sean to sit to her right. He remained standing, studying the maps. Did he get a different perspective from looking down at them? Like a fly-over or something?

"But he makes it sound like I personally placed that dynamite." Felix's voice wore a coat of discouragement, buttoned up to the collar.

Sean unrolled the maps again. He studied them, then walked around the table a couple of times, and stopped. When Felix cocked his head toward Sean, Claire shrugged. She had no insight into his thoughts. This called for caffeine. She fixed Felix and herself coffee and brought it to the table, along with a Coke for Sean.

He sat down abruptly, pulled out his cell phone, and brought up the Internet. Claire leaned toward him to see. More maps. He slid the paper map closer and squinted at the cell phone.

"Bingo." He pressed a button and his screen went black. "I believe I have a fix for you. It'll cost some money, but it will save that farmland, not to mention correcting the warm springs." He turned to Felix. "This will make you a hero."

Claire almost laughed. The boy had Felix's number all right.

Sean drew a small circle on the map. "This is about a quarter mile before Benson Creek goes underground. We can divert it by digging a channel to alter the flow, so instead of going underground, it will turn here"—he pointed to the circle—"and will stay above ground. The best way would be to start digging where it comes above ground, and dig backwards to where it goes subterranean."

Poor Felix turned pale. "What do you think this will cost?"

He loved this town, and as much as Claire butted heads with him, she felt sorry for him.

"I'd have to study it, but my guess is around half to three quarters of a mil. A contractor will need to measure, but it looks like about two miles. However, remember, you're not talking deep. You probably only have to dig about four or five down and maybe six wide, and lay a gravel base. So, that's a decent ballpark figure."

What if someone—Claire turned to Felix. "Don't we know somebody with that kind of excavating equipment? Wait ... Sean, would a Bobcat handle it?"

He didn't seem sure. "It's possible, but that would take an awfully long time."

The mayor brightened. "Forget a Bobcat. Norm Akins has a backhoe that makes easy chomping of Georgia red clay. I'll call him tomorrow and have him come meet with you."

Claire saw a ray of light in all this dark business. If they could pull this off, they might get rid of Howie and his ridiculous bid for mayor. Even more, they'd finally have a fix for the warm springs, and then Lydia could offer therapeutic treatments at the spa. She already had Vince on retainer as the doctor.

Chapter 11

Keeping her distance so she wouldn't disturb him, Carin followed Norm Akins through the house. He was methodical. And quiet. JJ shadowed the contractor, chattering like a magpie, from the moment he came in.

Her heart squeezed. Her baby needed his daddy. Where was Wick right now? Was he ready for tomorrow's race? Or had he partied all night? Tears blurred her vision as she trailed Norm and JJ, but she blinked her eyes dry, refusing to cry anymore.

With his foot, Norm tested an area of the floor in the bathroom around where Claire fell through. "Water damage but not too bad. It didn't spread further."

Her stomach rolled over and she saw dollar signs. Behind Norm, JJ tested the floor like the contractor did.

"What do you think, little buddy?"

JJ nodded. "Yep." He looked at Carin. "Didn't spread."

He was so stinking cute, mimicking all that Norm did. How could Wick have walked out on this little guy?

"It's not as bad as you think, ma'am. The floor's not great, but the water damage is just surface, and there isn't as much mold as I thought there would be. The subfloor is still okay. Your grandmother took good care of the place. I noticed the roof isn't very old. Probably not more than five years."

He took another hour to complete his inspection, then they talked about what kind of appliances she wanted in the kitchen, countertops, and the bathroom fixtures. "I'll have an estimate for you later this afternoon. For now, be careful with the electrical. It's all the old knob and tube with a few things tied in illegally."

Carin sucked in a sharp breath. "Is it safe for us to be here?" What would she do if he said it wasn't?

"The quicker we can rewire the better I'll feel, but you'll be fine. I'll come back this afternoon and install a couple of battery operated smoke detectors, just in case."

"Thank you. I'll sleep better."

He smiled then ruffled JJ's hair. "So, are you going to be part of my crew when you get home from school?"

JJ looked up at her, his eyes hopeful. "Can I, Mama?"

"Since Mr. Norm says so, how could I say anything but yes?"

JJ threw his arms around her waist. "Thanks!" He quickly released her and reached out his hand to Norm. "It's a deal."

"Then I'll have to find you a tool belt." He nodded to Carin. "That okay?"

More than okay. She nodded. "Thank you, Norm. I appreciate it. As soon as you get me the estimate, I'll go to the bank and start the loan process." She crossed her fingers behind her back and her toes inside her sneakers.

After Norm left, she helped JJ into his jacket and they headed out to get him registered in school.

"Mama, I'm scared." JJ jumped over a sidewalk crack. "A little anyway."

"Why, buddy? Is it because you'll be the new boy?"

He nodded.

Carin squeezed his hand. "JJ, all the kids liked you at your old school, right?"

"Yeah, but what if they don't here?"

"Doodle bug, you're one likable kid. I think they'll all want to be your friend. Look, here we are."

The school consisted of two buildings, one for elementary students and one for middle school. The high school kids went to Pineridge, if she remembered right.

A few minutes later, she and JJ sat in the principal's office. It looked like the same office from her elementary school. She liked Mr. Morris immediately. He was warm and approachable. Plus, he made JJ laugh by telling him a silly joke and wiggling his large ears.

He then explained the year-round school in Chapel Springs. "The children have nine weeks of school then three weeks off. We've found their retention much better, and they test the highest in the state. I'm placing JJ in Miss Tresler's class. She's a wonderful first grade teacher. Her class is small enough that she can give lots of personal attention. I've asked her to send another boy to escort JJ to class."

Carin glanced at her son. He'd relaxed and now seemed ready to start "real" school, as he put it. Before she could tell him to have a good day, the secretary opened the door and a towheaded boy bounced in.

"Hey, Mr. Morris. I'm here for the new kid."

JJ stood and faced him. "I'm JJ."

The other boy grinned and fist-bumped him. "I'm Mikey Akins. My daddy's working on your house."

"Cool! I like your dad." JJ and Mikey walked out, talking away like best buddies. JJ didn't even look back.

She turned to Mr. Morris. "How did you know?"

His smile bore witness to years of understanding kids. What a good man to have as the headmaster. She'd bet he was a wonderful father to the boys in the photo on his desk.

"After you arrived, while my secretary was getting JJ's transcript from his other school, she did a little checking. Remember, this is a small community. She was pretty sure she remembered you. Her mother and your grandmother were close friends. She suggested Mikey."

Did the people in Chapel Springs all have some kind of supernatural powers or something? Everywhere Carin turned, someone helped her. Tears stung the back of her eyes, and she had to swallow the lump in her throat before she could speak. "Thank you. Y'all have eased a horrible situation for my little boy."

"That's my job, Ms. Jardine." He shook her hand and escorted her out. "The school bus will deliver JJ home each afternoon."

"He'll love riding the bus. It's something he's always wanted to do."

After lunch, Carin sat with Norm on the porch in the Adirondack chairs he brought for her. On the table between them, his laptop lay open with the plans for the house. She loved what he proposed for the downstairs and her bedroom, adding a walk-in closet and master bath.

The old contractor didn't have those additions and wanted to charge her more.

"I can have it all done in seven weeks for eighty-five thousand."

She swallowed. Her need of a story loomed even larger. Still—it was lower. "That's a lot better than the other contractor." *Sixty thousand better.* "Thank you, Norm."

"I'm putting temporary supports in downstairs today. That should have already been done. Let me know what the bank says so I can order the engineered beam."

"I don't know what I'll do if they don't approve my loan."

Norm tapped the keys on his laptop, then closed it. "I wouldn't worry too much. I just sent over the plans to Ward. He's the loan officer you'll be seeing."

"I can't thank you enough, Norm. You've found ways to cut costs without sacrificing anything I need." She didn't care about custom cabinetry or high-end granite. Those were Wick's must-haves, not hers. She could do everything on tile that she could on stone.

"Wasn't that hard," Norm said. "Now, I'll get those supports in before I go."

Carin followed the blonde receptionist from the bank's lobby. The clacking of their heels on the marble floors echoed over hushed voices, making her want to tiptoe. None of the tellers behind the counter seemed to notice them, though. They wound down a hallway to an office, where the name on the door made her stop.

"Ward *Cleaver*? Really?" She raised an eyebrow in question as she said the name.

With a chuckle, the blonde nodded. "It's for real. His mama was a hoot." She opened the door and ushered Carin in, then closed it behind her.

The banker rose from behind a large mahogany desk and walked toward her, his hand thrust out. "Ms. Jardine, I'm Ward Cleaver. Come on in."

His thick gray hair coupled with his handshake and down-home manner made her chuckle, putting her at ease. "Being a writer, names are important to me. I'm sure you must get a lot of questions over yours."

"I do. It's funny, though. My mother must have had some intuition that I'd become a banker. My name has opened a lot of doors for me in the investment world. People naturally trust me."

Carin took the seat he offered, tightly clutching the manila envelope that held her paperwork. She sucked in a deep breath. "Norm Akins told me he emailed you the plans and the budget for the renovation."

"He did, and it's a hefty loan but not impossible."

She had to convince him. "I think you'll find my income to be more than sufficient. I can get references."

Who was she kidding? Her only income was the royalties from her old books, which didn't cover more than food. This latest book wouldn't even earn out her advance. She had to buckle down and write another one—fast. And references? Who would give her one?

"I received references for you from Ryan Graves, Claire Bennett, and the Holcombs."

He did? They did? How did the Holcombs know? The light from his office window cast a glare and made it hard for her to read his expression.

"I've gone over everything, but I have a few questions. Did you bring your past three years' tax returns?"

Uh-oh. She purposely hadn't put Wick's name on anything, but his credit probably tanked hers too. She pulled out the requested paperwork and handed it to him, holding her breath as he looked them over. After a couple of minutes and a frown or two, he stacked the papers together.

"Ms. Jardine, can you tell me about the—" His phone rang. He glanced at it. "Hold on. I need to take this."

He turned away from her. She didn't mean to eavesdrop, but being a writer, it was automatic. "Jim, what can I do for you?" He listened, nodding. "I see. Well ... oh. Uh. Uh-huh. Hmm. It's a bit irregular, but ... oh. I see. You sure about this? You'll come in? Very well."

Carin's mind spun for a moment, working on a story of the mysterious caller. An elusive plot thread hung in front of her. She reached for it. Mr. Cleaver hung up and turned back to her. The thread broke.

"Now, where were we?" He glanced over her paperwork. "Ah yes. Well, everything seems to be in order." He called an assistant to come copy her returns. "While she makes the copies, we can go ahead and sign the papers."

Wait. What? "Just like that? It's approved?"

"It is." He smiled. "We're a small town bank. We don't have more than an inch of red tape." He tapped the pile of papers. "I've got what I need. *Your* credit is good and your tax returns verify your income. Now"—he turned some papers around so they faced her—"if you'll sign here, here, here, here, and here, then initial here, here, and here, we'll be done. This gives you an equity line of credit. When you need to, you can request funds transferred to Norm's account, or you can write a check on the account. Your payments will be calculated on the amount withdrawn."

Her head felt as if it was spinning like that girl in *The Exorcist*. What happened to the question he started to ask her? "Are you—" She bit off the question. Carin trusted him, and whatever it was, she wasn't about to rock the boat. She picked up the pen. Without this loan, she and JJ would be living on the street, and she'd do anything to keep that from happening to her little boy.

When the assistant came back with her tax returns, she shook Mr. Cleaver's hand and left with her copies of the loan documents and a checkbook. She disciplined herself not to run before they could change their minds.

Outside on the sidewalk, she turned her face up, letting the sunshine warm it. Maybe God was listening to her again.

Thank you.

Apparently, her credit rating remained good. She wasn't sure how, with what Wick had done, but she'd take it. Now, if she could just get started on a story. An idea had better land and take root soon. She had a mortgage to pay.

Carin called Norm as she walked home. He said he'd order the supplies and give her an invoice for that plus a third of the labor. After she hung up, she changed her mind about going home. She was on the prowl for a story and the center of the village was a good place to start.

Chapter 12

Claire kept her ears on her friends and her eyes on the bakery door. Yesterday, she invited Carin to join them this morning. That girl needed friends, ones she could trust. She didn't let anyone get too close. Why, Claire wasn't sure, but she had her suspicions and they began with that rat of a husband.

Patsy nudged her. "You're frowning. What's wrong?"

"Was I?" Claire pinched off a piece of the enormous cinnamon bun sitting in the middle of the table. "I'm hoping Carin Jardine comes in. Some of you know her. She spent summers up here as a kid. Although Adrianna's several years younger, she and Carin were good friends."

"Adrianna was born mature," Patsy said.

Lydia leaned forward. "Do you mean the author Carin Jardine? I read one of her books and really liked it."

"Don't ask her for an autograph, whatever you do." Claire sucked frosting off her index finger. "Ryan Graves told me he took her to church with him Sunday, and she's wary of the attention her celebrity status receives. I think she's starved for real friends."

"She'll find them here," Patsy said.

"Patsy"—Lydia leaned her chin on her cupped hand—"how are the wedding plans coming?"

"I think everything is on track. Nicole is a whiz at organization."

"That's unusual in an artist, isn't it?" JoAnn asked as she passed the sugar to Lacey.

The bells on the door jingle-jangled, and Carin came in, wearing a ball cap and large dark glasses. Claire waved as Carin looked around the room. She nodded and wove between the tables to reach them.

Claire patted the chair next to her. "Gals, this is Carin. I think you remember Patsy? And this"—Claire gestured to her right—"is Lydia Sanders. You'll want to get to know her. She owns the spa. Next to her is her sister, Lacey, who works at the bank. And finally, next to Lacey is Nancy Vaughn, who owns *Sunspots*, the most wonderful boutique."

"Hey." Carin sat next to Claire. "I'll try to remember all your names, but forgive me—"

Patsy waved her apology away. "Don't think a thing of it, Carin. I'm delighted you've moved here." She smiled at the circle of faces. "Y'all have got to meet Carin's little boy, JJ. Talk about cute."

Claire studied Carin's body language as she responded to the ladies welcoming her. She set her purse on the floor and then wrapped her arms around her waist. There was a definite protective wall around her.

Lydia picked up a clean mug from the center of the table, filled it, and offered it to Carin. "However are y'all managing in your grandmother's house? The last time I walked by there, you could look straight through the front window and out the back."

That drew a laugh from Carin, and she relaxed her arms. "It's an adventure, that's for sure. My little boy told me it can't be haunted because there's no place for a ghost to hide." She took the coffee, thanked Lydia, and added some cream.

Good, she opened up a teensy bit. Claire pushed the cinnamon bun toward Carin. "That's for all of us, so have some. Nancy, I saw a truck in the alley behind *Sunspots*. What did you get?"

"Wait till you see the adorable new swimsuits and shorts collection. There's something for everyone." She gave them an exaggerated wink. "Including those of us who want to leave a little hidden."

"That's me, all right. I've tried working out, but y'all know what happened last time." Claire patted her kneecap. "I'll stick to walking and hiding the flabby parts."

"I read an article about you and Patsy in *American Art Review*," Lydia said. "It was by Avery Chandler. He's become quite the loyal follower, hasn't he?"

Claire rolled her eyes. Patsy laughed and told Carin about how one of Claire's vases fell on the art critic and knocked him out. "We thought our careers were over, but he ended up giving us a great review."

"You're not telling her all of it." Lydia turned to Carin. "His review brought them national interest and made them famous."

"I'd heard that." Carin slid her dark glasses to the top of her head. "There's been a lot of news about Chapel Springs the last few months."

"Don't let that bother you, sugar." Claire squeezed Carin's hand. "We realize we all scrub toilets at the end of the day. Besides, we're one big family here and watch out for each other. You don't have to worry." The bells jangled and Claire turned toward the door as Felix walked in. "Well, all but that one. He's more like an in-law."

As they continued to chat, Carin appeared to grow more relaxed. Claire wanted her to know she could trust these ladies. They'd all protect her like a gaggle of mother hens. Lacey hung on every word of Carin's, being a writer too. Hmm. Claire's gaze went from one to the other. Could they become good friends?

"Lacey, you and Carin are about the same age, just a couple of years' difference. What? Why are y'all looking at me like I'd lost my marbles? I just made an observation."

"Totally out of nowhere, too." Patsy pushed the cinnamon bun to Claire. "Occupy your mouth with that and let Carin and Lacey choose their own friends."

Heat mounted in Claire's cheeks. "Oh. Sorry about that." Her mouth overrode her brain again. "But they *do* have a lot in common. Carin, Lacey is a writer, too. She's a playwright and has written several wonderful murder mysteries that have been performed in theaters all over the state."

Carin brightened and looked at Lacey. "Really? I've never attempted a play."

"They're not hard." Lacey shrugged. "It's all dialogue."

Lydia laughed. "Says she who hardly speaks."

Claire bristled at Lydia's teasing but relaxed when Lacey laughed with her sister.

"She carries on her conversations with her characters."

"You do that, too?" Carin's interest had obviously been piqued. "Do you have trouble shutting them up?"

Lacey's giggle was infectious. "My husband thinks I'm certifiable. Maybe we could have lunch sometime." Lacey's face grew pink. "That is, if you'd like to."

"I'd like that, Lacey."

For the first time that morning, Carin's smile was genuine and made Claire's heart happy. She pushed away from the table. "As much as I'd love to stay and chat, I've got a serving platter calling my name." She put her hand on Carin's shoulder. "We meet every morning during the week, sweetie, and would love to have you join us if your schedule lets you."

She picked up her Chartreaux Katz tote and raised a brow at Patsy, who sat frowning and staring out the window. "You coming? What's wrong?" Claire glanced toward the front. "Uh-oh."

Howie Newlander and Peyton Murdoch stood across the street with their heads together. Howie pointed and Murdoch nodded. They crossed the street and veered into the alley between shops. It looked like they were headed for Springs Park. They were up to something, and Claire intended to find out what.

"Come on, Patsy. We're going to trail those two."

Patsy jumped up and followed her. "We are? Where do you think they're going?"

Outside the bakery, Claire kept close to the wall. "The springs."

"Why?"

"Because that's the direction they're going."

"No, I mean why are they going there?"

"Oh. I don't know, but I intend to find out. We don't want them interfering with Sean's work, and I wouldn't put it past Howie to do something like that."

Patsy stopped. "Sean's not working at the springs. Besides, why would Murdoch be involved? Sean's work will solve the farmers' problem."

"Hmm, you're right." Claire reached for Patsy's hand and pulled her forward. "But I don't trust Howie as far as I could toss him. He'll spin it so Peyton won't know who's on whose side."

Patsy stood her ground and wouldn't budge. "Has Sean started the trench?"

"Next week. He's using Norm Akins's backhoe and a couple of his men. Come on."

"Well, shouldn't we call Felix or somebody to come with us?"

"What's gotten into you, Pat-a-cake?"

"Remember those goons who were with Howie's investors? What if they're in on this, too?"

"Whoa, I hadn't thought about that." Claire couldn't just let Howie go without knowing anything, though. She owed it to Chapel Springs. "Come on, we'll be careful, but I've got to know what they're doing."

They hurried toward Springs Park. When they entered the grounds, Howie was nowhere to be seen. Claire tiptoed up to the Springs House and carefully peered in the window. Howie and Murdoch were at the pool's edge.

"It looks like they're checking the water for something," she whispered.

"But for what?"

Claire moved to the next window. "I don't know, but they took a sample with them. Duck!"

She pulled Patsy behind a bush as the door banged shut. When she was sure Howie and Murdoch had left the park, Claire peeked out from behind the foliage. "It's okay. They're gone. I've got to warn Felix and Sean about this."

Chapter 13

"Anyone here?"

Carin turned at the sound of Ryan's voice coming from the open front door. The morning sun backlit his broad shoulders. "Come on in. Norm and I are going over the plans. Maybe you can help."

Ryan stopped to give Edgar a good petting then shook Norm's hand. "Hey, buddy. How's it going?"

"Good. I'm showing Carin a couple of alternatives." Norm pointed to the blueprints. "I've saved enough money in some areas that we can wire an office for her. Now, she has to choose where she wants it."

Ryan looked over the plans then turned in a slow circle. "What type of insulation are you putting in the attic?"

"Spray foam with a forty-eight R-value. I see where you're going. It could work. We could add a wall-mounted AC unit."

Ryan nodded. "Right. How many BTUs?"

"Twelve thousand. With a small space heater, she'll be cozy in winter and cool in summer."

"Wiring it shouldn't be much of an expense."

"A few extra feet of cable, no additional labor."

"It's a great spot for an office. She'd have a fantastic view from up there."

Carin looked from one to the other. "Hellooo? You two having fun?" They looked at her like they'd forgotten about her. Which they had. "It looks like you've chosen for me."

Norm's ears turned red. "Actually—" He glanced at Ryan. "It's a perfect spot, Carin. Your grandfather chose the way the house sits on the property to take best advantage of the view. The attic is wide, and we can put a custom dormer in that's ten feet wide. Think of the natural light."

"I love that, but I can't go a penny over the loan amount and, in case neither of you noticed, I don't have furniture."

"Are you averse to good quality secondhand stuff?" Norm pulled out his cell phone. He took off his baseball cap and stuffed it in his back pocket.

"I'll take anything that's cheap right now." Losers couldn't be choosers.

"I don't think there's much need," Ryan said. "Have you looked in the garage? Your grandmother's furniture is stored in there."

"Really? I'd love to use Nana's furniture." That would almost be like having her here with her and JJ.

"And anything else you need, you can find at *Déjà Vu*." Norm tapped on his phone then turned it for her to see the display.

"It's a great place," Ryan added. "My sister's a realtor and trades with them a lot."

Carin jotted down the name. "Thanks. Realistically, how long do you think it will be until the renovations are done?"

"Give me six more weeks. I might be able to push that up, though. Since the deconstruction is done, that cuts my time. I've got all the permits already. The electrician is coming tomorrow to rewire, and the plumber starts today. Once they're done, it's a straight road to finishing. You're sure you're good with your office on the third floor?"

"Yes. I'll love having a view. After I look in the garage, I'm fixing to go into town. If I need to, I'll stop by *Déjà Vu*. After that, I plan to sit in the coffee shop to write. I've got my cell if you need me."

"I'll give you a hand in the garage," Ryan said, following her out the door. After a few tries, the key turned in the old padlock, and they each pulled open a creaky carriage door.

The garage was stacked high with boxes and furniture. Ryan pulled a string hanging in front of them and a weak light shone down.

"I'll replace that bulb with a brighter one for you." He ran his hand over an old dresser, brushing some of the dust off.

Carin sneezed. Most of the items were covered in old sheets, and after a half-hour of looking it all over, she'd have to buy new mattresses, since the mice got to Nana's. A few pieces were crumbling from age and poor quality. The rest just needed a good cleaning. JJ would need a whole room, though. There was nothing that suited a six-year-old. Her credit card groaned.

Fifteen minutes later, Carin peered through the window of *Déjà Vu* before heading inside, just to get an idea of how gently-used the furniture truly was. She liked shabby chic, but she wasn't into moth-eaten. The pieces she was able to see, like that living room display, looked new. She pushed open the door.

"Welcome to *Déjà Vu*. I'm the owner, Vic—Carin? Carin Rice?" She pointed to herself. "Vicky Adams ... well, Stolz now. How fun to see you again."

While Carin tried to grab a memory of her, Vicky pulled her into a hug. Did everyone in Chapel Springs hug? Then it landed. Carin babysat her when staying with Nana.

She pulled back but kept her hands on Vicky's shoulders. "Look at you all grown up. It's been what? Fifteen years? You look wonderful." Carin looked over the shop. "And your store is great. That's quite an accomplishment at your age."

Vicky still blushed the cutest shade of pink. "Mom helped me. You know what a yard sale fan she's always been. By the time I was twelve, I got the bug." She gestured around her. "*Déjà Vu* is the result. Mom and I turned a hobby into a business when Daddy died."

Carin's heart wrenched. She dropped her hands from Vicky's shoulders. "I'm sorry. I didn't know about your daddy."

Her smile was honest and bright. "It was nearly six years ago, but we'll see him again, one day. Now, what can I help you with?"

How could she put it without laying out her dirty laundry? Oh fiddle, Vicky would hear anyway.

She took a deep breath and blew it out. "I'm having to start all over alone. Well, alone with my little boy. I've moved into Nana's house, and while I have her furniture, I need a few other pieces, especially mattresses. I can't afford to buy new, but Norm and Ryan said you have things from model homes."

"I'm delighted. No! Wait." Vicky face-palmed herself. "That came out wrong."

Carin chuckled. "No offense taken."

"I meant I'm glad you came here. I've got some special things from home stagers. They buy, trade, and rent from me." She pulled a small pad of sticky notes and a pen from her pocket. "Anything you're interested in, slap a sticky on it with your name in case anyone else comes in. If you have any questions, I'll be at the counter."

"Thanks, Vicky. Uh, you do take credit cards, don't you?"

"Absolutely. Have fun."

Armed with her list and Vicky's notepad, Carin began in the bedroom side of the store. She quickly found a chest of drawers for JJ. Nana's dressers were either too antique for a growing boy or deteriorating. She spied a desk that could double as a nightstand if she placed it next to his bed, and a bookcase.

Norm was fitting her walk-in closet with an organizer, and with Nana's dresser, she didn't need any bedroom furniture for herself or the spare bedrooms. She spotted the most interesting hexagonal table with a bottom shelf. It appeared to be an antique.

"That was my great-grandmother's." Vicky came alongside her. "It's hardrock maple but isn't either Mama's or my style. Grandma ruined the antique value by painting it." Vicky yanked off the price tag and wadded it up. "You can have it for fifty bucks."

"Are you sure? I love it, but I know it's worth more than that."

"Not to me. I'd rather have you love it." Vicky stuck on a sticky note with "Sold-Carin" written on it. "I've got to run next door for a minute. Keep on looking and if someone comes in, just tell them I'll be right back. That is, if you're okay with that?"

"Sure, go ahead."

Carin found the perfect bed for JJ. She didn't see one that suited her, but Norm had rescued some old wood from a pile in the back of the garage—shiplap, he called it. It was beautiful. She wasn't sure why it hadn't been trashed, but she was grateful. When he showed it to her, he said she could probably sell it. First, she would make herself a headboard, and because she liked the look, a feature wall for her office. Then she'd let him sell the rest. It would help with the bills.

She'd just lowered herself onto a chair to try it out when a man entered the shop. He looked around for a moment then made eye contact with her.

"Do you work here?"

Funny, he sounded surprised. "No, the owner's next door and should be back in a moment."

"Ahh. I didn't think I'd seen you here before."

"Do I know—"

The door opened and Vicky stepped inside. "Thanks, Carin. Hey, Mr. B. How can I help you?"

"Looking for something special for my grandson."

He and Vicky went to another part of the store, and Carin continued to tick off her list. By keeping a running tally, she was doing well enough but would max out one credit card. She needed a story idea and she needed it *now*. If she wrote fast and pumped one out in eight weeks, she'd save on finance charges.

Vicky came back alone. The man, Mr. B she called him, must have left. Carin showed her the things she'd picked out. When given her total, it was much less than she figured.

Vicky shrugged. "It's my prerogative to have a babysitter's discount."

Carin was touched by the kindness. "I appreciate it more than you know, Vicky. If there's anything I can ever do for you ..."

"There is something." She reached under the counter and pulled out three of Carin's books. "Autographs? You're Mama's and my favorite author."

"I'd be honored." Carin wrote a personal and heartfelt note then autographed the books.

"I'll deliver the bedroom furniture next week, and hold the other pieces until your house is finished and ready for them."

Carin thanked her and while walking home, decided to order online whatever else she needed but couldn't find in Chapel Springs. She didn't feel like making the long trek back to Atlanta to her favorite housewares stores. Besides, she couldn't afford those places now, even with what Vicky saved her. Carin stopped in her tracks.

Vicky. She and her mother went in business together after daddy/hubby died. Hmm. It could work, but what was the goal? It had to be more than simply making a living or having something to do. Where was the conflict? Without it, it wouldn't make a good story. Carin walked and thought. And thought some more. By the time she got home, the idea had unraveled.

"Snap."

Chapter 14

Carin smoothed the comforter on JJ's bed and stepped back to view the room. He'd be so excited to see his furniture. They had made do with the air mattresses until Norm had the bathroom finished upstairs. He'd saved her money there when he found a large box of antique subway tiles in Nana's garage, so she could afford the racecar bed she found at *Déjà Vu*. When she saw it, she tossed out the idea of the shiplap headboard for JJ. Instead, Norm would use that to make one entire wall a feature in her office.

He'd finished the bathroom this morning. Then he and Ryan helped her bring Nana's bedroom furniture from the garage upstairs to her room. After that, they helped Tommy Holcomb carry up JJ's furniture and the mattresses from *Déjà Vu*. It would be nice to sleep in a real bed again.

Back downstairs, she tackled the sanding Norm had left for her to do. Any way she could save money was worth her time and effort, and sanding wasn't hard. At least she could noodle story ideas while she worked on the old trim Norm had saved for use as crown molding around the kitchen cabinets.

The doorbell rang, startling her. Who could that be? She hadn't had time to make any friends except the ladies at the bakery. Could it be one of them? Lacey, maybe? She dropped the sanding block and brushed the debris from her hands. Hopefully, it wasn't a reporter. But then, no one knew where she was. She hadn't even told her agent.

Edgar beat her to the door, his tail whapping the wall. A man stood on the porch, holding flowers and a bag from *Déjà Vu*. Her gaze travelled above the flowers. It was him, the man she'd seen—Mr. B, Vicky called him. But she'd seen him before in town. She opened the door. Who was he? And why—

A memory surfaced from her childhood. Carin's hands started shaking. Edgar pushed his big head against Mr. B. At least she knew he was okay, whoever he was. Not bothered by the dog, he patted the beast's head without taking his eyes off her.

"Carin."

His voice. It played along with the memory, belonging to it, like a voice-over. A nice man and a sad lady. She'd wanted to go with them. Her heart beat against her breastbone and echoed loud in her ear.

"I … I remember you. You came to my house when I was four. Who … who are you?"

He shifted his feet and glanced down. When he looked up at her again, his eyes glistened. "I'm your father."

Her gaze darted back and forth between his eyes, then to his mouth, and then back to his eyes. They were green with gold flecks, exactly like hers. They even crinkled like hers when he smiled. And he had her chin, or she had his chin.

She licked her lips, but her tongue was dry. "My father." Her flesh and blood. Family. How was she supposed to act?

He opened his mouth then closed it. Finally, he smiled. "May I come in? We have a lot to talk about."

Did they ever. She had a thousand questions for him. Like why he'd abandoned her.

She held the door open a little wider, shoving boxes out of the way with her toe. "It's a mess in here. I'm in the middle of a renovation. This was my grandmother's—well, my *adoptive* grandmother's house. I inherited it. My husband—"

Good grief, she was rambling. She'd never been so nervous, not even when she pitched her first novel. She bit back what she'd been about to say and gestured toward the door to the deck.

"We can go out on the back porch. I have a couple of chairs there."

His soft chuckle followed her through the door, Edgar on his heels. Before they sat, he handed her the flowers. "These are for you."

They were already in a vase of water. She hadn't noticed that when she opened the door. Had he known about the house?

"Thank you. Spring flowers are my favorite."

"I know."

"You do? How?"

And if he knew so much, how come he waited so long to contact her?

"I've read every interview you've given. I've read all your books. I've read every blog you've posted and follow your fan page on Facebook." He held out a bag. "If you'll allow me, this is for my grandson, JJ." His voice cracked and his eyes filled. He swallowed.

JJ's grandfather. His blood flowed through her veins and JJ's. She never had a close relationship with her adoptive father. He was always gone. He and her adoptive mother didn't get along, and he stayed on the road as much as he could. She always thought it was because of her—that he hadn't wanted her. But this man, her father, whose name she didn't even know, he came to her. With flowers. But he gave her away as a baby.

Unable to think straight, she took the vase and set it on the table between the chairs and placed the bag for JJ next to it. Edgar plopped down at the man's feet. She couldn't keep calling him that, even in her own mind. And Mr. B wasn't enough.

She rubbed her hands together then stuck them in her pockets. "I—" She blew out a breath. "Please, I don't know your name." She lowered herself into the other chair.

"Jim Buchanan. Your mother's name was Sue—Susan."

Buchanan. She was born a Buchanan. She was *Irish*?

Carin jumped to her feet. "Wait, you said *was*?"

"She died nineteen years ago of ovarian cancer."

When Carin was thirteen. "I didn't know. I'm—" What was she? Shell-shocked, that's what. How could he waltz into her life after following her—

She sank into the chair and lowered her head. Jim Buchanan. JJ's name was James. How had she ... did God ...? It was too much to work out. After a moment, she raised her eyes to his.

"Why now? Why did you wait?"

"I wanted to contact you earlier, but your sisters—"

"I have sisters?" She'd always wanted a sister. Now she had more than one. This was so much to take in. Her right leg bounced.

He nodded. "Three." He sat in the chair beside her, perched on its edge. "Julie's the eldest. Leanna's next, then Darcie." He reached for her hand. "Carin, your mother and I loved each other. We wanted to get married and keep you, but we weren't allowed the opportunity."

Bitterness etched his voice. She had to know. She ached to know. "Tell me."

"I met your mother when I was fourteen. She was a year younger. We knew right away that we loved each other." He looked out over the lake and his expression grew wistful. "I was barely seventeen, and your mama sixteen when you were born. We were still in high school. They whisked you away from us."

He cleared his throat and swallowed. "Your mother cried for weeks. As soon as we were old enough, we got married and started looking for you." He gave her a half smile. "Your memory is good, because you were four when we finally found you."

She understood why they had to give her up, but knowing she had been loved and wanted meant more than she could verbalize. "I thought you were so nice. I was sad when you left, and then I never saw you again."

"That's because your adoptive mother refused to allow us to come again. She threatened us, and we were afraid she'd take it out on you. So we stayed away but followed you every step of your life."

"You know about my husband?"

Her father frowned. "Yes, and I've wanted to throttle him."

He did? She got up and walked to the porch railing. "I've got so many emotions right now, I can't seem to land on any one of them for more than a second." She turned to face him. "I'm angry that you had to give me up, yet I understand it. I don't like it, but it is what it is. And you know, I used to pray that God would give me a sister. I was so lonely as a child. Mom was distant and cold. Dad was rarely around, and if he was, he scowled all the time. Now, I find I have sisters who got to be raised by loving parents—*my* parents."

I'm jealous. Jealous of sisters that she wanted over a man she didn't really know. She couldn't help it. She laughed. "Talk about dysfunctional."

There was something about him—her father—that drew her. He seemed vulnerable yet open to her. He risked her rejection, something she knew all too well. Anger was a wasted emotion, at least in this situation. It wasn't his fault. So, she could either stay mad and send him on his way … But why? To punish him? Forget that. She finally had a chance to have a dad who *loved* her. Had always *wanted* her. She wasn't about to waste any more time on anger. It was stupid. She was going to forget the past and love him.

She crossed the deck, reached for his hands, and pulled him up and into a hug. A Chapel Springs hug. That made her smile. This town had an effect on her. His arms closed around her. He smelled familiar. That was silly, and yet, she knew his scent. But how could she? He squeezed her tight. She wanted to stay there, safe in his arms—a grown woman, but for a moment, Daddy's little girl.

"Your mother will be smiling down from heaven right now." There was a catch in his voice.

"There are so many things I want to know." She released him, laughed, and wiped her eyes. "Where do you live? Will you be able to see us a lot? JJ is going to be so excited to meet you. He's never had a granddaddy." JJ would want him to stay over. It was all so new, but still, they both had always wanted a dad and grandaddy. It would be ridiculous to wait.

Her dad chuckled. "Carin, sweetheart, you are just like your mother. Whenever she got nervous or excited, she'd start to chatter just like that. You remind me so much of her. I was so happy when your adoptive parents kept the name we gave you."

She blinked. "You named me?"

"We did. It was your mama's great-granny's name. They were very close."

She'd always wondered about the unusual spelling. He looked over his shoulder at the inside of the house. "I think my grandson is here."

Carin turned. JJ stood in the open doorway, his eyes wide. She went to him. "Hey, doodle bug. How was your day?" She squatted and gave him a kiss.

"Good. Who's that?" He pointed to her dad.

Carin couldn't stop smiling. "Do you remember how I told you how God is trustworthy with your dreams?"

He tilted his head up and narrowed his eyes. "Yeah …"

"I have someone special you need to meet."

JJ's feet seemed glued to the floor. "Who is he?"

"Love bug, he's your granddaddy."

His eyes changed from suspicious to sunshine bright. "Really? For real, Mama? My very own granddaddy?" He skidded past her and stopped just in front of her dad. "Are you honest and truly my granddaddy?"

"That I am, Grandson. How do you do?" Her father held his hand out and JJ solemnly shook it.

"I've never had a granddaddy before, but for my whole life I've always wanted one."

"And now you have one." He pulled JJ onto his knee. "And think of the adventures we'll have. I'll take you fishing and teach you to ride a dirt bike, if your mama will let you."

"Aw, she'll let me. She lets me do all kinds of neat things. She's not a scaredy cat."

"She isn't? Well, good for her."

"Did you know my daddy's a racecar driver?"

Her dad glanced at her. She had no idea what to say, so she shrugged. One side of his mouth rose, and he turned back to JJ. "I do know that. I know all about you, JJ."

"How come I didn't know about you, Granddaddy?"

"Because God told me it wasn't time until now. He knew you'd need me more now than ever before."

Carin's heart skipped a beat. She hadn't been sure if God watched out for them or not, but she couldn't deny the timing was perfect.

JJ leaned against his grandfather. "Yeah, I think so, too." He put his little arms around his granddaddy's neck and hugged him. "I've decided I'm gonna love you, Granddaddy."

"Well, now that makes me plumb tickled. I love you too, JJ. You and your mama. Now, pick up that bag and see what I brought you."

While JJ and her dad played with the truck he brought and got to know one another, Carin called Claire. After telling her about her dad, she asked, "Would I be completely out of my mind to ask him to stay?"

"Wow, sugar, I think it might be better to ask where he's staying. If it's in town, then have him come back for breakfast."

"I guess you're right. I know JJ's going to want him to stay."

"And you can ask him, but only after you've had a day or two with him."

"Thanks, Claire."

Chapter 15

Claire sat at the Town Council table and studied the audience. Everyone involved in the Lakeside Players had passed the word to come tonight if they wanted the *Lola Mitchell Opera House* reopened. While she didn't want to be involved in every production, she loved going to see the plays. Apparently, she wasn't alone. A sizable crowd had assembled. Great Aunt Lola would have been pleased.

Joel stood in the back, talking to that reporter who had covered their town revitalization. What was her name? Jacqueline Ford, that was it, from WPV in Pineridge. Had he invited her? It would make a good local interest story.

Claire counted over thirty of the summer residents, too. That was good. She might have a chance at getting Felix to go along with their plans. What was Mel doing here? Her stepmother was supposed to pick her up after work. Maybe she got held up. Claire could have Joel run the girl home. She didn't want her hitchhiking or walking alone.

Boone banged his gavel and brought the meeting to order. After the pledge of allegiance, Ellie Grant read the minutes, yada, yada, yada. This part of the meeting always bored Claire beyond reason. She stifled a yawn.

"I move we accept the minutes as read," Doc said.

Claire twisted off the top from a water bottle. "I second." *Let's hurry this up.* She took a drink and screwed the top back on.

"All those in favor?" Each board member raised a hand.

"Opposed?" Now why did Boone bother to ask that? Roberts and his rules needed some adjusting.

Boone called for new business. Claire bided her time. She didn't want to be the first. Finally, after some reports on the financial gains they'd made from the tram and parking, Claire raised her hand.

"A lot of people from Chapel Springs have been going to see live theater productions in Pineridge. I often recommend the *Pineridge Playhouse* to tourists and summer residents." Claire nodded to the covey of renters in the audience. Motor-mama—uh, Hazel Jones—waved at her. Huh, when had she come back?

"And?" Felix drummed his fingers on the table.

Her right eye twitched. "And those of us involved with the Lakeside Players have begun to wonder why we always *rent* the *Pineridge Playhouse* for our productions, when we have a perfectly good theater here in Chapel Springs."

The audience murmured. Jacqueline Ford sat straighter and poised her pen over her notepad.

Felix harrumphed. "I wouldn't call that old place 'perfectly good.' Why it's dilapidated, boarded up, and haunted."

"That rumor died years ago, although I suppose a rumor could haunt it." Claire chuckled at her own joke. But maybe Felix made a good point, albeit in ignorance. By the look of the audience leaning forward in their seats, people loved a so-called haunted theater.

"Ain't a rumor. I saw a light in there the other night." Felix thumbed his suspenders. "At first I thought it might be one of them college boys, so I peeked through the winda'. I saw your great-aunt Lola's ghost."

Boone laughed out loud. "Felix, you're imagining things. Claire, I know y'all fixed up the outside of the old theater when we revived the town. What is the condition of the inside?"

"To be honest, I haven't been inside for decades. It's been boarded up for close to forty years."

Howie Newlander stood. "And it should have been torn down and something useful built instead. That's the kind of waste I'll address if I'm elected mayor of Chapel Springs."

The room erupted. Claire almost danced a jig. Howie had sorely miscalculated the residents' feelings for the old opera house. Felix, his eyes wide with panic, turned to her for help. That alone was worth her efforts. She passed a note to him on which she'd listed her guestimate of the cost to refurbish the theater. There were plenty of used items in good condition they could purchase from large theaters that upgraded their interiors every few years.

Boone banged his gavel for quiet. "Newlander, you're out of order. And this isn't a campaign rally."

Howie sat down with a scowl. Nancy Vaughn, Lakeside Players' stage manager, and Kelly Appling, the director, sat next to Lacey. All three held their thumbs up in support. They wanted this theater reopened. It would save everyone involved a lot of time, not to mention gas money.

Felix raised his hand, and Boone gave him the floor. "Claire, you've done some research on the cost of refurbishing the old place. How do you propose to fund it?"

"The building belongs to the town. If the town funds the remodeling"—she held up her hand to stop any protests—"the Lakeside Players could rent it, bringing in more revenue. We could also rent it to other companies or for concerts when the Lakeside Players aren't using it."

Felix brightened at that, but Howie shook his head and walked out of the meeting. That chalked one up for Felix's team. Claire pulled another copy of the costs involved from her tote.

"If the Chairman will look this over, I think by the next meeting, we could have a vote on this issue." She passed the paper to Boone. "If need be, we could do another fundraiser. I'd donate some of my artwork to see the theater revitalized."

As soon as the meeting was officially over, Jacqueline Ford approached Claire before she had a chance to find Mel. "Ms. Bennett, I'd like to ask you a couple of questions."

Claire smiled. "Of course."

"Lola Mitchell was your great-aunt?"

"Yes, on my daddy's side."

"And the theater is named after her?"

"Yes. She and one of the early homesteaders in Chapel Springs, Cora Lee Rice, were good friends. When Aunt Lola retired and moved here, they funded the building of the theater, and the community named it after her."

"What was she like?"

Memories flowed over Claire like warm honey. "She was larger than life. I was in awe of her." She chuckled. "Aunt Lola could keep us entertained for hours with her stories of Hollywood in its early days."

Jacqueline scribbled her notes. "It would be a wonderful tribute to her to reopen the theater. My own great-grandmother was in one of her movies and thought the world of her."

"Really? I didn't know that. Will you help us raise some outside funds? Maybe cover the reopening if it happens?"

"I'd be honored, Ms. Bennett."

"Claire, please."

Jacqueline nodded. "Claire. I'll write a story and include a way for people to donate. Now, another question. What is the story behind Howard Newlander's bid for mayor?"

Claire couldn't help it. Her eyes rolled of their own volition. "Last year, Howie tried to sell some land owned by his grandmother to a group of investors with the idea of building a high-rise hotel here in Chapel Springs. We discovered the mayor's brother was the instigator of it all. He had invested drug money."

Jacqueline stopped writing and stared at Felix.

"No." Claire drew the reporter's attention back to her. "Felix had no idea of any of his brother's activities." She went on to explain what happened and how Howie's grandfather had willed the land to Chapel Springs, so the whole thing fell through. "He's been mad at us ever since, acting as if we'd stolen the land."

"I'd love to hear his side of it, to see how he tries to spin it." Jacqueline held out her hand. "I'll send you the story before it runs, Claire, so you can check any facts."

Jacqueline left her and went over to Felix. Once again, Great Aunt Lola brought Claire an ally. Tomorrow, she'd get the keys to the theater and enlist Nancy and Kelly to help her go see what was needed to fully renovate it inside. Then they could give a true estimate to the council.

Felix's ghost story floated through her mind along with *The Phantom of the Opera*. The ghost of the *Lola Mitchell Opera House*. It was silly, but people liked the idea of theater ghosts. It added to the mystique.

Claire searched the dwindling crowd. "Joel, did you see Mel leave?"

"No. I didn't know she was here."

"I hope she didn't walk or worse, hitchhike. I don't think that stepmother of hers cares much for her."

Joel took her hand as they strolled home, making her heart pitter-patter. Public displays of affection went against his nature, and to take her hand was a blatant I-love-you. They crossed Church Street and wandered through a short stretch of woods to Pine Drive.

"Look, honey." Claire pointed out Carin's house as they walked down Pine. She waved at Carin, who was sitting on the front porch. "Oh, she's got someone with her."

"Hey, Claire." Carin waved. "Come up and meet my dad."

Her dad? Hadn't Mr. Rice passed away? She tugged Joel's hand and they turned up Carin's walk. The man stood as they approached. It wasn't Mr. Rice. She glanced at Joel, who either didn't remember Carin's father—wait. Carin had been adopted. Was this—?

They stepped onto the porch. Carin beamed. "Claire, Joel, this is my birth father, Jim Buchanan. Dad, these are my friends, Claire and Joel Bennett."

"It's good to meet you. Carin and JJ have told me about you, Claire. I'll have to come in to see your artwork. JJ thinks you're magical. And my grandson and I are going to come rent a boat so I can teach him to fish." He motioned toward the chairs on the porch. "Will you sit and join us?"

Joel shook his head. "We just finished a town council meeting and are on our way home. But maybe you'd join us for supper." He looked at Claire. "Thursday next week? Is that good?"

Claire nodded, but Jim deferred to Carin, who looked unsure.

"We'd love you to bring JJ, too." Joel chuckled. "We have plenty to keep him occupied. In fact, bring Edgar, too. He and Shiloh will have a blast in the backyard together."

Carin smiled. "All right, then. And thank you."

An idea snapped. Claire reached out and stopped Joel, who had started down the porch steps. "Hang on a second." She turned back to Carin. "Would you be interested in helping us refurbish the old theater? I don't mean do the work, but help pick out things? Lacey will be helping."

"What theater?"

"It's just up the street, next to the church."

Carin blinked. "Oh. Well, I'm … I mean, I'd like to—oh sure, why not?"

What was the indecision about? Tilting her head, Claire studied her. "I'll let you know when we meet, then. If you're busy, that's okay." She didn't want to push Carin. "I'm going there tomorrow to see what all has to be done."

"I'd love to come with you."

First she seemed hesitant, now she was eager. Chapel Springs was breaking through that girl's defenses.

"I'll call you." Claire and Joel headed home.

"Why didn't you tell me you were going into the old opera house?" Joel asked.

"I didn't particularly think about it. What's wrong?"

He took her hand again. "It could be dangerous. After all, it's been what? Forty years since it was boarded up? The floors could be rotted."

"I'll be careful."

"And I'll be with you, to make sure."

Claire leaned over and kissed his cheek. He scowled and pulled away. Public displays only went as far as hand-holding, apparently. She laughed and leaned toward him again. He sprinted ahead of her. Silly man. She dashed after him, just like she did when they were in high school. Joel vaulted the garden gate, and they ended up on their porch, winded and laughing.

He threw his arm around her as they stumbled into the house. "We aren't as young as we used to be, babe."

No, they weren't. But Claire wouldn't turn back the clock for anything. She loved the changes in her husband. She only hoped, as she switched off the porch light, that Melissa realized that before she made a huge mistake.

Chapter 16

The afternoon sun cut through the pines, its rays painting JJ and his granddaddy in mottled stripes. Dad—Carin had finally started thinking of him that way—reached out and ruffled JJ's hair, making her heart swell. Finding him—or having him find her—after all these years of wondering, well, she wasn't going to waste another minute. She joined them on the porch.

"Hey, you two. If JJ's finished with his homework, how about a walk down to the lake? Edgar wants a swim I'm sure, and we can show your granddaddy the special spots we've declared ours."

JJ grabbed Dad's hand. "I've even got one Mama hasn't seen yet. Me an' Mikey found it. Come on."

While JJ ran ahead of them with Edgar, Carin walked beside her dad. After a moment, she took his hand and held it out in front of her. She put hers up beside it, comparing the two. "I've got your hands."

His grin filled her with joy. "Ah, that you do." He reached for hers and kept hold of it. "Your mother's were a bit daintier, but these long fingers of ours are better for typing. Now, you may favor me more in looks, but you've got your mother's mannerisms. You and Leanna share that."

"What about Julie and Darcie? Do they share those?"

"Not so much. Julie takes after my mother, I'm afraid."

Carin called for JJ to slow down then looked at her dad. "In what way?"

"She ..." He seemed to struggle for the right words. "My mother never allowed anyone to know things weren't perfect in the family. Everything and everyone was always fine."

"Isn't that good?"

Dad stopped. He searched her eyes. "No, honey. It isn't honest, and it doesn't let anyone help carry your burden by praying for you."

They walked on toward JJ. "I don't know if anyone is praying for me, but I've had to share my shame. Wick leaving forced me into it."

"And don't you find it a relief not having to hide your situation?"

She stopped. "No, Dad, it isn't a relief. It's an embarrassment. It's like wearing a brand on my forehead." She made an "L" with her thumb and index finger against her forehead. "Loser."

He pulled her hand down and put his arms around her, squeezing her tight. "Sweetheart, you're not a loser. He is." He kissed her forehead. "Look at me. I wish so much I could have talked you out of marrying Wick. I saw the way he was with women."

"I didn't, and my parents didn't know, or more like they didn't care."

He groaned. "Oh, Carin, I'm so—"

"Don't. We said we'd forget the past. It's futile to wish and spend time on what ifs. I've laid it to rest. You need to, too. We have our future—" How ironic. She quoted words from her last novel. The one that failed. She shook it off. "And JJ and I have you now. Speaking of that little imp, let's go get him before he decides to catch a fish with his bare hands."

On their way back up to the house, JJ walked between them. "Mama, can Granddaddy stay at our house? Overnight? Pleeeease?"

No reason to refuse. Not anymore. They'd spent the last two days getting to know him better. She smiled. "Dad? Do you think we should make this kid's day?"

He stopped, laid one finger beside his nose and cradled his chin. Studying JJ, he winked. "Yes, I believe that's a fine idea."

Carin started walking. "What about your clothes?"

He looked down at his pants. "I'm not sure I ... what do you mean?" Mischief twinkled in his eyes.

She swiped back a strand of hair that had stuck to her lip. "If you're going to stay for a few days, you need your clothes and things."

"Ahh." He turned and grinned at JJ. "Can't I borrow some of yours, buddy?"

JJ's giggles were infectious. "You're silly, Pop."

Carin blinked. "Pop?"

"Yeah. Pop and I decided 'granddaddy' sounds too babyish for a big kid like me."

"Ah, I see." It tickled her to see their fast bond. Dad was good for him. "Tell you what, your *pop's* room is almost ready, so how about we go get dinner at one of the restaurants in town. Then we'll stop and pick up his things on the way home and he can check out."

As soon as they got back to the house, she punched *Déjà Vu's* number into her cell phone. "Vicky, this is Carin. I need another double mattress set." The guest room had an antique bed, dresser, and nightstand of Nana's in it. Norm had tossed the mouse-eaten mattresses in the dumpster.

JJ's laughter floated in from the porch where he and his granddaddy played with Edgar. "I need it right away."

"Sure. Tommy is delivering some things for his dad a few doors down from you. I'll have him bring them then. What about linens and pillows?"

"Those I've got. Thanks, Vicky. I owe you dinner. Plus the mattresses." Carin surprised herself by suggesting dinner, but then, Vicky was someone she'd known for years. Even though it had been a long time ago, Carin trusted her. Maybe it was Chapel Springs that made the difference. Or her dad. Whatever it was, she liked it.

Vicky snickered. "I'd love that—dinner I mean. Although getting paid is a good idea. Let's plan it."

"Which, the payment or dinner?"

"You nut. Good-bye." Vicky hung up, but Carin could hear her giggles until the line cleared.

They went to dinner at *The Pasta Bowl* and then checked Dad out from Eisler's B&B. Dad teased Faye about staying in the Roosevelt Bedroom. Said he'd channeled FDR all night, making Faye blush. According to Claire, there was no basis that FDR actually stayed at the old Inn, but the Eislers insisted he had.

Tommy was waiting for them when they got back to the house. When the mattress set was in her dad's room, Carin handed Tommy a folded ten-dollar bill. "Thanks, I didn't want to ask my dad to help carry that upstairs."

"Aw, that's okay, Miss Carin. It's nice that your daddy can stay with y'all."

"Yes, it is." *It really is.*

After Tommy left, she made up the bed and added drawer liners to the dresser and nightstand. With JJ finally settled for the night and Dad's things put away, Carin fixed them both some tea in her room. She had a small, temporary office area set up, complete with a Keurig and electric teakettle, so she could be cozy while she wrote. It would have been perfect, except she couldn't write. Every time she opened her computer screen, her mind froze. All she could see were the bad trade reviews.

She spooned the teabags out of the water. "How do you want yours, Dad?"

"Without the string."

So that's where her dry sense of humor came from, although lately, she seemed to have lost that too. She handed him his cup. "You never finished telling me about my sisters."

He settled into the settee by the window. "Ah, yes, your sisters. Well, after your mother died, Julie, being eldest at the ripe old age of seven, took her place in raising Leanna and Darcie. Sweet Leanna didn't need a lot of hands on. Though only four, she was already the family peacemaker." He paused and took a drink of tea. "Ah, that hits the spot." He set the cup down on the side table next to him.

The thought of finally having sisters was strangely daunting to her now. As a child, it was all she wanted, but now? Would they love or reject her? She tried to put herself in their place. How would she feel?

"Darcie, on the other hand, was spoiled by everyone. She was an adorable baby and not quite two when your mother died. Everyone pampered her, thinking it a tragedy. She hardly noticed. From the moment she was born, Julie was infatuated with her. Your mother had a hard time holding her own baby. It's unfortunate Julie and Ted—that's her husband—don't have any children. She substitutes Darcie and considers herself her mother. I'm not all that convinced it's healthy."

A shiver quivered through Carin. It didn't sound healthy. "Tell me about Leanna." Maybe the family peacemaker would welcome her when the time came to meet them. As much as she had wanted sisters, she coveted time with her dad first before adding any more family. Dad drained his teacup. He looked drawn.

Carin lowered her cup. "Are you okay?"

"Just tired and ready to call it a day."

"Call it a night and I'll tuck you in."

He rose and gave her a bear hug. "Good night, daughter. I promise, we'll spend a few months together before I tell your sisters about you. I'm selfish enough to want that, too."

How had he known? She kissed his cheek. "Good night, Dad ... I love you." And she did. More each day. Could love be built into the DNA of a person?

"And I love you. More than you can imagine."

After she was alone, Carin couldn't sleep. Her mind overflowed with the day's events. She tried to journal them but couldn't capture her thoughts. Like humming birds, they'd flit away before she could grab hold of any. Settling on her sisters, she tried to picture them one by one, burning them into her memory.

She finally fell asleep, dreaming of a woman pointing her finger and screeching. Carin couldn't make out what she was saying but awoke suddenly, tangled in the bed sheets.

Chapter 17

As soon as JJ was off to school and her dad busy helping Norm, Carin sat down at her computer. First, she sorted through some email then opened a new document. She set her fingers on the keyboard and stared at the blank screen. It stared back without yielding any ideas. A kernel of fear took root in her stomach.

Lost her edge.

Her fingers hovered over the keyboard, trembling. If anything, she always had an overabundance of ideas but now, her mind was blank. Okay, the writer magazines said to simply BICHOK. But the acronym, Butt In Chair Hands On Keyboard, wasn't helping. Her behind was firmly centered in her chair. Okay, her fingers weren't exactly *on* the keyboard. She lowered them and typed. "The quick brown fox jumps over the lazy dog." That was it? An old typing exercise? That was all she could come up with?

Dear God, help!

She'd never faced this before. That kernel in her stomach sprouted branches. *Type anything.* She lowered her fingers, closed her eyes, and free typed. After a couple of minutes, she peeked at the screen. It was total nonsense. And bad nonsense at that.

It was the renovation, the upheaval in her home and her life. That had to be it. She shut down the computer. Once the renovation was done, she could settle in and work. She was sure of it. For now, she'd try to help out and speed up the process.

The phone rang before she got out of her room. Her agent's name appeared in caller I.D. "Bobbie Jo? How are you?"

"I've been better." Her voice was cold, like icicles, sending an involuntary shiver up Carin's spine. "Have you seen the papers?"

"No, I've been—"

"You haven't been keeping up with your email either. The trades are filled with your divorce and goings on that are frankly in violation of the ethics clause in your contract."

Divorce? Wick was divorcing her? "But I didn't—"

"It doesn't matter whose fault it is, Carin. The fact is you're in the middle of a scandal as far as the agency is concerned."

"That's ridiculous. He walked out on me and I'm scandalous?"

"I'm sorry. The agency is voiding your contract."

She heard a click as Bobbie Jo ended the connection. Severed was more like it. What just happened? She'd been with her for six years. She was lost without an agent. Some people managed, but she never had. Was this the end of her career? Would her publisher call her next?

God, why? What had she done to cause all this?

The implications seemed insurmountable right now. She couldn't deal with it. After shutting down her computer, she went downstairs where she found Norm by the front door.

"Hey there. Want a pair of extra hands?" Maybe she could start a new career in construction.

He looked up from the box in his arms. "You bet. Have you ever tiled?"

"No." Carin eyed the box. "Is that the backsplash?"

"It is. It's a classic white subway tile that will suit the era of the house." He pulled one out and held it up.

"I like it. It's simple and clean."

"You and your dad can put it up this afternoon. Oh, and I've got something to tell you about your countertops."

She took a half step back. "Uh-oh. That doesn't sound good."

"Oh, it's good all right. I got a call from a buddy at a stone yard. One of his clients refused the marble countertops they cut for her. Said the veins weren't going the right direction or something." He laid the box on the worktable he'd set up in the kitchen. "Anyway, he offered them to me at cost. It's pretty close to your layout. Look here." He walked over to the end cabinets. "I'll have to put a spacer between these two, extending the counter by two inches and move the stove top over a few inches to the left."

"And that's not a problem?"

"Piece of cake, and we save you nine hundred."

"Over tile?"

"Yep."

She wanted to kiss him, but controlling herself, she wrapped her arms around her middle. "Thank you. For that kind of savings, you could move the stove into the laundry room and I wouldn't complain."

"No need to, just four inches to the left."

"When do we get them?"

"This afternoon. Once they're in, we can start the backsplash."

"Well, if there's nothing I can do yet, I think I'll go to *Dee's 'n' Doughs*. Do you want me to bring back something for you?"

"Coffee and an apple fritter."

"Make mine a pear tart and coffee." Her dad's voice carried in from the porch.

"Okay, but I might be a little while." She pulled out her phone and checked the time. "I'm meeting a few ladies there."

Dad walked in through the open door, wiping his hands on a rag. "I'm glad to hear that. Friends are important."

"Why do you say that?"

He put his hand over hers. "They'll help you get through this hard time."

They might turn her friendship away, too. Although they hadn't … yet. Not like her agent. That still stung.

Dad smiled and handed her twenty dollars.

"Dad, I—"

"Humor me, daughter. Don't rob me of a blessing."

She reluctantly took it, still feeling like a loser. As she walked toward the bakery, she turned the conversation with her agent over in her mind. She'd thought Bobbie Jo was calling with an offer. Carin kicked a pebble on the sidewalk. She thought her agent had been her friend. It served to prove what she'd discovered. People only wanted her celebrity status or what they could get out of her. And once she wasn't worth anything to them, they severed the connection.

Carin turned around and walked toward *Grounds for Delight*. She could get Dad and Norm a pastry there. The ladies at *Dee's 'n' Doughs* would do fine without her. They probably wouldn't even miss her. She cut between Cottage Row and the movie store to Sandy Shores Drive. A twinge of guilt niggled at her for going into Tillie's rival bookstore, but it shared its space with the coffee shop.

As soon as the barista handed Carin her chocolate raspberry frappe, she chose a table on the patio and settled in to people-watch. The front patio, separated from the sidewalk by a low wrought iron fence, was covered with a wisteria-laden trellis. The wisteria's heady scent chasséd a ballet with the coffee's aroma, one minute upstaging the java and the next pirouetting behind it.

She could sit here for the next couple hours, shaded from the hot sun, and see ... not as much as she'd hoped. The left bay of the bookstore's window was to her right, and across the street was Moonrise Cove and the boat launch. Besides that, all there was to see was the bait shop, *The Happy Hooker*.

It seemed a strange spot to place a coffee shop and bookstore. Why did they choose this lot? Was there a story in it? She quickly pulled out her notepad and scribbled. After a moment, she laid down her pen. There wasn't a story. Anyone with a lick of sense could see there wasn't any more land in the center of the village.

Esther Tully stood in the bookstore's large bay window with a muscled carpenter who worked on a new display. Wisps of gray and brown hair had worked their way loose from the bun at the top of her head. The carpenter came down the ladder and studied a paper she held. They both gestured to opposite sides of the window, making Carin laugh.

What made Tillie dislike Esther? Both their lives revolved around books. Tillie sold used books, Esther new. It couldn't be simply competition. There had to be more. And the new store's name, *Leave the World Behind*—there had to be a story behind that. Surely Esther had a story, and what did Carin know about Tillie? She never married. Why not?

Her pen stalled. If books were Tillie's only friends, then there wasn't a story, at least not a Carin Jardine novel. As for never marrying, that only invited a failed romance. She scratched out Tillie's name. Esther might be worth investigating, but the story didn't intrigue her.

Carin leaned her elbows on the table and absently sucked on the straw. The glass empty, it gurgled at her. With the loan funded, her financial need loomed large, like one of those cartoon bubbles, a shark following her, waiting to swallow her. What if she couldn't come up with another story? Had the well gone dry? Desperation settled in her stomach and made the frappe she'd just finished threaten to spill.

The street was empty. Her plan hadn't worked at all. There weren't many people in the village today. Since it was close to three o'clock, she got the coffee and pastries for her dad and Ryan, then walked home to wait for JJ.

Walking everywhere was something she hadn't realized she missed while living in Atlanta. She normally sat so much, either at her desk or in her car. Walking invigorated her, and energized, maybe she'd find her muse on the way home.

Chapter 18

Claire locked the door of the gallery and headed straight to Felix's campaign office. 'Lissa had promised to bring her some dinner, but they needed help with a mailing before the town council meeting. The late afternoon air made Claire yawn as she strolled the sunlight-dappled sidewalk.

She climbed the outside stairs of the post office building to the cramped space Felix rented for his campaign. He'd only been challenged twice in the fourteen years he'd been mayor, so the need for a campaign office was usually nil. This unused space was as old and dilapidated as the theater. She pushed open the door and stepped inside.

As fast as Bobby folded the campaign donor letters, 'Lissa stuffed them, and Patsy slapped on a stamp.

"What am I here for? To crack the whip? Y'all look like you have everything under control."

'Lissa didn't even look up from her envelope-stuffing. "Aunt Patsy came in your stead."

"Didn't you hear me tell you that when I left the gallery?" Patsy slapped another stamp to an envelope, then moistened the flap with a sponge-bottle. Felix refused to waste money on a stamp machine that could seal an envelope.

"I guess I missed that. Say, if you really don't need me, I want to take a look inside the theater. I got the keys last week from the bank but haven't had time to get inside. I really need to so I can give a decent report tonight."

Bobby stopped folding. "Do you want someone to go with you?" He looked at 'Lissa.

Was he looking for her approval? Claire grudgingly gave this boy a couple of man-points for that—emphasis on grudgingly.

"That would be nice, Bobby." 'Lissa pointed one thumb at Pat-a-cake. "Aunt Patsy and I can handle the rest, and we'll come over to the council meeting when we're done. Momma, there's a sandwich in the cooler for you."

Claire didn't need an escort, but it appeared to be a done deed. She pulled out the sandwich and unwrapped it. Ooh, pimiento cheese. Yum. She took a bite and grabbed a can of sweet tea.

"Let's get going then, Bobby. I don't want to be in there in the dark."

Bobby clambered down the metal staircase after her, his footfalls making the whole thing rattle and vibrate. At the bottom, Claire stopped.

"Okay, what's the real reason you wanted to come? And don't try to tell me it's to protect me."

Bobby scratched his head. "That's actually the reason, Miss Claire. The other night, I saw a light or what appeared to be a light, moving from one part of the theater to another. I peeked through a window, and it looked like ..." He glanced around. "Like a floating lantern."

Claire didn't know whether to believe him or laugh. She started walking toward the theater, which stood next to the church. "What exactly do you mean by floating? Was it hanging on something?"

"No, ma'am. It moved."

Claire stopped. "You mean somebody is in there?"

His face was solemn. "If there is, they're invisible. That lantern moved from one place to another without anyone holding it."

"Bobby, you've got to be mistaken, caught up maybe with the ghost rumors." She lengthened her stride. She wanted to see for herself. If he was trying to move her attention from him and 'Lissa with this lantern business— "Take me to the window you looked in."

From the outside, it appeared perfectly peaceful and ready for patrons to be entertained. Hmm. Could this ghost business be perpetuated by the owners of *Curtain Call*? They stood to lose revenue if Chapel Springs reopened the *Lola Mitchell Opera House*.

She followed Bobby around to the side of the building. Weeds grew tall against it and were the only sign the building wasn't occupied. If she asked Joel, maybe he'd get a few of the men together to clean up the grounds.

"That second window is where I saw it." Bobby pointed to a tall window. It was two panes wide by ten high with antique wavy glass. It was only about ten feet back from the front of the building.

Claire tried to think of where that particular window was on the inside. It couldn't be the actual theater because of the light it would let in.

She peered in through dirty glass. Nothing. However, a mirror stood a few feet from the window, facing it. This had to be the rest room.

"I think I found your ghost. Come look. See that mirror? I'll bet the sunlight shone off it or off a lantern hanging in the room and bounced off the mirror. With the windows so dirty, that made it look foggy and ghostly, and the wavy glass could account for the movement."

"Except that it was dark out." Bobby looked inside. "And there's no lantern there now."

"This is ridiculous. I'm going in. Are you coming?" She didn't wait for his answer but went around to the front door, inserted the key, and—nothing happened. The key wouldn't budge. She pulled it out, turned it over, and reinserted it, bumpy side down. It still wouldn't turn. Either the bank gave her the wrong key, or the lock was frozen from years of neglect.

She yanked the key out of the lock and shoved it back in her pocket. "I guess we're not getting in today. The lock is rusted out or something, and I don't want to force it. I'll talk to the council."

They left the theater and Claire headed to the bank, where the council meetings were held in the Community Room on the third floor. She was early and hoped Felix would be too, so she could talk to him about the key. Bobby went back to the campaign office.

She finished off her sandwich as she walked. Claire didn't really believe in ghosts, but neither did she disbelieve. She'd never seen one. Then again, Jesus talked about not being a ghost in the Bible. Were his words symbolic or fact? The jury was still out on that. However, she was pretty sure what Bobby saw could be explained with the science of light bending or something. Maybe Wingnut—Sean—would know.

She entered the bank's lobby, ignored the elevator, and climbed the stairs to the Community Room. Bud Pugh was there, helping Happy Drayton set up chairs. Bud drove the tram part time and was the parking lot guard, too. One of the town's elders, he always had a smile for everyone.

"Evenin', Ms. Claire. How be you?"

"Much better for seeing you, Bud. You always brighten my day. Is Felix here yet?"

"Haven't seen him yet."

Happy Drayton set the gavel at the end of the council's table on the raised dais. "I think I hear the elevator. Might be him now."

A moment later, Felix stepped from the elevator, hitching up his pants. His signature suspenders were patriotic tonight and actually went well with his red shirt. Eileen, his main squeeze, must have helped him. He had no sense of style on his own. Claire motioned him to join her, and when he did, she held out the worthless key.

"Either this is the wrong key or the lock is frozen, and we need to get in for more than an inventory. Did Bobby tell you what he thought he saw?"

Felix slid his thumb under one suspender strap, leaned close, and whispered, "Bobby ain't the only one. I had a call from one of the summer folks. They saw a light too. I went over to investigate, but I couldn't get inside. I didn't see anything, though. Figured it was their imagination. But I've had a few other calls with people saying they've seen things."

Claire furrowed her brow. What was going on? "We need to get in there. Since the town owns the land, doesn't that make the council the caretaker? Can we get a locksmith with a simple vote?"

"Yep, we can."

The door opened and Joel came in, followed by several other townsfolk. Felix moved to greet people, and Claire welcomed her husband.

"We've got some issues with the theater. I'm beginning to suspect someone from the Pineridge theater doesn't want us opening up again."

Joel frowned. "Why's that?"

Claire shook her head. "They stand to lose revenue. So what's better than to start a ghost rumor?" She told him about Bobby's lantern-sighting.

Joel put his arm around her. "Promise me you won't go inside without me or the sheriff."

Claire crossed her eyes. "I certainly won't go with Jim Bob. He'd try to arrest the lantern and end up shooting me. I've got to get to my seat."

She kissed his cheek before he could move away and left him red-faced but grinning.

Boone called the meeting to order. When they got to new business, Claire told them the lock had to be fixed or changed on the theater so she could get inside to do an inventory of what they needed to do to get it open again.

A hand went up in the back of the room. Boone gave the woman the floor. It was one of the cottage renters, a fortyish brunette. "What about the ghost? Y'all are going to need a paranormal sleuth."

"A what?" Boone asked.

"I'm a certified paranormal sleuth," she said.

Certifiable, if anyone wanted to ask Claire. Hey, maybe she was the one keeping the rumor alive so she could make some money. She disciplined herself to not roll her eyes and pasted on a smile. "I don't think we need a whatever sleuth just yet."

Boone agreed and the Council voted to call a locksmith. They would shelve the vote on refurbishing until Claire could give her report.

"Next on the agenda"—Boone ran a finger down the paper in front of him—"is the creek diversion. Does Sean have a report for us?"

Tall and lanky, Sean unfolded himself and stood. "It's going better than I anticipated. We should be finished in a couple of weeks with the tie-in to where the creek comes above ground and flows down to the farmlands. When that's complete, we'll go back to where the creek goes subterranean and dig the connector. The final step will be to dam the entrance to the underground and fill in the few yards of dry creek-bed. That should solve the springs' temperature problem and the farmers will have a full creek."

When Boone adjourned the meeting, Felix asked if any of the council members had seen Howie around lately. "When I can't see him, I get nervous."

"He was in my office last week," Doc said.

"Was he sick or campaigning against me?"

"Now, Felix, you know I can't tell you that. I can tell you he didn't leave any campaign literature in my office." Doc sure was good at letting them know what they wanted without violating his Hippocratic Oath.

"He's up to something. I can feel it in my knower." Felix tapped his gut.

Chapter 19

"Norm, the house is fantastic." Carin stood in the great room and turned in a circle. The color palette was neutral but warm, and she felt welcomed each time she walked through the front door. That door caused a lot of arguments between her and Norm. He thought making the top half glass wasn't smart for a single woman. She argued back it gave everyone a view of Edgar, and she didn't need anything else to deter an intruder. With a glance at the mastiff, Norm had given in.

Having reversed the original contractor's layout, the kitchen was now in the front of the house to the left of the front door, making the lake the focal point when she cooked since the stovetop was on the island. When she and her guests—or she and JJ—ate and relaxed in the great room, they had both the lake view and the mountains. Her little guy liked to count the boats on the lake while they ate.

They'd run into a few problems, but Norm had managed to keep to the time schedule. There were other projects she hoped to take on in the future, but her renovation money had run out. Now, she had to find a way to pay the mortgage or she'd lose this too. Royalties on her past books weren't enough. And people thought every bestselling author was a millionaire. If they only knew.

Norm slid a hammer and some other gadget into his toolbox. "I'm glad it all worked out for you, Carin. Our boys have become best friends, and Mikey would have my hide if I didn't make JJ's mama happy—not to mention my wife. You're her favorite author."

"You're safe. It's beautiful. I didn't think I'd find beauty in my life anymore."

He closed the lid on his toolbox. He cocked his head and smiled at her. "You've got JJ and now your dad. Don't forget to count your blessings, Carin. It helps to see past the trials." He picked up his things. "See you at church?"

She nodded and went to a table in the entry. "This is for Sheryl." Her cheeks grew warm. "She asked me to autograph it."

Norm took the book, glancing at it. "Thanks, that will make her day. Enjoy your home. Allow for God to bless it and all who enter." He turned and went out the door, leaving her under an umbrella of benediction.

With the house to herself for the first time in nearly eight weeks, Carin didn't know what to do. Oh, she knew she *should* start writing, but at that moment, she wanted to play in her new home. There was a box filled with old photographs in Nana's—her—garage. Hanging some of them on the walls would be a good place to start. She grabbed the key off the hook by the back door.

Ryan must have done something to the old lock, because the key slipped in and turned with ease. She pulled the string, and a bright light lit the gloomy old space. He took care of that, too. The same way he took care of Nana. Ryan was a good friend, one who didn't want anything from her other than friendship.

The garage was filled with treasures she needed to explore, but she'd wait to do that with JJ. She picked up the box of photos and balanced it on one raised knee while she turned out the light.

Back in the great room, she pulled out the old pictures, dusting each then laying them on the floor around her. It was a photo journal of family history. Not having had a close relationship with her adoptive father, Carin was surprised how connected she felt to his mother. Nana.

The dog plodded into the room and flopped down next to her. She rubbed his ears. "Nana was the only one who really believed in me, Edgar. She never made me feel like I was in the way."

Edgar gave her a sloppy doggy grin, then snapped his head toward the door.

"Somebody coming?" Carin glanced over her shoulder, and Edgar's tail began a loud thumping against the floor. It was Ryan. Seeing her through the door, he raised his hand and came in. Edgar jumped up to greet him.

He gave the beast a thorough petting. "What have you got there?" He grabbed one of the towels from a basket by the door, and holding one end between his elbow and ribs, he wiped his hand dry of slobber.

"I found them in the garage. I need to get something of Nana's on the walls."

"Need a hand? I've got one, and it's dry now."

She rolled her eyes. He was so easygoing. If she'd lost half her arm, she wasn't so sure she could joke about it. She'd lost half her life and wasn't anywhere near as jovial.

She handed him several of the pictures. "Help me figure a layout for the stairway wall."

They moved the framed photos around on the floor until she was satisfied, then she got out a hammer and a box of hangers. Ryan held the first photo in its assigned spot, and Carin marked the wall then pounded in the nail. She reached for another hanger.

"Did you ever check with your principal to see if there's an opening to teach?"

Ryan held up the next frame. "That's why I came over. He doesn't have a permanent one right now, but he does need a good substitute, usually a couple days every week. He'd love to have someone close. There's only one other who lives close enough to get there on time. He said to come in."

That lifted a bit of the weight off her shoulders. She marked the wall and pounded in the hanger. At least she'd have some income. If he hired her. "Can he hire without going through the county or something?"

"Pineridge has its own school system, so yeah, he can."

They continued to nail and hang the photos until the box was empty and the wall going up the stairwell was filled with old photos. Ryan nudged her shoulder with his.

"Looks like a family lives here."

"It's perfect." She bent and picked up the empty photo box. "I'll go see him in the morning. I'm going to need the income."

"Anybody home?" Her dad's voice sent Edgar into a wild dance of joy. Silly dog wiggled all over when he wagged his tail that hard. He charged over to her father, who braced himself against the doorframe. "Good to see you too, fella." He didn't release his hold on the door until

Edgar settled down. "You'd think I'd … been gone a year. Instead of … a few weeks."

His speech sounded thick. If she didn't know better, she'd have thought he'd been drinking. Carin kissed his cheek. There was no odor of alcohol. It was probably fatigue.

"Come see the final product of your labor, Dad. Your help saved me a chunk of change."

"I didn't do much."

Carin led him into the kitchen. His feet scuffed against the hardwood floor as he walked.

"Dad, have you been having trouble sleeping?"

He glanced at Ryan then back at her. "Not really, but traffic was bad. Maybe I'll go up and take a short nap before my grandson comes home."

He stumbled on a stair tread but caught himself. Carin's alarm grew. She threw a glance at Ryan, but he looked as bewildered as she was. She motioned him out to the porch.

"Okay, I realize I've only known my dad for what, two, three months? But something's wrong, Ryan. Do you really think he's just tired?"

"He's what? In his fifties? It could be just tired. And it could be the writer is seeing things that aren't there."

Carin scrunched her mouth. "You might be right. I do have an over-active imagination. Normally. It's been dormant recently."

"Maybe it woke up."

She rolled her eyes heavenward. "From your lips to God's ear." God hadn't been listening to her lately.

"Anyway"—Ryan picked up the hammer and box of picture hangers—"if something is wrong, he'll tell you." He wiggled the hammer. "Where does this go? In the drawer closest to the side door?"

"I hope you're right."

"Why? You think that's the wrong drawer?"

She slapped his shoulder. "No, I mean about Dad."

Ryan slid the things in the drawer then put his hand on her shoulder. "Quit borrowing trouble. You know what the Bible says. 'Tomorrow has enough trouble of its own.'"

"It says that?"

"Close enough. Anyway, I've got to get back to school."

She followed him out onto the porch where a large pot of dahlias had finally blossomed. She plucked a dead bloom before turning to him. "Thanks for the help."

"Anytime, string bean." He ducked the deadhead she threw at him.

Chapter 20

JJ and Mikey ran through the front door. "Mama, is Pop back yet?" JJ tossed his backpack at the base of the coat tree.

"He is, but he's taking a nap, so keep your voice down."

"No more napping for me. Not when I have a grandson and his best buddy to fish with."

"Hooray!" JJ and Mikey shouted in unison, jumping up and down.

Dad stepped off the bottom stair. He seemed steady as he approached the boys. Maybe Ryan was right and he'd simply been tired.

"Y'all be back by supper, you hear?"

All three saluted her as they trooped through to the mudroom for their fishing gear. She'd pulled out what she needed to make taco salad, one of her dad and JJ's favorites. She'd started frying the ground beef, when JJ's scream rose over the sizzling meat. She turned off the burner and sprinted out the door as JJ ran toward her.

"What's wrong?"

"Pop fell down and hurt hisself. Come on, hurry!"

Something *was* wrong with Dad, she felt it. When she reached him, he leaned against a tree, rubbing his left ankle. Mikey stood next to him, his face pale.

"Dad, what happened?"

"My knee gave way or something. I've twisted my ankle, that's all."

"Can you put any weight on it?" She helped him up.

He tried and winced. "A little."

She got on his left side and wedged herself beneath his arm. "Lean on me, Dad. Let's see if we can get back up the hill. I'm taking you to the doctor. Mikey, I'll drop you off on the way."

"I don't need a doctor for a twisted ankle."

"You're going."

JJ walked close by his grandfather's side. "No use arguin' with her, Pop."

"No?"

"Uh-uh. Mama's stubborn when she thinks you're hurt."

"Is she now?" He winked at JJ. "I guess I'd better behave then."

"He's right, Dad. I want to be sure nothing's broken. Just because you can put some weight on it, doesn't mean you don't have a fracture."

They reached the driveway without any more mishaps. "JJ, go get my handbag. Make sure my keys are in it." She opened the door and helped her dad into the passenger seat. JJ returned with her keys in one hand and her purse in the other. He and Mikey jumped in the car, slamming their doors. She started the engine. Where was she going to take him?

"Mikey, where's the closest hospital?"

"Ya don't need a hospital. Take him to Dr. Vince."

"Where's that?"

"I'll show you. It's behind Miss Patsy's house. Go down Sandy Shores Drive."

"Why is a doctor behind her house?"

Mikey giggled, his color returning. "'Cause her daddy and Mr. Joel's brother are the doctors."

Oh. She didn't remember Joel having a brother. So, he was a doctor with Patsy's father. Interesting.

"Turn left here." Mikey pointed to a driveway. "Then go past the house to the back."

She followed his instructions with a glance to the house, which appeared to be an old craftsman style two-story bungalow. Though she'd love to see the inside of it, she drove past it to the house in back. "Is this it?"

"Yes, ma'am. Doc's office is on the first floor. Him and Mrs. Doc live upstairs."

Carin didn't bother to correct Mikey's grammar. They got her dad inside and into a chair. Carin went to the frosted glass window and tapped on it. The door opened instead.

"How can I help you?"

Carin turned and found herself face to face with a good looking man in a white doctor's coat.

Mikey stepped in front of her. "Hey, Doctor Vince. This is Miss Carin and her daddy. He fell and hurt his ankle. I brought 'em here." He swaggered a bit with the importance of his mission.

Dr. Vince put a hand on Mikey's shoulder. "Good job." He turned to her dad. "Let's get you in back and take a look at your ankle. Then I'll get an x-ray."

He helped her dad up and got on his left side. "No weight until I know how it is. It's possible you tore some ligaments." He turned to Carin. "Why don't you wait here with your son? I'll come get you if we need you."

She wanted to go with them but didn't want to leave JJ alone. "Okay, but please do whatever he needs."

She and the boys took seats, and Carin pulled out her cell phone. She tapped in Mikey's number. "Hey, Sheryl. My dad took a fall and I've got him over at the doctor's office behind—oh, you know where that is. Of course. Anyway, I have no idea how long I'll be. Do you want him to wait or—oh, that would be wonderful. Thank you." She put her phone away.

"Boys, Mikey's mama is going to pick up both of you. JJ, I'll get you after supper. How's that?"

JJ didn't get as excited as she thought he would. "What about Pop?"

"I promise to call you as soon as I talk to the doctor, okay?"

That seemed to satisfy him. He and Mikey stood near the door. Within five minutes, Sheryl came and collected the boys. Carin sat back to wait. After what seemed like hours but was only thirty-five minutes, a nurse came for her.

"Doctor wants to see you in his office." She held the door open for Carin then showed her into Dr. Vince's office. Her father was already in one of the chairs. Something about the set of his shoulders alarmed her.

They were slumped, turned in.

She laid her hand on his arm as she sat next to him. "Dad? Are you all right?"

His lips didn't quite make it into a smile.

"What's wrong?" Her eyes darted between her dad and Dr. Vince. She licked her lips. "Is something broken?" Or was it worse?

"His ankle will be fine." He nodded and smiled. "It's sprained but the ligaments aren't damaged. However ..." His face grew serious, the smile fading. "Your father shared with me that he has been diagnosed with Amyotrophic Lateral Sclerosis, commonly known as Lou Gehrig's disease. I concur with that diagnosis, based on what your father has told me."

Horrified, she grabbed her dad's hand. ALS was fatal. This wasn't fair. She'd just found him. "How do you know? I mean, no offense, but you haven't even run any tests. What if he's just tired ... or maybe he's diabetic ... or ..." She squeezed his hand.

"Sweetheart, my doctor in Atlanta has done every test possible to rule it out." His eyes filled. "I couldn't tell you. I'm sorry."

Dr. Vince slid a box of tissues across his desk. "His doctor prescribed Riluzole, which will help slow his symptoms."

That sounded positive. Carin plucked a tissue from the box and dried her eyes. "Then he's in the early stages?" She searched her dad's face. "How long have you known?"

"Just a few months." He squeezed her hand again.

Dr. Vince folded his hand on top of Dad's chart. "It's fairly early, but your father needs to be careful. He has some muscular degeneration in his legs and can stumble like he did today. I'm prescribing a cane."

Her dad's reluctance was heartbreaking. "Please, Dad?"

"I know it's not what you'd like, but you have a beautiful daughter here who hasn't had much time with you. Let's give her all we can."

Her father gave them a sad little smile. "I promise I'll use it."

Dr. Vince handed Carin a list and called in a prescription for a cane and more riluzole to keep at her house. "You can pick this up at Chapel Lake Drug Store. Tom will have it ready for you."

She looked over the list. It was long and detailed. She sought the doctor's eyes. "Can I call you if I ... get confused, I—"

"You can call anytime." He took out a card, jotted something on the back, and then slid it across the desk to her. "That's my cell number. If you need to call me for any reason, you can always get me, day or night."

"Thank you." Carin leaned forward and shook Vince's hand. She glanced at the prescription.

"Wouldn't crutches be better?"

The doctor shook his head. "To be honest, he'd have more trouble maneuvering them. The sprain isn't bad, and the cane will be all he needs. I'll help you get him to the car. Then go straight to the pharmacy."

She helped her dad out of the chair. "Thank you, Doctor. We'll see you again."

After they were in the car, Dad watched Vince go back inside his clinic. "I like that young man. He's got good all the way down inside." He glanced at her. "Remember that, daughter."

"I'm still married, Dad."

"For now. But that husband committed adultery."

"I could forgive him for that. I ... when I get deep into creating a book, well, I guess I closed him out. I asked him to come home."

"And go to counseling?"

"He declined. To come home and counseling." As her eyes filled, Carin adjusted the rearview mirror she couldn't see through. "What hurts the most is his utter lack of caring."

"Not all men are like him, sugar."

"Maybe not, but I don't think I'll ever trust another one."

"Never say never, Carin. Look at us."

That was true. She'd thought she and JJ would be all alone, and now she had her dad. But for how long?

They picked up JJ on the way home, and once he was in bed, she and her dad sat on the sofa. "Dad, I want you to move in here with me. I can take care of you. I've got a lead on a substituting job, so we'll be fine."

"And I'd love that, sweetheart. I also think the time has come to tell your sisters about you."

Carin's heart raced and she curled her shoulders inward and hugged her waist. Would they accept or reject her? She swallowed. "I know you're right, but I'm nervous."

"Why?"

A waterfall of words cascaded out of her. "Because I've been rejected by so many. I know you and mom had no say, but for most of my life, I felt abandoned. You know my adopted parents withdrew emotionally. Then Wick left. Even my agent left me. Of course I'm nervous."

He put his arm around her. "Carin, listen to me carefully. You know God loves you, don't you?"

"Sometimes I have to wonder."

"Do you think maybe you put all those others before the Lord?"

She didn't like this line of questions. "I don't know." She got up and straightened the pillows in the chairs. "Tell me more about my sisters. What should I expect? What should I not say to them?"

Dad sighed and allowed her to sidetrack his questions. He told her stories about her sisters until she knew them fairly well. Then they decided he would invite the girls to Chapel Springs for the weekend, letting them think he'd rented a place. He would introduce her when they arrived.

To give him privacy, Carin paced the kitchen while he put in a call to Julie, inviting her to come up Friday and stay until Sunday. Finally, using his cane, he limped into the kitchen to join her.

"Julie suspects something." He snorted a laugh. "I think she thinks I'm getting married again."

Carin gasped at that then had to laugh. "I hope you set her straight."

He merely smiled.

"Dad, you *did*, didn't you?"

"Yes, I did. She's still not happy with me. I've kept her in the dark a lot in the last few months." He sighed and sat down in the window seat. "Julie likes to control things and the people she loves. Once I learned about the ALS, I didn't want my last years to be under anyone's control but my own. Mine and God's. That's why I haven't told your sisters about it. Now, I'm ready for bed."

She made him a cup of chamomile tea, and carrying the cup, she helped him upstairs. "Tomorrow, if you're okay with it, we'll move you to the downstairs bedroom."

"I won't argue that." He huffed and puffed. She came back into his room once he was settled in bed with his tea.

"Carin, I'd like to pray a blessing over you. I didn't get to do that when you were born, and I sense your faith is low at the moment."

He wasn't off base there. God seemed to have turned His back on her. She let him pray, accepting the mantle of blessing he settled over her, then kissed him goodnight. After checking on JJ and snugging his covers up to his chin, she went to her room. In the window seat, she stared up at the stars twinkling through the trees. They were so much brighter here than in Atlanta. It was almost as if she could touch them.

"God, if you're listening to me, help me love my sisters. I want that so badly. Everyone else has been taken away from me. I don't know who to trust anymore, except Dad. And You."

She sat there for a few more minutes, not hearing anything. But somehow, she was at peace.

Chapter 21

The locksmith Claire hired to open the theater sprayed something into the lock then wiggled the key, but it didn't budge. She hoped this wouldn't take too long. There were commissioned pieces she had to make this afternoon. But when the man—Ralph—called and said he had time now, she ran over. Young, maybe in his early thirties, he stood, scratching the back of his neck. His brown hair curled over his collar.

"Graphite nearly always works." He squatted, pawing through his toolbox. "Let me try this." He pulled out a different spray can, stuck a skinny plastic straw in its top, and sprayed inside the keyhole. Then he sat back on his heels.

"How long does that take?" Claire forced her toe to stop tapping.

"It's normally pretty fast." He tried it again. The key wouldn't turn. He stood hunched and grunted as he tried once more. The key snapped off. "There's got to be something wedged in there. Normal rust would have dissolved and that key wouldn't have broken."

"Now what do we do?"

"You'll have to get somebody else to take the door off."

"Can't you do that?"

"I could, but I'd break the doorjamb. Then you'd have a broken doorjamb and no door on the theater. I'm not a carpenter, either."

Well, thank you Billy Sunday. "Send your bill to the town."

After he left, Claire called Norm Akins. After explaining the problem and what the locksmith suggested, she asked if he had someone who could do that for them, and when they could come.

"Not for a couple of weeks. They're all tied up on projects. I could check with another contractor."

"No hurry, really." She wanted someone they could trust. "A couple more weeks won't hurt. Thanks, Norm."

She walked down the block and turned onto Sandy Shores Drive and smack into a madhouse. Protestors blocked the street and the tour bus trying to get into town. Gauging by their overalls, it was the farmers' union. Murdoch rose above the crowd with a bullhorn. She was right. He was the local union leader. She yanked out her cell phone and called Jim Bob.

"Get over here. The farmers are keeping the tourists from getting into town."

He and Farley must have been close by, because it wasn't more than two minutes when one of them fired a blank into the air—at least she hoped it was a blank. You never could be sure about a yahoo like their sheriff. The crowd shut up.

Jim Bob got in Murdoch's face. "Who told you that you could have this here gathering?"

"It's a peaceful protest and our right as citizens." Murdoch crossed his arms and widened his stance.

"Yeah, our right!"

"Don't forget the first amendment!"

The murmur swelled as the farmers agreed, fists raised. At least no one Claire could see brought pitch forks. Most of the mountain farmers were peaceful folk. She'd bet Sunday's chicken that Howie put them up to this.

"That may be so, but y'all don't have the right to stop traffic. Besides, you lack a permit." He turned to the crowd. "Now, y'all can holler and stomp all you want but on the other side of the street and out of traffic's way."

There wasn't much traffic since they instituted the trams, but tour busses and local residents could drive through town. And a bus with tourists wanting to get into the shops waited by *Front Row Seat*.

But the crowd didn't move. Jim Bob glanced at Farley, who pulled out a can of mace. Jim Bob grinned. "Now, if'n y'all don't start moving off the street in thirty seconds, I'm gonna try me this new can of mace.

It says here it can shoot up to twenty feet away and has a wide spread. I could get a lot of y'all with this."

The crowd scattered to the opposite side of the street. They shouted and grumbled, but they moved. Claire still hadn't heard their beef.

She joined Jim Bob. "Did anyone say what they're protesting?"

"I'm not sure if anyone but Murdoch knows. I heard water, but the creek's being fixed and they know that. My guess is they're paid protestors and not real farmers. Do you recognize anyone other than Murdoch?"

"No. I wondered about that. Thanks for coming so fast, Jim Bob. Will you let Felix know?"

He grunted an affirmative—at least, she thought it was a yes—and went over to join Farley. They waved the bus through, and within minutes, the gallery was filled with senior citizens. She recognized the tour driver. He always included Chapel Springs in his tour. He came down the bus steps.

He took off his hat and wiped his brow with his sleeve. "Thanks for getting us out of that mess. I was afraid one or two of my passengers would have a heart attack. Some thought it was a hoot, but others were frightened."

"I'm glad everyone is okay. I'll be sure to tell the mayor about this." She'd also tear into Howie the next time she saw him. Felix could use this as an example of Howie's wisdom. What might he do as mayor?

When Claire got inside, 'Lissa, Nicole, Mel, and Patsy were elbow deep in sales—mostly small items like coffee mugs, trivets, and Patsy's miniatures. Finally, the seniors carted off their treasures and the bus disappeared. The displays were left all askew, and Claire began to straighten them.

"Did you get into the theater?" Patsy asked, swishing the feather duster over a shelf filled with pottery. "Mel, bring the stepladder for Claire, please."

"I didn't."

"How come?"

"The lock is frozen or something. The locksmith tried to tell me it's been jammed from the inside, but I don't believe that." She climbed to the second rung.

Patsy frowned. "Why not?"

"Nobody's been inside for forty years." Claire removed a small whimsy vase from the shelf and replaced it with three coffee mugs. Wait. That wasn't right. All this ghost talk had her discombobulated.

Mel stopped what she was doing and stared at Claire. "What about the ghost?"

"What do you know about that?" She exchanged the coffee mugs for vases then stepped off the ladder. A mosquito buzzed past her nose. She tried to grab it but missed.

"Well, I've heard a lot of people say they've seen things there. That gives me the creeps. Would you go near that place, Nicole?"

Nicole shook her head, her braid swinging over her shoulder. "I never have. It's off the main street, so unless there had been a play there, I had no reason to go." She leaned over the counter, her chin on her clasped hands. "I think it's kind of romantic, an old actor or actress wandering the theater at night. Maybe she plays the part she always wanted."

Mel's eyebrow piercings wobbled. "Or maybe there was a murder in there and the ghost wants revenge."

"Enough of this talk." The mosquito buzzed Claire again. This time, she tried to catch it between her hands, but they clapped together without squashing the insect. At least, maybe, she could squash this ghost talk. It was as pesky as the mosquito. "There was never any murder there, Mel."

"Could it be your great-aunt?" Nicole asked.

"No way. She's in heaven, and if I know her, she's dancing with the Lion of Judah. She's most definitely not wandering the earth." Claire had had enough of this. "I've got consignments to make." She left them in the gallery and went to the workroom.

Nicole's voice followed Claire. "Still, it would be romantic to let it be rumored the theater's namesake watched over it every night."

Claire snorted. "Y'all's imaginations are running amok," she called over her shoulder. "Ghosts, my foot."

Patsy tapped her shoulder and Claire jumped, yelping. "You scared the fire out of me." She opened her clay barrel and pulled out a large hunk and a second one. She'd do the lower part of the whimsy vase on her wheel, then complete it freehand.

"It's all this ghost talk that's got everyone a bit off center." Patsy slipped into her painting smock, an old shirt she'd commandeered from Nathan. Claire couldn't understand why Pat-a-cake still wore it. It was caked with paint and had to be as stiff as her palette. She needed a new one. Maybe that's what Claire could buy her for her birthday.

She punched and kneaded the clay to soften it. "Do you believe in ghosts?"

"I've never seen one and want to keep it that way."

"You didn't answer my question." Claire slammed the larger hunk of clay on her potter's wheel. The larger the chunk, the more force it took to make it stick.

Patsy's hand paused, her brush midair. "I'm not sure. I know the Bible mentions ghosts several times, but it's always someone saying something about them, so it isn't clear."

With one hand on the clay, Claire started the wheel turning and formed the clay into a cone. She rewet her hands and pressed the pedal, moving the speed to moderate. Now she leaned in and over the clay, her muscles tight, and forced it to dead center.

"I'm on the fence, as they say, but I'm over more to the disbelief side. Unless I ever see one, and like you, I have no desire to do that. I just can't help but think it's the Pineridge theater peo—oh." she stopped the wheel. "Patsy, you don't suppose Howie's involved in this, do you? He said he wanted it torn down."

"Huh. That's a possibility. Do Jim Bob or Farley patrol at night? Have they seen anything?"

Claire started her wheel again. "Jim Bob is as superstitious as an old mountain granny and Farley's almost as bad. They won't go anywhere near the theater at night. Jim Bob told me being next to the church ought to keep it safe enough."

They worked in silence for a while. Patsy's brush, stroking the canvas, and the hum of Claire's pottery wheel were the music of the day. Sometime later, strains of classical rock filled the air, and Nicole took a seat next to Claire.

"I haven't gotten to see you do a large piece yet, and the gallery is quiet. Mel said she'd call me if it gets busy."

Claire didn't look up from her work. "That's fine."

"Besides, I'm sick of talking about ghosts. Mel seems fascinated by it. She keeps making up stories of who it could be and how they died.

It's gruesome."

"She does have quite an imagination." Claire would give her that, even if it did run wild sometimes. She worked until she had the vase as far as she could on the wheel. Nicole handed her a length of piano wire, but Claire shook her head. She removed the wheel head with the piece attached.

"I'll use another wheel head for the next part, then join them. Right now, I'm going to see the mayor. What time is it?"

"It's five o'clock."

"Great. Let's close up." She walked over to the easel. "Patsy?" Ooh, her new painting was going to be melancholy. "You coming?"

"I'm going to stay and finish this. Nathan is coming by a little later."

Nicole closed the register while Claire helped Mel pull the shades. As they left, Claire walked toward the campaign office. At cottage row, she cut between the cottages to Church Street. Mel waved goodbye and walked toward the parking lot where her stepmother picked her up.

Claire found Felix in the campaign office, bent over the table, examining a poster with Bobby. A stack of yard signs stood near the door, ready to be handed out. She'd have to remember to take some with her. A fan in the corner lifted the corners of a stack of papers each time it rotated that direction.

"Did Jim Bob tell you about today? I asked him to."

"He did, and if I could find Newlander, I'd jerk him a new tail."

"Calm down, Dad." Bobby pushed a bottle of water toward Felix. "We can use this to our advantage."

Felix glared. "How?"

Yeah, she'd like to know what he had in mind, too. Probably some harebrained scheme that would backfire.

"The whole protest was stupid, and it put some old people in danger. What kind of wisdom is that for a mayor?"

"Oh, com—" Claire blinked. Wait ... that wasn't harebrained. That was the same idea—hey, was he listening to her thoughts? Wait, no. He couldn't do that. She peered at him. Could he?

Chapter 22

After a day of fishing with her dad and getting ready for her sisters to arrive tomorrow, Carin was curled up in a corner of the sofa, reading a new novel by a friend. She envied Susan's ability to turn out books every six months and not compromise quality. Carin laid the paperback in her lap. Why couldn't she come up with a new story? The day Wick left, her life fell apart, that was why. She couldn't concentrate.

Dad came down the stairs, went to the kitchen, and pulled Edgar's leash from the junk drawer. She had to organize that drawer. The contents were multiplying.

"Carin, I'm going for a walk. I'll take Edgar with me."

"All right, Dad, but be careful. Have you got your key?" With Edgar along, she wouldn't worry about him as much. The meds Dr. Vince gave him seemed to be helping. She hadn't noticed him dragging his feet as much as he had been.

He patted his pocket. "I've got it and my cane. It's the perfect walking stick. We'll go north along Sandy Shores Drive. It's a balmy evening, sure you don't want to come along?"

"I've got cookies in the oven. Maybe tomorrow night."

As the back door closed behind Dad and Edgar, the aroma of snickerdoodles baking drew her back to the kitchen. The timer had only a few seconds left. She opened the oven door and withdrew the cookie sheet.

JJ skidded to a stop beside her. "Oh boy, I've been waiting for these.

Can I get the milk out?"

"'May I' and yes, you may. But be careful, it's—"

The gallon jug fell to the floor, the lid popped off, and milk splattered.

JJ's eyes welled. "I'm sorry, Mama. I tried but it was too heavy." Poor baby still quailed from his father's harsh belittling when he dropped things.

"It's okay, love bug. Go grab the mop and we'll clean it up." She lifted the jug with a third of its contents left inside. "There's still enough for a glass for both of us."

After the floor was clean and they'd had their cookies, Carin tucked JJ into bed and listened to his prayers. They were the prayers of the innocent, full of faith, before life slapped you down. Before the people you cared about abandoned you.

"Sleep tight, sugar." She kissed his forehead then closed the door.

Back downstairs, she read for a bit then decided to take her book upstairs. She turned out all the lights except the porch and stairwell lights. Dad could turn those off when he came in. She expected him soon enough.

Once in bed, she tried to read, but with all the day's activities, her eyes grew heavy. She set her alarm and realized Dad had been gone about an hour. But that wasn't unusual. He'd made a lot of friends since coming to Chapel Springs. He was probably sitting on a bench by the beach with a couple of his cronies. Edgar would be investigating the wildlife along the shore. Her last thought before drifting off was hoping the dog didn't come home all muddy.

The doorbell rang. Her sisters couldn't be here already. She hadn't showered yet. She jumped up. Wait. Something was wrong. It was dark out. Who could be ringing her doorbell at—she glanced at the clock. It was two-fifteen. She grabbed her robe and crept down the stairs. Through the door's window, she saw no one—then Edgar jumped up and his paw hit the doorbell again.

"Edgar!" She pulled open the door. "How did you get back out?" He refused to come in but sat on the porch and whined. Then she saw his leash dangling and broken. "What happened, boy? How'd you break your lead?" And where was Dad? She managed to get the beast inside and went upstairs to check on her dad.

His bed was still made and he wasn't in his room.

Carin raced back downstairs and out onto the porch. "Dad! Dad? Where are you?"

She held her breath and listened. Nothing but tree frogs answered her. Then a light came on in Ryan's house. The back door opened.

"Carin? What's wrong?" He cinched the belt of his robe and crossed the driveway separating their houses.

"Edgar came home with his lead broken and he's full of mud and weeds. Dad's not home. I need to find him."

"Let me throw some jeans on. You do the same."

"What about JJ? I can't leave him in bed alone."

Ryan put his hand on her shoulder. "Carin, this is Chapel Springs. I'll let you search around the perimeter of the house where you can still see it. JJ will be fine. I'll look farther afield."

Carin quickly threw on some jeans and a shirt then checked on JJ. He was fast asleep. On her way out, she grabbed a flashlight. Ryan headed toward Sandy Shores Drive while she crossed Pine and checked the woods between her house and cottage row. JJ and Mikey liked to play in those woods. They'd taken Dad with them a few times.

"Dad!" She shined the flashlight back and forth. Something crunched to the right of her. She swung around. "Dad?" She strained to hear any sounds. Nobody had said anything about any bears or wolves in this area, but she'd heard something. Her heart pounded.

"Who's there?" A light shone in her eyes. "What are you doing out here in the middle of the night?"

Carin took a step backward then saw the squad car. "Sheriff?"

"It's Deputy Farley Taylor, ma'am. And you're …?"

"Carin Jardine." She raised her hands in a plea, her fingers splayed. "Deputy, my dad is missing. My dog came back with his leash broken. Dad has ALS. He may have fallen. Please, can you help me find him?" Her voice broke.

"Take it easy, ma'am. We'll find him. You live in the old Rice house?"

"Yes."

"You go on home. We don't want the whole town awake."

Yes, she did. She wanted them to help her.

"Most likely, your dad took his date to a bar—"

"He's not in a bar. He doesn't drink. And he was walking." What date? The deputy wasn't taking this seriously. "My father is ill."

"Why didn't you say that in the first place?"

"I did. I told you he has ALS."

"Oh. I thought you said he had Alice, and that's why I figured he took her to a bar for a nightcap."

Would she be arrested for battery if she clobbered him upside the head? "Please, call somebody for help and find him."

Ryan walked toward her. "Hey, Farley. I've gone along the shoreline from Main to the north end of town. I didn't see any fresh footprints or any sign of Edgar's struggle. Carin, you go home and stay with JJ. I've got a few buddies coming over to help search." He put the flashlight under his arm and his hand on her shoulder. "Don't worry. We'll find your dad. He probably got lost."

Please let that be all it is. She nodded and started back to the house. She paused at the edge of the yard. "Ryan, wait. Come get Edgar. Maybe he can help you find Dad."

"Good idea."

They went in the back door, and Carin got another leash from the laundry room cabinet. They found Edgar sound asleep outside JJ's bedroom door. She clipped his lead on and pulled. "Come on, Edgar. Help find Dad."

The mastiff looked at her like she'd lost her mind then laid his head back on his paws. "Come on." She pulled harder. "Get up. Go find Dad." He lumbered to his feet.

Ryan took the lead. "Hopefully, once we're outside, he'll get the idea." He left with a reluctant Edgar.

Carin paced the house. They had to find him. *Please, find him.* After all the years of longing for a loving dad, was God taking him away? *Why?* She finally sat on the couch. Her eyes were heavy from crying. She didn't want to scare JJ when he woke up. She put her head back but opened them at every sound until they wouldn't stay open any more.

"Carin?" Ryan was shaking her gently.

She startled awake. "Did you find him?"

Ryan shook his head. "But we're going back out. Sheriff Taylor called in the U.S. Forest Service Search and Rescue Team to help."

Carin stood. It was dawn. "Can I make you some coffee before you go back out?"

"No. Dee Lindstrom has set up a table in front of the bakery and she's supplying coffee and breakfast for everyone."

"How did she find out?"

"She starts work around four a.m. She saw us and called Jim Bob to see what was happening. She told him she'd keep the search team caffeinated and fed."

Carin frowned. "Why?"

Ryan scratched Edgar's ears then pulled up on the leash as the dog tried to lie down again. "Because that's what we do for our friends, Carin. You're one of us. Friends help friends. Surely you understand that."

She studied her bare toes. "I haven't had a friend since I was in high school."

"Well, you've got a lot of them now, string bean, and they're out helping Dee. Now, I need to get back out there, too. Come on, Edgar." He pulled the lead and the mastiff gave her one remorseful glance before plodding after Ryan.

Carin ran upstairs and went to wake JJ. She needed to break this gently. She sat on the side of his bed, smoothing his hair off his forehead. He stretched and yawned. A sweet smile spread, but his eyes remained shut.

"Hey, Mama." He snuggled deeper into his covers.

"Hey, yourself." She pulled the covers down a little way. "JJ, Pop went out with Edgar last night for a walk, but he didn't come home. I'm sure he's fine, but I think maybe he got a little lost. The sheriff and Mr. Ryan are looking for him. We need to get dressed and go help them, okay?"

JJ jumped up. "Where did he get lost?"

She helped him pull his clothes on. "We're not sure. He hadn't come home when I went to bed, but you know how he likes to sit out by the lake and talk to the other men in town."

"Yeah, He talks to Mr. Happy and Mr. Joel about fishing."

Though JJ could tie his own shoes, she needed expediency and did it for him. "And they're out looking for him. Everyone is."

"Then we need to go help." He pulled her hand.

When they got to *Dee's 'n' Doughs* Carin stopped. Half the town huddled around the coffee pots or handed out Styrofoam cups to the searchers emerging from the woods. Dee was busy orchestrating the coffee and breakfast sandwiches team so no one went without. When she saw Carin, she thrust a coffee cup at the pharmacist and put her arms out, pulling Carin into a hug.

"Now don't you worry. We'll find your father. These men know every corner of the area surrounding the lake. If he took any trail, they'll find him."

Carin's words clung to one another in her throat, trembling, refusing to come out. "Thank you," she managed to whisper through her tears. "Thank you."

A hand rubbed circles on her back. She turned to find Claire, who had JJ by her other hand.

"Don't you worry about anything. I'm going to take JJ to the gallery and teach him how to make a buddy for Timothy."

How did she know exactly what to do? "Thank you." Carin kept saying that but the words felt so inadequate.

Claire smiled. "After five kids, you learn how to keep them distracted. I'll keep him with me until you come for him."

Carin kissed JJ and told him to be good for Miss Claire and have fun. "I'll come get you after we find your granddaddy—your pop."

She spent the day handing out coffee and sandwiches. By four o'clock, when he still hadn't been found, the sheriff told her they would call off the search for the night when the sun went down.

"We have another hour and that's it for today. We can't search in the dark, Ms. Jardine."

"I understand, Sheriff." She didn't like it but she understood. She'd have to wait at home. She went to the *Painted Loon* to get JJ.

Pasting a smile on her face so she wouldn't pass her rising fear to JJ, Carin opened the gallery door.

"Come on in, Carin." Patsy greeted her with a hug. "I'm praying they find your dad quickly. JJ's in back with Claire."

When she walked into the workroom, JJ sat between Claire's legs at the pottery wheel. His little face was scrunched in concentration as Claire guided his hands. They looked up and saw her. Claire steadied his hands as she stopped the wheel.

"Mama, look what I'm making. It's a baby Timothy."

"It's wonderful, doodle bug." She put her hands in her pockets then pulled them out again. "I need to talk to Miss Claire for a minute. Why don't you—" She glanced up at Claire.

Claire put her arm around JJ. "Sugar, pull a little more clay from the barrel and make some worms. Baby unicorns like to play with them." Claire wiped her hands on a towel and motioned for Carin to follow her into the gallery.

"Did they find your dad?"

She rubbed her hands down her pant legs and then against each other. "No, and soon they're calling off the search for the night." Her right foot bounced.

Claire grasped Carin's fidgeting hands. "Sugar, you're exhausted. JJ knows his grandfather is missing, but he's not that worried, being a little boy. Why don't you let me keep him for the night? Joel and I will have fun with him. We have a house full of things little boys love. That will keep his mind off this and you can get a bit of rest. You'll need it for tomorrow."

Carin searched Claire's eyes. Her gaze was steady and filled with compassion. "I don't know what I did to deserve your friendship, but thank you."

Claire placed her hand on Carin's cheek. "You don't have to deserve friendship. It's given because I like *you*." She winked. "And I adore your little boy. He reminds me so much of my Charlie when he was this age."

Carin reached out for the first time and hugged Claire, then they went back to tell JJ he was spending the night with his hero, sending him into an Indian war dance of whoops.

Back at home, Carin drew a bath. She was about to lower herself in when the doorbell rang. Had the sheriff found Dad? Slipping on her robe, she moved the curtain aside and peered out the bathroom window but didn't see a squad car.

She called out, "Coming!" and ran down the stairs.

On her front porch stood three women. They looked exactly like their pictures. Carin's heart stumbled.

It was her sisters.

Chapter 23

Carin opened the door. A brunette, whom she recognized as Julie from the photos her dad had shown her, narrowed her eyes and looked Carin up and down.

"And you are?"

She wasn't about to give them her last name. "I'm Carin. Would you like to come in?"

Julie didn't budge. "We're looking for our father, Jim Buchanan. Is he here?"

The "here" came out like her house was a garbage can.

"Not at the moment." How was she going to tell them? Julie may have a nasty superiority complex, but she was still Dad's daughter and her sister. Her blood pressure rose a good two notches. Why did Dad have to take a walk last night?

She opened the door wider. "Please come in."

Leanna stepped around Julie and held out her hand. The blonde streaks that hadn't shown in Dad's photos gave her a halo that matched the sweet spirit radiating off her. "I'm Leanna. Daddy called us to come meet him here. These are my sisters, Julie and Darcie." She moved through the door. "What a lovely home you have."

If she only knew what it had looked like two months ago. "Thank you." She inhaled a deep breath, trying to no avail to calm her nerves. "Please, come in. Have a seat."

Julie didn't budge from the doorstep. "Just who are you?"

Carin faced her. It was now or never. "I'm—"

"If you think you're going to marry my father—"

"Julie!" Leanna's face turned rosy red. "Please excuse her. She's been speculating all the way up here until she worked herself into a rage."

I'll just bet she did.

Carin held up her hands, palms out. "You can all relax. I'm not trying to marry your father. That's not who I am."

"Well, where is he?" Julie sailed to the stairway. "Dad? Come down here." She whirled around. "Where are you hiding him?"

"I'm not—"

Before she could finish, Julie stormed upstairs. Thank the good Lord Claire had taken JJ for the night.

"Oh my word, she's got a kid." Julie flew back down stairs. "Whose kid is that?"

Dad had said Julie was protective, but frankly, she was a witch with a capital "b."

Carin clenched her jaw so tight she was fearful of breaking her teeth. "That is my son's room."

Julie stood toe-to-toe with her, arms akimbo. "And just who is his father?"

Okay, she'd had enough of this one. Carin balled her fists at her sides, ready to use them if she had to. "That. Is. None. Of. Your. Business."

"If you're trying to get child support because of some trumped up idea that he's our father's son, you're sadly mistaken."

Carin sucked in her lips. "I'm not after anything and my son is—"

Darcie, who had been examining the room, spun around, a photo of JJ in her hand. "Well, just who are you, then? You look familiar."

Carin's heartbeat increased to a frightening rate. She took a deep breath in an effort to regain control. She had to tell them. She didn't want to. But she had to.

"I'm your sister."

The silence roared in her ears. Julie's eyes couldn't decide whether to squint or bulge wide open. Each one chose the opposite, giving her a grotesque expression of horror. Leanna's delight made Carin take a step back. Darcie dropped JJ's photo. The shattering glass broke the silence and chaos erupted.

"I don't believe it."

"But ... when ... his ... who?" Leanna couldn't seem to land on any one thought. Carin almost smiled. Almost.

As for Darcie, Carin got the impression she was calculating something in her head. What, she had no idea.

In three steps, Julie crossed to Carin. "I don't know what you expect to gain by lying, but I think it's despicable. Our father never had an affair with anyone. He adored our mother."

"I know." Carin kept her voice soft. She had expected some rejection, but if Dad had been here, it would have been a little easier. At least he would have lent credence to her claims.

"Please, sit down so we can talk." Carin sat at one end of the sofa.

Julie stood rigid behind Darcie, who chose the leather club chair Dad preferred. Did she know that was his? Her hand rubbed its padded armrest as if stroking Dad's arm.

Leanna sat beside Carin. "Are you really our sister?"

Carin nodded. "I was as surprised as you are. Your father found me several weeks ago."

"Humph. I don't believe a word."

"Julie, give her a chance." Leanna reached out a tentative hand, touching Carin's arm. "Please, tell us."

She didn't want to. She wanted to keep her dad tucked tightly beneath her heart, hers alone, for a while longer. Now they were here, and he was no longer just hers. Presenting a calm exterior tightened the muscles in her shoulders and beat a small drum in the base of her skull.

"I'd always known I was adopted but had no idea who my birth parents were. Then, in the middle of March, a man came to my door."

Carin told them what Dad told her about their story. When she finished, Leanna had tears rolling down her cheeks. Carin plucked a tissue from a box on the side table and handed it to her.

"That's so beautiful. I remember Mama would sometimes look out the window and seem so melancholy, like she was looking for something or someone." She turned to Carin, her smile wistful. "Now I know who she was looking for."

"That's crazy. You were too young when she died to remember that." Waves of rejection and distrust from Julie's eyes rolled over Carin.

"I was not," Leanna said. "I was four *and a half* when Mama died. In fact," she turned sideways to face Carin, her eyes bright, "I remember one of the times I sat with her not long before she died. She was in and out of consciousness. She grabbed my hand and told me, 'Find your sister.' Her voice was so urgent, I said I'd find Julie, but she held my hand tight and said, 'Not Julie.'"

"That's ridiculous. You're making that up." Julie's eyes shot fireworks at Leanna. She had remained standing behind Darcie, one hand on Dad's chair. Carin bit back a weary smile. Her sister would have to give in sometime.

Darcie reached up and grasped Julie's hand. "You know, Jewels, she does look like Daddy and like Grandma Buchanan."

Leanna grabbed Carin's hand and pulled it to her, examined it, then grinned at Darcie. "She's got Daddy's hands."

Julie walked away from Darcie and collapsed in the wingback chair. "I won't believe a word of this until I hear it from Daddy's lips."

Rising from the club chair, Darcie went to the bookcase and perused the books. Suddenly, she whirled around. "That's who you are. You're Carin Jardine, the author. I went to your book signing in Atlanta. You autographed a book for me."

Darcie tripped over to the sofa and plopped down between her and Leanna, squeezing her sister out and wrapping Carin in a hug. "You're my sister!"

The last thing she wanted was false hero worship. It was untrustworthy. She pulled away and rose. "Can I get anyone something to drink?"

Julie's face puckered like she'd eaten a lemon. Dad had said she was particularly close to Darcie. The transferring of allegiance wouldn't sit well if it kept up.

"Please, I'd love something," Leanna said. She was exactly as Dad had described. A peacemaker. Carin's heart opened a crack. She understood this one. Always on the outside, longing to be on the inside.

When she brought in a tray with glasses of sweet tea, Julie and Darcie had their heads together, whispering. Leanna was looking at JJ's photos on the mantle.

"Is this our nephew? He looks like Darcie when she was six."

Darcie jumped up and went to see. Something about her interest urged Carin to gather the photos and hide them.

"Darcie, a lot of people look like other people. That doesn't mean she's our *sister.*"

The distaste Julie added as emphasis on sister wasn't lost on Carin. Could she claim sisterhood with just one of them or were they a package deal?

Julie stood. "I've had about all I can take of this business. Carin, just where is my father?"

Carin closed her eyes and sank onto the sofa. "I don't know."

Julie squinted and folded her arms across her chest. "What do you mean? You don't know, or you won't tell us?"

Tears filled Carin's eyes, tears she didn't want them to see. She wanted to pull her heart back inside and hide it. She kept her head down, blinking until she could control her emotions.

"Last night, he went out for a walk and never came back."

"Ahh, he must have come to his senses and left. Come on, Darcie, Leanna. Let's go home. This"—her lip curled—"distasteful interlude is over."

She picked up her purse and headed to the door. Darcie hesitated but finally stood.

Leanna didn't move. "Carin, what are you saying?"

"Your father ..." Somehow she couldn't say "our father" yet. She swallowed and started again. "Your father has ALS. He was diagnosed in Atlanta. The other day, he stumbled and sprained his ankle. The doctor here verified the diagnosis. He's been on medication and had gotten better, but last night—"

Julie stomped toward her and stopped in front of her. One hand reached down and dug into her shoulder and pushed Carin into the cushions. "You've been giving my father drugs? Is that what happened? How do we know these drugs were really what the doctor prescribed?"

Leanna's eyes rolled. "Oh, Julie. Do you hear yourself? You're acting like the Witch of the West. Or was it the east? The wicked one, anyway. You're so far overboard, you're wet."

Julie turned on Leanna, her fists planted on her hips. Her face twisted into an ugly mask. "You'd throw away family loyalty to have this imposter as a sister?"

What was the reason behind her hostility? It was so over the top. Yet Leanna just rolled her eyes. Was Julie always this angry?

"I'm not throwing anything away." Leanna smiled at Carin. "I'm opening the door wide. I'm sure she can explain and verify everything."

Julie turned her back and walked to the door. "We're going home."

Carin rose and gestured toward the stairs. "His medication is in his room and the pharmacy can tell you what it is."

"I'm sure they can, Carin," Leanna said. Her soft voice eased the tension a little. "And I'm glad he had you to help him."

A breath-stealing lump had lodged itself in Carin's throat. She swallowed. "The thing is, he hasn't returned. The sheriff and a search and rescue team looked all day for him."

At the door, with one hand on the knob, Julie turned pale. "This ... this is all your fault."

Carin had had enough. Pulling up to her full five-foot-seven-inches—taller than Julie by a good two—she was suddenly grateful for her height. "Tell me just what is all my fault? Being born? Being abandoned by my parents to be adopted by a couple who withheld love and encouragement while *you* were raised by *my* loving parents? That's somehow my fault?" She stalked to the fireplace, keeping her back to them.

She wanted Julie and Darcie to leave, to get out of her house and her life. She didn't need them.

But he was their father too.

Leanna crossed the room to Julie. "Honey, you can't deny this away. Carin is our sister. I know it. Daddy will confirm it when we find him."

Julie's gaze went from Leanna to Carin and back. Her eyes narrowed and her face became hard as granite. She walked back to the chair and sat down. She wouldn't make eye contact with Carin but looked at Leanna.

"Look, I'm sorry about Carin's parents, but that's not my fault, either." Julie dropped her gaze but not before Carin saw the defiance and disdain.

Weariness weighed her. The sun had set long ago, and while she'd prefer to crawl into bed and pull the covers over her head, her sisters hadn't eaten.

She motioned toward the kitchen. "Your dad had planned to take everyone to dinner at *Jake's Rib Cage*. Somehow, I don't think any of us want that. I can throw together some spaghetti and a radish salad. Will that do?"

Her sisters nodded and followed Carin to the kitchen. Julie sat at the island while Darcie put garlic spread on a French baguette, and Leanna made the salad from the recipe Carin gave her.

Carin dropped a pound of ground beef into a skillet, its sizzle sounding so normal. Like a real family, cooking together. But they weren't. Not really. But maybe one day, after Dad was found and let them know it was for real.

After dinner, Carin made up the guest room. Julie and Darcie slept in there while Leanna chose Dad's room. As Carin showed her the room, she eyed the blankets at the end of Dad's bed.

How was he keeping warm? *God, please … keep him warm.*

Chapter 24

In the morning, Claire called Carin. When she told her about her sisters arriving, Claire decided they'd meet at *Dee's 'n' Doughs.* That Julie wouldn't bully Carin, not while Claire was around. They'd have to deal with her first.

"That way, you're on safer ground," Claire said, keeping her voice light. "People tend to not make a scene in public." And she and the gals would have poor Carin's back.

"I hope you're right. Julie is a pressure cooker without a safety valve. I'm glad JJ wasn't here to see it. Was he good for you? Did he have any trouble going to sleep?"

"He was a delight. He and Joel had such fun pulling out the boys' old train set. They had them running all over the family room, carrying popcorn to me. I think Joel had as much fun as JJ." Neither of them could wait for Charlie and Sandie's twins to arrive. "Joel wants to take him to the marina for the day. It might be wise, sugar, depending on how the day goes."

"You're right. How can I thank you, Claire?"

Bedsprings squeaked through the phone. Claire hoped that meant Carin had slept some.

"Last night was pretty ugly. Julie, the eldest of the three, hates me. Darcie, she's the youngest, and well, I can't read her. She scrutinizes everything. It's rather weird. Leanna is the only one who seems open to me. My nerves are strung so tight, worrying about my dad and treading on fault lines around my sisters."

Claire paced the kitchen. How could anyone not love Carin? "Bring them down to the bakery for breakfast. We'll set them straight."

Lighten her burden, Lord.

Claire pulled out a couple of doggie treats for Shiloh. "That poor girl needs some laughter in her life, you know that, Shiloh?"

He gave her a doggie grin and politely held out his tongue for the treats.

"Oh, no you don't. You get these in the laundry room on your bed." He could get outside through his doggie door if he needed to. "I'm going to work."

The big goof knew the word "work" meant he couldn't go. He hung his head then looked to see if she was watching him.

"You are such a drama king." She tossed him another treat and left him happily chomping it as she closed the door.

The spring air still held a nip this early in the morning. She slipped her arms into the sweater she'd tossed over her shoulders. As she rounded the corner, her cell phone rang. "Claire? It's Helen Grant."

"Good mor—"

"I went to bingo last night, and when Ellie dropped me off, I spent a moment enjoying the sunset before I went inside. At my age, you have to enjoy all you can while you're still alive. Anyway, something caught my eye over at the old *Lola Mitchell Opera House*. I wish they'd reopen that theater. I love to go see plays."

Ellie's mother would talk the hind legs off a donkey if Claire didn't get her back on track. "What was it?"

"What was what?"

Claire stepped up onto the boardwalk. "What did you see at the theater?"

"I didn't go to the theater. I went to bingo."

Patience was a virtue, especially with Miss Helen. "And you said something caught your eye at the theater."

"Did you see it too? It liked to have frightened me to death. The curtain in one of those upper rooms moved. I. Saw. The. Ghost. I'm certain it's your great-aunt."

Of course she was. Helen always said Lola Mitchell was a heathen. And in her younger days, Claire supposed she was. But when she came home to Chapel Springs, Great-Aunt Lola mended her ways, made peace with God, and was in church every Sunday. From what Claire had read in her aunt's journals, she became a fervent believer. It definitely wasn't her great-aunt that Helen saw.

"Miss Helen, if you think you saw something, you need to call Sheriff Taylor."

"I don't want him to arrest Lola. I just think you need to know she's scaring folks. You talk to her, now." The line went dead.

Claire pocketed her phone and went over to the search team. Jim Bob Taylor was getting his prerequisite donut and coffee while talking with a captain from the Search and Rescue Team.

She snatched the donut from his hand. "Once you find Carin's daddy, I need to talk to you about this ghost business. You can eat donuts then."

The captain snorted and walked back to his team. Jim Bob swallowed a mouthful of coffee.

"We've got three teams in the woods, Claire. We've got this covered. And I didn't think you believed in ghosts."

"Not in the ghost, but someone is trying to scare people, and I think it's either Howie Newlander or the Pineridge theater people. They stand to lose revenue if we reopen the opera house here."

For lack of the donut, Jim Bob chewed on her comment. "I have to say there's a possibility with both. I heard what Newlander said about the old place. I'll look into it, Claire."

"Thanks. How's the search going?"

Jim Bob shook his head. "Not good. We've swept all the trails around the lake, and there's miles of them. We've had dogs out, sniffing. Even had Ms. Jardine's dog, since he'd been with her daddy. We stayed out as late as we dared. We can't risk losing the searchers, too. I hate to say it, but our next step—"

Carin and her sisters rounded the corner from the alley next to *Halls of Time*. Claire grabbed Jim Bob's elbow and whirled him around. "Shh, Carin's here with her sisters."

He tipped his hat, retrieved his donut from Claire's fingers, and said, "Morning, ladies." He then executed an about face and headed toward the S & R Team captain, leaving her alone to greet Carin and her sisters.

"Any word?" Carin asked as she stopped beside Claire.

"Nothing yet, but they'll find him." *Alive for Carin's sake, please Lord.* "Ladies, I'm Claire Bennett. Let me take all y'all to breakfast. *Dee's 'n' Doughs* has the best pastries and breakfast sandwiches in the state of Georgia."

She pushed the door open for them. Carin gestured that she was going to talk to the search team. Claire wished she wouldn't do that, but she ushered the sisters inside. She could handle them.

The women hesitated as Carin walked away. "Shouldn't we help them search?" Leanna asked.

Claire shook her head. "Honey, you don't know the terrain and they've got the Search and Rescue Team from the U.S. Forest Service. They're top notch—none finer. They don't need to worry about y'all being out there and getting into trouble."

Inside the door, the three women stopped. Leanna closed her eyes and inhaled. She elbowed Darcie, who did the same. Julie hesitated but finally tested the air. Her eyes grew large and she smiled.

"That's how it always affects me, too." Claire showed them where the coffee pots were. "Choose your java, then breakfast. Hey, Dee, these are Carin's sisters …" Claire lifted an eyebrow and looked them over one by one. "I'm sorry. I'm not sure which one of you is which."

She was sure, but she'd let them introduce themselves and see if she was right.

The rigid one stepped forward. "I'm Julie Knowles. This …" She gestured to the one Claire thought was Leanna by her open, sweet smile. Their dad's smile. "This is Leanna. And beside her is Darcie, our baby sister."

Well, la-di-dah. Claire *had* been right. Even her voice, with its affected modulation, demanded recognition. Like a ship's captain. Or women's club president. She and Patsy had run into a few of those. Claire held in a snicker for Carin's sake. Oh. Claire eyed Julie again. Maybe not a ship's captain but like the firstborn and used to being looked up to. Could it be her anger was due to having lost her position in the family? Usurped by Carin through no fault of her own?

As soon as they got their breakfast, they found a table near the window. The bells jingled as Carin entered. Claire had seen Carin's smile, and the one she wore now was a poor imitation pasted on for her sisters. What had Jim Bob and the search team told her? She joined them with a cup of coffee and dropped into the chair beside Claire.

She patted Carin's knee in silent support then directed her attention to the sisters. "Julie, tell me about yourself. What do you do?"

She'd let Carin regroup before she had to tell whatever news she'd received. She'd save her revelation for later, but she'd definitely share it with Carin. Maybe it would help her with Julie. If Julie allowed herself to *be* helped.

"I volunteer with various groups and of course, my church. My husband owns a Honda dealership and we live in Dunwoody."

Well, Claire now knew her worth, but not much else. Except, maybe, that this one kept things hidden—presented a perfectly ordered life to the world. With her back straight as an arrow, and her forearms, not her elbows, resting on the table, she gripped the coffee mug with both hands. Beautiful, she carried herself as a model might. Her hair was parted in the middle and swept back into a French twist, but not in one of those banana clip things Claire saw young women wearing—the kind they twist and clip, letting the ends hang out willy nilly. Julie's 'do had every hair smoothed in place. Did she pluck out the mutinous ones? Her ivory skin didn't dare have a blemish. And her makeup appeared to have been applied by someone of Patsy's artistic caliber.

"Leanna, how about you?" Would this one give up more information?

"I teach eighth grade English. My husband's a middle school principal, so we're both very involved with kids. I'm an avid gardener and noticed some lovely yards as we rode in the tram to get to Carin's house. That tram is such a fun way to get around. It allowed us to really see Chapel Springs instead of watching traffic or street signs. But Carin mentioned you're a potter."

Carin startled at her name, and coffee splashed over her cup. She shook it off her hand and plucked a napkin from the dispenser on the table. "Sorry about that. I guess I was, uh, not paying attention."

Claire patted her hand while Julie scowled. Leanna kept looking out the window. Darcie was more interested in the people in the bakery.

"Claire's a well-known pottery artist," Carin said. "She's the one who made the vase you admired, Darcie."

Julie's right eyebrow lifted. Claire always wished she could do that. She strained her forehead but nothing happened. Both her brows worked together.

"Darcie works in an art gallery in Buckhead. Do you carry her work, honey?"

"Bennett? Why yes, we have a few of your small whimsy line." Darcie exposed perfectly even teeth. Some Buckhead orthodontist got a trip to Tahiti.

The bells jangled wildly and Jim Bob stuck his head in the door. "Ms. Jardine, may I see you out here?"

Carin's color drained and her eyes grew round. Her chair scraped the floor with a skin-crawling screech as she rose and rushed outside.

"What was that all about?" Julie asked.

Her tone demanded more than an "I don't know" but Claire didn't know. She might have an idea, but she wouldn't say. *Lord, let my intuition be off.* She shook her head and shrugged. "Would you like me to go see?"

Those same brows that rose singularly now drew together in a scowl. "Maybe I should go."

Claire wasn't about to let Carin be alone with this sister. She reached the door first and pulled it open, colliding with Patsy.

"Girlfriend," Claire whispered, "Carin needs us. Now. Come on."

Julie, Leanna, and Darcie trailed them.

As they approached, the S & R Team captain pointed to the lake. "They're bringing up the body now."

"No!" Carin took a step back, shaking her head. "Please God, no!" Tears streamed down her face.

Claire wrapped her in her arms and held her tight. Over Carin's shoulder, she saw Julie showing her ID to the search captain.

"I just got him," Carin whispered against Claire's shirt. "Why is God punishing me?"

"Carin, I'm so sorry, honey." Claire rubbed circles on her back.

Julie grabbed Carin's shoulder and wrenched her away from Claire's arms. Her perfect make-up was now a clown's mask of brown mascara and eyeliner. "This is your fault. If he hadn't come up here to see you, he'd still be alive."

Her former modulated tone had turned into a shrew's screech and spittle flew from the corners of her twisted mouth.

Carin flinched but didn't retaliate. Her eyes were raw with naked sorrow. Julie drew back her arm, but Claire stopped it. "That won't make you feel better."

Julie scowled and turned away. She reached for Darcie and wept on her shoulder. Just beyond them, Leanna stood alone with tears trailing down her cheeks. That poor baby. Claire caught Patsy's attention with a tilt of her head, and her BFF moved to console Leanna. They had a gruesome job ahead of them.

Chapter 25

"I can't begin to imagine what all poor Carin is going through." Claire closed her eyes against the bright sunshine streaming in the windows of *Dee's 'n' Doughs*. It was wrong. The sun shouldn't be shining at all. The sky should be grieving with Carin instead of celebrating. "She was overjoyed to have found him, and now she's lost him already. It doesn't seem fair, Pat-a-cake."

Patsy tore her pastry into bits and pieces. "And to have to tell her sisters who she was without her dad—"

Claire opened her eyes. "That Julie is a piece of work. I was itchin' to give her an attitude adjustment."

"My word, is there something wrong with my apple fritters this mornin', Patsy?" Dee untied her apron, draped it over the back of a chair, then slid off the hairnet she wore when baking. She pulled out the chair and dropped into it, stuffing the hairnet in her pocket.

"The fritter's fine." Patsy reached over and smoothed down a lock of Dee's hair the net had left standing straight up. "I'm out of sorts this morning."

Dee nodded. "We all are. Carin's father is all the town's talking about. It's the first drowning we've had in three years."

Claire frowned. "Why did the coroner have to take him?"

"Rule out foul play," Dee said.

"Oh."

The bells on the bakery door jingled and Lacey stepped inside, followed by Ellie Grant, JoAnn Hanson, and Lydia. They picked out pastries, poured their favorite coffees, and crowded around the table. How did Carin manage without good friends like these ladies? Claire hoped the seed of friendship between Lacey and Carin would bloom. Glancing between Lacey and her sister—

Claire leaned on her elbows. "Lacey, you and Lydia didn't always get along. You might be able to help Carin with her sisters. Ouch!" Claire glared at Patsy who had kicked her ankle. "What?"

Patsy slowly shook her head.

Oh.

Claire frowned. "I guess that *was* a bit tactless. But Lydia and Lacey know my intentions are good, right?" She sent the sisters a plea for forgiveness. "I only want to help Carin."

With a sidelong glance at her sister, Lacey smiled. "We know. I haven't talked with her all that much yet. We were going to go to lunch tomorrow, but then all this happened."

"When are they going to perform the autopsy?" Ellie asked. "And does anyone know what they're looking for?"

"I heard the dark-haired one—what's her name?" Dee asked.

"Julie." Her name tasted bad on Claire's tongue, like New York barbecue.

"Right. I heard her ask them to check for drugs." Dee paused, eyeing each of them. "I think she's trying to accuse Carin of—"

Claire jumped out of her chair. "She wouldn't dare. I'll—"

"Sit down." Patsy pulled on Claire's arm. "Julie's already gone. I saw her car pulling away from the lot on my way over here. Only she and the youngest sister were in the car, though. The middle one must have stayed."

"Leanna." Claire took a piece of Patsy's apple fritter and popped it into her mouth. "Carin told me she was a sweetheart. That Julie better not accuse Carin or—"

"I heard he had Lou Gehrig's Disease." Ellie dug in her purse, pulling out a tissue. "That's fatal." She blew her nose then stuffed the tissue in her pocket. "Although, I believe he wasn't that far advanced to cause his death. Most likely, his legs gave way and he collapsed. He probably hit his head and fell in the water."

"How do you know all that?" Staring at Ellie, Lydia bit into the last half of her bagel.

"I've read every book in our library."

"Do you have one that tells how to make Carin's sisters nice? Ow! Oh, for Pete's sake." Claire glared at her BFF. "That wasn't tactless. That was truth. At least in Julie's case."

Patsy gave her a grin with only one side of her mouth. "Maybe Ellie has a book on diplomacy."

Claire ignored that. "Or ghosts. Do you have any on ghosts?" She drained her coffee and rose to get a second cup. "Reliable ones. Books, I mean, not reliable ghosts." She stepped to the coffee bar and chose mocha. She needed chocolate's comfort today.

"Is the theater ghost acting up again?" Ellie asked.

Claire rolled her eyes. "The last time rumors flew around town I was in the third grade. All of us kids were scared but fascinated. We'd stand on chairs in Sunday school to look out the window at the theater, hoping to see it."

"I remember that," Patsy said. "But didn't we discover a vagrant had gotten inside?"

"No. They thought that was what it was, but there wasn't any evidence of a break in. The only entrance remained locked." Claire gave a nod to Ellie. "That's why I want some answers. I don't really believe in ghosts. At least I don't think I do. Your mother says she saw it, though. There has to be a logical explanation."

Ellie slipped on her sweater. "My mother is always seeing something. At her age, it's mostly her imagination giving her something to talk about." She pushed her chair back and rose. "I've got to pick up Mother's prescriptions before I open the library. I'll pull some books for you, Claire."

"And I've got to get to work, too." Lacey got up. "See you tomorrow."

Amazing. Lacey was beginning to talk a little more. Did Patsy and Lydia notice? They were both chatting with JoAnn. Anyway, it was nice she opened up a bit.

Patsy nudged her shoulder. "You're in your head again. JoAnn asked about Bobby and Melissa."

She did? "Oh. They're working on Felix's campaign."

JoAnn laughed. "You know that's not what I meant. Are you still dead set against Bobby and Melissa dating?"

Claire gave a half-hearted shrug. She disliked admitting he wasn't so bad. The boy had changed. But was it enough? She and Joel spent too many years on opposite sides spiritually. It broke her heart to think Melissa might do the same, even though she said she wouldn't accept Bobby's proposal until he became a believer.

"What if he lies to her, tells her he believes when he doesn't?"

Patsy slapped her hands on the table, making Claire jump. "That girl is as level-headed as you are looney. She'd cotton onto that quicker than instant grits."

Claire gazed past her BFF to JoAnn. "Do you think he's really getting close to believing?"

The consummate pastor's wife, JoAnn's smile was genuine but never gave any confidence away. "We're praying for him, and I believe it will happen. Someday. He and Seth's nephew Vaughn have become friends, and from what I understand, Vaughn keeps trying to steer a lot of conversations around to faith."

"Well, you'd better warn Vaughn." Claire looked at JoAnn then Patsy, then JoAnn again. "This is the same boy who quoted Marx, saying faith is the opiate of the masses."

JoAnn gave Claire's hand a squeeze. "Have faith, my friend. Remember Saul of Tarsus." She pushed back her chair. "I've got to make hospital rounds with my husband. See you."

"Come on, Claire." Patsy chuckled. "Bobby's not so bad."

"I guess not. I just can't get the high school Bobby out of my head. He was such a peacock, spouting atheist views that weren't even his own."

Still, JoAnn had a point. If Saul became Paul, then maybe there was hope for Bobby. A spark of faith grew to a small flame.

Patsy smirked. "And which among us had a brain when we were in high school?"

Claire snorted. "I guess you're right. As much as I hate saying it, Bobby *has* grown up. He's not a peacock anymore, at least." She picked up her tote. "Dee, before I go, can I get a quart of your pearl pasta salad? Joel loves it."

A moment later, with the salad in hand, they stepped outside into the sunshine. Claire slid on her dark glasses and turned toward the gallery as Felix exited *Halls of Time*.

"Claire, hang on a second." He lumbered toward them. "Sean should have the trenching completed in another week or two. That boy's doin' a bang-up job. I haven't seen hide nor hair of Newlander, though, and that worries me."

A frown tugged at Claire's brows. "I haven't either. I wonder what he's up to. He always was a sneaky one. His last attack was on the theater. He's still yapping about tearing it down."

"Hogwash. Costs less to refurbish the old one. Besides, it has history here."

Claire could've almost kissed Felix for that. Almost. That was as good as an approval for the funds to remodel. She composed herself. Knowing he pleased her could make him change his mind. "It does, and that adds to the value. I'll keep my eyes and ears open for Howie."

When they reached *The Painted Loon*, Patsy opened the cash drawer while Claire turned on the lights. Mel was late this morning.

"Patsy, have—"

The door opened and Mel rushed in. "I'm sorry I'm late. I couldn't, well, uh, my stepmom was late."

"That's okay, Mel, but Nicole is at an art sale for us, so she won't be in today. You'll have to cover for her, too."

"I'm good with that." She stowed her brown bag and picked up the newspaper.

When Claire entered their workroom, Patsy was already at her easel. She poked her head out from behind it. A brush in one hand held crimson paint on its tip.

"I had a thought about Howie and his campaign. Since we've disarmed his water rights argument, what's he got against Felix now?"

"Money wasting. He's using the theater as part of that ridiculous argument. Anyone with a shred of sense knows Felix makes every nickel cover a dime's worth of business."

Claire slid into her potter's apron then opened the kiln. She withdrew two vases and set them on her workbench.

Patsy waved her brush. "But the summer people don't really know that."

"What difference does that make?" Next, she withdrew a platter from the depths of the kiln.

"Any landowner can vote. Oh, Claire, those colors turned out spectacular."

"Thanks. But how did you come to that conclusion? About the landowners, I mean." She set the platter by the vases and then pulled out a chunk of clay from her barrel. She threw it onto the counter and began to soften it.

"I checked the county records. It seems back when the town incorporated, most people only stayed here during the summer months. So that first council decided all landowners got the vote, even though they were only in residence three months out of the year."

"So what does that mean for us?" Claire took the softened clay to her pottery wheel and plopped it down.

"Eighty-six percent of those landowners rent their property to other people." Patsy disappeared behind her easel. "They don't live here or vacation here. It's merely income property to them, passed down by their grandparents."

"And since last year, it's bringing in good money for them. Hoo boy." Claire stopped the wheel and released the clay, tossing it back in the barrel. "I've got to get to Felix with this."

Chapter 26

Carin handed her sister a cup of coffee. "What can I give you for breakfast? I've got chocolate cereal or toast and eggs." Would she even feel like eating? Poor Leanna. Last night, after Julie and Darcie refused to stay another night under Carin's roof, Leanna alone stood by her side, telling her sisters she'd rent a car to get home later. Then she called her husband and explained what happened. He was going to come get her tomorrow afternoon.

The front door opened and JJ barreled in. "Mama? I'm home. Miss Claire—" He skidded to a stop in the kitchen, his eyes solemn. "Are you my new aunt?"

Leanna squatted to eye level with him. "Yes, I'm your Auntie Leanna."

"Was Pop your daddy like he was my mama's?"

Her sister glanced up at her then back to JJ. "Yes, sugar, he was. But he told me all about you."

Carin startled. He did? She thought he'd kept her a secret. "Leanna, when did Dad tell you about JJ?"

She rose, keeping one arm around JJ's shoulders. "Early last week. He needed me to be prepared. To help with Julie. And Darcie. But mainly Jewels. She's used to being Queen Bee."

"I wonder why Dad didn't tell me that you knew about me."

"I don't know. But I was thrilled to learn about you and JJ."

"Why?" Carin didn't mean to be so blunt, but she wanted to understand.

Leanna moved to her side. "Growing up, it was always Julie and Darcie. I was on the outside. I wanted a sister of my own." She stretched her hand out and laid it on Carin's arm. "And now I have one. How I wish Mama could have seen this day."

Carin searched Leanna's eyes, not sure what she wanted to see. Finally, she smiled and gave Leanna a quick hug. "I'm so glad." She stepped back. "I didn't have any siblings. I wanted a sister after a family moved in next-door with three daughters. They were close to each other and always played together. I used to watch them over the fence."

JJ tilted his face up. "You got me, Mama."

Carin scooped him up in her arms and squeezed him. "I surely do and that's the best." She kissed his cheek and set him back on his feet. "But having an Auntie Leanna is pretty nice, isn't it?"

"It sure is." He took her sister's hand. "You aren't going to leave us, are you? Everybody leaves me and Mama."

"Oh, sugar," Carin said. She and Leanna bumped heads as they bent at the same time to comfort JJ. They all ended up laughing and sitting on the floor.

Leanna took JJ's hands. "Sweetie, I will have to go back home, but I'll be back to visit you. And maybe sometime, your mama will let you come stay with me and your Uncle Scott."

That would take a while before Carin would trust enough to allow that to happen. Before JJ started begging to go, she needed to change the subject. She hoped Leanna would understand.

"What did you do with Miss Claire and Mr. Joel last night?"

While he regaled them with stories about the trains, Carin made French toast. After breakfast, the three of them played Candyland. Leanna was good with him and didn't seem to tire of his chatter or games. She shared stories from her childhood that made Carin wistful. It was so different from her own. She couldn't remember being hugged or kissed, except by her grandmother.

She tried hard to make sure JJ got plenty of hugs and kisses. He felt the loss of his daddy and now his grandfather. She swallowed, trying to keep her tears from falling.

"How about some more coffee? Does this establishment provide second cups?" Leanna asked JJ, who giggled.

"Mama always has second cups." He carried her cup to the counter.

Her sister was intuitive. Compassionate, too. Carin's heart opened another notch. She wasn't sure where their relationship would go, but she wanted it. She only hoped Julie and Darcie would come around.

Shortly before noon, they finished playing games, and JJ went outside to play with Mikey. Carin stood next to her sister in the kitchen, pan-searing chicken breasts while Leanna fixed the vegetables for the salad. It was a unique experience, and Carin liked it. It made the chore of cooking fun. The phone rang, and she turned off the heat under the pan.

"Hello?" She turned to Leanna, covered the microphone and mouthed "the coroner" to her. Carin put it on speaker phone.

"Your father's death was a simple drowning. We believe the leg muscles, weakened from ALS, couldn't support him as he climbed over some rocks. He collapsed and hit his head. He rolled off the rocks into the water and drowned. I'm sorry. We're releasing the body. Whom should I contact to retrieve it?"

Carin turned to Leanna for help. Her sister took the phone and gave the coroner the name of a funeral home in Dunwoody. When she hung up, she went back to sautéing the veggies. Did she feel as numb as Carin?

"Julie insisted on that funeral home. I didn't argue. It's where Mama was taken."

They worked in silence for a few moments.

"JJ should come with you."

"Come where?"

"To the funeral. He's Daddy's only grandchild. After dinner, I'll contact our attorney if Julie hasn't already. She'll want the reading of the will right after the funeral."

"We don't need to be there for that."

Leanna laid down the knife. "Carin, you're his daughter, too."

She might be Leanna's sister, but Julie wasn't about to accept her as a Buchanan daughter. "That may take more strength than I have at the moment."

"You're stronger than you think, sister."

Carin tried to smile, but it collapsed. The tears she'd held at bay for the last hour spilled over. "When Daddy knocked on my door, I opened my heart to him. He loved me and JJ, and we were so happy. Why did God take him? We only had a few weeks together. And now he's gone."

Her sister held her while she wept, their tears mingling. But as much as she'd like to stay there being comforted, she had to dry her tears before JJ came inside. It upset him when he saw her crying. She fought for composure.

"Carin, I don't know why God let Daddy die, but I have to believe it's for the best."

That dried up her tears. She frowned and moved back to the stove. "How can you say that?"

"Daddy would have hated to become crippled and dependent on others."

"He was going to move in with me here so I could take care of him."

Love filled Leanna's eyes. She smiled. "And he would have loved being here. But he wouldn't have wanted JJ to see him decline." She tossed the chopped veggies into the salad bowl. "Daddy had a weird outlook on that. Maybe it was male pride, I don't know. I remember when Mama's brother, Uncle Marvin, lost his legs in an accident. Daddy said he'd rather die than become dependent on others."

"You don't think he … he did it on purpose, do you?"

Leanna moved the salad bowl to the island. "Absolutely not. This was an accident. But what if God decided it was for Daddy's best?" She lifted her hands and shrugged her shoulders. "I'm not saying I know that was it, but I'm supposing. Maybe trying to convince myself."

"But what about our best? JJ's best?"

"Sweet sister, I don't have an answer. I only know God is trustworthy." Leanna washed her hands. "And now you have me."

Sweet sister. Carin loved the sound of that. It brought a smile to her face. "I guess I'm a bit at odds with God right now. He's taken so much away from me." First her husband and now her father.

"I wouldn't be so quick to blame God for your husband's own choices," Leanna said, almost as though she heard Carin's thoughts. "He has a free will, you know."

Leanna's cell phone rang in her pocket. She pulled it out, glanced at Carin, and answered it. "Hey. That was fast. Yes, I'll be home. What? Hold on." She placed her hand on the speaker. "I need to go outside for this. Excuse me, please."

Out on the deck, Leanna gestured wildly with one hand. "You can't do that."

Carin couldn't hear anything else as her sister had moved to the far end of the deck. She went to set the table for lunch.

Leanna came back inside, a frown on her pretty face. "Julie makes me tired."

She found the plates and lifted them from the large drawer. Carin loved those drawers and was glad Norm talked her into them, but how did Leanna know that's where the dishes were stored?

"Why's that?" She stopped placing the flatware when Leanna didn't answer. "What did she say? That she doesn't want me at the funeral?"

Carin actually agreed with Julie on this. Nobody knew about her except her sisters. Everyone would want to know why Carin Jardine was at Jim Buchanan's funeral. Then the gossip about Wick would start, and she didn't want JJ hearing it.

Biting her lip, Leanna nodded.

"I'm going to give her this round. Don't—" Carin stopped her sister's protest with an upraised hand. "She's right. No one knows I'm family, but everyone in Atlanta knows who I am."

Her sister smiled at that. She was glad, since it removed the sting of her declining.

"Look," Carin said. "I don't want to be the center of attention, and we both know that's what would happen. And that would alienate Julie further."

Leanna drew near. "I hate to admit you're right, but I think it may be the wisest. I keep forgetting *who* you are, other than my sister."

At that, Carin's heart opened all the way. "That's the sweetest thing anyone has ever said to me." She grabbed Leanna into a bear hug. How about that. Chapel Springs was wearing off on her. "My very own little sister." At the very least, she'd have one sister who loved her. "Now, call your nephew in for lunch. Mikey, too. I'll call his mother."

Carin called Sheryl about Mikey having lunch with them, assuring her there were no peanuts involved. Mikey had a peanut allergy. The boys made a good team, since JJ was the world's strangest child—he hated peanut butter. Carin sliced the warm chicken and tossed it into the salad, promising the boys Chocolate Lovers Fantasy for dessert if they ate their salad. That always worked with JJ.

After lunch, the boys went over to Mikey's house to play, so she and Leanna took a walk and talked. Carin shared more about her childhood, and Leanna told her about how her sisters always left her out of their confidences and play if they could get away with it.

"I made up a sister of my own, instead of an imaginary friend."

"Really? I had a slew of imaginary friends, too. Did Dad tell you they came to see me when I was four?" Carin stepped over a log.

"No. What happened?" Leanna stepped on the log and jumped to the ground.

Carin told her about remembering the incident. "After they left, my adoptive mother changed, became withdrawn. We moved shortly after that. I think she was afraid they'd keep coming. We moved two or three times in the next couple of years. Then she seemed more relaxed and we stayed in one place."

"But Daddy kept tabs on you."

"Yes, so it seems. He knew everything about me."

"Moving so much must have been hard."

"I couldn't bring any friends home from school. My mother kept the house looking like a museum. She was always cleaning and wouldn't tolerate anything out of place. I kept my dolls in my father's shed outside."

"Carin, that's awful."

She shrugged. "Anyway, I never formed any close friendships, except for once in high school."

"What happened?"

"She stole my boyfriend." Carin stopped at a "y" in the trail. Which way would take them away from the lake? She chose the left trail. "Anyway, that was in our freshman year. After my first book hit the *New York Times* bestseller list, she came to a book signing, telling everyone we were BFFs since high school."

Leanna stopped and planted her fists on her hips. "That stinker."

Carin had called her a lot worse than that.

"No wonder you're cautious."

Carin thrust her hands in her pockets. "I never wanted the attention. When I hit the bestseller list, I was pleased but had no idea it would change my life so much. Some who have made it said theirs didn't change at all. Others did. Maybe it was only in Atlanta, but I couldn't go to the store without people approaching me as if I owed them something. One woman frightened JJ and that did it for me."

They walked in silence. As the trail wound around back toward the church steeple, Carin bore left again, which led them past Dee Lindstrom's cute chalet to Pine Drive. They crossed the street, cut through her rear neighbor's yard, and arrived at the house.

This place, the house and Chapel Springs—she glanced at her sister—was beginning to feel like home.

As they entered the back door, the front doorbell rang.

Chapter 27

Claire found Felix in his office at *Flavors*. She sometimes forgot he had a business besides being mayor, but it was a great place to work in the summer since the air conditioner was always on to keep the ice cream frozen. Today, however, not so much. This time of year could be so fickle in the mountains. She shivered and slid her arms into the sleeves of her lightweight sweater.

"Here's where I found the clause." She pointed to the paragraph. "I talked to Ellie and she said every one of the owners is registered to vote, and most have voted in every election. If Howie gets to them …"

She left that hanging. She hated to think of what he might do.

Felix yanked his ball cap off and whomped it against his desk. "Dagnabit! He'll lie through his teeth." He slapped the hat back on his head. "How many of them are there?"

"Not as many as full time residents. But if Howie gets to any of them, it could be close. Have you heard anything from his camp lately?"

"Nope, not a peep, and that worries me. I don't like an opponent I can't see."

"Well, I have an idea. I called Sean on the way over here to see when his work will be done. He said two more days. I told him to hold up on opening the channel."

Felix gaped at her. "Now, why would you do something as dumb as that?"

"It's not dumb. I'm fixing to save your bacon."

"And how are you going to do that?"

"By holding a large press conference out at the site. We'll have the news there and show them what y'all have done for Chapel Springs and the farmers."

Felix went from mad to glad faster than Dale Earnhardt went from zero to sixty.

"That's downright brilliant. What day do you think would be best?"

"I'm thinking Friday. That gives us enough time, and Howie can't come back with anything. By Monday, it will be old news."

"Dang, that's smart, Claire. Can you set it up with Sean for eleven in the morning?"

"Sure. I'll have Ellie send out the press release."

"Have her do it pronto. I gotta hand it to ya, Claire. You did save my bacon this time. Without frying it to a crisp, too." He chortled at his joke.

"Instead of laughing, we need to try to find out what Howie's been up to. That water sample he took didn't gain him anything except wet pants and a cut backside when he tripped over the curb and the bottle broke. He didn't bother to go back."

"No, but the inspector came two days later." Felix grinned. "We passed with a ninety-eight-point-seven percent. So whatever Howie was hoping for didn't happen. Now git goin' and coordinate with Sean."

Claire called Sean on her way back to the gallery. He answered when she walked in the door—from the gallery. She tapped her phone off. "What are you doing here?"

His face turned bright red. So did Mel's.

"Uh, I'm here to pick up Mel. We're going to eat."

She raised a brow. "Oh, well, I won't hold you up, just be back by two, please. And Sean, I need to talk with you when you come back. It's about the timing on opening the channel."

"Okay, I can do that." The two walked out and turned toward restaurant row.

Patsy smirked. "What's with giving Mel a long lunch hour?"

"I'm merely helping Sean see that she's too young for him."

"And how will having lunch together do that?"

"Have you talked to Mel for any length of time? Her youth shows. She's not a conversationalist beyond the latest ghost story, or band, or movie magazine. I think she's a great kid, but the emphasis is on kid. I'd sure like to see her get some more education."

Patsy straightened one of Claire's small whimsy vases. "Since you're not playing yenta with them, what's up with 'Lissa and Bobby?"

Claire sat on the stool behind the front counter. "Melissa hasn't been home much lately. She finished her thesis. Now she's getting ready for graduation." *Whoa.* That meant their tuition bills would be over. After so many years of kids in college—"Do you realize we'll finally be rid of all the tuition and housing bills? I'm trying to work out how many years it's been. Charlie started in 2007, then Adrianna two years later. He graduated just as the twins entered. There was one semester when we had four kids in college at once."

"That was the semester you ate nothing but peanut butter sandwiches."

"And stone soup. Wow, I wonder if Joel has realized this yet. If he has, he's probably planning on a new boat." She stopped. A grin formed along the tail of an idea. "Do you think there's any way remotely possible we could talk our husbands into a cruise?"

"Not with all the potential weddings we have coming up."

Claire propped her elbows on the counter and lowered her chin onto her hands. "Do you suppose we could pay them to elope?"

"Your girls have always wanted a double wedding, and now they've both fallen in love. What do you think?"

Claire scrunched her nose at Pat-a-cake. "Killjoy."

"Ha. You'd be the first one to cry in your soup if they eloped and you missed all the fun."

"Y'know, it's downright unnatural the way you're always right." She climbed off the stool. "I've got work in the kiln I need to paint. What are you doing this afternoon—besides *being right*?"

Patsy snickered. "I'm going with Nicole's mother to help her do some decorating in Chase's apartment."

"And Chase knows about this, I hope."

Patsy wrinkled her nose. "It was his request. He said he wanted it perfect for when he brings Nicole there for the first time after the wedding."

"When did Chase turn into such a romantic?"

"The moment he met Nicole. It's how I knew she was the one." Patsy's smile was blissful.

"It seems so strange to have all our chicks falling in love and getting married. Soon, only Deva and Adrianna will be left unwed, and Adrianna brought her boyfriend home at Christmas, so I expect her to call us any day with the news she's engaged."

Patsy bent over and picked up a rogue dust bunny that had escaped Mel's radar. "I know. It makes me realize how fast time goes by. It seems like yesterday they were in diapers. But I don't feel any older. Do you?"

"Sometimes, but not really. No, I'm looking forward to taking a few trips with just us four."

"Well, if we have any money left after these weddings, we'll get the boys to take us." Patsy picked up her purse and left to meet Nicole's mother.

Claire wandered into the workroom. 'Lissa and Bobby. The only child who still kept her awake at night. If she could just know that Bobby would finally believe, she'd be okay. Even if it meant she and Felix would become in-laws.

What a mother did for her kids. Claire shook her head and opened the kiln.

Chapter 28

Carin didn't recognize the man on the porch, but her sister flew to the door and wrenched it open. "Scott! I didn't expect you until tomorrow."

She hoped this was her brother-in-law. He lifted her sister and swung her around. Had Wick ever done that to her? She couldn't remember a time when he'd been that delighted to see her.

"Put me down, silly." Leanna kissed him, then grabbed his hand. "Come meet my sister."

Together, they looked like a couple of college kids. Carin could definitely see them as teacher and principal. He looked like a man kids would trust. A man who listened to them.

"Sis, this is your brother-in-law, Scott."

He didn't hold out his hand but opened his arms instead. Carin surprised herself when she stepped into his hug. But it felt right. He kissed her cheek. "Welcome to the family, Carin."

Carin squeezed him back. "Thank you." She turned to her sister. "I have a feeling JJ is going to adore his Uncle Scott. Where's your bag? You're not thinking of driving back tonight?"

"Duffle bag's on the porch. I wasn't sure—then again, since Leanna stayed, I should have known it would be okay for me, too."

He reached out the door and grabbed a backpack. Carin called Sheryl to send JJ home. They were at the store, but when they finished, she promised to drop him off.

Scott and Leanna settled at the kitchen island, so Carin joined them there. He told her how much he had loved their dad. She heard more stories about her father's kindness and how much he had loved their mother and that he'd never gone on another date after she died.

"His life was full," Scott said. "We played golf every Saturday with Ted."

"That's Julie's husband, right?" Carin pulled out glasses for iced tea. "Sweet tea?"

"Please, and yes, he's Julie's husband. He's a good guy. A patient man."

He'd have to be, married to her.

"Which," Scott said, "brings me to the reason I came this afternoon instead of tomorrow. Besides missing you." He tugged Leanna's ponytail. "David Lawler called. He wants to do the reading of your dad's will tomorrow afternoon. Before the funeral on Wednesday." He turned to Carin. "He also asked if we knew about you. When I told him yes, he said to be sure you came."

"Why before the funeral?" Leanna asked.

"He leaves on vacation right after the service."

"Why do I need to be there?" Carin didn't want to go. Just imagining Julie's reaction if she showed up to a will-reading made her shudder.

Leanna gripped her coffee cup with both hands. "Sugar, if David says you need to be there then you need to be there. Daddy probably left you something."

Talk about a conundrum. She was desperate for money. She had a mortgage and had nearly maxed out her credit cards. Worse, she still didn't have a story. Yet the idea of sitting in a room and having a lawyer tell Julie part of her inheritance went to Carin? She'd rather—

She'd rather what? Have JJ be homeless? She had more than herself to think about.

"I'm not looking forward to it, I can tell you that."

"We'll be there for you," Scott said. "Leanna told me you don't want to go to the funeral and why. I don't blame you and I think it's a good decision." He glanced at Leanna and smiled. "You'll stay with us, and then you can remain at our house during the funeral. We'll bring you back here afterward."

Though bookended by Scott and Leanna as they entered the lawyer's office, Carin felt vulnerable—exposed. Explosions were coming. Accusations for sure. If Leanna was right, would Julie try to contest the will if Carin were left anything of value? Would she feel the same if she were in Julie's position?

The outer office held plush sofas, dark paneled walls, and a large mahogany reception desk behind which sat a fifty-something receptionist with a jaw-length, gray bob. Just what she expected from a Dunwoody law office. Even—Carin glanced at the desk's placard—Mrs. Nelson radiated professional but grandmotherly care. Other than Mrs. Nelson, the room was empty. Either they were very early or late. She hoped it was early.

"Good afternoon, Mrs. Wallace, Mr. Wallace. And this must be Mrs. Jardine." She blushed and pulled out a copy of one of Carin's earlier titles. "Before you go into Mr. Lawler's office, may I please get an autograph?"

Slapping on her author smile Carin signed the novel, trying to control the trembling in her hand. Mrs. Nelson read the personalized autograph and, beaming, thanked her.

"Your sisters are already inside."

They were late, then. Carin's stomach took a nose dive.

Mrs. Nelson led them down a hallway and stopped in front of a large door. She tapped then opened it, ushering them inside. Carin steeled herself for the first round.

Julie watched as they walked in. When she caught sight of Carin, her head snapped back to the attorney. "What is *she* doing here? This is private, for immediate family only."

A man whom Carin assumed was her husband, Ted, put his arm around Julie's shoulder and whispered in her ear. She sat back, rigid, and crossed her arms, clearly fuming. Whatever he said silenced her, though, and for that Carin was grateful.

Mrs. Nelson bustled about, serving coffee or water to everyone. Ted and Scott took coffee, and a tall glass of ice water for the attorney. Darcie whispered with Julie while Ted rose and bumped fists with Scott.

Carin took the bottle of Evian Mrs. Nelson handed her. "Thank you."

Mr. Lawler—Carin couldn't help but wonder if he chose to study law because of his name—opened a folder on his desk.

"Now that we're all here, shall we begin?"

Julie gave him a sharp nod. He glanced at Ted then each one of them. "Girls— ladies, I mean. I've known you Julie, Leanna, and Darcie since you were small." He glanced down at the file. "I have known about Carin since shortly before your mother passed away."

"What? And you never told us?" Julie machine-gunned the accusation.

Mr. Lawler cleared his throat. "You know I couldn't do that." He took a sip of water, and the crushed ice made no sound in the glass. "I came to the house and your mother made her wishes known to me and your father, in the presence of their pastor as a witness. She was firm that any money her parents left to her would be equally divided between all four of her daughters."

Julie leaned forward, her nostrils flaring. "That's not fair. She wasn't there to help with Mama. I did it all. Though I was only six, I cared for her. I fed her when she couldn't hold her head up any longer." She turned and glared at Carin. "You weren't there."

Leaning on her professional persona, Carin didn't say a word, but neither did she back away from Julie's glare. She silently blessed Claire for insisting on keeping JJ so he didn't have to witness her sister's malicious behavior. Now she understood the saying, "Money is a necessary evil."

Mr. Lawler folded his hands on top of the folder. "Remember, Julie, you were all small children. Carin was a pawn of your grandparents in this. Your father was barely seventeen and your mother sixteen when Carin was born. Both sets of grandparents insisted on adoption." He gazed at each of them over his readers. "Later, they came to realize the depth of your parents' love for one another and for Carin. They were the ones to suggest setting up trusts—one, to avoid the tax consequences of a will, and because, through a trust, they could include Carin without the worry of someone"—he stared pointedly at Julie—"trying to contest a will."

He paused and waited until Julie looked at him. He seemed to be well aware of the family dynamics. "You can put away any thoughts of trying to contest this. It was written many years ago, with the directive to set up and fund the trusts for all four daughters upon his death. The only codicil was the recent addition of Jim's only grandchild, James Allen Jardine."

He read the simple document then. It included a trust of fifty thousand dollars for JJ's college education, the trustees to be Mr. Lawler and Carin. When he told them the size of their trust funds, Carin was flabbergasted. She could pay off the mortgage and have enough to live on for a long time, if she were careful. Tears of gratitude stung the back of her eyes, and only a lifetime of hiding her emotions enabled her to remain outwardly calm. While her daddy couldn't take care of her in her childhood, he provided when she needed it most.

"The terms of your trust funds, with the exception of his grandson's, is the monies are to be held in trust until your thirtieth birthdays."

Julie jumped up. "So out of all of us"—she turned and pointed her finger at Carin—"this interloper is the only one who gets Daddy's money now?" Her face turned dark red. She lunged for Carin. Ted and Scott stepped between them and grabbed her.

"Stop this right now, Julie." Ted had his arms wrapped around her. Her breath came in heaves. She finally broke down and sobbed.

Over his wife's shoulder, Ted caught Carin's eye. "I'm sorry. I'm hoping it's just grief that has her so overwrought."

He could hope all he wanted, but it was greed not grief. Did he have the slightest idea how much money his wife gave to Darcie? On the way down to Atlanta, Leanna told her more about Julie and Darcie's relationship, and unfortunately, Julie couldn't say no to *her baby*. And as spoiled as Darcie was, she couldn't hold on to a penny.

It was no wonder Dad had made the age requirement on the trusts. He knew his daughters well. Leanna had to wait six years to get hers, but she wasn't bothered at all. Money wasn't important to her. It wasn't to Carin, either, until Wick walked out and thrust her into a position of need.

Mr. Lawler handed her an envelope. "Here is all the information you need, Mrs. Jardine. My card is in there and I will manage the trust for JJ. Since yours has already funded, I imagine you will want it transferred to your bank account. See Mrs. Nelson on the way out, and she'll give you the instructions."

Carin shook his hand. "Thank you. I'm sorry for the—" A word merchant, yet here she was at a loss for the right ones to describe what happened with Julie.

Mr. Lawler sandwiched her hand between his. "Carin—may I call you Carin?" She nodded. "I understand more than you know. You see, your dad and I are distant cousins. Were distant cousins. I found you for him when you were little. I kept him informed on your whereabouts and what was happening in your life. Together, we followed your career and your family. I feel like I know you as well as the other girls. The only thing I didn't tell him was how cold your adoptive parents were. That wouldn't have helped. He couldn't have done anything."

"I understand. And I appreciate all you've done. Thank you. Did he tell you he was planning to move in with us? I wanted *time* with him, not his money." Her voice broke, and she clamped her lips together. Leanna's hand slipped into hers.

"We need to go. Goodbye, David." Leanna gave the lawyer a hug and kissed his cheek. "I'll call Lauren and invite you two over for dinner. It's been too long."

They stopped at Mrs. Nelson's desk, and she gave Carin instructions for the wire transfer. A moment later, they were in the parking lot.

Scott paused with his hand on the car door. "Carin, this took a bit longer than we anticipated. Is there somewhere you would like to wait out the funeral?"

She nodded. "There's a park where I used to love to sit and write. I'll be fine there for a couple of hours." And she'd appreciate the time alone to sort out her emotions.

They dropped her off, making arrangements to be back at four to pick her up. After they left, she found her favorite path through the woods. There, she mourned her dad alone. She wept, prayed, and soaked two hankies and a pack of tissues. It was a good thing the park was empty. If anyone had come around, they would think she was having a nervous breakdown and call the funny farm. Finally, she got up and made her way slowly back to the entrance. It wasn't long before Scott and Leanna arrived.

"How about I take you two lovely ladies home and order Chinese?" Scott opened the car door for her.

Carin didn't know about her sister, but she was utterly and totally exhausted. Chinese at their house sounded good—better than a restaurant. They got on the interstate and headed north. Forty minutes later, they exited.

Gainesville, Georgia, was the quaint county seat in Hall County with tree-lined streets and country roads. Within ten minutes, they turned into a driveway. The house didn't have a stately appearance like the photos she'd seen of Julie's home. This was middle America, a brick ranch with a long front porch, popular in Georgia. It was warm and inviting, and the respite Carin needed.

Once settled inside, Scott called in their order, and she called JJ.

"How did everything go, Carin?" Claire asked while Joel went to get JJ.

"Awful and wonderful. Daddy has left me well cared for and JJ has a trust. Julie was … Julie."

"I was worried about that. Ah, here's JJ. I'll see you when you get home."

"Hi, Mama!" His voice squeaked with excitement. "Guess what? Daddy called me."

Carin clutched the phone, her mouth void of all moisture. Wick called JJ? At Claire's? How did he get the number? "JJ, did you call your daddy first?" If Wick thought he could waltz back into her life, he—he what? Was there a chance they could repair their marriage? Her heart began to beat a little faster. She still loved him. And JJ needed his daddy.

"Yes, Mama."

"Well, I'm glad he called you back, sugar. How is he?"

"He's fine and he wants to come see us." Carin inhaled and let the breath out slowly. She didn't know how she felt about that, but she didn't want to get JJ too excited. "I'll give him a call, love bug. I'll be home tomorrow. I love you." After speaking again with Claire, Carin turned off her phone and set it on the coffee table. She picked up her plate of Chinese.

Leanna's eyes held sympathy and an invitation to talk. Finally, a sister to talk to. Scott rose and kissed Leanna.

"You gals can talk all night if you want, but I'm fixing to watch the game, then go to bed."

That made her smile. "Goodnight." She held the mug of green tea and sipped, then set it on the end table. "JJ said Wick called. He wants to come see us."

Leanna nodded. She pulled her feet up and tucked them beneath her. "How do you feel about that?" She took a bite of egg roll.

"You sound like a counselor." Carin set her now empty plate on the coffee table. "I don't know. I still love him, even after all he's done. I don't think you can unravel ten years of loving someone in a few weeks." She picked up a throw pillow and hugged it to her middle.

"Even when you find out the person you loved isn't who you thought they were?"

"How did you guess?"

"We're a lot alike in more ways than you'd realize. I've watched your reactions to various things. You feel deeply, deeper than the average person. So do I. I think it's in our DNA. Believe it or not, Julie is the same, but she hides everything. I don't think that's very healthy, but she won't listen to me."

Carin couldn't help smiling. She "got" Leanna. There was still a lot to learn, but this sister was easy to care about. "I sensed that about you from the beginning. So, little sister, what do you think I should do?"

Leanna put her feet on the floor and leaned forward, resting her elbows on her knees and her chin on her fists. "I don't know enough to advise you. Oh, I've seen the newspapers, but I don't believe all I read there."

"Smart girl." Carin relayed all that had happened from the moment she first found the letter from the HOA with the eviction notice. "I didn't understand what was happening. Wick cheated on me. He's hurt me, humiliated me. But worse, he hurt JJ." Anger clawed her again. "He stole all my money, walked out, and didn't give a flying fig for his son's welfare. If it weren't for Nana's house, we'd be living on the street, homeless."

"Daddy wouldn't have let that happen."

"Wick didn't know about Daddy. JJ could be living in a car for all he knew."

"Do you think you could ever forgive Wick? You know for your own sake, you need to, right?"

She knew, but was she ready? Would she be able to? Inside her heart, a still small voice said, *I can through you.* If he was truly sorry ... "I'd have to see him prove it. I could forgive him, maybe, but can I trust him again?" She wasn't sure.

Her sister waited, not saying anything.

"It's so hard, Leanna. But ..." Carin reached for her sister's hand. "I'm so thankful I have you. I've never had anyone to share my heart with. Wick couldn't share feelings."

Her sister laughed. "Scott's not the best at it, but he tries, bless his heart. Sometimes, I can actually see his eyes glaze over if I go longer than about five minutes."

"At least he tries." Her heart squeezed. Would Wick try?

Chapter 29

C laire pulled off the road into the meadow through which Benson Creek flowed shortly before it went underground. Today, Sean would make the final whatever-it-was to divert the creek away from going underground and send it down to the farmers. Anticipation had kept her awake most of the night. The field was already swarming with workers and reporters.

"Do you see where we're supposed to park?"

'Lissa turned her head to peer out her window. "It's over there." She pointed to the corner of the field where Felix had a large sign set up to direct the media. Typical of Felix, it read:

Felix Riley, Mayor of Chapel Springs

Welcome to the Benson Creek diversion.

Park here.

"All righty, here we go." Claire pulled into the parking area. Snatching her tote off the front seat, she opened the door and climbed out.

"Wait for me." 'Lissa jumped out.

An indistinct hum of voices washed over them. Sean stood beside the backhoe, talking to a reporter while several others thrust their microphones closer to him. WPV had sent a satellite truck for Jacqueline Ford to do a live feed. A makeup artist made a last minute touch up to the reporter's face. Next to WPV's truck stood a large motorhome with the logo of a large cable news channel.

Claire checked her list again. "Wow, every single newspaper and TV station in the area sent reporters. And look, 'Lissa." Claire pointed.

"There's Jacqueline." This was a feel-good story in the midst of a world gone crazy. Hilary Tallord from cable news stood next to Felix.

A festive atmosphere permeated the air as much as the TV cables crisscrossed the ground. Careful not to trip on any of those, Claire joined Felix at his beckoned invitation, and 'Lissa walked off, presumably in search of Bobby.

Hilary poised the microphone in front of Claire. "Mayor Riley tells me you spearheaded this event. Tell us about that."

Her brows shot up so far, her bangs tickled her eyelids. He did? Did he expect something to go wrong? "Last year when we investigated a temperature decrease in the warm springs, we discovered that the state's road work caused a cold stream to split, sending half its water into the springs. When the farmers complained that Benson Creek didn't have the flow it used to, I called in a geologist who had worked with us before. After his surveys, and whatever else he does, he came up with this solution." Claire spotted Sean and waved him over. "Here he is now."

She left Hilary talking with Sean and Felix looking like a proud papa. Yesterday, he told her he was going to hire Sean full-time. Living on a lake in a national forest, he'd have a plethora of problems he could solve. He'd be a nice addition to the town.

Joel arrived and waved at her from beneath a tree next to the creek. She hurried over. "Did you see how many of the media have turned out?"

"I also see a few farmer representatives. But the one I don't see is Newlander."

Claire snorted. "There's nothing for him to object to here. We've pulled the plug on his arguments."

Joel slid his ball cap off and scratched the back of his head. "Don't be so sure. Newlander isn't stupid. He's clever."

"And sneaky."

Claire turned. "Oh, hey, Happy." On the grass, she hadn't heard him approach. "What makes you say that?"

"He's down in the hollow yonder with the farm union. They plan to come up here and disrupt things."

That dirty dog. They'd better warn—

Felix tapped the microphone. "Testing. Okay, we're ready. Ever since Chapel Springs discovered the warm springs had cooled, we've been working on the problem. We hired Sean O'Keefe, a geologist, who investigated and found the problem had been caused by the state DOT when they dynamited to build the new road. Those blasts caused Benson Creek to alter its underground course, sending half its water into the warm springs. It caused the town trouble, but it also caused the farmers a heap in lower water tables. Today, right this very minute, that's about to change. Sean, go ahead."

She was glad Felix gave Sean credit—and in a campaign year, too. Wait—Sean wasn't— "Joel, look!"

'Lissa stood staring at Sean on the backhoe, her eyes sparkling as if a thousand stars lit them.

Claire elbowed Joel, continuing to watch her daughter. "Do you see what I do?" She waved, but 'Lissa didn't see her. Her gaze never moved off Sean.

"Yep."

"And look at Sean. He hasn't taken his eyes off her." Claire giggled. "If this were a movie, right now, the sound track would be playing some romantic theme, and everything but those two would blur out."

Joel's gaze ping-ponged between 'Lissa and Sean. "I'm thinking God just answered our prayers. Did I ever tell you his parents were missionaries?"

Claire tore her eyes off her daughter and stared at her husband. "You knew that and never told me? When? I mean when did you find that out?"

"Shortly after he arrived with the professor. We fell to talking, and I noticed he has a slight accent and asked where he was from. He said he was born in Africa and his parents were missionaries. They're retired now. Sean is the youngest of six."

"And just why did you not tell me this?"

"Because, Yenta, I knew what you'd try to do. I figured if God was in it, it would happen."

Boy, when her hubby became a believer, he sure became wise— and a bit of a wise guy. She wrinkled her nose at him and returned her attention to 'Lissa and Sean—who still hadn't stopped staring at her daughter but now wore the cutest grin.

"Hey, Wingnut," Felix bellowed. "You gonna sit there all day or get this creek flowing?"

Sean shook himself, his face turning red. The backhoe rumbled to life and a thrill ran down Claire's back. A cheer went up from the crowd as the machine made its way into position. The warm springs was about to go back to the way it was, but above ground. Lights flashed on and cameras rolled. He lowered the bucket and removed the last barricade to the water entering the new channel. Dirt, rocks, and mud dumped into the old channel, and a metal door closed, damming the water's flow to the underground. Later today, they'd put in a permanent structure to close the old hole. Water gushed into the new creek bed, and the crowd erupted in cheers.

While the crowd went wild, 'Lissa walked calmly over to the backhoe. Joel patted Claire's back in congratulations. Lydia and Graham, who were near the creek bank, hugged each other. She'd wanted to advertise the health benefits of the springs but couldn't until it got fixed. Claire waved and clasped her hands together over her head in solidarity with her friend, even as her eyes followed her daughter.

Sean climbed down from the backhoe, stood beside 'Lissa, and together they watched the channel fill. Within a few moments, Benson Creek looked like it had before the state started the new road.

But Claire couldn't take her eyes off 'Lissa and Sean. They seemed to have forgotten the crowd around them and stood, talking. After a couple of minutes, they wandered off together.

My, my, my. Claire couldn't wait until tonight to talk to 'Lissa.

"Now just you hold on a minute, Newlander." Felix's voice rose above the sound of water and cheering, his microphone still live. "That's a flat-out lie."

Claire blanched. When had Howie snuck over? He stood with a wide stance, his hands on his hips, and nose-to-nose with Felix, who had his index finger jabbing Howie's shirt buttons. Reporters thrust their microphones as close as they could to get the argument.

"Hogwash, Riley. Everyone knows you want to raise taxes to pay for this. And the farms will be hit the hardest." He turned to the crowd. "A vote for me will mean lower taxes. If you vote for Felix Riley again, you'll get more trouble and higher taxes."

Claire couldn't stand it another minute. Felix may be a pain in the behind, but he was *her* nemesis. Newlander had no right to lie about him. She shouldered her way between the men and the microphones.

The cameras zoomed in on her as she grabbed Howie's shirt by the collar and gave it a twist. "Howard Newlander, we go way back. I can tell a few stories about you that are gospel truth. But I won't stand here and let you slander this town and its mayor." Howie's eyes bulged and his face grew red, but she didn't loosen her hold. He could still breathe. "You couldn't wait to get out of this town. When you did come back, you tried to hornswoggle us all, but your granny knew what you'd do and fixed it so you couldn't. Now, you're ticked off at Chapel Springs, so you think you'll fix us by lying and cheating. You'd better be careful, Howie. There is *no* plan to tax anyone. You say that again, and I'll personally sue you for slanderin' our fine mayor."

Van Gogh's ear, did she just say "our fine mayor?" Felix stared at her like she'd grown another head. Joel laughed and slapped his cap against his thigh. Jacqueline Ford pushed through the crowd. As she approached, Howie jerked away from Claire and stormed off.

"I hope he doesn't go and do something worse." Felix frowned, watching Howie depart.

"Claire, a word for our viewers. That was quite a dressing down you gave Mr. Newlander. Care to comment?"

"As a member of the City Council, I couldn't let it go by. All our doings in town are open for everyone to attend. We don't do anything behind closed doors. For Howie to say we were going to tax people is a downright dirty lie. I don't always agree with our mayor, but I can tell you he is honest and cares about this town as much as anyone, maybe more." She'd said enough. Felix would start to think she liked him.

"Thank you Mrs. Bennett. This is Jacqueline Ford in Chapel Springs. Back to you, Grover." She handed the microphone to her cameraman. "Claire, that was wonderful. You're a loyal friend." The reporter grinned. "And I'm glad you're one of mine." She walked away, chuckling.

An arm slipped around her shoulders. She knew it was Joel's without even looking and leaned against him.

"I'm proud of you, babe. Of course, our mayor might think you've gone sweet on him."

A laugh bubbled up and flubbered her lips. The idea was absurd. She turned and kissed Joel's cheek before he could react and pull away. "Thanks, I needed that to get the mad off me. Let's watch Sean finish up." And see if 'Lissa was still with him. If she was, she'd invite Sean to go to dinner with them.

"Joel, look at your daughter now." 'Lissa was up on the backhoe with Sean. She wore a hardhat, too.

"It seems to me like we'd better invite him to dinner."

Claire squeezed his hand. "I already thought of that. And it's perfectly natural, too, what with our past with Sean and him fixing the creek."

"Sure you don't want to ask Felix instead?" He darted away before she could slap him. As he loped off, Felix walked toward her.

"Uh, Claire? I, uh, well, umm, thanks." He turned and scurried away as fast as could, his belly bouncing.

Well, what do you know about that? She made her way over to the water's edge. Benson Creek was like most streams, deeper in some places and only a few inches in others. When they dumped the rock base into this new section, they used all sizes and shapes from small river rock to boulders. The water splashed and danced around the boulders in the shallower areas, creating music that made her want to sit and dangle her feet in the creek.

She glanced over her shoulder. Not too many people left, not enough to notice her, anyway. She took off her shoes, rolled up her pant legs, and sat on the bank. *Oh bother.* The sides here were too high for her feet to reach the water. Would the bank eventually wear down so someone who sat here years from now could dangle theirs?

"Not thinking of jumping, are you?"

Claire patted the ground next to her. "Hey, Patsy." Her BFF sat beside her. "I love the bubbling symphony the water makes and thought a good foot-splashing was in order."

"Knowing you, you'd probably slip and fall in. That's why I came to find you."

"You always have my back, don't you?"

Patsy's shoulder bumped Claire's. "Like you always have mine."

They sat in silence for a few moments. Blue jays flew from branch to branch in the trees lining the banks. Sean had worked hard to not disturb the tree roots. It hadn't been easy and they lost a few in the process, but the majority survived. Kind of like her and Joel. They'd survived the years of construction on their marriage.

"I happened to see our 'Lissa when she discovered Sean. I almost thought I heard fireworks go off." Patsy swung her feet, getting mud on her heels.

Claire pulled one leg up and tucked it beneath her. "You too? So, you think it's really something? Not just a 'Howdy, you're new in town' thing?"

"Girlfriend, Cupid gobsmacked your daughter."

"She said she'd been praying that God would take away her love for Bobby, if it wasn't His will for her. God sure took his time, though."

"Maybe he was trying to teach you to have a little faith."

"You're always right, aren't you?"

"Only when you benefit." Patsy swatted Claire's knee. "Poor Bobby. I hope he still comes around to believing one day."

"Me, too. But he's lost 'Lissa, if we're right about what happened today."

Patsy giggled. "Her expression reminded me of a movie when the knight in shining armor rides up and rescues the princess."

"It was something, wasn't it? She was more like Megan at that moment than she's ever been. Meg goes with her feelings, but 'Lissa has always thought everything out first."

Patsy rose, grabbed Claire's hand, and pulled her up. "Not this time. God's in control and gave her exactly what she needed to see the light."

Dusting off the seat of her pants, Claire glanced up. *I should have realized You would work it out perfectly.*

He always did.

Chapter 30

The alarm jarred Carin awake. The aroma of coffee and bacon helped clear the cobwebs. She and her sister had talked into the early hours of morning. It was a remarkable thing, sharing her heart with a sister. Her smile stayed in place as she showered, then dressed, and followed the scent of coffee.

Leanna sat at the breakfast table, reading the newspaper. She must have heard the shower, because two steaming coffee mugs sat next to her elbow. Carin pulled out a chair. "How is it you're up and clear-eyed?"

"I'm used to it. Scott and I are youth group leaders at church. We have the kids here from time to time for overnights."

"That sounds like ... work. It makes me tired."

Leanna chuckled. "Not everyone is cut out for it. The funny thing is, it was Julie who got us involved."

"You're kidding."

"Nope." Leanna got up. "Eggs?"

Her stomach growled. "Sure. Can I help?"

"You make the toast. So, Julie was working with Darcie's high school group at church. They needed more chaperones, and she talked us into it."

Carin opened the breadbox and pulled out a loaf. "Figuring you already worked with kids for a job, so you should spend your free time the same way?" That was nuts. Wasn't it? She popped the bread into the toaster.

"We love it." Leanna shrugged her shoulders, then dropped the eggs into the pan. "Until we have kids of our own. Then we'll probably be involved where our kiddos are."

Those would be very lucky children. "Speaking of kids, I need to head home after breakfast."

"I know. Scott left us the car. I'll drive you home."

Carin hated to make her do that drive but it was a wonderful thing to be able to count on a sister. Something stirred within her heart. She knew Leanna like she knew herself, and she loved her. How could that be? They hadn't known each other more than a few days.

As if reading her thoughts, her sister turned and their eyes met. "Maybe because we're so much alike, and the same blood flows in my veins as yours." Leanna grimaced. "And mine didn't have enough sleep to drive both ways today. I'm going to bring my PJs and spend the night with you. That okay?"

Carin couldn't begin to explain how okay that was. Her sisters had a lifetime of assuming on each other's love. It was all so new and amazing to Carin. "You know it is."

They hurried through breakfast and were on the road twenty minutes later. The ride home was filled with stories and laughter. Carin couldn't remember ever feeling so free with her thoughts and heart. Would she ever be close to Julie and Darcie? She'd like to, but Julie held the door shut so far.

Halfway to Chapel Springs, Leanna got sleepy, so Carin took over driving. The news about Wick had her wide awake. They arrived at the entrance to town just before noon. Carin parked Leanna's car in the lot, paid Mr. Pugh the parking fee, and they boarded the tram.

The driver, a high school student, looked familiar. She glanced at his name tag. Rick Lindstrom. "Are you Dee's son?"

"Yep." And a boy of many words. They chose seats just behind Rick.

"This is fun," Leanna said. "Ooh, I didn't notice those flowers before." She pointed to Claire's front yard as the tram pulled to a stop. It was awash with color. Petunias, impatiens, and daylilies bloomed in abundance.

A woman Carin didn't know climbed aboard and the tram started to move. A moment later, they arrived at Carin's driveway. They gathered their bags and hopped off after thanking Rick.

Leanna paused in Carin's front yard. "You should plant wildflowers.

It's a perfect setting for them."

Carin tried to see the yard through her sister's eyes. She was right. The large trees filtered the sunlight, and there were a lot of varieties that would grow well there. "I'll do it. JJ would have fun planting a garden."

Her phone rang and she dug in her purse for it. Wick's face popped up on the screen. A shot of adrenaline pulsed through her stomach. She glanced at her sister and mouthed "Wick."

She strove for a casual tone. "Hello?"

"Carin, it's me. I'd like to come up and see you and JJ."

"Why?"

"Do I need a reason? You're my wife and he's my son."

She needed to know, that's why. "The wife and son you stole from and abandoned."

"You gonna hold that over my head forever?"

She couldn't believe his gall. "That depends on you."

His exaggerated sigh blew loud in her ear. She yanked the phone away. "Come on, Carin. I'm coming up. I'll be there tonight." He clicked off, not waiting for her response. "He's coming up tonight. I'm glad you're here to lend me some strength."

"Do you think we need Scott to come up?" Leanna's frown touched Carin.

"No. Wick wouldn't hurt anyone, physically. And Ryan's next door."

"You don't think he wants to take JJ, do you?"

"No, he's not good with little kids. Poor JJ tries so hard to get his daddy's attention, but Wick just tosses him his iPad or brings him a new toy, usually something inappropriate. But that's what worries me, Leanna. I'm afraid JJ will be hurt again. When Wick left, the poor baby thought it was his fault."

Leanna dropped into an easy chair and dangled her legs over the arm. "It happens in all separations and divorces. Every child believes it's their fault."

"I was pretty adamant with JJ that it wasn't. I think he believed me." She hoped.

Carin's arms were loaded with dinner dishes when a key rattled in the lock. She whirled around and the stack wobbled, but Leanna steadied them for her.

"It's Daddy!" JJ jumped up and ran to the door, throwing it open. Edgar growled a low, threatening rumble in his throat.

Frowning, Wick walked right past JJ. "Why won't my key work? And tell that beast to shut up."

Carin stood beside Edgar and stroked his head. "First, this isn't your house. Secondly, Edgar's a good judge of character." JJ still stood in the doorway. Devastation covered his face like a layer of dirt. "And can't you greet your son?"

He glanced over his shoulder. "Oh, hey, JJ. What do you mean it isn't my house? I designed it. I'm your husband. Of course it's mine." He looked around, turning in a circle. "I knew you'd get the money to do it." He walked to the sofa and smiled his "woman-killer smile" for Leanna. "And who is this lovely lady? Do I know you?" He reached for her hand.

Too smart to be taken in by him, her sister pulled back. "I'm Carin's sister, Leanna Wallace."

"Sister? You don't say? So the stories in the paper are true?" He dropped to the couch and put his arm on the back. "I heard you came into a fortune."

The last part of Carin's heart broke. He wasn't here for her or JJ. He was here for more money. JJ hadn't moved from the doorway. She went to him and pulled him out on the porch. Wick didn't even notice.

"Love bug, would you like to go to Mikey's?"

"No, Mama. I want to stay with you, and I want to know why he doesn't love us anymore."

"You know it isn't your fault?"

"Yeah, I know that. And it isn't yours, either. It's his." JJ pointed at his father. His face was a mixture of dislike and sorrow. She put her arm around her little man and together, they walked back inside.

Wick had picked up the remote. He aimed it at the TV, but nothing happened. "Why doesn't this work? And buddy, get your daddy a beer, huh?"

That's it. "Wick, you're not welcome here. There is no cable or satellite because we can't afford it. You stole my money and walked out on us without a thought for your son or me. You lost your rights. Get out. Now."

Wick laughed. "Good one, babe." He got up and started toward the kitchen. Edgar jumped to his feet and faced Wick, growling, his teeth bared. "Call this dog off, Carin."

"He's never liked you. I should have paid more attention. Please leave."

The nice slid off Wick like melted popsicle off its stick. "Half of what you got is mine, Carin. You owe me."

"JJ, take your Aunt Leanna upstairs. I know she wants to call Ryan. Show her the phone up there." She turned back to Wick. "Owe you? We'll see how much you're owed when I show my lawyer the receipts of what you stole. Be glad I didn't press charges then." She couldn't have, but he didn't know that. "The fact that you abandoned your son and your wife for another woman has lost you all rights."

His tactics changed. She could almost see the wheels turn in his head. "Carin, I need money. I owe some guys."

She went to the door and opened it. "Try your girlfriend."

"She hasn't got any." He turned away, his eyes searching the room. Where had she dropped her purse? On the kitchen counter, but it wasn't there. Leanna must have picked it up. Carin blessed her sister's foresight. Had JJ and Leanna understood her reference to Ryan? She needed him.

Wick started towards the stairs, but Edgar beat him to it. There was no way he'd get around the dog. She spotted Ryan coming onto the porch and met him at the door. Her husband stopped his searching and stared at Ryan. He changed in an instant to racecar driver star. Walking toward Ryan, hand outstretched, he pasted on a big smile that didn't reach his eyes.

"Hey there. I'm Wick Jardine." He threw his arm around her shoulders. "Carin's husband. And you're ...?"

"Ryan Graves, next door neighbor." He looked to Carin. "You okay?"

"Yes, thanks, Ryan." She stepped out from under Wick's arm. "Wick was just leaving."

"Naw, I think I'll hang around. Carin's got a nice sister you might like, Graves. That is, if she's okay with a cripple."

JJ stood at the top of the stairs. "I don't like you anymore. Mr. Ryan is a war hero and lots nicer than you. Go away. Get out of my house." JJ stormed down the stairs. He tugged Edgar's collar and the dog followed him. They stopped in front of Wick. "Sic him, Edgar."

Edgar growled and took a step toward Wick, who took a step back. "Call him off, Carin."

"I couldn't if I tried. He's obeying JJ's command." She could get that dog to do anything, but she wasn't about to tell him that, either.

Edgar stepped closer. He bared his teeth. Wick backed up. "JJ, call him off. Now."

"No. I divorce you. You're not my daddy anymore. Go, Edgar."

Wick leaped out the door as Edgar haunched up, ready to spring. Ryan slammed the door and shot the deadbolt.

JJ brushed his hands together as if getting rid of dirt. "Good riddance to bad garbage." He came over to her and hugged her. "I'm sorry, Mama, but that had to be done."

Tears pooled in Carin's eyes. Her baby grew up in the last half hour. He shouldn't have done that for another ten years. Blast Wick Jardine.

"Don't cry, Mama. We got Auntie Leanna and Uncle Scott, and Mr. Ryan and Mr. Joel and Miss Claire. Why, we gots lotsa friends."

Ryan put his hand on JJ's shoulder. "You're a good soldier, JJ. I'm going to give you a medal for your bravery. We'll have the ceremony tomorrow."

"Wow, Mama, you hear that? I'm gonna get a medal for bravery."

"A well-deserved one. Where's Auntie Leanna?"

"Getting in the bathtub."

Carin laughed. Her sister must have figured the trouble was over, at least for tonight. But she couldn't help worrying that Wick would be back.

Chapter 31

C laire surveyed Patsy's dining table. It was beautiful, with candles, her BFF's best china, and her mother's silverware. She thought the dinner was a July fourth celebration, but a bit of mystery surrounded it. All their combined kiddos were there, with the exception of Adrianna, who couldn't make it from Nashville on such short notice. Claire talked to her every week, but that wasn't the same as seeing her. All her chicks were leaving the nest. At least the twins were home since graduation, but that wouldn't last for long.

"Hey, you. You're daydreaming." Patsy elbowed Claire.

"Oh, sorry. It's nice having everyone together and that got me thinking about Adrianna."

With Patsy's three kids and four of Claire's, plus the various spouses and significant others, along with Patsy's parents, there were twenty around the huge Kowalski dining room table. After Nathan said the blessing, Dane and Patsy exchanged glances. With a wink at Claire, Patsy nodded to her son. What was going on?

Oh! Dane pushed back his chair and rose. Oh, my. Claire gaped when he dropped to one knee beside Megan. *He's going to—* Everything blurred. As Dane formally proposed to Megan, Claire's memory banks released a scene of her and Patsy, each with a set of twins in matching double strollers, walking along the beach. They had dreamed about truly uniting their families with a marriage one day. And now it was happening.

As soon as Megan said, "Yes!" and threw her arms around Dane,

Claire jumped up and hugged first Dane, then Megan, and then Patsy. Dane's twin, Deva, embraced her brother, squealing. Then she grabbed Megan. "Now we're truly sisters!"

Joel stood, waiting to congratulate the kids. Poor man. His eyes looked bright with moisture. His girls were close to him. Was any boy-man going to be good enough for his babies? After he finally got a chance to shake Dane's hand and kiss Megan, he returned to his seat.

Claire leaned closer to him. "Are you pleased with her choice?"

His eyes warmed with happiness. "Yeah. Dane's almost like one of our own kids. I couldn't have chosen better."

Claire's gaze traveled to Megan's twin. "I'm crossing my fingers for another engagement in the not too distant future."

Joel glanced at their other daughter sitting next to Sean. Her hubby nodded. "She sure looks happy."

"She and Megan always talked about a double wedding." Claire took the casserole dish Charlie passed her and dished out a large helping of the fragrant enchiladas, Dane's favorite dish. "Yum." Patsy-cooked anything was Claire's favorite.

After the last enchilada had been devoured and the other serving bowls empty, they went to the family room to make some plans. Thank goodness Dane and Megan chose next May for the wedding. That would give her and Patsy plenty of time to plan the event. Megan, Deva, Costy, and 'Lissa talked bridal showers and poured over a magazine Deva produced. Apparently, her twin had taken her into his confidence.

Patsy brought the dessert and coffee into the family room. She'd baked an engagement cake, and Claire grabbed a few photos of the kids cutting it. These would make the opening page of a scrapbook. Through the viewfinder on her phone's camera, Claire stopped at Sean and 'Lissa. Her daughter's hand was entwined with his, and contentment was written all over her face. The fact that Sean wasn't uncomfortable with all the wedding talk spoke loudly to Claire. She had to blink away her happy tears.

She went into the kitchen to find Patsy and help with the clean-up. Joel came to find her as the last dish had been dried. Nathan stood behind him in the doorway.

"Good timing, your lordship."

Joel snickered. "I try to oblige. Hey, I wanted to tell you that Sean caught me alone for a moment and asked if he could formally court

'Lissa."

Nathan clapped Joel on the back. "That boy has his head on straight."

"Did he say when he was going to ask her to marry him?" Claire dried her hands on a dish towel.

"I didn't ask. That's up to him. What I did ask was did he love her and would he cherish her all his life?"

"And?" Patsy and Claire said simultaneously.

Joel grinned. "He promised he would. I think he's going to plan something special for the proposal."

"He's perfect for 'Lissa, isn't he?" Claire glanced at Patsy and Nathan. "Do you remember how he never got angry at Professor Sokolov when he called him 'Wingnut'? Sean never retaliated."

Joel glanced over his shoulder at all their brood in the family room. Sean hovered over 'Lissa. "He'll make a wonderful father, too." Patsy joined them in the doorway. "We've done something right, or God gave us a lot of grace," Joel said. "All the kids have turned out okay."

A chuckle rumbled deep in Nathan's chest. "Some would say dumb luck, but I agree with you, buddy. God's grace covers a lot."

"'Lissa is just like Claire." Patsy reached over and squeezed her hand.

"How's that?" Joel asked.

"I think I know what she means." Claire looked up at him then back at their daughter. "The moment I saw you, even back when we were what? Fifteen? I knew you were the one. I felt exactly like 'Lissa looked—head over heels in love."

Joel squeezed her shoulder. "We made a commitment when we married. A lot of kids these days don't understand that you have to work at love. The first glow fades. Then what? That's where commitment comes in, and that's what I wanted to see if Sean understood."

Good gravy, who was this man, talking about love? As if he just realized what he said, Joel's face turned pink.

"It's a little early to start that. They've been dating for only a few weeks." Claire and Patsy went back to the kitchen to put away the clean dishes.

Claire handed her a stack of dishes. "Have you heard anything more from Howie?"

"I got a flyer today. He's off the creek and onto the theater as his money wasting theme." She opened a drawer and withdrew a paper.

"This one is aimed at the property owners whose houses aren't their primary residence." She handed it to Claire. "He brings up the so-called lost opportunity to expand Chapel Springs by that hotel. He cites the mayor and council's lack of foresight."

"Why, the dirty devil." She opened the flyer. "This says the theater's a waste of money. 'The town would benefit more from a hotel. The taxes paid by commercial property outweigh the usefulness of a dilapidated, empty building owned by the town.'" She locked eyes with Patsy. "You'd better be watching my back closely, girlfriend, because I'm gonna give him an attitude adjustment with my bare hands. One his granny would have applauded."

"I'll help you. By the way, when are we getting into the opera house to see what's there?"

"Monday morning. Want to come with?"

Claire waited with Patsy and Felix while the carpenter, Ash Neville, removed the door from the theater. She was more than ready to get inside. It had taken an extra week to get the door off, since they had to order a replacement door once Ash saw what they had. What was the big deal? A door is a door, but Norm said they needed a steel one.

"I'm about done." Ash picked up a chisel and hammer. "Y'all can head on in. I'll get this new door on. Here's the key." He handed it to Felix.

"Let's go." Claire grabbed Patsy's hand, and they stepped inside with Felix trailing them. Only a little light filtered through the dirty windows in the lobby, leaving it gloomy. Ghostly even. "Felix, give me the flashlight."

"I don't have one. I thought you did."

"No, you were going to bring one. We can't see inside the theater without one, unless you want to turn on the power."

"Oh, bother. Stay here. I'll go get one."

Claire wandered the lobby. "It isn't too bad, Pat-a-cake. A good cleaning—" A loud thud came from the will call office. "Hello? Felix?"

Patsy grabbed her arm. "Let's get out of here."

"Don't be silly. Something just fell down in there." Claire walked over to the ticket window and peered through the opening. A box of papers lay upside down on the floor. The left window shutter blocked her view. Just as she pushed it back, something flew at her from an upper shelf. She screeched and jumped back, her heart pounding.

Patsy screamed and grabbed her hand. "Come on!" She pulled Claire out onto the porch where Ash stood dead still. His toolbox lay on the ground and the tools were scattered. His eyes bugged out of his pale face.

Felix took the steps two at a time. Claire didn't know he could move that fast. "What happened?"

"Something—or somebody—doesn't want us in here." Now that she was outside in the light, the whole thing seemed absurd. "That was no ghost, I'm sure of it." Wasn't she? She traded glances with Patsy. "Did you see anyone go through there?"

Patsy shook her head. "There was nobody in that lobby but you and me. At least, no one we could actually see."

"Ash? You see anyone follow us in?"

He didn't speak but shook his head.

Claire held her hand out to Felix. "Let me have that flashlight. I'm going to look inside the will call booth. It's probably a squirrel or something." She told him what had happened.

Felix harrumphed and didn't give her the torch. "I'll go first."

Well, what do you know about that? She stepped back and let him take the lead.

The approached the booth cautiously. Felix shined the light inside. It was empty, save for the box and papers on the floor. And something else. Below where her head had poked through the window lay a large wooden and iron weight from the old block and tackle system used on the stage. It had to weigh a good seven to ten pounds. If that had hit her … Claire moved back.

Her phone rang. She pulled it from her pocket and checked the caller ID. It was the gallery. Frowning, she answered it. Patsy watched her while Felix roamed the lobby, shining his light into all the corners.

"Where are you, Claire? Patsy isn't here either. Is something wrong?"

"Nothing's wrong, Mel. We're over at the theater, looking around."

"Oh. Did you find anything? Did you see the ghost?"

"No ghost. Did you need us for something?"

"Yeah. There's a delivery guy here with a package that you have to sign for."

"All right. I'll be there in a few minutes." She clicked off the phone and turned to Patsy. "I've got to—what's wrong?"

Her BFF was as pale as a sheet. Wide-eyed and trembling, Felix pointed to the far corner of the lobby. Claire turned. A woman, dressed in a flowing gown from a bygone era, hovered above the floor, swaying back and forth. Something about her looked familiar. A screech clawed its way up Claire's throat.

It was her Great-Aunt Lola.

Cold water trickled down her neck. Why was Aunt Lola giving her a bath in bed? She wasn't sick.

Aunt Lola! Claire's eyes snapped open and she struggled to sit up. Patsy held her down, and Felix had his cell phone out, talking to someone.

"Claire, be still." Patsy pushed her back down. "You fainted."

"I'm fine and I want to get back inside."

"Why? Do you want to faint again?" Felix put his phone away.

Patsy quit pushing her down and Claire scrambled to her feet. "I'm not going to faint again. I admit seeing that apparition caught me off guard. But I don't believe for a minute it was real. There's a perfectly good explanation for it. I keep telling all y'all that somebody doesn't want us in there. I want to know who and why."

Joel ran up the street toward them. Claire glared at Felix. "Why'd you call Joel?"

The mayor snorted. "You were out cold. I didn't know if you'd died of fright or just fainted. I mean, I've known you all my life and you never fainted. You had your Charlie in the backseat of Joel's old Mustang and never whimpered. What was I to think?"

Claire blinked and glanced at Patsy to see if she heard the same thing. Felix actually sounded worried.

"I thought you fainted." Joel glared at Felix. "You said she fainted."

Joel was so cute when he worried about her.

Felix snapped his suspenders. "She did. But she's okay now."

"I see that." Joel bent over and put his hands on his knees, catching his breath, then straightened. "What made you faint?"

Felix and Patsy answered in unison for her. "We saw the ghost of Aunt Lola." Only Felix said, "Lola Mitchell."

Joel's eyes snapped wide open. "What?"

Claire's rolled of their own volition. "You don't believe that, do you?" Was she the only person in Chapel Springs who didn't believe in this ghost?

"Not your Aunt Lola's, anyway. I know where she is. But the jury's still out on the subject." He crossed the porch and peered in the window. "So what do you think it is?"

"I've been trying to tell everyone that I think it's either Howie, bent on revenge against the town—" She joined Joel at the window. There was nothing in that lobby now. "Or it's the theater group in Pineridge. They stand to lose our rent money if we reopen our theater."

"Nobody is going in there again until we have the sheriff with us." Felix locked the now-installed door, held up the key, and then with a flourish, thrust it into his pocket. "I'm gonna call Jim Bob and see when he and Farley can come over. But right now, I've gotta go speak to the Kiwanis Club." He stomped down the steps.

Claire stood on the theater porch, arms akimbo. "In the middle of this, he has to go speak? I think our mayor really believes he saw a ghost." She sighed and turned. "Patsy, you don't really believe that do you?"

"No, but we saw something and it scared me witless."

"There's no use standing here," Joel said, taking Claire's hand. "I've got to get back to work. Don't you two have some art to create?"

"I want to wait. I've got to get in there and find out who's trying to stop us."

"You can't get in without Felix unlocking the door." He slapped his ball cap on his head. "He won't do that until Jim Bob comes, you know."

"Okay, okay. Come on, Pat-a-cake. I've got to sign for a package anyway. Let's go back to work." Joel headed down Church Street toward the marina. Claire and Patsy cut through the woods. After a couple of minutes, Claire pulled out her phone. "I'm calling Jim Bob. Maybe I can light a fire under him." She dialed and waited.

"Chapel Springs Police Department."

"Faye, where's Jim Bob?"

"Hey, Claire. He and Farley are out at Peterson's Gas Station. Vern's drunk again and overfilled a customer's tank."

"Tell him to call me."

"What's the complaint?"

"Just have him call." Patsy shook her head and frowned at her. "Hang on, Faye." Claire put her hand over the microphone. "What?"

Patsy held her finger over her lips and raised one eyebrow.

Oh. "Right." Faye was the town gossip, and if Claire didn't tell her, she'd let her imagination go wild and broadcast the results all over town. What was Jim Bob thinking when he hired Faye Eisler as his answering service?

Claire crossed her eyes at Patsy. "Faye, it's the old opera house. Somebody's trying to keep us out. I need Jim Bob and Farley to come with Felix and me to investigate."

"Did someone break in?"

"There's no evidence of that."

Faye gasped. "Do you think it's the ghost?"

Claire groaned. "No, I don't. If I did, I'd call Pastor Seth, not Jim Bob. Please, Faye, just have the sheriff call me as soon as he's got Vern locked up."

Chapter 32

The afternoon sun made Carin's eyes heavy. She'd been on her front porch since the school bus picked up JJ, trying to come up with a story. She chased a half dozen ideas, only to end up deleting them. Phone calls to a few select writers ended in frustration. Nobody was available to brainstorm with her. They were either on deadline—oh, how she wished—or not answering the phone. Not one had time for her. Even Lacey was at work. Carin closed the lid to her laptop and her eyes.

She must have dozed off, because the thud of something weighty landing on the porch awoke her with a start. Her laptop slid off her thighs and landed on its corner with a loud thunk. Oh, great. She bent over and picked it up.

"Hey there, sister." Darcie sashayed over to her. "Oh dear, you've got to be careful with those things. Did you break it?"

What was she doing here? "I don't know." Carin left it closed and slid it under her chair. She'd examine it later. "What brings you back to Chapel Springs?"

Darcie lowered herself into the chair next to Carin, smoothing the skirt to her blue and yellow sundress. She crossed her legs and slid one foot out of a strappy sandal, dangling it from her toe. The name "Choo" flashed in and out of sight as Darcie wiggled her foot. Even when Carin got her largest advance, she never forked out that kind of money for footwear.

"To visit my big sister, of course. Silly." Even her blue toenail polish matched the blue on her dress.

It was two o'clock on a Thursday. Didn't she work? And shouldn't she have called first?

"I decided I wanted to get to know you better, so I told my boss I needed to take two days vacay." She slid her foot into her sandal and stood. "I need to use the bathroom. I remember where it is." She picked up her purse and wandered inside. A second later she screamed.

Carin ran inside and saw her sister leaning against the wall with Edgar in front of her, tail wagging and drool dripping from his jowls. "Back, Edgar." She grabbed his collar. "You remember him from last time you were here. He remembers you, too. He won't hurt you."

Darcie's face screwed up. "But he's wet and nasty."

Oh, grow up. "Then grab a towel from that basket"—Carin pointed to the corner—"and carry it around with you."

Darcie sidled away from Edgar and flounced upstairs.

Carin sat on the bottom step for a moment to sort through her thoughts. What did Darcie really want? A better question, why was she so suspicious of this little sister? Because this one calculated everything, gauging its worth. Leanna saw it but Julie didn't. Did that come from being spoiled? Carin wasn't so sure.

She went back to the porch and picked up her laptop and her sister's heavy suitcase, which she set beside the stairs. How long did she plan to stay? In the kitchen, she laid her computer unopened on the island. Right now, she didn't want to know whether it worked or not. She glanced toward the stairs. Darcie was taking an awfully long time in the bathroom.

Carin went upstairs and tapped on the door. "Hey, you okay?"

"Hmm? Oh yeah, I'm fine. Just"—the door opened—"freshening up after the long drive."

Carin peered over her sister's shoulder. The medicine cabinet was ajar. A warning flag waved. Darcie was nosy. Still, she was a sister. Were they allowed to be nosy? Was that how sisters acted in each other's homes? Carin had no idea. A slow smile took over her lips. She'd give Darcie a chance.

"Come on, little sister. Let's get you settled then make a snack. Your nephew will be home soon." She stepped back and let Darcie precede her out the door. Before closing the door, she looked back over her shoulder and groaned inwardly. Darcie had left the sink with smears of makeup and dark eyeliner.

Downstairs, her little sister walked around the kitchen, opening drawers, running a finger along the countertop, and peering into cabinets. Carin tensed. "Can I get you something?"

Darcie turned to her, blinking long, false eyelashes. They made Carin want to blink. "Oh, um, how about some sweet tea?"

"Sure. Have a seat." Carin pulled out two glasses, filled them with ice and sweet tea, and set them on the island.

"With all your money, why don't you have high end furniture?"

If she only knew. "Those aren't to my taste, Darcie. These are Nana's—well, my adoptive grandmother's heirlooms. They mean a lot to me."

"Really?" Her sister's nose wrinkled. "If I had your kind of money, I'd buy all new stuff and sell this off. Or dump it."

Carin stretched her lips into what she hoped passed for a smile. "And in your own house, you'll be able to do that." JJ skipped up the driveway. "Here comes my little guy."

Darcie looked over her shoulder as JJ bounced in the door.

"Hey, Mama." He stopped. "Oh, hey. Who are you?"

Darcie stared at JJ for a moment. "I'm your aunt, but I'm really too young for you to call me 'Aunt,' so just use my name. Darcie."

Carin caught JJ's gaze and gave him a small nod. He shrugged. "Mama, can I go to Mikey's house? His mama said it was okay."

Darcie waved a hand in dismissal. "Don't stay on my account, kid."

No way was this sister going to override Carin's authority with her own son. "Darcie, please. JJ, do you have homework?"

He lowered his head. "Yeah." He looked up. "But Mikey and I can do it together."

She struggled not to laugh. "I've seen you two do homework together. Tell Mikey you'll come over as soon as you finish. I'll help you."

Darcie huffed and drained her glass. "What am I supposed to do while you help *him*?"

Frankly, my dear— "Darcie, if I'd known you were coming, I could have suggested a better time. Since you didn't give me any warning, you'll have to make do." It was like having two kids.

"Maybe I won't—" She stopped. "Never mind. I'll manage." She pulled out her cell phone and started tapping.

"Whatcha playing?" JJ stood on his tiptoes, trying to see the game.

"Candy Crush." Darcie turned her shoulder so he couldn't see.

What do you call sibling rivalry between aunt and nephew? "JJ, let's get your homework done."

While he got his books out, Carin moved to the small game table. JJ sat by her and opened his math book. She stared at the page. Math. Lovely. It was basic, but math gave her a headache, even if it was only adding or subtracting fruit. That was the problem. It was apples and oranges.

JJ frowned at the page. "I hate math, Mama."

"Me, too, love bug."

"I'm a whiz at it." Darcie abandoned her cell phone and stepped over to the table. "May I?"

That was a quicksilver mood change. "Sure." Carin slid over and let her sister help JJ. Within five minutes, the penny dropped and he "got it." He flew through the rest of the lesson. Darcie appeared quite pleased with herself.

JJ slammed the book shut. "Done!" He leaped out of his chair. "Can I go to Mikey's now? I can explain this to him now that Darcie helped me."

And Carin was grateful. "Yes, go ahead. Be home by suppertime."

Darcie observed his quick departure. When the door had shut, she picked up her cellphone again and turned it off. "Sister, for a kid, he's a wonderful little boy." She rose and crossed to the wall of photos by the stairs, touching each.

And? When he first came in, she wasn't interested in him. "Thank you."

"He looks a lot like I did as a baby." She sauntered over to the bookcase, perusing the titles and photos there.

"I noticed that when Dad showed me pictures."

Darcie stiffened ever so slightly. "Speaking of family, you should see how stingy Julie's become. Well, it isn't really Julie. It's Ted." She flounced down on the sofa. "He's just plain greedy. He won't let her lend me any money. It's not like they don't have plenty. It wouldn't hurt to lend me some against my trust fund. I mean ..." she pulled her feet up and tucked them beneath her. "I have to wait for years before I get any."

Her pout would draw a nine-point-five from an Olympic judge.

"She has the same restriction. So does Leanna."

Darcie peered at her through lowered lashes. Was she trying to be cute? "But you don't. You're old enough. Will you lend me a couple thousand? Please? My paycheck doesn't go far enough."

If she only knew. First of all, Carin's trust hadn't landed in the bank yet, so she had next to nothing in her checking account. "Why don't you have enough?"

Darcie's face lit up. She thrust out her foot. Blast, she'd had those shoes on the sofa.

"See? Jimmy Choos. Are they to die for? You don't get Jimmy Choos cheap, you know. Anyway, I need it for my rent."

"Darcie, you don't buy shoes like that if you don't have the money. That's exactly why Dad put the restriction on the trusts. He knew by the time a person reaches thirty, they've usually gained some smarts on how to handle money." Unless they're an egotistical racecar driver—or a spoiled brat. Maybe he should have set Darcie's at forty.

"Oh, fiddle. You just don't understand." Her sister's tone bordered on whining. JJ knew better than that.

"I'm sorry, I guess I don't. I also don't have the kind of money you seem to think I do."

Darcie waved that away. "Oh, don't give me that. Bestselling authors have scads of money. Plus you now have some of ours. I mean your portion. Of the trust."

"I need to use the bathroom. Excuse me." Carin went to the master bathroom. Help was needed. She called Leanna for a little insight.

"Do you need me to come up there, sugar?"

Always ready to help her, Leanna was fast becoming a *real* sister in Carin's heart. "Is there any way you can? I hate to ask you, but I'm lost here. I … I want to tell her to go home. At the same time, I'm trying to remember she's my sister, like you are. But this is really weird, Leanna. I'd never be friends with Darcie."

"Nor would I."

"Really?" Is that how sisters were? Could you choose whom to love?

"Really. I don't like Darcie one teensy bit. But I love her."

Sure, but they had history. "It's hard coming to this sister relationship as an adult. How can I love her if I don't even like her?"

"Hold on a sec." Leanna put her hand over the microphone and muffled her voice. "Okay. I'm coming up. Scott's going out of town, anyway. I'll see you tonight. Don't tell her I'm coming."

"I won't, but she's pestering the daylights out of me for money."

"Don't give her any, whatever you do."

"Don't worry. I've got her number."

Leanna's laughter rang as she hung up. Carin breathed a sigh of relief. Family drama was one thing she hadn't expected. As she descended the stairs, Darcie's voice reached her ears.

"Julie, you've got to come help me. She's stingier than Ted."

Carin debated whether to warn Darcie of her impending return but decided not to, just to see what her sister did. When Darcie caught sight of her, she screeched and her phone flew out of her hands and landed on the carpet.

"Darcie? What happened? Are you all right?" Julie's voice rose from the floor.

Baby Sister glared at Carin and bent to pick up her phone. "What'd you do that for? You scared me." She turned her back. "I'm here, Julie." Her voice broke and she sniffed.

Carin rolled her shoulders to ease the tension gathering her muscles into a knot. *What a drama queen.* She went to the fridge and pulled out hamburger meat. She'd make burgers for dinner.

"I don't eat red meat."

Carin counted to ten. "And I didn't know you were coming. This is what I have planned."

"Can't you change it?" Darcie laid her hand on Carin's shoulder. "For me?"

She'd play nice. "Honey, I don't have anything else defrosted, and I don't have much in the freezer."

Darcie brightened. "I know. We can eat out."

"I can't afford it." How could she make that more clear?

"Oh, fiddle. You've got pots of money. I've read about you. You're a *New York Times* bestselling author. They make millions."

She couldn't help it. Carin laughed. "You realize we only get a small portion of what the book sells for, don't you?"

Darcie's mouth twisted and her nose wrinkled. "That stinks."

"Not really. The publisher pays to have it edited, printed, distributed, and for promotional marketing."

"Yeah, yeah. You've sold a lot of books, though. I read an article."

Bully for you. "Those articles aren't always correct, Darcie. Especially if you're reading the magazines you find by the grocery store checkout."

"They do too tell the truth. You're just being like Ted. Stingy."

On her way back to the fridge, Carin sighed. This sister thing was a lot harder than people made out. "I'll make you a salad."

"That'll work. I love salad." She hopped into a chair at the island.

Chapter 33

Carin left Darcie in the great room putting away Candy Land while she put JJ to bed. She would have liked to have gone to bed herself. Darcie wore her out. When Leanna stayed with her, it had been easy, comfortable. But this—this had her tense and cranky.

"Amen." JJ jumped up and hopped into his bed. Carin tucked him in and kissed him.

"Sweet dreams, buddy. Do you know how much I love you?"

"Three teapots full."

"Try fourteen."

"That's a lot. And I love you forty-teen gatrillions."

"You win. That's the most I've ever heard of. Night, doodle bug. I'll send Edgar up."

"Night, Mama."

Carin turned out his light and went downstairs. She had just stepped into the great room when the doorbell rang. Darcie jumped up.

"I'll get it." Before Carin could protest, she opened the door. "Oh, it's you."

Leanna walked inside, laughing. "Love you too, Darce. Hey, Carin. Forgive the impromptu slumber party. Scott has an out-of-town seminar, and I decided I'd come see you instead of sitting home alone, feeling sorry for myself." She set her weekender down and kissed Carin's cheek. Then she gave Edgar his due with a good ruffling of his fur.

"You're the best dog in the world, Edgar." He rewarded her with a doggy kiss, after which Leanna plucked a towel from the basket and wiped her face, laughing.

"JJ will be excited to see you when he wakes up." Carin hugged Leanna, whispering, "I'm so glad you're here." That's when it hit her. She loved Leanna. Really loved her. Why? What made her love one sister and not another? Leanna was lovable, there was no denying that. Julie hadn't displayed one lovable trait. Carin would watch Leanna with her and see how she did it.

Darcie watched their exchange. "JJ was glad to see me, too. I helped him with his math homework."

"You always were the math whiz." Leanna joined Darcie on the sofa. "That's why we wanted you to go to college."

"I hate school. If I could have taken just math and art, it would have been okay, but they made me take English. I already speak English, for pity sake."

Math and art? What an odd combination. "I was just the opposite, Darcie." Carin went to the stove and turned on the burner beneath the tea kettle. "I loved all my English and writing classes but hated the math." She pulled out the tea caddy. "Who'd like tea?"

Leanna's hand went up. "Me, please."

Carin looked at Darcie, waiting for her answer.

"I liked the computer classes, too." Darcie inspected her fingernail polish. "But I have more fun working at the gallery. My boss adores me, and I meet some cool people."

Okay, no tea. "You met my friend, Patsy Kowalski. Have you seen her paintings? She's very talented."

"I've seen a couple of them. Oscar—that's my boss. Oscar Savage. Isn't that a great name? He's got two or three of hers in our gallery." Darcie pulled out her phone and focused on email, a game, or something. "I'll be outside." She unfolded herself from the sofa and went out onto the deck.

Leanna grinned and came into the kitchen. "Don't let her bother you. If she's not the subject of conversation, she's not interested. You lost her at Patsy."

"Don't her friends see through that?" The teakettle whistled and Carin poured the water over the teabags in their mugs.

Leanna moved the sugar bowl next to their cups. "That's the

strangest part. They don't seem to." She went to the fridge and opened it. "Maybe they're all that way."

"Milk's in the door."

Carin set out two napkins on the island, and Leanna plopped the milk carton next to them. This sister was comfortable. Carin knew her. Could it be because they were so much alike? She added milk to her tea but shook her head when Leanna pushed the sugar bowl toward her. Her sister shrugged and added two heaped spoonsful to her tea, making Carin's teeth hurt.

Leanna laughed. "Well, I see we have one area where we aren't exactly alike."

Carin pulled out the stool next to her sister and sat down. For a few minutes, they sipped their tea in a comfortable silence. On the deck, Darcie paced. She was on her phone, one hand sweeping with broad gestures.

"I'm really trying to love Darcie, but she makes it so hard." Carin wrapped both hands around the warm mug.

"I've often wondered what her friends see in her. She's completely self-centered. She can pitch a hissie fit over the silliest things, and you never know what will set her off. Still, it's not all her fault. Daddy told you how everyone spoiled her. She honestly thinks it's her due."

"Come on. Are you saying she really believes that?" Carin didn't buy that. Darcie was sweet on herself. "She's so stuck up, she could drown in a rain storm."

Leanna didn't seem to mind the insult or maybe she didn't see it as one, since after all, it was the truth.

"That she is. I don't know, Carin. Maybe she does realize it but still wants all the attention. I've never spent a lot of time trying to figure her out. She's who she is."

"Well, it's going to take a miracle for me to love her. She annoys me."

Leanna picked up a spoon and stirred another half spoonful of sugar into her tea. "If I were in your shoes, I'd feel the same." She reached over and gave Carin's hand a squeeze. "Sometimes, love is a choice. We may not like Darcie's personality or her behavior, but because she's our sister, we choose to love her."

"I'm going to have to chew on that for a while." Carin glanced at the wall clock. It was nearly eleven o'clock. "How about we all call it a night?"

Leanna agreed and called Darcie to come inside. After everyone was settled in their rooms, Carin checked on JJ. Edgar lifted his head when she entered. "It's okay, boy," she whispered. She patted his big head, then checked JJ's covers and kissed his forehead.

Once in her own bed, she lay there awake, mulling over Leanna's comment about choosing to love. With Leanna, it had been easy. To begin with, she was likable. Julie and Darcie didn't have one likable trait, as far as she'd seen. Carin hadn't made a conscious choice to love Leanna—it simply happened.

This sister thing was a maze that made little sense. She could choose all she wanted, but she doubted she'd ever love Julie or Darcie.

Chapter 34

C laire rounded the corner onto Church Street and stopped. Up
ahead, a crowd had gathered in front of the theater and spilled
over onto the church lawn. Where had all these people come
from? She jogged toward the mob. Jim Bob's car was parked in front
and he stood beside it. She had wanted to get in the building with him
and Felix. But who—Claire frowned. Faye Eisler stood near the theater
steps. Of course. She should have known.

"Here's Claire now." Faye pushed the people back so she could
pass through. Couldn't Jim Bob arrest her for interfering with police
business? Or at least for gossiping about it? She glared at Faye and took
the steps two at a time with Jim Bob following.

Felix met them at the door. "Jim Bob, you go first. Claire and I will
be right behind you. And watch out for the ghost. Claire, stop rolling
your eyes. You saw it too."

Had she rolled her eyes out loud? "Felix, that was no ghost and you
know it. Somebody made an image of Aunt Lola and hung it there. Or
they used a projector or something. That's what we're here to find out."
She grabbed Jim Bob's elbow. "Do you have your fingerprinting stuff?"

"Farley's bringing it, but I don't see how we'll get fingerprints from
a ghost."

Claire balled her fists at her side and looked heavenward, growling.
Had everyone in this town gone ghost-crazy? "I hope you're kidding,
Jim Bob. Felix, do you have a flashlight?"

Felix nodded as he unlocked the door then stepped aside for Jim

Bob to enter first. Claire followed right behind him, but he was taking his good time, shining his flashlight in all directions before moving ahead.

"Felix, lock the door," Jim Bob said. "I don't want some thrill seeker coming in and messing with our investigation."

Felix stood his ground and didn't move. "But what if the gho—"

"Just lock it." Jim Bob put his hand on his holster. "I've got us covered."

Really? If he believed in the ghost, what good was a gun? Claire came close to laughing out loud but held it. "Over there was where we saw whatever it was." She shined her light to the far corner of the lobby. "Your light's stronger. Shine it over there." He had a large LED police light.

He did, but the apparition was no longer there. She knew it wouldn't be. Whoever did this had taken it out. They weren't dumb, that was for sure.

She tapped her foot. "How long are we going to stand here? Let's get moving."

"Give me a minute to look around."

She bit back a retort and followed him. After he studied every bit of the lobby, he moved toward the far corner. He shined his light from the ceiling down. Something caught the light. What—

"Look," Claire aimed her light and reached out, picking up the end of a long string. "At least we know how the apparition was hanging above the floor. Fishing line."

Jim Bob tugged the line. "It's either caught or tied or something." He moved the light up its length. "Well. Look at that." He pointed the beam at the ceiling where a small hole about the size of a quarter could be seen, and the fishing line disappearing through it. "How do we get upstairs?"

Claire used to go up there with Aunt Lola. She was only seven or so the last time, but the memory hadn't faded. The world of theater and Aunt Lola was magical to a little girl. "Over here." She led them up the stairs. "That door to the left leads to the balcony. This one goes to the rest of the floor."

"What's up here?" Felix asked.

"Office, dressing rooms, prop room. The mechanical room's on the other side of the stage. There's a rear set of stairs. Archives are in the attic." Claire thought she remembered another door somewhere, too, that Aunt Lola showed her. Where was it? That memory wasn't surfacing.

Jim Bob aimed the light at the floor ahead of them while keeping his hand hovering over his holster. Felix gripped a nightstick. Did Jim Bob give it to him? Why didn't she have anything other than her flashlight?

They slowly climbed the stairs. At the top, Jim Bob paused. "Where would that corner of the lobby be? I'm turned around."

Claire spent a good bit of her early childhood in this place. She and Patsy used to run all over while her great aunt rehearsed. "It's this way. Come on." She took the lead to the first hallway on her left.

They crept along the ragged carpet, keeping close to the wall. Claire almost giggled. Their three lights bobbed around, up and down, right and left. All they needed to complete this circus was the ghost on horseback.

When they reached the last door, Jim Bob pushed it open cautiously. The room was empty. Jim Bob crossed to the corner and squatted. "Look at this. You were right, Claire. This ghost is flesh and blood."

On the floor was a spool of fishing line and a small mirror on the end of a stick. Claire picked it up. It had been glued onto a thin dowel, and the back of it had been painted black.

"Claire!" Jim Bob's growl startled her, and she dropped the mirror. "If there were any prints on that, you just compromised them. Don't touch anything."

"Sorry. I forgot about that. This little mirror looks familiar, but I'm not sure where I've seen it."

"I know." Felix held a baggie open for Jim Bob to drop it in. "Kelly Appling sells them at her gift shop. They're to set little figurines on so they show up better." He glanced up at her and Jim Bob, whose mouth was quirked in a smirk. "Eileen told me about them. She's got some at her house."

"Well, I don't think Eileen's our ghost."

"And it sure isn't Kelly." Claire studied the mirror. "As the director, she's got a stake in the theater opening."

Jim Bob took the baggie from Felix and stuffed it in his pocket. What was he planning to do if they found something big? He lumbered to his feet. "Let's keep looking."

They searched all the dressing rooms on the second floor with no results. "Where is that prop room?"

"Here." The last door on the left stood ajar. Claire stepped back for Jim Bob to open it. The creaking hinges raised the hairs on Claire's arms. Felix glanced at her with trepidation in his eyes. She swallowed.

Stop it! Claire gave herself a mental shake. All this ghost talk would make anyone jumpy. She turned her light to the right while Jim Bob moved to the left. Double-sided racks of costumes lined the right side of the long room. Claire moved down the line, touching some. There was the Peter Pan costume. She stopped.

Memories whisked her away to the balcony of the opera house. She was five years old. Great-Aunt Lola brought her. Patsy had the chicken pox and couldn't come. Claire had stood at the edge of the balcony in complete belief. When Peter asked them to believe, she almost jumped off the balcony, certain she could fly. Only Aunt Lola's hand grasping the hem of her dress stopped her. Oh, how she missed her flamboyant great-aunt.

"Claire? You find anything?"

"No, Jim Bob." Only memories. "Not yet." She moved on.

Felix rummaged through a trunk across the room. "Nothing here."

Claire came to the end of the clothing racks and turned to go back up the other side.

Someone touched her in the dark.

She screeched.

Lights swept over her and footsteps thundered.

Oh. It was a costume on a dressmaker's form. Jim Bob and Felix reached her side. "Sorry. I didn't see it in the dark and ..."

Felix had his hand to his chest and scowled. "Y'all scared the dickens outta me, Claire."

"Yeah, well, you would have been startled, too."

"All right, let's keep looking. This isn't a matter of ghosts." Jim Bob pulled his gun from its holster. "Let's stick together, now."

They continued to search. There were long shelves of props, things someone could use to concoct ghostly apparitions. They came to the end of the room without finding a thing. Claire stopped and studied the last shelf. If she were going to hide things, where would she do it? She shined her light beneath the bottom shelf. A large, dark lump lay next to the wall.

"Jim Bob, look here."

He clambered down to his knees. The man had to stop eating so much fried catfish and hush puppies. He reached under the shelves and pulled out the lump. When he unwrapped the clothing, Claire stared in disbelief. A hoodie, its ragged sleeves tied around a shirt with an equally frayed collar. Her stomach sank.

She knew that shirt.

"Aw, it's just more costume stuff." Jim Bob tossed it aside. "Where's the attic stairs?"

The door to the attic was on the other side of the theater. Claire led them to it. "I'm going back to the costume room. There's something I'd like to find."

Felix glanced at Jim Bob. "You think that's okay?"

"Yeah. There's nothin' in there."

Claire returned to the clothing they'd found. She picked up the shirt and tucked the bottom of it into her waistband, then lowered her shirt over it. Now, she only had to think of a way to confront its owner and find out where that owner's brains were. What was the point?

Claire waited in the hallway until Jim Bob and Felix returned empty-handed.

"Are there any other floors? What about a basement?"

Of course. The basement. "The old scene shop is in the basement."

Felix pulled on his ear. "What's that?"

"It's where the carpenters build the scenery." Claire led them to the door where the basement stairs were. She opened it, and a musty blast of air assaulted their noses.

Felix sneezed. He pulled out a handkerchief and breathed through it. "I'm allergic to mold."

The stairs ended in a large, open space filled with wood. Against one wall stood rolls of rotting muslin. They'd have to get rid of that. It was a shame, too. Still, they didn't use muslin flats anymore. They used a thin sheet of wood. They called it something Hawaiian, like a luau.

"So they made all the scenery down here, eh?" Jim Bob toed a stack of lumber.

"They used to make a frame, then stretch muslin over it. Now they use something different, uh—"

"Luan. It's called luan," Felix said from behind his hankie.

That was it. Huh, how'd Felix know that? Jim Bob and Felix flashed their lights around, but nothing could hide down here.

"Let's go. There's nothing of interest." Jim Bob trudged toward the stairs. She and Felix trailed him.

"Did you see anything suspicious?" she asked Felix.

"I'm not sure. Never having been in the place, it's hard to know if anything was missing or shouldn't be here." He glanced up at Jim Bob's back. "He thought it might, though. Said it looked like the dust had been disturbed. What do you make of this, Claire?"

"It's definitely a living being. What I can't figure out is how they're getting in. There's only the main door and the two side fire exits. Those can't be opened from the outside. Only the main door, and you know how that was. *We* couldn't even get in." And those fire exits had been padlocked from the inside and boarded over when they closed the theater.

"It's got me stumped." Felix resettled his ball cap. "It's like they were a ghost or could vaporize or … somethin'."

They reached the lobby and went outside. The people stopped their chatter and drew close to the porch to hear what Jim Bob had to say. Carin Jardine was on the sidewalk with her sister, Leanna. Claire slid into the crowd and toward them.

"Show's over, folks. There's no ghost. There has been, however, somebody in there, up to mischief. I'll be staking out the place until I catch the culprit." Jim Bob and Felix walked down the steps to the sheriff's car.

"Hey, Carin, Leanna. What brings you out to this madhouse?"

"We were heading out for a walk when we saw the crowd." Carin glanced sidelong at her sister. "Curiosity got the best of us."

Leanna nodded. "So, no ghost?"

"No ghost." Reluctant to say more, Claire excused herself. "I need to get back to the gallery. Have a nice walk."

Whirling around, she hugged her waist. Blasted shirt was starting to slip. She hurried back to *The Painted Loon* and into her workroom. She needed time to think.

Chapter 35

Carin stared at Claire's retreating back. "That was odd. She's usually more chatty. I wonder what they saw inside." It was a bit nerve-racking to think somebody had broken into the theater. Chapel Springs was free of any real crime. It was one of the reasons she'd started to relax. Now, if she could only find a story. Since the ghost seemed to have flesh and blood, even that idea dried up. Not that she had really given it a lot of thought.

"Come on, let's walk. Want to go through the woods?"

"I'd love to." Leanna bent to tie her sneaker. "We don't have enough woods left at home to really hike through. They're all broken up with subdivisions." Rising, she inhaled deeply. "I love it up here."

"I'm beginning to. It's still not really home to me yet, though. Maybe once I find my next story ..."

"Why? What does finding a story have to do with feeling at home?"

Carin kept walking. The crunch of dry leaves beneath her feet reminded her of her arid creativity. Her sister was right. What did a story have to do with home? Because she equated home with success. "That's dumb."

"What is?" Leanna looked at her expectantly.

Had she said that out loud? "Me. I've been thinking of Buckhead and success as home. But I'm starting to realize, I think, that home is where you decide it is. You make a decision to put down roots and make friends." She stopped and turned to face her sister. "Does that make sense?"

"Of course. You've made friends. You met Daddy here. And you spent your summers here as a kid. It should feel like home."

Carin started walking again. "But that doesn't solve my problem of not having a story. I'm afraid I've got a bad case of writer's block."

Leanne gaped at her. "Carin, you're kidding, right? Girl, you're living a story."

They came out of the woods and into Carin's backyard. Before she could question Leanna, her sister pointed to the large windows.

"Julie's here."

What was she doing here? Darcie must have called her. Maybe she'd had a chance to calm down and was ready to be a sister. Carin could only hope. "Let's go."

When Carin opened the door, Julie startled and jumped, dropping her glass of sweet tea. The glass didn't break, but tea and ice cubes flew everywhere. What had she been doing that made her so jumpy?

"Oh! Don't sneak up on me like that."

"Julie, it's Carin's house and we only opened the door." Leanna hurried to the kitchen and grabbed a towel. Carin got the mop from the mudroom.

"Well, y'all scared the fire out of me."

What did she feel guilty about? And— "Where's Darcie?"

Julie blinked. "Darcie? Oh, yes. She went up to her room to get something."

Carin hated to be suspicious, but with Darcie asking for money, and Julie showing up uninvited, her thoughts naturally went to the devious side. "I see. Well, since y'all are here, I suppose I'd better figure out something for lunch." What she could give them to eat, she didn't know. She needed to shop. Had the trust money check cleared yet? The bank said even with it being a cashier's check, they needed a few days for one that large to post to her account.

Leanna met her by the fridge. "Let's go out. Dutch treat."

Carin checked the fridge and nodded. "It'll be slim pickin's here. Unless you like lettuce sandwiches." She made a face.

"Hey, Darcie, get down here. We're going out to lunch." Leanna turned to Julie. "What do you feel like?"

Julie shrugged. "I don't know. What's around here?"

"There are several restaurants." Carin pulled out a business directory card. Chapel Springs wasn't big enough for a directory book. "There's *Jake's Rib Cage*, a gourmet burger place, *Pasta Bowl*, and the *Krill Grill*, a seafood place. Then there's *Dees 'n' Doughs* for sandwiches."

Darcie ran down the stairs. "Pasta's my favorite. Do they have pizza, too?"

"I guess. I haven't eaten there." Carin put the card back in the drawer.

"Why not?" Julie asked.

Darcie rolled her eyes. "She claims not to have any money."

Julie looked Carin up and down. "That's ridiculous. Look at this house."

"Julie!" Leanna shaded her eyes with one hand and lowered her head. "You're embarrassing me with your judgmental assumptions. Carin was left the house by her adoptive grandmother. She didn't buy it."

"Some people have all the luck." Darcie's nose wrinkled.

"Luck? Oh yeah, you must mean the kind of luck when my husband walked out on me and stole what money I had. JJ and I were evicted because he didn't pay the lease. He was paying for his mistress's apartment instead. Or maybe the kind of luck when I arrived here to find he'd stopped paying the contractor. I came to a gutted downstairs and no working bathroom. Yes, you're right. All that luck was mine." Carin tossed her keys to Leanna. "I've lost my appetite. Y'all go on to lunch without me."

She turned, walked upstairs, and into her room. How was she ever going to love Julie? For that matter, what about Darcie? That girl was spoiled beyond redemption. She didn't even want to change. Carin slumped to her knees beside her bed.

"I've tried, God, and I lost it. I'm sorry, but Julie and Darcie are so ... so ... *trying*. Are you sure I can't just claim Leanna?"

Three days.

What?

You've only had three days with your sisters.

Oh. She turned her legs and sat on the rug. She chose this room because outside the window lived seven different species of trees. It was like sleeping in a tree house. God created those trees, each with different colors of green. Some kept their leaves year round while others shed theirs. How could anyone, seeing them, deny that God created all that?

"I think I see what you're telling me. It took you seven days to create the world, right?"

You're catching on.

Carin smiled and her anger cooled. "All right. I'll give them some more time. But you're going to have to help me."

When her sisters got home from lunch, the atmosphere had cleared. They had gone shopping and sported bags from *Sunspots*. Swimsuits, according to Leanna. They wanted to take advantage of the lake.

Carin was glad but remained on guard. She wasn't going to let Julie or Darcie spoil her time with Leanna. Nor would she let them bait her. She set her weather vane to sunny disposition.

Shortly after two o'clock, the front door burst open and JJ ran in, trailed by Mikey. "Hey, love bug. Your aunts are all here. Isn't that fun? Mikey, call your mama and ask if you can go to the beach with us and stay for supper. Tell her I'll see you home after that."

"Oh, boy!" JJ high-fived Mikey. While his buddy called his mama, JJ scurried to hug each of his aunts. Leanna teased him and kissed his cheek. Julie appeared to have lost her aversion to him once she discovered who Carin was—or wasn't. She accepted his hug and returned it. Darcie fist-bumped him, which made her baby giggle. JJ might be the catalyst they needed.

"My mama said it's okay, Miss Carin." Mikey hopped from one foot to the other in excitement. "Can we ask Mr. Ryan to go with us? I saw his car a minute ago. He likes to fish with us."

"Yeah, can we, Mama? Please?"

How would Julie and Darcie react to Ryan? "Do y'all mind if my neighbor joins us?" Carin hoped they'd behave and not be rude. She'd better prepare them. "He's a wounded warrior."

Julie shrugged, clearly uninterested.

"Is he young?" Darcie asked. That got Julie's attention.

"He's about my age, early thirties."

"Hmm, it might be interesting to meet him." She fluffed her hair. Julie hadn't taken her eyes off Darcie. Now, she smiled at Carin.

"Sure, invite him along."

Carin prayed he'd serve as a buffer, or at the very least, keep the boys occupied so they didn't hear any arguments. "Okay, I'll call while I get changed."

Ryan agreed. She'd told him about her sisters last week, anyway, so he wasn't without a clue.

"I'll bring the fishing rods and all my boyish charm."

Carin laughed. "Thanks, buddy. I hate to foist the boys off on you, but I don't want JJ or Mikey subjected to any arguing. I don't know Julie or Darcie well enough yet to know when I've hit one of their hot buttons."

The women converged in the great room. Julie wore a red and blue bikini under a white shirt that looked as if it belonged to Ted. She carried a red, floppy straw hat and one of the large beach towels Carin had left stacked in the hallway. Leanna was adorable in a turquoise one-piece suit with a wrap-around sarong. She'd grabbed a matching towel, as had Darcie, who outshone them all in a yellow, polka-dot bikini and a white straw hat with yellow daisies on the band.

"If y'all are ready, let's go." Carin crossed her fingers and opened the side door.

They met the boys in the driveway with Ryan. She had to give Julie points. She was charming and didn't react at all to Ryan's missing arm. Both Leanna and Scott had met Ryan last time they were here and hit it off. It turned out they had mutual friends in education.

It was Darcie who made Carin smile. She slid between the boys and Ryan. "Carin told us she had a neighbor, but she never said you were so handsome."

Ryan's ears turned red. Boy, was he in for it.

JJ, skipping backwards, looked at Darcie like she had two heads. "He's not handsome. He's Ryan."

Her son had a future in diplomacy. They all laughed and within a couple of minutes, crossed beneath Sandy Shores Drive. They walked out of the tunnel and onto the beach.

Leanna turned around in a circle. "It's absolutely gorgeous here. This has to be the most beautiful lake I've ever seen. And with a sand beach, too. Hmm-hmm." She flipped her towel and it floated down then twisted. Carin helped her lay it straight then put hers out.

"Where do y'all fish?" Darcie angled her hat on her head so one corner hid her right eye.

Ryan and the boys all pointed to the dock by the boat launch. "Over there. Did you want to come?" Ryan sounded dubious and the boys didn't look pleased.

"Of course I want to come." Darcie never caught the boys' displeasure nor Ryan's surprise. She was on pursuit. "I've never been fishing."

For fish anyway. JJ threw his aunt a disgusted look and he and Mikey stalked off. Ryan was quick to catch up with the boys, and Darcie followed. Even Julie chuckled.

"She's very focused when there's a man around."

Carin wasn't surprised. "Does she bother to find out if the man is married?"

"Don't be catty." Leanna swatted her hand.

Somehow the rebuke didn't bother her, coming from Leanna. It was natural. "Sorry, I really didn't mean it. I'm actually in a bit of awe. I've never seen anyone like her."

Julie chuckled. "Our Darcie is a natural flirt. Sometimes I wonder if she'll stop flirting when she finally marries." She sighed. "I hope she does. Otherwise, it could spell disaster for her."

"Does she flirt with every man?"

"Even our husbands, right Jewels?" Leanna handed Carin a bottle of sunscreen. "Would you do my back?"

"Yes, even them. She's not trying to steal them, though." Julie was quick to defend Darcie. "It started when she came to live with Ted and me. Daddy was in a bit of depression, so I took her. She was fourteen. Old enough to begin experimenting with her feminine wiles. Ted understood and told her to save her flirting for boys and leave the 'old men' alone." Julie made air quotes.

"Scott wasn't so gracious." Leanna took the sunscreen and squirted some on Carin's shoulder blades. "He told her to cut it out. Period. I think he scared her."

"I'm sure Ted wanted to do the same, but since she was living with us, he kept quiet. I had a talk with her and explained a little beyond the birds and bees. It worked, because she left our husbands alone after that. Mostly. Like I said, it's natural, not intended. It's just her way."

And a cheetah's a natural carnivore. "I hope she leaves all married men alone." Carin stretched out, letting the sun warm her back.

"She's not like that. You don't know her, so don't judge."

These sisters were grown women, yet Julie acted like a jealous teenager if Carin said anything about Darcie. Why? Should she come out and ask her? Leanna nudged her elbow and closed her eyes, giving the slightest shake of her head.

Carin caught her meaning and would leave it for now. She laid back and closed her eyes. Strains of music from an oldies station floated over them. The tension began to leave as the sun warmed her. She must have dozed off, because she startled awake with Darcie whining and her skin prickling from the sun. It wasn't too much longer until the boys came back, holding high a line with a fish attached. She sat up.

"Who's the lucky fisherman?"

"Mikey was." JJ grinned. He and Mikey were such good buddies, JJ didn't mind that it wasn't him. If only Julie and Darcie could be like that.

"Mr. Ryan said we need to get it in the 'frigerator." JJ started for the house.

"Wait up, love bug. We're coming." She picked up her towel. "Y'all can stay down here for a while, if you want. I'll take the boys up."

"I'm coming," Darcie said.

Poor Ryan. "You sure?" Carin tried to rescue him.

"I'm sure, Carin. Jewels? You coming?"

"Yes, dear. I'm coming. I'll catch some sun from the deck."

Carin waited but neither of them asked Leanna. She bent down and tickled Leanna's ear. "You coming, sis?"

Leanna beamed and picked up her towel.

Chapter 36

Claire sat in the workroom, staring at the shirt in her hands. She didn't show it to Jim Bob or Felix. Not yet. First she had to know why. Why would she try to sabotage the theater? What did she have to gain by it? It made no sense whatsoever. As much as she hated it, she would have to confront her.

"Patsy?" This was going to be harder than she imagined.

Her BFF's head poked out from behind her easel. "Hmm?"

"We've got a problem. Can you stop and come over here?"

"Sure." A brush splashed into a jar of terpenoid. A second later, Patsy approached her.

Claire held up the shirt. "Do you recognize this?" She held her breath.

"Sure. It's Mel's. Why do you have it?"

Claire's heart sank. She had hoped she was wrong. "I'm afraid Mel is our theater ghost. We found it inside the prop room, stuffed underneath some shelves."

"What did Jim Bob say?" Patsy fingered the shirt's collar.

"He thought it was an old costume. I didn't enlighten him. What I can't figure out is why? What would make her do it?"

Patsy's face was a study of confusion. "Are you saying she's trying to stop us from reopening the theater?"

"That's how it appears. The other thing I can't figure out is how she gets in and out. There's no other access but the front door." Claire folded the black shirt.

"What about the fire exits?"

"There isn't even a keyhole in them. No handle. No way *in*. Only out. And Jim Bob checked. They hadn't been pried open."

Patsy moved to the small table beside her easel. "What do you think her parents will have to say about this?" She picked up a rag, dipped the corner in her jar of terpenoid, then scrubbed the paint from her cuticles with it.

"That's what really worries me. I have a feeling her stepmother will wash her hands of Mel. I don't know anything about her father." She slid the shirt into a drawer. "Has she said anything to you about him or any other family?"

"No." Patsy slumped onto her painting stool, her legs stretched out in front of her. "What are you going to do?"

"Right now, nothing. I'd really like to return to the theater without Jim Bob or Felix."

"Do you think that's a wise move?"

Claire shrugged. "Since we know who the 'ghost' is, why not? There's no danger."

"You can't be sure about that, Claire."

"Oh, come on. Mel's about as dangerous as Shiloh. She just looks that way, and you know as well as I do, that's just a defense."

"What if she's not alone in it?"

Had Pat-a-cake lost her marbles? "Have you ever seen her with anyone other than us?"

"I guess not. But we don't know what she does at night."

"Until now, it hasn't been any of our business. That's changed." Claire drummed her fingers on the counter for a moment, taking the time to form a plan. "I've got it. I'm going to follow her tonight when she leaves work. I'll take 'Lissa's car and leave it at the parking lot. When her stepmother picks her up, I'll follow them."

Patsy didn't say anything right away. She tilted her head, squinted, and cast her gaze back and forth. She was in think mode. "So, you're going to follow her home. And do what? Spend the night parked outside her door? How long can you keep that up?"

"Do you have a better idea?" Claire didn't want to confront Mel without more evidence.

"I guess not. But what are you going to tell Joel?"

"That's the worm in this apple." She mulled it for a moment, then brightened. "If I tell him I was *going* to try to steal the key from Felix and get into the theater by myself, but then thought of *following* Mel instead, maybe he'll think this way is safer."

Patsy didn't look convinced. "Be careful, girlfriend. I've got an uneasy feeling about this."

"I've decided to talk to him before I do anything. I'm pretty sure I can talk him into letting me follow her."

They spent the rest of the afternoon working, but Claire's mind was never far off Mel. She'd grown to care for the girl a lot. And Mel was beginning to shed some of her Gothness. Still, something wasn't right.

Claire opened the front door. The house smelled wonderful. What could Joel be cooking? "Honey? You inside?"

"In the kitchen."

She dropped her *Painted Loon* tote at the base of the hall tree and went to join him. He had his head in the fridge, rummaging.

"What are you making? Can I help?" She knew the best approach to her man. He loved her to be his sous chef, not that she could do much more than chop and stir—and the stir was suspect.

"I felt like taco salad, and I've always loved your Aunt Lola's recipe. You can help chop."

"Her recipe isn't gourmet, though. It's down-home."

"Sometimes the simplest are the best. Grab the avocado while I get the chips."

They soon had all their—what had Chef Thornton called it? Oh yeah, their *mise en place* together. Claire chopped the lettuce, tomatoes, and avocados, while Joel cooked the meat. She'd wait until they had eaten before—

"Babe, whatever it is you're trying to tell me is burning a hole in your tongue. Just spit it out."

Blast, he was on to her. "What makes you think I have something to say?"

"Because normally, you're Chatty-Cathy, telling me about your day."

"I don't chatter."

"Do too."

She raised an avocado half and threatened him with it. He laughed. "Come on, it can't be that bad."

It could, but then again, they'd been through so much with their kids, this was pretty mild. "I've discovered who the ghost is."

Joel stopped tossing the meat. He removed the pan from the burner and turned to face her. "Who is it?"

She met his gaze. "It's Mel."

He frowned. "Mel? Why would she fake being a ghost? What's in it for her?"

"That's what I'm trying to find out." She told him the whole story while they mixed the salad ingredients together. He plated their dinner, and she poured sweet tea over ice. After he asked the blessing, they dove in. It was wonderful, but her appetite was hindered.

Joel laid his fork down. "Babe, what is it you want to do?"

She took a sip of the sweet tea. It would be best to plunge in headfirst. "I want to follow her, Joel. I want to catch her inside or trying to get in or something. I can't just hand her a shirt and say we found it. I don't want to give her the opportunity to lie to me."

He didn't explode. His lips rose to a half smile. "Yeah, I can see that. So how are we going to do it?"

Her jaw dropped. "We?"

Claire and Joel huddled down in the front seat of 'Lissa's car, parked in the lot at the edge of town. Claire had slipped out the back door of the gallery a half hour before closing. Patsy would text her when Mel left work. Joel enlisted Bud Pugh's help to not give them away. He was tickled to be part of a stake out again. It had been over thirty-five years since they'd had an attempted robbery at the bank. Bud had been a guard there at the time and became a hero, saving the bank manager and capturing the robber, not to mention saving the money.

"Just signal us when Mel is coming to meet her mother." Joel shook his hand and climbed in the car.

"Don't you worry none, Joel. When I see Mel, I'll raise the guard arm twice."

"That's perfect. We can see it from the car." They'd parked behind an SUV and between a pickup truck and a Toyota.

Claire's cell phone vibrated. "She just left" showed in the display.

"She's left," Claire whispered, though she needn't have. It just felt right. "Get down. She should be here in three minutes."

Joel lowered down enough to be hidden but still see through the steering wheel. A minute later, the guard arm went up, then down, and up again.

"Mel's here." Joel whispered, too. "She waved at Bud."

"Evenin', Mr. Bud." Her voice carried across the lot.

"Evenin', Mel."

"See you tomorrow."

"I'll be here."

They waited. And waited. Bud appeared beside the car and tapped on the window. "Nobody picked her up. She waited a couple of minutes, then turned and disappeared into the woods."

"Does she always do that?"

He lifted one shoulder. "Don't rightly know. I've never truly watched her before."

Joel fired up the engine. "Which way did she go?"

Bud pointed toward the woods between the parking lot and *Lunn's Grocery*.

"Thanks." Joel backed out and almost fishtailed the car in his hurry.

"Careful there." Claire fastened her seatbelt.

"Don't worry. Just watch for Mel."

"Where are we going?"

"I'm going to try to get into the church parking lot, near the back. If you remember, Seth has this same car, so Mel won't know the difference."

"Oh, you're good." He really was, and it gave her the warm fuzzies. There'd been a time where he wouldn't bother with her schemes and such.

They drove into the parking lot, turned off the engine, and got out. They hid behind the church where they could see the front of the theater. Claire's breathing was close to normal now, but her heart still pounded.

A few moments later, Joel squeezed her hand and put his finger to his lips. He pointed. Mel crossed the street. She approached the theater but kept walking down the side of the building and out of their sight. Where was she going?

Claire glanced at Joel. He raised his shoulders. He crept forward, pulling her along behind him. All she could do was follow. Then Mel came into view. She was out behind the theater. She turned. Joel jerked Claire down behind a bush. They crouched, watching through its foliage.

Mel turned in a complete circle, then she bent over and thrust her hand into the forest floor. Claire took a sharp breath when Mel raised up and the ground did too.

"What in—?" Joel's hand stopped her whisper.

Mel disappeared into the ground. Joel took Claire's hand and pulled her up. He put his finger to his lips. She nodded. No more whispering out loud. They tiptoed to where Mel disappeared. Joel felt around, searching the ground. Claire tried to replicate Mel's movements. She turned in a circle, then her foot caught. She went down fast, face first into a layer of pine needles.

She came up spitting dirt. "I found it."

Poor Joel. He pulled her back ten paces and stepped behind a tree. He was trying very hard not to laugh, but each time he opened his mouth, he clamped it shut fast. Finally, he was able to maintain his composure. With his lips next to her ear, he whispered. "Sorry, babe. I knew you weren't hurt, but you bounced back up so fast, the humor got hold of me before I could stop it."

She laid her head on his shoulder. "What do you suppose this is?"

"A tunnel. Do you remember that old story about the underground railroad going through Chapel Springs?"

She lifted her head and stared at him. "Yes. And the old house it was supposed to be in was rebuilt into our theater. You don't suppose—?"

He nodded. "I'm betting this is the way they snuck people in." He leaned out from behind the tree then motioned her to come. "We'll wait a few minutes and see—look!" Joel pointed to an upper window.

A pale, ghostly light moved from pane to pane, then it went out. Claire was sure it came from the prop room.

"Are you ready to play cops and robbers?" Joel whispered.

"You're on."

They moved to the door and Joel lifted it carefully. There wasn't a sound. Not a creak or a groan. Mel must have oiled the hinges. There's no way a door used more than a hundred and fifty years ago wouldn't squeak at the very least. Joel went first. He cupped a keychain pen light, keeping the light down as he descended steps almost as steep as a ladder.

Claire followed, but had only made it a couple of steps before he motioned her to stay. He climbed back up, stepping around her. For half a heartbeat, she thought he was going to leave her there, but he closed the door behind them and rejoined her. He grinned in the dim light.

"Didn't want anyone to fall in accidentally. I won't leave you, babe. Not even as a joke. Not here."

How did he always know what was in her head? He couldn't even see her face.

"Wait until I get to the bottom, then come down."

She waited, then he shined the light back to the next step for her. She couldn't really see the steps but went by feel. On the fourth one, her heel slipped. She slid down the remaining stairs, bouncing her fanny against each one. Careful not to cry out and warn Mel of their coming, she couldn't let Joel know what happened until she landed on top of him. He went down with a soft thud into the dirt. That's when she realized she'd gone down the steps backwards.

Claire found his ear so she could whisper. "Joel? Honey? Are you okay?"

His arms came around her and squeezed. "You make life so surprising."

Of course, he couldn't see her grin in the dark, so she leaned down and kissed him. Because of the darkness, her kiss landed in his ear.

They scrambled up. Joel took her hand and they moved quietly forward. After a few feet, the ground began to slope upward in a slight incline. At the end of the long tunnel was a door. Joel didn't open it right away. He turned back to face her.

He put his lips next to her ear and whispered so softly, she had to strain to hear. "Where do you think this door opens into?"

She ran the theater through her mind. At the rear and in the basement was the scene shop and storage. That had to be where the door opened. It would be easy to camouflage behind the stacks of lumber and scenery doors.

"It's now or never." Joel turned the handle carefully and opened the door a crack. He peered inside then pulled it wide open. He motioned her to follow. After she was inside, he silently closed the door.

They were behind a large stack of flats. Claire motioned for him to follow. She had a good idea where Mel was. The question was why. She led him to the stairs and they ascended to the second floor. Finally, they stood outside the prop room door. Claire put her ear to the door and closed her eyes. Soft strains of guitar music accompanied by the muted beat of drums came from inside.

She nodded to Joel. Before he opened the door, he pulled out a little tube from his pocket. He squeezed it above the hinges, and then showed her the label. Graphite. Smart man. He opened the door slowly without a sound.

They tiptoed inside, and a moment later, Joel shined his light on Mel.

She screamed and burst into tears.

Chapter 37

Carin sat on the side of JJ's bed and listened to his prayers. After his "amen," she leaned down and kissed his sweet face. He smelled of sunshine and soap. If she had no one else on earth, she had her little boy. Love squeezed her heart to near bursting.

"Did you have fun today, doodle bug?"

"Yeah, but Mama, why is Aunt Julie so mean to you?"

She frowned. How did he pick that up? "What do you mean, sugar?"

"She's always nice to Darcie, but not you. Or Auntie Leanna."

His observations surprised her. She had no idea an almost-seven-year-old could be so astute. "Honestly, I don't know. I think she's jealous, but I don't know why."

"'Cause you gots me." JJ wiggled and giggled. He'd lost interest fast enough, thank goodness. That was too deep of a subject for such a little guy.

"I think you're right. Anyone would be jealous. Now"—she stood and tucked in his covers—"you get to sleep. Aren't you and Mr. Ryan going fishing in the morning?"

"Yep." He held up his arms.

She bent and kissed him. "You have to get up early to catch fish. Night-night."

"Night, Mama." His words were drawn out by a yawn.

She turned out his light and left the door open a crack so Edgar could get in later. She paused on the last stair tread before she could be seen and observed her sisters. Darcie sat on the floor between Julie's feet. Julie, in the chair her dad loved, was French braiding Darcie's hair. Leanna had curled up on the sofa, one leg beneath her and a book in her lap. Edgar laid on the floor by her, his head on top of her foot.

Every time Carin saw her sisters together, it was two and one. They were never a threesome. Leanna was always left out. How sad to have grown up with them but not quite part of them. How she managed to not resent Julie and Darcie was beyond Carin's understanding.

As if she heard Carin's thoughts, Leanna raised her eyes and patted the cushion next to her. Carin took the last steps into the great room. "Anyone want a cup of tea or decaf coffee?"

"I'd love some tea, thank you. And I'd offer to help, but I'm held captive here." Leanna pointed to Edgar.

Darcie wrinkled her nose. "Decaf is icky. Do you have any regular coffee?"

Julie wrapped a hair band around the end of Darcie's French braid. "How she can drink that and sleep, I don't know. But she can so it's okay."

Julie couldn't mean Carin should ask permission before giving Darcie coffee. Darcie was twenty-one, for Pete's sake.

"And I'll take tea. Herbal with honey." Julie leaned over and selected a magazine from the side table.

Carin turned the kettle on and set a cup in the Keurig, slipping a regular coffee into it. She pressed the brew button. When Leanna visited alone, Carin had been comfortable with her, but her other sisters were different. With them, she couldn't relax. The quiet was awkward. Julie and Darcie were company. They hadn't become sisters yet. How could she make that happen? Could she? Did she even want to?

Carin put their cups on a tray along with the honey pot, sugar bowl, and two small pitchers—one milk, the other cream. After setting it on the coffee table, she picked up her mug and joined Leanna on the sofa.

Leanna turned her book face down on her lap. "I love this room, Carin. It invites one to relax." She ran her hand over the large floral printed cushions. "I love the magnolia blossoms. Where'd you find it?"

Since Edgar had imprisoned her sister, she handed Leanna her mug of tea—no milk, lots of sugar. "It was Nana's and purchased not long before she died. I was so pleased the mice hadn't gotten to it."

"Eew!" Darcie didn't bother to wipe up the coffee she splashed onto the tray when she stirred in the sugar.

Carin waited a heartbeat to see if Mother-Julie would admonish her. She didn't. Come on. Did their manners stop because it was *her* house?

Leanna cleared her throat and pointed to the mess when Darcie looked at her. Julie didn't look pleased. The family prima donna grudgingly slapped a napkin on top of the spill.

There was a huge elephant in the room and Carin couldn't say a word. It made her tired.

"Ooh, look, Jewels." Darcie held a magazine up for Julie to see. "That's the red Jimmy Choo bag I want. And he has red sandals to go with it." She wiggled and grinned up at Julie.

"It would look scrumptious with your new sundress, but I don't think you can afford it. I'm sure there are some knock-offs that would be less expensive."

Darcie pouted. She actually stuck out her bottom lip and pursed her upper lip. Carin's gaze flicked to Julie, whose brows knitted in what appeared to be genuine concern.

The elephant was about to explode.

With a glance at Carin, Julie leaned over and whispered in Darcie's ear. The pout disappeared and a smile replaced it.

"Julie!" Leanna withdrew her foot from beneath Edgar and stood. "You didn't promise to give her the money, did you?"

Julie lifted her chin and stared at Leanna.

"You really shouldn't, Julie." Carin couldn't keep quiet any longer. "She asked me for it, too."

Darcie jumped up, her face bright red. "You're just jealous because I'm the prettiest." She aimed her words at Leanna, then turned on Carin. "And you have pots of money. Don't try to tell me different. You're just stingy. Jewels …" She slid next to Julie, who had risen, and wiggled beneath her arm. "She's the only one who really loves me." Their drama queen kissed Julie's cheek and ran upstairs, boohooing.

Julie drew herself up, her shoulders back, and peered down her nose at Carin. "I'll only tell you this once. Stay out of this. It's not your place, nor is it any of your business. You made Darcie cry."

Unbelievable. "You really don't see what you're doing to her, do you?"

"I don't know what you're talking about." She moved toward the stairs.

Leanna followed her and caught her arm. "Julie, come back here. Carin's right. If you don't stop, Darcie will never learn that she can't have whatever she wants." She put her hand up to stop Julie's protest. "And you'll lose your husband over her if you're not careful."

Julie blanched and glanced at Carin then back to Leanna. "She's my responsibility, not yours. I don't need you telling me how to raise her."

Did she hear herself? "Darcie's grown up. It's time she learns to stand on her own two feet." Poor Julie needed a child of her own.

Julie's face turned deep red. She was in front of Carin in a heartbeat, her finger jabbing into her chest. "You! This is all your fault. You encroached on our family, uninvited. We. Don't. Want. You." Her last words screeched, her face an ugly mask.

Edgar jumped to his feet and pushed his way between her and Carin. Julie turned and ran up the stairs. The beast followed her up. He would post himself at JJ's door.

God, please don't let JJ have heard that.

Leanna's arm went around Carin. "I want you and Daddy wanted you. One day, she'll come around, honey."

Reaching up, Carin squeezed her sister's hand. "Thank you. I'll be right back. I need to check JJ."

She found Edgar on top of JJ's bed, snuggled up to her sleeping boy. *Thank you.* "Good boy, Edgar." She petted the big head. "You and God watch over him, sweet beast." She went back downstairs.

Her sister was out on the front porch. Even in July, after the sun went down up here in the mountains, the air got cool. Carin plucked up two lightweight, cotton jackets from the coat tree and opened the door. "Want company?"

"Always." Leanna's smile welcomed her and the windbreaker. She draped it over her shoulders and they settled into Adirondack chairs. "I'm still in a bit of shock over Julie's reactions. A bit over the top, don't you think?"

Carin slid her arms into the jacket. "I try to put myself in her shoes. But it doesn't work. I always wanted a sister." She drew on her novelist hat. Maybe that would help. "If she were a character in a book, I'd try to climb inside her head, but—"

"Our Julie's a strange one. Did Daddy tell you how she took over Darcie from the day Mama brought her home from the hospital?"

"He told me some of it. Mother was ill. He told me he thought she probably already had cancer and they didn't know it, yet."

Leanna put her feet up on the porch railing. "I always thought so. She never recovered from Darcie's birth, anyway. So Julie became the little mother to Darcie. She never tried to mother me. At least not until I got in high school. Then she had an opinion on every outfit I bought, not that I bought a lot. That was a problem, too." Leanna chuckled. "She'd hoped I would at least listen to her fashion ideas." She rolled her eyes. "I could tell you stories—"

The door opened. "And I'm sure you will. All our private business." Julie turned her nose up and pulled her weekender down the steps behind her. "We won't stay where we're not wanted."

Darcie followed her out. A moment later, the tram arrived. They climbed aboard and left.

Carin stared at Leanna. "I keep running the evening through my mind, looking for what I did to make them think they weren't wanted."

"It wasn't you. The minute you disagree with either of them, you're wrong. That's enough."

"I wonder if we'll ever get to the point where we're sisters."

Leanna leaned to the left of her chair and turned her shoulders so she faced Carin. "Silly, we're all sisters. They can't get away from that even if they wanted to."

Carin sighed. "We might share the same blood and DNA, but they sure don't want a relationship. It's almost as if I've been divorced by them."

"Well, you've got me, babe." She hummed the old Sonny and Cher song, making Carin laugh. She joined her sister in the song, but because she couldn't sing a lick, they dissolved into giggles. How much fun she would have had growing up with Leanna. It made her melancholy for what she missed, yet grateful for what she had now.

Chapter 38

Claire squatted next to Mel and wrapped her arms around her. So much for the tough Goth-girl facade. She pulled out a hanky, silently blessing Patsy's mother for teaching her to always carry one, and handed it to Mel.

"Do you think you can tell us why you're here?"

Mel lifted a teary face and nodded.

"Let's wait until we're home." Joel held out his hand to Mel and helped her up. "You're coming to our house. Grab all your stuff."

Her Joel was a sap for kids. Claire didn't say a word but helped collect Mel's belongings. They went back down to the scene shop in the basement, slipped behind the pile of scenery flats, and into the tunnel. Joel pulled the door shut behind them and turned on his penlight.

Claire tucked her hand through Mel's arm.

"Are you afraid, Miss Claire?"

Should she say she was? "Not really. I just don't want to lose you."

"I'm sorry about all this." Mel sniffled.

"Shh, don't worry, sugar. We're not angry. We just want to understand. But wait until we're home. We don't want to alert anyone."

"Okay."

They reached the trap door. Joel aimed the pen light on his hand and motioned for them to wait. He turned off the tiny beam and cracked the door open. After a moment, he lifted it all the way open and motioned for them to come out. There was no moon, thank goodness. Nobody should be able to see them.

After Mel showed Joel how she covered the door with pine straw and branches, they went to the car and drove home. Two minutes later, Joel pulled 'Lissa's car into the driveway.

"You go get Mel settled in Adrianna's room. I'll make us some popcorn. Then we'll talk."

Once Claire got Mel settled and showed her the bathroom, they went back down to the den. Joel already had a bowl of popcorn on the coffee table, along with a pitcher of sweet tea and cans of Coke.

Mel chose a Coke. She popped the top and took a small bowl of the popcorn. After a swig of her drink, she took a deep breath.

"I'm sorry for all the trouble I've caused. I've been living in the theater."

Claire exchanged glances with Joel. "Why?"

"When my dad left, my stepmom kicked me out. I was staying in the woods, but then I found that trap door. I explored the tunnel and discovered where it came out in the theater. It was dry and safe."

Claire's heart ached for her. "Have you heard from your dad at all?"

She shook her head. "He's never been around much. It wasn't so bad when my mom was alive. After she died, I went to live with him and Kandy."

"When did you lose your mother, sugar?"

"She died when I was twelve. She got Hep C from a dude who used a dirty needle to do her tat." She raised her chin. "I've always been very careful. I won't go into a dirty parlor. Anyway, Dad left when I was ten. Mom started drinking. The combination was really stupid. When she died, I ran away before the authorities found her."

Claire tried to keep her mouth from gaping. *Lord, the grief this child has suffered.* "Why did you run, honey?"

Mel's lip curled. "I wasn't going to let them put me into foster care. I'd heard the horror stories."

Claire and her friends lived a sheltered life, that was for sure. When her mom died, her dad was there and Great-Aunt Lola, too. "How did your dad find you?"

"He didn't." Mel snorted. "I found him in Franklin, Tennessee. He'd married Savannah by that time. She wasn't happy about having to raise a kid and left within six months."

Claire was confused. "I thought her name was Kandy."

"Kandy came later. After Betsey."

How many times was this man married? Oh, maybe he didn't marry them all. "How did you get to Chapel Springs from Franklin?"

"Hitchhiked."

She and Joel both gasped. "You hitchhiked?" Joel asked. "Didn't your dad tell you not to do that?"

The smile she gave him was sweet. *She's never had anyone care like that.*

"He taught me how."

Claire let that go. "So why Chapel Springs?"

"Actually, it was Pineridge, not Chapel Springs." She tossed a couple of popcorn kernels into her mouth. When she'd swallowed them, she continued. "Dad was out of work. Kandy saw an ad in the newspaper for a bartender in Pineridge. That's what she did—tend bar. So we hitchhiked there. Dad got a job at a gas station but got bored. He hated the mountains. So he took off one night."

And left his daughter with a stepmother or whatever she was. Claire wiped the butter from the popcorn off her hands. "When did Kandy kick you out?" She still couldn't imagine a woman doing that to Mel. Goth stuff aside, this was a good kid.

"About a week before I got arrested. Then I met some kids who came to Chapel Spring to party."

December? How could she? It made Claire's blood boil. "Who bailed you out?"

She gave them a shy smile. "Hazel and her old man. They let me stay with them for a couple of weeks. Then they moved on. Said they'd be back, but I didn't have enough money for the rent."

"Wait." Claire worked out the timing. "Weren't you working for me by then?"

Mel gave the slightest nod.

Terrific. Talk about a schmuck. She didn't pay her employee enough to rent an apartment or a room at the very least. "I feel like I could stand tall beneath a toadstool. I wish I'd known. We'll remedy that right away." Somehow. She'd talk to Nathan and Patsy. "So after Hazel left town, you stayed in the woods? How did you shower? You're always clean."

"I was only there for two nights. I showered at the springs park.

But I stumbled over the trap door on the third afternoon. It was kind of cool." Her brown eyes went back and forth between Claire and Joel. "I always loved an adventure. I read mystery books as a kid. I read every Meg Mackintosh Solve It Yourself mystery. I had a flashlight, so I opened the door and went down. It was fun to explore the theater. Then someone saw my light. I heard the door rattle, so I hightailed it back into the tunnel."

She stopped for a drink of her Coke. "Anyway, I heard y'all talking about the ghost, so I figured if I kept the rumor going, I could stay there long enough to save up some money so I could rent a place. That's all, Miss Claire. Honest. I wasn't trying to stop you from renovating. I was fixing to move out of there in a few more weeks."

Claire had read bestselling novels with less conflict than Mel's story. What were they going to do? "Mel, how old are you? Truth, sugar."

Her face grew pink. "Sixteen."

Oy vey. That brought DFACS into it. No way would Claire let that happen. "Did you graduate from high school?"

"No. We moved too much, usually to a different state."

Claire blanched. This child's life was a mess. She turned to Joel. "So what do we tell Jim Bob?"

Mel's face lost its color. "He told me if I got in any trouble, he'd have me convicted."

Claire snorted. "I'm not condoning trespassing, but there are extenuating circumstances involved here." She sent a pleading glance for help to Joel.

He cleared his throat. Were his eyes misty? He wouldn't let her see, silly man.

"I'll handle Jim Bob," Joel said. "And Felix. I'll simply let them know the ghost has been exorcised." He grinned. "Now, Mel, did we get all your things out of the theater? Nothing left behind?"

She shook her head. "I didn't have much at all. I kept everything in my backpack so I could scat in a hurry if anyone came in."

"Good." Joel stood. "Now, I'm going to—Mel, did you eat any supper?"

She shook her head. "I didn't have time to." She grinned. "Y'all caught me before I could."

Claire rose and took the bowl from Mel. "We'll remedy that, and more than popcorn. Would you like to shower before you eat? You can use Adrianna's robe. She leaves some clothes here for rare visits." She showed Mel where to find what she needed and left her with the robe in the bathroom.

In the kitchen, Joel was making more taco salad.

"Honey, what are you going to tell Jim Bob?"

He handed her the lettuce to chop. "Not rightly sure yet. I think he'll understand, though, since other than trespassing, no laws were broken." He put down his spatula. "She did not break into the building, technically." He held up his thumb. "She didn't do any damage." He raised his index finger to join his thumb. "I think we can handle the sheriff."

She didn't want to ask but she had to. "What about DFACS? Do you think Jim Bob would insist on bringing them in?"

"Child services? Naw. Well, maybe. By the letter of the law, he should. But we'll vouch for her."

"What do you mean?"

"She can stay here until she finds a good place to rent or someone to live with."

She laid down the knife and hugged him. "You're a good man, Charlie Brown."

He chuckled and kissed her cheek. "Did you think I'd toss her out?

"Nope. You're too soft where kids are concerned. Even Goth teenagers."

A few minutes later, Claire called Mel to her supper. She skidded into the kitchen, her hair still damp and her face scrubbed clean. After she was finished eating, and over dessert which Claire and Joel hadn't had earlier, Claire told her their plans.

"You'll live with us until you find a place." Claire crossed her fingers beneath the table. If Jim Bob insisted, DFACS would be brought in and Mel would have to go into foster care.

Mel's eyes grew large. "Wow. Thanks." She lowered her gaze and shoveled in another bite of ice cream.

"But you have to promise me when that happens, you'll let us know where and with whom."

Mel grinned. "Okay, Ma. I promise." She held up three fingers.

"You were a girl scout?"

"Yeah. For two weeks."

They ate in silence for a moment, then Mel dropped her spoon. "I forgot to tell you this." Excitement sparked in her words. "When I was exploring the theater, there was an old trunk in the prop room, way back in a corner. Had a bunch of boxes and junk on top of it. Anyway, I cleared the junk away and opened the trunk. It was filled with old letters from way back. A few of them talked about the underground railroad."

Now Mel's excitement infected Claire. "That would validate the historical value. Did they mention the tunnel at all?"

"Yep. Talked about digging at night. They even described where the entrance was and carved some marks in the trees to lead folks to it. And before you ask, yes. I checked. Those trees with the marks are still there."

Joel leaned forward. "How were they marked?"

"The letter said they 'scarred' the trees. I found carvings. They were really strange. Looked like Indian stuff or Egyptian. Then they'd hang a quilt on the back porch if it was safe to enter the tunnel."

Claire exchanged glances with Joel. They needed those letters. She wondered when the back porch had been removed. Probably when it became a theater.

He sat back. "If you'll tell me exactly where the trunk is, I'll go get it. You gals can wash the dishes while I'm doing that." He opened his eyes wide. "What? You don't think I'm going to let y'all have all the fun, do you?"

Dee's 'n' Doughs was busy this morning, even at the early hour. If Claire were on vacation, she'd be sleeping in, not schmoozing. Last night, she tossed and turned, worrying about Mel and if Child Services would come take her away. Of course, that would depend on whether they found out about her. Van Gogh's ear, she hated secrets. She broke a crumb donut in half and slid the larger part to her BFF.

"Thanks." Patsy took a bite. "These are good. So." She set the donut on a napkin. "What has you twitterpated this morning?"

"You're not going to believe it." She let her gaze travel around the table at her friends. "You have to promise to keep this to yourselves."

Lacey nodded and Lydia said, "Of course."

"Promise." Dee slid her chair closer to Claire's.

Ellie Grant's eyes grew wide and so did her grin as she nodded her affirmation. She loved a secret.

Claire was just glad that Faye wasn't here today. "Joel and I found the ghost."

Eyes popped and jaws dropped all around the table.

"Whose ghost is it?"

"Where?"

"How?"

"It's not a real ghost." Claire lowered her voice and leaned in. "It was Mel. She's been living in the theater."

Patsy frowned. "Why?"

"It seems her stepmother is of the wicked sort." Claire relayed what Mel had told her and Joel. "Right now, we've got her at our house, but I know she won't be able to stay with us."

Lydia reached for a mini-pot of cream. "Why not, Claire? Doesn't Joel want her? I thought he likes kids." She opened the cream and poured it into her cup.

"He loves them, and it was his idea to bring her home. But ..." Again, Claire leaned in. She didn't want anyone outside her friends to hear anything. "She's only sixteen. Once Jim Bob finds out it was her, DFACS will have to be brought in. She's run away from them more than once in her life, poor kid." Why did Ellie have a Cheshire-cat grin on her fa— "Ellie, why are you smiling?"

"Because," she raised her fingers and counted off. "First, Mel and I have become friends. Second, she's been in the library a lot. And ..." Ellie poked one ankle out like a coquette, showing off her ankle tattoo. "Third, she helped me fulfill a bucket list item."

"That's great. I'm glad she has a friend." Claire's frowned. "But how does that help us right now?"

"That's number four. Have you forgotten that years ago I went through the training to be a foster parent?" She sighed. "Before I could act on it, Mother worked herself up into a hissy fit. I realized it wouldn't be a good environment for a foster child. But now ..."

Ellie and Mel? The more she thought about it, the more she liked it. It could work.

"But what about your mother?" Patsy asked then popped the last of her donut in her mouth. "Won't she do that again?"

Just when Claire thought Ellie's grin couldn't get any larger, it did.

"That's number five and the most providential part of this. My eldest sister—you remember Donna? Her husband died a year ago. She's finally decided to come back here, after all these years." Ellie smirked. "Guess her conscience is bothering her. Anyway, she's moving in with Mother to care for her. Says it's her turn."

Claire snorted. "I say it's about time."

"There's that." Ellie put her cup beneath the coffee thermos and pumped another cupful. "But ..." She paused, waiting for their attention. "I've bought the pharmacy building from Tom. There's that large apartment above it for me. I close next week. Don't worry. Tom's leasing the pharmacy space now. He wanted his equity for a winter home in Florida. Anyway, I'd love to foster Mel. We'll be great roommates. And I can homeschool her until she graduates."

Well, butter my fanny and call me a biscuit.

If Claire had chosen anyone in town, she wouldn't have thought of Ellie. Yet it seemed just right. Providential, like she said. Now, if they could convince Felix not to press charges against Mel for trespassing, and if DFACS agreed on Ellie, they'd all be in high cotton, as Aunt Lola used to say.

Chapter 39

"Speak slower, Julie. I can't understand you." Nor could Carin understand why Julie called her, unless she was trying to blame her for whatever her problem was. She did a lot of that.

Leanna stood beside Carin, trying to hear. She poked the speaker button.

"I said I went out for a while today and when I got home, the police were here. They were looking for Darcie. They … had … a … warrant …. for her arrest." Her words were broken with sobs.

"For being spoiled?" Leanna mouthed to Carin.

She smothered a laugh. "What did the police say, Julie?"

"They … they said the charges were embezzlement."

Embezzlement? Carin stared at Leanna who took over the conversation. "Jewels, did they explain anything to you?"

Julie's answer was incoherent.

"Honey, we can't understand you. Is Ted there?"

"No, he's talking with the police. Oh, Leanna." Julie's voice was thick with tears. "Is she up there with Carin? We've got to do something. Help her. Hide her!"

"Until I can understand what's happened, we can't do anything. And no, she isn't here."

"You've never loved Darcie like I do."

"Oh, Julie. Grow up. Have Ted call me when he's through talking with the police." Leanna swiped her finger across Carin's cell phone screen and handed it back.

"Did anything Julie say make sense?"

Leanna shook her head. "Not completely. Something about Darcie embezzling. I hope it's a mistake."

So did Carin. Her stomach roiled. Her publisher had stuck with her so far, but if this was real and it got out? There was a morals clause in her contract. They'd have no choice but to drop her. Without an agent, she'd have a tough time getting another publisher, at least in the inspirational market. And she believed the charges were probably true. Darcie was pretty determined to get whatever it was she wanted.

Leanna handed Carin the phone. "Ted will get me back on my phone. Funny how the minute there was trouble, Julie called you."

"I don't get it." Carin pocketed her phone. "Why do you think she did?"

"She's always been the 'big sister' and loves to hand out advice. She thinks she knows everything. That's the reason she resents you. But in this case, she had to look to someone for help—you."

"I don't know everything."

Leanna chuckled. "No, I mean you're now the 'big sister.' She's lost that position in the family. It's not easy for her."

Not easy for *Julie*? "That's the silliest thing I've ever heard."

"Not really, Carin. She defines the classic birth order characteristics for the firstborn. That's always been Julie's identity, and after Mama died, it took on life. She was mother and big sister rolled into one. Then, in one day, she lost it. You're the firstborn, now. She's not sure who she is anymore."

Carin couldn't take her eyes off Leanna. "You don't think that, do you? That I stole her place?" She couldn't stand it if she did.

"Of course not. Julie needs therapy." Leanna paced the great room. "Ted's been trying to get her into a doctor for a while. If she'd had a child of her own, it wouldn't be so bad, but she has issues with her self-esteem because of it. She's so afraid of losing Darcie's love, she gives her everything she asks for." She flopped down on the sofa, pulled a hair binder out of her pocket, and pulled her hair into a ponytail.

"That's obvious."

With her hair up like that, Leanna looked all of sixteen.

"But it's been more, lately. Finally, Ted put his foot down. He showed

Julie how much she'd given Darcie over the last year. It was obscene. Over fourteen thousand dollars."

"You've got to be kidding."

"I wish I was. Ted works hard and makes good money, but that much hurts."

"Didn't she see what she was doing to Darcie?"

"Nope." Leanna went to the fridge and pulled out a Diet Coke. "Want one?"

"Please. So what did she spend it on?" She took the can and popped the top, taking a long drink. "Thanks."

Leanna nodded. "Clothes. Most everything she wears is designer. You've seen her shoes. Jimmy Choos aren't cheap."

"Has Darcie always played Julie like that?"

Leanna's lips thinned to a straight line. "That's what makes me the angriest. She has. She knows how to push Julie's buttons. She quit trying on me years ago. I never thought she was that cute." Leanna sighed. "Darcie is narcissistic. She has no thought for anyone but herself."

Leanna's phone rang. "Hey, Ted. Hang on a second. I want to put you on speaker so Carin can hear, too. Is that okay?"

He must have said yes, because his next words were audible. "Okay, first, I'm sorry it took me so long to get back to you. I had to give Julie a sedative. Anyway, when the police find her, Darcie will be arrested for embezzlement. Her boss filed the charges. He claims she's stolen over fifty thousand dollars."

Carin stared at Leanna, her stomach churning. There was no way this would stay hidden. Her career was over. She'd seen it happen to other authors. Somebody in the family did something wrong, and the author disappeared from the literary world's sight, never to be heard from again.

"Wow. Will you post bail for her?"

Their brother-in-law's sigh was deep. Poor Ted. He sounded defeated.

"I'm not. It's time she learn the consequences for her actions. I love my wife, but I'm through putting out money for Darcie. If it were for an education, or a business, or a charity even, I'd be fine with it. But she doesn't even care about Julie. She only cares about having the latest toy or designer purse. It doesn't bother her if anyone gets hurt." He sighed again. "I'm sorry."

Carin liked her brother-in-law and thought him longsuffering to be married to Julie. But something in her sister had made him fall in love with her. Carin wanted to see that part of Julie.

"Don't be, Ted. You're doing the right thing. "Scott and I ..." Leanna paused and raised one eyebrow at Carin. She nodded. "And Carin all support what you're doing. It's the right thing. Tell Julie I'll be over tomorrow afternoon. And Ted, tell her I love her."

"I will." Leanna clicked off her phone. She raised her eyes to Carin's. "I just thought of something. You told me your agent dropped you because Wick filed for divorce. Will your publisher do the same over this?"

Does a duck quack? But Leanna didn't need to know that right now. "Let's wait to see if it's actually true. Maybe their accountant made an error on the books. Or maybe he did it?"

Leanna's face lost its color. "Darcie did the books."

"Oh, boy, that's not good. Did he say how long it had been going on?"

"No, but—"

The doorbell rang. A marshal stood with his finger poised to ring the bell again. Fear shot through Carin. Had something happened to JJ? She pulled open the door. "Yes?"

"Are you Carin Jardine?"

"Yes. What is—"

He thrust an envelope in her hands. "You've been duly served."

"What is this?"

"Ma'am, I simply deliver what the court tells me to." He turned around and marched back to his car.

She shut the door and moved to the couch, having the premonition she should be seated to read whatever it was. With a glance at Leanna, she slid her nail under the flap. Her heartbeat accelerated as she read the heading: Divorce Decree. She dropped it in her lap.

"Wick is divorcing me."

"I'm sorry. I know you loved him, at least at one time, but from what you've told me, it doesn't seem like a huge loss."

It wasn't, not really, yet it was another failure. For JJ's sake, one she would rather have avoided. If only Wick would have agreed to counseling.

"May I?" Leanna held out her hand for the papers.

"What? Oh, sure." Carin handed the papers to her sister.

After a moment's study, Leanna gasped. "Did you read this?" She shook the papers.

"No. I stopped on the heading."

"Wick is suing you for a million dollars. If you give him the money"—she curled her upper lip—"he won't fight for custody of JJ."

Carin jumped up. "What?" She grabbed the papers from Leanna and scanned them. "He cares about JJ all right. He cared enough to walk out on him. This—" she dropped back on the couch holding the missive aloft. "This is like he's selling JJ. What am I going to do?"

"We're going to fight this."

Where are you, God? "I don't know a lawyer."

Leanna sat sideways on the sofa, one foot tucked beneath her. "Sure you do. David."

"David? David who?"

Leanna slid the papers back into their envelope and handed it to Carin. "Silly. David Lawler. Daddy's lawyer."

"Oh, right. But do you think he'd take it? Does he do things like this?"

"I'm not sure, but for the family, I think he'd do pretty much any kind of defending. Or he'd bring in a colleague. Don't you worry, sister. We'll send Wick's tail skedaddling."

Carin gave a half smile, wishing she had her sister's confidence. Her students must love her get-it-done attitude. "This was the last thing we needed right now, though. First Darcie, then this." She couldn't help it. She laughed. There wasn't much mirth in it, though.

"Darcie brought on her own problems." Leanna laid an arm on the back of the sofa. "You and I refused to enable her. I hadn't realized how bad she'd gotten. When she was little, it wasn't that big of a thing. People spoiled all three of us. But Julie and I didn't start expecting things. Darcie acts like the world owes her everything." She caught Carin's gaze. "What really surprises me, though, is that Ted saw through Darcie."

"You mean that she doesn't really care about Julie?" Carin had seen it, too.

Leanna nodded, her brow knit.

Carin leaned over and squeezed her sister's hand. "You're too close to see it. You love her." She released Leanna's hand and sat back, pulling a throw pillow into her lap. "Being on the outside, I could see it. Darcie calculates everything and everyone to see what value they have to her. When I told her I didn't have any money to give her, she decided I was either lying or wasn't worth anything to her."

Leanna stared at her. "That's a perfect description of her. I hadn't realized it, but that's it. She weighs each person's value to *her*. That's a horrible way to view people."

"It's a sick way, Leanna. Darcie is mentally ill."

"Well don't tell Julie that. She'll barbecue you."

"We have to. And Ted needs us." Leanna stared at her like she'd never seen her before. "What?"

Her eyes warm and loving, Leanna smiled. "You sound like a sister."

Chapter 40

The silence was palpable in the town council meeting as Boone called for the vote. "All in favor of renovating the theater, raise your hands." Claire held her breath and lifted hers. She glanced around the table. Not a single hand remained on the table. Doc even raised both his, and everyone laughed. They did it. The council agreed to spend the money. Even Felix was for it.

"Let the minutes show the vote was unanimous. Now, who is going to head up the renovations?"

Claire put her head down. No way was she going to make eye contact with anyone. Her plate was full enough. What with Megan and Dane's engagement, and now it seemed 'Lissa and Sean were headed that direction, too. No, her—

"I think Kelly Appling should be on it. She's the creative director for the Lakeside Players," Ellie said. "And Nancy Vaughn. She'd have good reason to be involved as the stage manager."

"What about Claire?" Faye Eisler asked. "It's named after her great-aunt."

Claire couldn't have stopped her eyes from rolling if she'd tried. "And that's my only involvement. I don't know anything about how it should be done."

Felix cleared his throat.

Boone nodded to him. "Felix? You have a comment?"

"Lester Gordon has built a lot of the sets. He should probably be involved."

Boone tapped his gavel. "For the minutes, Ellie, we'll ask Kelly Appling to head up the renovation committee, and appoint Lester and Nancy to help. The council will need to approve all bids. Now …" He ran a finger down his agenda. "Is there any more new business?" When no one had any, Boone banged his gavel down. "Meeting dismissed."

"You can't do that, Boone," Ellie said. "You have to call for a motion."

Boone's exasperation blew out his cheeks. "All right. If we must. Do I have a motion to end this here meeting? And a second?"

Doc motioned and Claire seconded it.

"All in favor raise your hands. Good. Now can I go get my supper?"

Claire pushed back her chair. For once, she got out of chairing a committee. Ellie scurried toward her.

"Claire, have you told Mel yet?"

"No, I didn't have time today, but I'll talk to her after we eat."

"Thank you. I want to do a bit of painting and I'd like to know what color she'll want her room."

Claire could have hugged Ellie for caring about their Goth Girl, though there was little left of the Goth. "I'll have her come see you tomorrow."

"One more favor. Will you call Kelly about the theater?"

Kelly would be so excited. "I'd be delighted to."

Joel had stayed home tonight, so Claire walked home with Doc. They waved good night to folks as, one by one, they turned off the sidewalk to their homes.

"Well, Clairey-girl, are you pleased about our Dane and your Megan?"

Her heart warmed, making even her fingertips tingle. "You have no idea how much, Doc. When Patsy and I were little girls, we used to say we'd grow up and have kids who'd marry each other so we could be real sisters. But I never thought it would be Dane and Megan."

"Was I the only one not surprised by those two?"

Staring at him, Claire tripped on a sidewalk crack. Doc caught her arm. "You weren't surprised at all?"

"I know our Dane. He's been in love with Megan since they were about thirteen. I also know his tenacity."

Claire smiled. "Meg said that's what won her. She knew his was a lasting love, that they'd grown up together and would grow old together."

She stopped to swallow the lump in her throat. "That's what you dream of for your children." She hugged Doc's arm.

He wrapped her hand in his. "God's been good to us all. Now, here's your house. Good night, girlie."

She kissed his weathered cheek and went up the path to her front door. Inside, a delicious aroma of … it took her a moment to identify it. Curry. That was it. Subtle, so it must be Joel's chicken and curry recipe. One of her favorites. Husband-cooked anything was her favorite. She dropped her tote by the stairs.

"I'm home."

"We're in the kitchen, babe."

She stopped in the doorway. Joel was demonstrating to Mel how to safely hold a knife and chop vegetables. His girls may be grown, but he had a new student. Claire's heart swelled with love for her Joel. God sure had picked out the right man for her.

Joel raised his head. "Hey, there." He came over for a kiss. "How'd the council meeting go?"

"We approved the renovation, which brings me to some news. If you don't need Mel, then she can come sit down."

"Sure." Joel took the knife from one very nervous girl.

Claire patted the seat next to her. "Don't go getting worried. It's all good."

Mel sat on the edge of her seat. "Really?"

"Yes, really. Felix isn't going to press charges against you for trespassing. He actually said he felt there were extenuating circumstances that warranted it. Besides, you technically didn't break in." Claire smiled at Mel's surprise. "Anyway, Jim Bob made a personal call to a judge friend, who agreed to get involved for you. He talked to DFACS, and they said they had a foster care home right here in Chapel Springs."

Mel backed away, fear and distrust in her eyes.

"Before you run, sugar, the foster mother is Ellie Grant."

Mel's eyes grew large. "The librarian, Miss Ellie?" Her lips twitched like she wanted to grin but wasn't sure.

Claire nodded. "That's the one. You can't believe how relieved I was to hear that. I was about to break the law, and not tell anyone, and keep you here."

Mel blinked. "You would have done that for me?"

"Well, of course."

"Why?"

"Oh, sweetie. Because we care. We've grown to love you. Besides," she nudged Mel with her elbow—"I don't want to have to train another assistant."

Mel's eyes filled with unshed tears. "Nobody has told me they loved me since my mama died." Those tears spilled over, and she ducked her head.

If Claire ever saw Mel's stepmother or her father for that matter, she'd—well she wasn't sure what she'd do, but it wouldn't be pretty. She put her arm around Mel and gave her shoulders a squeeze.

Joel snorted and made eye contact with Claire. "Makes two of us, babe," he mouthed. With his fists clenched, he turned around before Mel saw him. "If you two are finished, I could use some help."

Claire and Mel grinned at each other. She dabbed her eyes and they got up and got busy. As they worked, Claire filled them in on Ellie's purchase.

Joel stopped stirring. "So Tom's finally buying his Florida home. Hmm, we may have to take a trip and do some deep sea fishing."

"I've always wanted to see Miami Beach." Claire poured three glasses of sweet tea. "Mel, go see Miss Ellie tomorrow. She wants to talk to you about what color to paint your room. I hadn't realized you two had become such friends."

"I've spent a lot of time in the library. I didn't have much else to do after work, and I love to read."

Joel handed Mel the flatware and she set the table. Claire hadn't noticed the extra plates before now. "Who's coming to dinner?"

"Melissa and Sean. She called me this afternoon. Said they wanted to talk with us."

Claire held his gaze. "Does that mean what I think it does?"

He nodded.

"Well, say something. Is it too soon?"

A smile tugged at one side of Joel's mouth. "I don't think with these two you need to worry. They've prayed together and alone about it. The thing that pleases me is the part about praying together."

Mel looked at Claire then Joel. Poor kid probably never heard anyone talk like them. She didn't know about those twenty-five years before Joel became a believer. "Mel, have you ever heard about praying for the person you'll marry?"

"Uh, no. I don't go to church. I mean, I hadn't until I moved here."

She'd gone here? "When?" Oops. She hadn't meant to say that out loud.

"Miss Ellie invited me the second week I worked for you. I figured since she didn't seem to mind how I looked, she might be on to something." Mel's eyes grew warm. "And after I got to know y'all, I knew she was. But ..." She frowned slightly. "I'm not sure about it all yet."

Wisdom whispered in Claire's ear. She listened and left it at that. For now. "I imagine our 'Lissa's heart is rejoicing. I haven't seen her this joyful since her second year in high school." She glanced sidelong at Mel. "That's when she met Bobby, who, a few months later, broke her heart."

"What a rat. 'Lissa's one of the nicest girls I've ever known. She and Nicole both are real. Y'know what I mean?"

Claire nodded. "I do."

"They never judged me, or at least I never felt they did."

The front door opened. "We're here."

Claire moved to the kitchen doorway so she could see the foyer. "So you are. Hey, Sean. How are you enjoying working for the town?"

He had one arm draped over 'Lissa's shoulder, looking for all the world like they'd been together a lifetime. Soulmates. Claire's momma-heart thrilled for them.

"It's good. Felix has a lot of great ideas. He's got me working for both the town and the U.S. Forest Service. That keeps things interesting."

"Come on into the kitchen. Supper's about on the table." Her daughter stopped and kissed her cheek as they passed. Those two weren't even nervous. She'd never seen 'Lissa so content. God sure answered their prayers. In spades.

'Lissa hesitated a fraction of a second when she noticed Mel. Her recovery was quick. "Hey, girl. How fun to see you here."

Mel shot a fast glance at Claire. She winked back to let her know it was okay. "I guess you'll hear fast enough anyway. I'm the theater 'ghost.'" Mel made air quotes.

'Lissa and Sean burst out in laughter.

"What?" Mel was clearly surprised by their reaction.

Claire eyed them. "What do you two know about this?"

"Sean happened to see her disappear in the woods," 'Lissa said between giggles. "He found the trap door but didn't follow her. He just applied some math."

Math? "What do you mean?"

"He put two and two together."

Claire face-palmed herself. Mel cracked up. Joel fist-bumped Sean.

Claire sat at the banquette. "Did you know about the Underground Railroad going through Chapel Springs, Sean?"

He joined her while 'Lissa and Mel helped Joel. "I guessed it might be either that or it led to a hidden still."

Claire liked this young man's dry sense of humor. He was down-home and would fit in with their family. She lowered her voice. "Don't say anything about that to anyone, yet, okay?"

He nodded.

"So, I hear you want to talk with us after supper."

Again he nodded. He wasn't one to waste words. "I hope you're okay with this."

"I'm more than okay with it, Sean. I know of your faith, and most importantly, I've seen the change in 'Lissa. She found herself again."

Sean's pleasure turned his cheeks and ears pink. Claire heard wedding bells in her heart.

Chapter 41

The door clanged shut behind Carin, making her jump. It was the sound of imprisonment—loud and final, even though she was only a visitor. She shuddered and shared a glance with Leanna, drawing in a breath to calm her nerves. Leanna appeared calm, but the old adage about appearances being deceiving was true.

"How are you doing?" Leanna squeezed Carin's hand as they followed the guard down a long gray hallway.

"Remembering an old documentary I saw called *Scared Straight*. They took a bunch of kids who'd gotten in trouble to a prison and let the convicts scare them out of committing more crimes. That's how I feel." Their footsteps echoed.

"I'm still surprised you suggested coming."

"Something shifted when you told me I sounded like a sister." Carin hooked a finger and captured a strand of hair stuck to her lip. She tucked it behind her ear. "I made a decision." She gave Leanna a half smile. "I'm choosing to love *all* my sisters." *No matter how hard.* "But that doesn't mean I have to like them, right?"

The guard stopped, unlocked a door, and opened it, pointing. "In there."

Leanna's chuckle put Carin at ease as they walked into a large room filled with chairs. One woman had turned her chair to face the wall. The rest sat waiting.

A brunette caught her attention. Her head was bent and her shoulders slumped. The posture of lost hope. Thank the good Lord for

Claire. She put her foot down over Carin bringing JJ along, said she'd keep him overnight. She'd hate for him to see so many people without hope.

Something familiar about that woman bothered Carin. "Leanna, is that Julie?"

Julie startled and looked up. Carin turned to Leanna. "Did you know she was coming today?"

"No."

Julie looked a mess. Strands fell loose from the chignon she always wore. Ted stood across the room at a vending machine.

They stepped over to her. "Hey, Jewels." Leanna bent over and kissed her cheek.

Julie glanced at Carin, narrowed her eyes, then turned to Leanna. "What's she doing here?"

Carin wasn't about to let Julie cow her. She sat down on the bench beside her and gave her a one-armed hug. "I came to see *our* sister."

"Why?"

"Because that's what sisters do."

Julie raised her head to Leanna, who stood in front of them. "Did you put her up to this?"

"Try to put yourself in Carin's shoes for once. Just for a minute." She sat on Julie's other side. "You might see something different."

Julie stared at Leanna for a moment and then returned her attention to her clasped hands.

She was buying time, either to form another attack or just maybe do what Leanna suggested. Carin waited, giving her however much time she needed, and turned her attention to the people around her, looking for a story.

She hadn't heard anything from her publisher. When the trial started, Darcie's attorney asked Carin to stay away, but the press got wind of it anyway. Darcie reveled in the publicity, posing and playing up to the press. The whole thing was a big joke to her until the jury found her guilty and sentenced her to ten years in prison. Then the media saw her fury and camped out in front of Carin's house. It took a couple weeks for them to move on to another story.

"I'm trying to see it from your side, Carin." Julie still hadn't made eye contact with her. "Mama and Daddy never gave any hints that we had another sister. Never told us about you. Nobody did. Not even our grandparents." She finally looked at Carin. "It was natural not to believe you."

"I would have felt the same way, Julie."

"I never stopped to think about it from your viewpoint."

Carin gave her a one-sided smile. "It would have been a lot easier if Dad hadn't gone for that walk."

"Even then, it would have been hard to accept." Julie picked at her nail polish.

That simple act broke Carin's heart. Julie cared so much about her appearance. "What about now?"

"I don't know how I feel. I'm not mad at you anymore. I realize it wasn't your fault. But I sure wish I'd known about you a long time ago."

A guard called Julie's name and motioned her over to a window. Julie left without a glance back. Darcie approached the window from the inside and sat down. She picked up the phone and began to talk, gesturing wildly. Julie startled and talked into the phone. Carin tried to overhear, but the noise level in the room turned everything to a low hum. Whatever Julie said calmed Darcie.

Ted came over and joined them. "Has the press stopped bothering you?"

"I'm last week's news, thankfully. How are *you* doing?"

"We're … doing. Julie agreed to counseling. It's helping us."

"I feel so bad about all of this. I can't help but wonder if I compounded it."

Leanna slid over next to Carin. "Stop thinking that. We all could say that, but Darcie has always been … Darcie. And her stealing started way before we even found out about you."

"I meant Julie's reaction to things. Would she have been able to cope better before?"

Ted leaned over, his forearms on his knees, and clasped his hands between them. "I don't think so, Carin. Julie's problem comes from wanting a baby. It's complicated. She played mama to Darcie and was able to keep the longing hidden, even from herself. I would have adopted long ago, but she didn't want to do that. Now, I don't know if we'd qualify or if she'd make a good mother. For some reason I can't figure out, she lacks self-confidence. She's so afraid of losing Darcie's love, she tried to buy it."

Leanna put her arm around Ted. "I think through the counseling and prayer, Julie will see through the lies she's believed."

"I hope you're right. I love her, you know."

"We know, Ted." Carin kissed her brother-in-law's cheek. "And we love you for it."

At the window, Julie pointed to them. Darcie shook her head, scowling. After a moment, they both hung up, and Darcie walked out of sight.

Julie rejoined them. "I'm sorry, she won't see you. She barely tolerated seeing me." Julie gave a dry, mirthless laugh. "All she did was complain about the clothes they gave her and the shoes she had to wear."

Carin rose and pulled Julie into her arms. "We'll come again next month. Maybe by then, she'll feel ready."

Julie pulled back and searched Carin's eyes. "You're coming back? It's a long way for nothing."

"That's okay. Let's come together next time, though. It will make the trip more fun. A sister road trip." Carin couldn't believe she said that. A smile tugged her lips, curving them upward. She meant it, too.

Julie considered it before nodding. "I'd like that."

She didn't sound completely convinced, but that was okay. Choosing didn't change things overnight. But commitment wore down the hardest of defenses.

Leanna and Carin followed Ted and Julie as the guard led them out. Ted put his arm around his wife and she leaned into him.

"They'll make it," Leanna whispered. "Ted loves her."

The hallway blurred. Why couldn't Wick have loved her that way? Would she ever know the kind of love like her sisters did?

I've loved you with an everlasting love. The words reverberated in Carin's heart and gave her peace. Whatever the days ahead held, she could trust her Heavenly Father. And love the sisters He gave her.

They walked out into the sunshine. "So, do all y'all want to come up for the weekend? JJ hasn't had much time with his uncles."

"Thank you, Carin." Ted glanced down at Julie, waiting for her response.

She nodded. "I'd like that." Ted squeezed her and kissed her temple.

Carin withheld a fist pump. "JJ will be delighted. Leanna? Can you and Scott come?"

"Wouldn't miss it for anything."

In the parking lot, Ted offered to take Leanna home, but the drive was a long one, and she opted to ride with Carin to keep her company.

Carin started the car and waited for Leanna to buckle her seatbelt before leaving the parking lot, then she pulled out behind Ted.

Leanna turned, looking over her shoulder as they drove away. "It feels so strange leaving Darcie there. It's sad, even though she needs help. Her lawyer said they were going to make her see a psychiatrist. I wonder if it will help her."

Carin doubted it but one never knew. "It's considered a personality disorder. I read up on it." She glanced at Leanna for a second. "I took a test online and answered the questions by what I'd observed of Darcie's behavior. The score revealed 'highly narcissistic.' The treatment is psychotherapy."

"Darcie will probably think that makes her special." Leanna wrinkled her nose exactly like JJ did when he made a wisecrack.

"Let's just pray for her. At least she hasn't been self-destructive."

"Hasn't she?" Leanna turned sideways in her seat. "I think theft is pretty destructive."

"It sure is if you're caught." Carin chuckled then sobered. "Poor Darcie. This had to have come from more than simply being spoiled. I've known plenty of spoiled brats that don't have narcissism. We need to make sure Julie understands that." Up ahead, the sign for Atlanta indicated she needed to be in the right lane. She checked her rearview mirror and changed lanes. "I think Julie's carrying a huge amount of guilt."

Leanna opened her purse and pulled out a tissue. "Call Jewels and tell her what you've learned. I think she'd appreciate it coming from you."

"Why?"

"Because she's *starting* to look at you in a different light. I think today made an impression."

Carin hoped so. It would be nice to have a close relationship with Julie like she had developed with Leanna. Both would still take more time to grow deep, but Carin felt like she could ask Leanna anything. It was amazing.

This is what it feels like to be a sister.

She couldn't wait for next weekend.

Chapter 42

laire and Joel walked into the town council meeting. Old friends milled with summer people who had become new friends. Mel scooted over to them as soon as she saw them. Claire smiled. To think this was the same Goth girl she'd met in jail less than a year ago. Oh, she still had a tiny nose jewel and four earrings, but the rest had gone. Her makeup wasn't black and heavy anymore, either. Mel was a pretty girl, and now she shined.

She greeted them. "Nobody has been mad at me for living in the theater." Her amazement tickled Claire.

"Chapel Springs is like that. When you came to work for us, you became one of us. We protect our own."

Mel laughed. "That makes y'all sound like a pride of lions."

Joel winked at her. "Try crossing Claire over one of her 'chicks' and you'll see a momma lion."

Claire swatted him. "How's it going, living with Ellie? We were so busy today, I didn't have a chance to ask you, and then you were gone." She'd moved into Ellie's over the weekend.

"It's great. She reminds me a lot of my mom. She's older than Mom would have been, but still reminds me of her. She's great. I feel …" she searched for a word. "At home." She tilted her head. "You know, it's like Chapel Springs adopted me." She grinned and hugged Claire then went to the refreshment table where Dee had just set out a platter of pastries.

Joel squeezed Claire's hand. "I thought you'd lost your marbles when you hired her, but it appears God had a hand in it. You sure did a good job of it, though." He let go of her hand and went to talk with Happy.

"Jacqueline Ford from WPV-TV" entered the room. She waved then chose a seat near the front this time.

"She must think Chapel Springs has lots of newsworthy happenings," Patsy said from behind Claire's shoulder.

"Hey, girlfriend. Is Nicole still at the gallery?"

"Yes, she's locking up. Let's get some coffee before the meeting begins. I've got something to tell you."

"No more kids getting married, is it? We've got three weddings between us in the next twelve months."

"No, it's nothing to do with the kids. This is about Howie."

That got her attention. Claire followed her. They got their coffee and moved into a side room.

"So what about Howie?"

Patsy's eyebrows did the Groucho Marx thing, waggling up and down. "He was outside talking to Peyton and Elva Murdoch. Naturally, I eavesdropped—from behind a car." She snickered. "Anyway, Howie asked where the farmers were. He'd apparently arranged a protest, but nobody showed up. Elva told him they didn't have any more beef with the town. The water level is back to normal."

"I'm glad. I hated to see the farmland suffer."

"It was really funny. Elva's a driving force. Then Peyton capped it by telling Howie they weren't coming in for the meeting. The town had done right by them, and they were going to a movie instead."

Claire glanced toward the main room. "We'd better go in there. This should be a very interesting meeting." As far as she could tell, Howie only had one more gripe against Felix and the town. That was the theater. She would relish removing that platform from his campaign. He'd have nothing left.

She slid into her place at the council table. Doc and Ellie were already there and waiting. Nancy Vaughn arrived next, and Tom Fowler stood talking to Boone. Vicky Adams, from *Déjà Vu*, had taken Faye Eisler's seat when she decided not to run again. Warren Jenkins hadn't run again either, and Earl Appling won that one. Boone nodded at Tom and they settled at the table. Felix sat in the last chair as Boone banged his gavel.

"Let the meeting come to order. Pastor Seth, will you open in prayer?"

Pastor Seth stood and asked God to grant them wisdom in all their decisions. At his "amen," Boone called for the reading of the minutes. Why couldn't they just email them to everyone on the council? Then they could read them and email back their vote. They always approved them, anyway. It seemed such a waste of time.

She rolled her eyes when Boone called for the vote. She was anxious to get on with the theater business. 'Lissa and Sean sat in the front row and Sean gave Claire a "thumbs up." She winked in response.

"Any new business?"

Claire raised her hand. "Kelly Appling got the bids on the renovation of the theater. We went over them and found that Norm Akins has the best bid, and that's because he's donating the materials to the project."

Howie Newlander jumped up. "Even with donations, this is a waste of taxpayer money. Why, that old building could be torn down and something useful built. Like a convention center." He crossed his arms, looking mighty pleased with himself.

Claire loaded both barrels. This was going to be fun. "Can't do that."

Howie's gaze bore into her. "And why not?"

"Well, for one, it's right next door to the church, and two, it's way off the main drag. Why would anyone want a convention center back there?"

Felix pushed his ball cap back and wiped his forehead with a handkerchief. "Nothin's that far off the main drag in Chapel Springs, Claire." He pulled the cap back into place.

Whose side was he on? "My point is we don't want a convention center in Chapel Springs, but we do want a theater, which we already have. It simply needs a bit of restoration."

Howie snorted a laugh. "A bit? I'd be surprised if the foundation isn't cracked. It's wasting taxpayer money on personal preference of the council members. I vote to tear it down."

"Well, you can't vote for that." Felix snapped his suspenders.

"And why not?"

Felix shot Claire a "help me out here" look. She could do that and took aim. "Because the building is a historical landmark." *Fire one.*

The mayor's mouth gaped. "Really?"

"Why? Because it's named after your late great-aunt?" Howie

sneered at her. "Ha. Some historical landmark."

Fire two. "No. Because the original house was part of the Underground Railroad."

Now Howie gaped. *Bullseye.* She was leaving jaws gaping all over the room. Jacqueline Ford scribbled madly on her notepad. This could be a great story for Chapel Springs.

Howie recovered. "And just what do you attribute that distinction to?"

He wasn't going down without a fight, but Claire would have the final shot. "Because we found the tunnel entrance in the woods. Exactly where it was supposed to be."

"What do you mean by 'exactly where it was supposed to be'?"

Oh, he walked right into that one. "Joel? Will you and Sean bring that trunk up here?"

Even Felix looked perplexed. He pushed his cap back on his head and scratched his scalp. Faye Eisler stretched her neck to see, and Jacqueline moved a few rows closer. Joel set the small trunk on the council table in front of Claire.

She put her hands on its top but didn't open it yet. "What started out as a 'ghost sighting' turned out to be a boon for Chapel Springs. I hired Mel a few months ago. Unbeknownst to me, her stepmother had kicked her out. She had no place to live. She spent a couple of nights in the woods, figuring on saving money enough to rent a cottage. Then she stumbled onto the door to the tunnel. An adventurous girl, Mel followed it and came up in the theater. It was dry and warm, so she stayed there. She found this trunk. And we found her, discovering the theater ghost." Claire smiled at Mel.

Howie narrowed his eyes. "Why wasn't she arrested for trespassing? Seems to me there's always some skullduggery going on here, and it always involves the mayor."

Claire fired back. "Our mayor applied some common sense to this. Technically, she didn't break in. And he used a little compassion for a needy kid. Yes, kid. Mel is only sixteen. And before you yap something else you'll be embarrassed for, she's gone into foster care. Ellie Grant is Mel's foster mother."

Claire opened the lid to the trunk. She withdrew a small stack of old letters, held together with a tattered blue ribbon. After untying it, she opened the top one and read.

"*My Charles came back from the church after the services, mightily upset. Some of the deacons admonished John William Benson—*" Claire stopped and stared at Doc. "This is your ancestor, Doc."

He smiled. "Yes, my great-great-grandfather John."

"Did you know about this?" Claire couldn't believe they'd never heard about it.

Doc shook his head. "No. They must have kept it quiet."

Claire returned to reading. "*...admonished John William Benson for givin' Cornelia her freedom. Said they were going to find her and sell her. Charles argued with them, quoted scripture, but they rode off without paying him heed. I'd never seen Charles so upset or determined. He told me, 'Celia, I'm fixing to do something I'd rather you not know about, but I can't do it without your help.' He told me we were joining the Underground Railroad to help folks like Cornelia get away. We both abhorred slavery. So Charles dug a tunnel from the woods to the house. It came up in the basement. He carved some old Cherokee symbols on trees to lead them to the trapdoor in the forest.*"

Claire stopped reading. "There are several more letters here, which we'll have encased and on display in the front of the theater so everyone can read them. We've found and photographed the trees and their carvings. So, Howie ..." Claire turned to him. "What do—where'd he go?" His chair was empty.

Felix grinned. "I believe he slunk out a moment or two ago."

Boone tapped his gavel. "Now that we've established the historical value of the building that houses the theater, let's consider the restoration bids. Kelly, may I see them?"

The documents were passed to Boone. He shuffled through the three bids, comparing them to one another. "It appears that Norm's proposal is the second lowest, but the lowest doesn't have as high quality materials as Norm's. And Norm Akins is a son of Chapel Springs. I'm going to recommend we go with his bid. Good work, Kelly. May I have a motion?"

Claire raised her hand. "So moved." She was finally getting the lingo.

Ellie seconded and it passed unanimously. Claire glanced over at Mel, who sat beside Joel, grinning like Garfield with a pan of lasagna.

Boone told Norm to come see him in the morning and ended the meeting. Jacqueline Ford rushed to talk with Mel while gesturing to Claire to come over. Ellie had already made her way to the girl's side.

Claire stepped to the other side of Mel and gave her a hug.

"You did it, kiddo."

She blushed a pretty pink. "Thanks. None of this would have happened if you hadn't seen through my wall of defense." She leaned close and kissed Claire's cheek. Claire then moved a step back, allowing Mel to have her moment and tell her story.

"It seems our girl has made herself at home," Ellie said.

Claire agreed. "There's no better place."

Chapter 43

C arin pulled out two boxes, one of pancake mix and the other cereal. "What's your choice this morning, sir?"

JJ giggled at being called "sir" and pointed to the pancake box. She always tried to make Mondays fun, since a whole week of school and work were ahead of them. JJ wasn't the problem, though. Her not having a story was the big problem. The school hadn't called her more than a half dozen times to substitute teach, and the money from her dad wouldn't last forever. She was desperate for a story, but her muse still evaded her.

With a smiley face in syrup on JJ's pancakes, she set the plate in front of him. He asked the sweetest blessing, thanking God for his mama and pancakes.

"Eat up now. The bus will be here in ten minutes." Carin poured syrup over a single pancake on her plate.

"Okay." He downed his breakfast and slipped the last bite to Edgar, who sat beside him, patiently awaiting his percentage. Just like the tax man. JJ washed his hands and picked up his backpack. "I like school here, Mama. I've got lots of friends."

"I knew you would. Now, have a fantastic day, doodle bug. And don't forget, we have a wedding to go to this weekend."

He cocked his head. "Whose wedding?"

"It's Miss Patsy's son. You met Chase, remember?"

"Yeah. I like him. He's marrying Miss Nicole. She's nice." He kissed Carin goodbye.

Her little man trudged to the end of the driveway, where the school bus waited. He turned and waved then jumped up the steps and onto the bus. She waved as it drove around the bend.

At her feet, Edgar whined. "I know, boy." Carin bent and cradled the beast's head in her hands. "Our boy's growing up, isn't he?" In moments like now, the desire for another baby gripped her heart something fierce. "Edgar Allen Poe, divorce is an ugly thing, sometimes necessary, but it leaves scars and broken dreams in its wake."

Edgar licked her chin, making her smile return. She ruffled his ears. "I love you too. Now, I've got my friends waiting at *Dee's 'n' Doughs.*" The dog cocked his big head. "Yes, I'll bring you one of Dee's doggie treats." Edgar loped over to his great room bed and plopped down. Carin laughed. "Not yet. I've got to go first."

Five minutes later, Carin walked down Pine and then cut through the alley between Halls of Time and the bakery. The bells jingled their merry hello as she opened the door. Claire and Patsy waved from their table by the window. Lacey dropped money in the box Dee kept for her early customers while Lydia carried her and her sister's coffee to the table.

How different this was from the first time Carin came in here. A few short months ago, she didn't think she'd ever fit in, and now she was one of them.

She pumped a cup of coffee from Dee's special roast and after a few moments indecision, selected an apple fritter. She'd save half for JJ for an afternoon snack.

"Oh, and I need one of your doggie treats in a bag, please. Edgar has gotten to where he expects them." She waited for the bagged treat then went to join the gals. "Good morning." She set her cup and fritter on the table next to the doggie treat and slid into a chair between Lacey and Claire, who pointed to the bag.

"Treat for Edgar?"

"You wouldn't believe that dog. He smells my breath when I get home to make sure I haven't been to the bakery and not brought him his treat."

"Oh, I believe it. Shiloh does the same thing. I'm not sure whether to thank Dee or boycott her for coming up with the idea." Claire chuckled and showed Carin the bag she had for Shiloh.

Carin pulled off a piece of her fritter. "I missed the council meeting.

Did they approve the theater renovation budget?" She popped the pastry into her mouth, savoring the crunch of glazed sugar frosting and the sweet cinnamon against the snap of apple.

Claire and Lacey answered at the same time, their words overlapping. "They sure did. They chose Norm as the contractor." Lacey laughed and took a sip of her coffee.

Claire spread a bit of cream cheese on half a blueberry bagel. "You missed the fun, though. We found our ghost."

"You what?" Carin couldn't have heard that right.

Claire laughed. "Don't worry. This ghost has flesh and bone. It was Mel." She explained how they found her. "The best part is the theater has been declared a historical site and can't ever be torn down."

"And the thanks for that goes to Claire and Joel," Patsy said. Her pride in her best friend was obvious.

"And Mel," Claire added. "If it hadn't been for her living in there, we never would have found out about it. She discovered the trunk and the letters."

"So what does that do to Howie Newlander's platform? If I remember right, he only had the creek and the theater as points of contention. What's he running on now?"

Claire raised her hands, palms up. "His legs?"

Patsy laughed. "That's about right. He gave up, withdrew his candidacy, and headed back to Greenville."

"Felix was almost sorry to have him give it up," Claire said.

Carin tasted her coffee and reached for the cream. "Why? I'd have thought he'd be relieved."

Claire shook her head. "I think he wanted to be able to have a landslide victory. He's crazy—a great mayor—" Claire clapped her hand over her mouth and glared at them. "Don't any of you tell him I said that. He'll get a big head."

Laughter rang out around the table as they shared a moment of levity over Claire's secret admission. Carin delighted in the warmth of friendship. How had she lived so long without this? But then, she hadn't really lived. Except for JJ, her marriage had been a farce. Coming to Chapel Springs was the best thing that happened to her and JJ. They both had good friends. And maybe someday—

Lacey bumped her elbow. "So, how did it go yesterday?"

"Both better and worse than I expected."

"What do you mean?" Claire asked.

These women cared. Really cared. Carin's eyes grew moist. "Darcie refused to see me. Actually, she wouldn't see Leanna either. Only Julie."

Claire frowned and stirred her coffee. "Ungrateful little twerp. Ow." She glared at Patsy. "Okay, I'm sorry. But she *is*."

Carin wanted to hug Claire for her defense.

"You aren't going to go back again, are you?" Claire laid the stir stick on a napkin.

"Yes." Carin's gaze took in each of her friends. "I made a decision to love my sisters. All of them. I'll keep visiting Darcie and hope she'll accept my love. But that doesn't mean I'll give in to her."

Lydia reached across her sister and squeezed Carin's hand. "You're right, Carin. It's what sisters do." She sat back. "I read in the paper about her diagnosis." She glanced at Lacey. "We had a cousin who was narcissistic. I understand there's medicine to help now. There wasn't back then when our Cousin Buford was alive."

"Isn't the jury still out on how helpful it is?" Claire asked.

Carin swallowed a bite of apple fritter, then wiped her mouth. "We'll have to wait and see, but she's also in psychotherapy. I'm not sure how cooperative she'll be. She's pretty angry."

"What about Julie? Is she any better?" Patsy passed the cream to Lacey.

"I think so. She was surprised to see me. Not pleased, but Leanna told her to grow up. Walk in my shoes for a bit. Julie did say she would try to see things from my side. I think—I hope my going cracked open the door a tad." She sighed. "I'm so happy with my relationship with Leanna. She's the answer to a lifelong dream."

Carin looked around the table as her cheeks grew warm. "I want to tell all y'all that you are too. I haven't had many friends." The heat in her cheeks intensified. "Not real ones, anyway. Since I started writing, everyone wanted something from me." She ran out of words. Her, a word merchant. She laughed. "I can't find the words to say how much your friendship means to me."

Four hands reached out and met over hers. Then they all laughed.

Claire snorted. "Do we need a rousing chant of 'all for one?'"

Lacey faced Carin. "You're the first person who completely

understands me." She glanced at her sister. "Sorry. But Carin gets it that stories and characters come to life in my head. You just think I'm nuts." She grinned at Lydia.

"Not nuts, dear." Lydia crossed her eyes. "Well, maybe a little."

Lacey stuck her tongue out, but the love in her eyes made plain Lacey almost pretty.

Carin winked at her. "And I could use a brainstorm session with you. I—" Her heart stirred. She looked at Claire, moved her eyes back to Lacey, then to each of the others, listening to her heart as they stared at her.

These women opened their lives to her. Claire adopted her and JJ as her own, caring for them. Shy Lacey offered friendship at risk to herself. Patsy protected her. Lydia wasn't jealous over her sister's friendship with her. None of them had asked or tried to take from her. They simply gave. They supported her when she lost her dad, and surrounded her with a defensive hedge when her sisters showed up. But they never once wanted anything from her but to be a friend.

God whispered to Carin's heart, and it whispered back. She found her story. More important, she'd found home.

Chapter 44

The church was packed, and Claire stood in the back, not sure which side to choose to sit. Chase Kowalski was like a son to her, but her new protégé, Nicole, was the bride. She sent a questioning glance to Joel.

"Chase, of course." He shrugged one shoulder at her raised brow. "I used math. We've known him his whole life."

Leave it to Joel to use logic, but she agreed and Nicole wouldn't mind. The church was decorated with bouquets at the end of each pew. Up on the platform, more flowers covered the wedding arch. Claire looped her hand through her son Wes's arm and smiled up at him. He and his siblings—except for Adrianna—were all in this wedding as groomsmen and bridesmaids. Wes led her and Joel to the pew just behind where Patsy and Nathan would sit.

Claire stepped into the pew next to her daughters-in-law, Sandi and Costy. After she settled next to the very pregnant Sandi and greeted both girls, Claire leaned close to Joel. "Patsy's all ditherpated. It took me a couple of minutes to calm her down. Oh, Joel. All our babies are getting married." She scrutinized her husband's face. Years of laughter and sun etched lines around his eyes. "I don't feel old. Do you?"

He laced his fingers through hers. "Not really. Although my body tells me different once in a while. I don't know why you're concerned. We aren't even fifty yet." He shoulder-bumped her. "We've got a couple more years until we're officially—whatever fifty is called."

Claire wrinkled her nose at him, laughed, then reached for Sandi's hand. "How are you feeling?"

"Full." Sandi rubbed her enormous belly and Costy giggled behind her hand. "If these two grow much more, I won't be able to reach anything. Even my large maternity clothes are getting tight."

"I wasn't as large with Megan and Melissa, but you've got a boy in there with his sister. Bennett boys are big. You don't think you'll be early, do you?"

"Doc and Vince don't think so … not too early, anyway."

The music changed. Patsy was escorted down the aisle by Claire's firstborn, Charlie. He looked so handsome in his tux that tears filled Claire's eyes. Her firstborn would soon become a daddy to his own babies.

A moment later, Patsy and Nathan stepped into the pew. Patsy reached back and squeezed Claire's hand. Then, Nicole's mother was escorted to her pew. As soon as she was seated, a new song played. Chase and his groomsmen—Charlie, Wes, and Nicole's brother—stepped out onto the platform. Chase had his eyes on the door, waiting for his bride. A lump lodged itself in Claire's throat. In front of her, Patsy sniffed. They were saps for weddings anyway, but when it was one of their own, they needed two hankies.

Claire's twins were bridesmaids and started down the aisle. Megan winked at her as she passed. The next bridesmaid was an old friend of Nicole's Claire didn't know. Chase's twin, Deva, was the maid of honor and came last. She'd grown into such a lovely young woman, the exact image of Patsy.

It would have been great for Adrianna to be in the wedding too, but she and Nicole didn't really know each other. Claire understood that. Still, hers and Patsy's kids grew up a tribe, a family. When they were little, Claire and Patsy never bothered to sort out whose were whose.

The wedding march began and they rose. Nicole and her daddy stood in the doorway for a second. Claire couldn't help it. Tears of happiness spilled over. She and Patsy had prayed for their kids for years. To see another one marry their soul mate gave testimony to God's grace. Beside her, Joel squeezed her hand. He was another testimony to God's goodness and mercy.

The ceremony was sweet. Nicole and Chase had written their own vows and followed scripture. Poor Patsy would need her makeup redone. Claire probably would too. Deeply felt emotions were all part of being an artist.

When the service concluded, Pastor Seth introduced Mr. and Mrs. Chase Kowalski and the congregation erupted in cheers and applause. A half hour later, they all entered the fellowship hall, and as soon as the line was through, Patsy sought out Claire.

Her BFF was radiant. "That's three weddings down and five to go. Except we'll get through three in one event."

Claire picked up a cup of punch from the table and took a sip. "That will leave just Deva and Adrianna, and I have a feeling Adrianna's won't be too far in the future. I wonder if she'll come home for hers or have it in Nashville." She'd been there for four years and had made so many good friends at her church, not to mention it was the very church her fiancé pastored.

Patsy emptied her punch in one long drink and refilled it. "I have a feeling it will be in Nashville. It's not too far for all of her friends here to go, and Andrew's church will want to witness their pastor's wedding."

Claire shrugged. "I suppose. I guess one out of five wouldn't hurt to do long distance."

Patsy got pulled away and Claire found Joel talking fishing with Happy. She wandered around the room, speaking to friends but not settling anywhere. JJ waved at her from where he and his mama sat with Jake and Lacey. Carin looked radiant.

Finally, Claire joined Sandi and Charlie. She picked up a napkin off the table and dabbed her eyes. "Why is it weddings always make me sentimental?"

Charlie put his arm around her. "You love us."

"Is that it?" She popped a mint into her mouth. "When it's one of y'all, they make me feel old. I can't believe the years have flown by so fast." She smiled at Sandi and Charlie. "You just wait. The next twenty years will go by in a blink, and you'll be left wondering what happened." She laughed. "Here I am, sounding melancholy. This is a celebration. Let's eat!"

Epilogue

Claire and Patsy stood on the boardwalk outside the *Painted Loon*. The late afternoon sun washed Chapel Lake and Sandy Shores Drive in golden light. Claire never understood how anyone could want to leave Chapel Springs. It was the most beautiful place on earth.

"I couldn't be happier that Carin feels at home here." Claire crossed her arms and leaned against the doorframe. "That poor girl had the rug pulled out from under her, but she landed on her feet. Her lawyer said Wick has no case. Something about the money she inherited from her dad was after Wick walked out on her. State law is on her side since he abandoned them for another woman."

Patsy stepped to the bench in front of the gallery and sat down. She lifted her face to the sun. "Have you read any of her new story yet?"

Claire joined her BFF on the bench. "She only let me read one chapter for clarity. I can't wait until it comes out."

"It's good, then?"

"Better than good. This one is inspired."

"I'm glad. Do you know if she's told her publisher about it?"

Claire nodded. "That woman was rightly named."

"What do you mean? What woman?"

"Her editor at the publishing house. Her name is Grace. Grace Duval. She reminded Carin that as a Christian publishing house, they valued forgiveness and love, and Carin demonstrated those. The story is about them. Grace sent her a contract."

Patsy poked her toe at a bug that meandered too close. "I'm so glad. I know she was afraid they'd drop her."

Claire's brother-in-law, Vince, waved as he drove past. She waved back. "Now, there's a perfect man for some lucky woman. Say, there's a new young widow who moved into a house on Hill Street. What's her name?" Claire tapped a knuckle on her forehead.

"Do you mean Haleigh Evans?"

"That's her. I wonder—"

"Oh, Claire." Patsy began to laugh. "You'll only stick your foot in your mouth if you try to play yenta for Vince. Let it happen by itself. God can handle it without your help."

Claire scrunched her nose at her BFF. "Even the best artist sometimes needs a bit of critiquing for input."

Patsy snorted a giggle. "I'm leaving that one alone, but speaking of artists, have you seen 'Lissa's new painting? Methinks love has something to do with it."

Claire couldn't help the smile that stretched her lips. It came from her heart. "If I didn't already love Sean, I would simply for what he's done for her. He returned our happy daughter to us."

"I'm glad the girls decided to wait until next May to have the wedding."

"I'm looking forward to some traveling. The PR group we hired entered us in that art show in Charleston in December." Claire picked at a ragged cuticle. She could really use a manicure, but what was the use? Her hands were in clay every day. "They want us to do a national tour after the weddings."

"That'll be fun. Nicole, 'Lissa, and Mel can run the gallery."

"More like Mel can run the store while the other two take over our workroom. We need to expand, Pat-a-cake." Claire pulled her legs up and hugged her knees. "Did you ever think we'd have two of our kiddos in the art business with us?"

"I suspected 'Lissa long ago. And Nicole was a delightful addition, wasn't she?"

"Chase thinks so." Claire laughed. "Ellie sure took to Mel, didn't she?"

"It makes me wonder if God has someone praying for Chapel Springs." Patsy laid her head back against the window.

"What makes you say that?"

"Well, Ellie's sister came back home and wants to take her place caring for their mother."

Claire flubbered her lips. "Something she should have done years ago. Poor Ellie lost her fiancé because he got tired of waiting for her."

"He didn't want to care for her mother." Patsy pulled her feet up on the bench and hugged her knees.

"There's that. Anyway, she and Mel seem very content in the new apartment. I wonder if she and Happy will continue dating."

Patsy snapped her head around to face Claire. "Mel and Happy?"

Claire couldn't help but laugh. "*Ellie* and Happy. They've been flirting with each other."

"Well, I'll be." Patsy grinned. "Love is blooming in Chapel Springs. I wonder who will be next."

"I have an idea, but we'll have to see." Claire didn't want to jinx anything, but— "Vince is such a great catch, Patsy. I'd love to see him fall in love."

"I know, Yenta."

Claire tweaked her lip and blew her bangs off her forehead. "Renovation starts next week on the theater. The Lakeside Players are all atwitter." Claire chuckled.

"It will be fun to have the theater open again. Are you going to take a part in one of the plays?"

"I don't know. Maybe. If you will." Claire raised and lowered her eyebrows. "Could be fun. Uh-oh, look. The mayor and Eileen are coming out of *Dee's 'n' Doughs*."

"You don't suppose they're going to announce they're getting married, do you?"

Claire turned her gaze toward Eileen's shop. Felix had a bead on her and was heading her way. "Naw. More likely he has something he's going to blame me for." She stood. "Come on, girlfriend. Let's see if we can outrun him."

Laughing, Claire pulled Patsy up and the two sprinted into the gallery and out the back door. Felix would catch up with Claire eventually, but right now, she wanted to savor all the happiness that was Chapel Springs.

The End

Discussion Questions

1. Claire and her friends begin their days at *Dee's 'n' Doughs*, sharing life. Do you have friends you can share life with? Do they make life more fun?

2. What's the best part of having friends like Claire's? How does sharing with them differ from sharing with your spouse?

3. Like Job, Carin has had everything, other than her son, stripped from her life. She thinks God is mad at her. Have you ever felt like that? What did you learn from it?

4. Mel showed up in *Chapel Springs Survival*, in the same jail cell as Claire and Patsy. Being the mother of five, Claire saw through her "tough Goth exterior" to a hurting kid. Now Mel has come to *The Painted Loon* and Claire hires her. Do you think that was wise or misguided? Why?

5. Carin had to tell her sisters who she was without her father there to back up her story. Why do you suppose God allowed that? What was He trying to teach Carin?

6. Was it easy for you to see why Julie was suspicious of Carin? Why do you suppose she felt like that when Leanna openly welcomed Carin?

7. What did you think when Carin's son, JJ, "divorced" his daddy?

8. Birth order can affect personality. What is your own birth order? How has that played out in your life?

9. Claire's daughter, 'Lissa, has been in love with an unbeliever since she was in high school. What did she do about that? What advice would you have given her?

10. Why do you think God warns us about being unequally yoked?

11. God rewarded 'Lissa's obedience. How did He do that?

12. What did Carin risk when she went to see her sister in prison? Why do you suppose she took the risk?

Pearl Pasta Salad

- 2 C uncooked acini di pepe pasta (I couldn't find it and used tiny stars)
- 3 C frozen corn
- 1 jar (14 oz) oil-packed sun dried tomatoes, drained and chopped
- 1 jar (6 oz) prepared pesto
- ½ C grated Parmesan cheese (don't use the green canned kind— too salty)
- ¼ C olive oil
- 1/8 tsp salt
- 1/8 tsp pepper

In a large saucepan, cook the pasta according to the package directions, adding the corn during the last 2 minutes. Drain and rinse in cold water.

In a large bowl, combine the tomatoes, pesto, oil, cheese, salt, and pepper. Add the pasta and corn; toss to coat.

Refrigerate until served.
Yields 15 servings.

Radish Salad

Serves 6

- 4 C radishes, washed and sliced
- ½ C thinly sliced onion
- 1 C diced fresh tomato
- 1¼ tsp salt
- 1 small clove garlic, minced
- 1/8 tsp pepper
- 1 tsp finely chopped fresh basil or mint
- 2 Tbsp lemon juice
- 2 Tbsp vegetable oil
- fresh chopped parsley for garnish

Combine radishes, onion, and tomato in a bowl.

Whisk together the salt, garlic, pepper, basil or mint, lemon juice, and vegetable oil.

Toss with salad and garnish with parsley if desired.

Chocolate Lovers Fantasy

- 1 pkg chocolate chip cookie mix
- 1 pkg Oreo Double Stuf cookies (must be Double Stuf)
- 1 pkg brownie mix

Following the package directions, make the chocolate chip cookie mix and layer it in the bottom of a 9 x 13 pan.

Next, layer the Double Stuf Oreos whole (do not crumble) on top of the cookie mix.

Following the package directions, make the brownie mix and spread it over the Oreos.

Bake at 350° for about 30 minutes, depending on how you like your brownies.

Best served warm, topped with vanilla ice cream.

Made in the USA
Middletown, DE
11 May 2016